*a novel*

# FAMILY POLITICS

John Buckley

**SIMON AND SCHUSTER**

NEW YORK   LONDON   TORONTO   SYDNEY   TOKYO

Copyright © 1988 by John Montgomery Buckley
All rights reserved
including the right of reproduction
in whole or in part in any form
Published by Simon and Schuster
A Division of Simon & Schuster Inc.
Simon & Schuster Building
Rockefeller Center
1230 Avenue of the Americas
New York, New York 10020

SIMON AND SCHUSTER and colophon are registered trademarks of Simon & Schuster Inc.

Designed by Jeanne Joudry
Manufactured in the United States of America

10   9   8   7   6   5   4   3   2   1

Library of Congress Cataloging in Publication Data

Buckley, John, 1957–
Family politics: a novel/John Buckley.

   p.   cm.
ISBN 0-671-63457-7
I. Title.
   [PS3552.U343F3 1988]
   813'.54—dc19      88-5088
                          CIP

Song lyrics from "We're a Happy Family" by the Ramones used with permission from ASCAP.

*To my mother,*
*Ann Harding Buckley (1928–1966),*
*my father,*
*John William Buckley (1920–1984),*
*and to*
*Mary Tarbet, who brought me up.*

"And you have nobody and nothing, and you travel through the world with a trunk and a carton of books and truly without curiosity. What kind of life is this: without a house, without inherited things, without dogs."

Rainer Maria Rilke

"We're a happy family, We're a happy family, We're a happy family, Me, Mom, and Dad."

The Ramones

PART ONE

# CHAPTER ONE

WE THOUGHT THE PRIEST was going to do just fine, until he got to the part about my grandmother. Here was a grand old Catholic woman who for years and years we had known was dying and the family hadn't even bothered to collect a priest who had met her a time or two. Either it was an example of the way we cared about our own or else it was just bad advance work.

"She was a wonderful woman." So far, so good. "Or at least so I'm told."

We groaned, looked at one another. The reporters who were traveling with us began to scribble on their pads.

"She was devoted to God and to her family. So everybody says. And she certainly was prolific!" he said with a silly grin, motioning toward us with his palms held up flat. There were seventy-three of her children, grandchildren, and great-grandchildren spread across the width of the incense-steeped stone church, and we began to glower at him as politely as we could, glower at this florid-faced bumpkin who hadn't known my grandmother, until first Aunt Lizzie's shoulders began to rock, and then she burst out laughing. Uncle Wolfy couldn't keep it in either, and so as reporters looked up from their notes, laughter spread from aisle to aisle, pew to pew. The priest was left to struggle on with the altar boys giggling into the sleeves of their cassocks.

"So I did not know Mrs. Daley. Yet I should have liked to have known her," he said with some dignity, and with that Lizzie's shoulders went rigid as a gravestone, and Wolfy turned to us with a disciplinarian shot of eyes. The insurrection ended until the priest had said the Mass.

We began to file out of the church, nodding to friends and to the elderly servants who summer after summer had migrated with my grandparents from South Carolina to Connecticut and back again in the fall. Now it was a beautiful March day and southern sunshine sent stained-glass shadows across the musty floor. The light brought cheer to what was a solemn occasion, but for the absurd eulogy by a priest who was well-meaning even if slightly out of it. He looked as if he'd been working on the altar wine well before the long procession of Lazzies roared up the drive.

That was a nice touch, and I saw Wolfy's hand in it. Someone had taken the time to round up seventeen of the original Daley Lazarus automobiles my father had designed and my grandfather had manufactured in the early sixties and had used them for our ride to the funeral. It had been so stunning racing from my grandparents' old mansion past policemen who stood directing traffic with their hats held dutifully, and rather wonderfully, over their hearts. These rarities that were being driven in an oddly colorful and unmatched revved-up line were almost psychedelic against the dogwood blossoms, for Lazzies did not come in conventional colors. As a family, we had ridden to the funeral of my grandmother down dusty back roads in mauve and chartreuse sports cars.

Now we were standing in front of the church, seventy-three of us, with my aunts and uncles stepping into the first of the cars. My brother Edward got into the next car that lurched toward us because now he was effectively the head of our family, and he held the gull-wing door open for a couple of my older female cousins. The rest of us in the third generation were left to fight it out for seats in these automotive relics, and it was just plain fitting that the losers in this scramble would be reduced either to riding crushed in the back of unwashed pickup trucks or to hanging from television vans that looked as if they were outfitted for safaris. You see, as word had spread among us of her death, even then consideration had to be given to how we would handle the news coverage of the event. My grandmother only a few years ago had been featured on *60 Minutes,* been joined by all of us on the cover of *Life,* and been written up in several similar venues as the matron of a great manufacturing dynasty, with racy children who had a penchant for controversy. And without her, this huge family was set to dissolve, and I was not upset. I was not upset.

We drove through the streets on the way out to the cemetery. I ended up sitting next to my cousin Camille, whom I had tended to loathe, not really knowing her all that well. She kept her distance from us, which was a feat in a family as close as mine.

Camille was my Uncle Wolfy's oldest daughter, a sardonic beauty who had celebrated adulthood two years earlier by posing in the buff for one of the raunchier men's magazines. I had not seen her, I was going to say, in the flesh, since our Uncle Blitz's funeral, and she had not come to the funeral of my parents last year, though she sent a letter to my brother Sam in far-off Oregon. It was a note that showed genuine sympathy and an understanding of how my family worked that was more insightful than that of any of the magazine journalists who had stayed around too long and written about us over the years of my grandfather's, and then my uncles', stunning American fame.

Recently there had been column items on Camille's affair with a front-rank rock star, and next, a movie director twenty years her senior, and there were rumblings about a band and a nascent film career. I attempted conversation. "I, uh, liked those pictures, Camille. You looked real good." I was thinking of this one in particular where she had her head hanging over the edge of a bed, her feet up in the air.

Camille looked at me, bored. She was wearing a gown more appropriate for an after-hours club, as well as lacy black gloves. She looked as though she would have been comfortable carrying a whip. Her brown hair had taken on a caramel frost and a life of its own, and lay around her shoulders like a wreath. "Hey, well, thank you, Charles. What a wonderful compliment. That means a lot to me." She said it as if she were answering some call-in guest on a late-night cable show.

The chauffeur was having a little trouble with the gears, and I realized it was for perhaps the final time that such a collection of us would drive through these streets. Surely we would no longer be coming down en masse for Easter, and it was even unlikely that we would pile into the Jungle Room of my grandparents' former home in Mingeboro, Connecticut, to celebrate Thanksgiving. It was entirely possible that I would never again be in this southern small town, its streets now swollen with what appeared to be demonstrators and riot police, replete with wooden barriers and horses.

"What is that?" asked Camille, pressing close to me to see what had slowed down our pace.

"Over yonder's troublemakers said they was out to protest Mr. Wolfy," said the driver.

"Oh, no," whispered Camille. "If Mother's out there, I am going to hit her."

As we drove up the street we saw the damndest thing. On one side, being held back by police, was a collection of UAW members holding posters protesting the Daley Motorworks, the family's now-struggling company. Other posters, which I won't relate, were more direct about feelings toward the family. Almost twenty years after my right-wing grandfather had crushed a strike at one of our auto plants, the union still caused us trouble, though it seemed a bit excessive that some members would be here now.

Up the street from the union representatives was a handful of women, standing there giving Wolfy the finger as he rode by. Wolfy was by turns waving to and cheerfully smiling at the union members who'd been bused in from God knows where just to protest at the funeral of a dead enemy's widow.

The women clearly wanted some piece of Wolfy, but at least they were calm about it, studied, almost phlegmatic, as though they were used to being on the demonstration circuit. We had seen such demonstrators over the last couple of years. They had given new texture to the forces that reviled us.

Across from them there was yet a third group. Behind another police barrier were these howling men surging against cops who held them back. They had come either to cheer Wolfy, the former stock-car champ, as he rode through the town in which he had been raised, or else they just wanted to rail against the women and the union members, Yankees most likely, who had dared invade the town. It seemed these men had much to rage at, as young black cops clipped them a couple of times to make them settle down. The tension between these supporters, the union members, and the protesting women lent a strange glint to the morning.

Camera trucks with the odd little Daley hanging from them rushed ahead of the convoy of Lazzies, and cameramen leaped into the street with umbilical tugs at their sound men. A siren went off somewhere, and as Camille and I pressed our faces to the glass, the driver hit the gas pedal and shot past the snarl of opposing demonstrations. Wolfy could be seen ahead leaning out a window, taking in the cheers from his fans. I guess we made the news today.

"Where is she? I know she's out there. I can sense her, I've always been able to," Camille gasped through tight lips, one lace-gloved hand on my woolen sports coat, which was far too warm for this

weather, these tensions. "I bet she's just tacky enough to show up
and try and get her last digs in at Grandma's funeral."

"I doubt they would be her last digs anyway," I said consolingly to
my cousin.

As we drove onto the almost antiseptically sun-bleached main
street, there was no sign of Camille's mother, my Uncle Wolfy's ex-
wife. Aunt Rose had made quite a name for herself with the best-
seller she wrote extolling the life she'd found after leaving those
race-car-driving Daley boys with their cruel and whoring ways. Part
feminist tract, part self-serving memoir, *Pit Stop: My Life with the
Daleys* had caused quite a stir. Rose had become a leader of the
movement of the self-defined abused, and she was awfully energetic
about it. She had only the month before posed for photos at the
White House with President Jimmy Carter and his wife, who had not
helped themselves any with the stock-car fans of the South. She was
a regular on "Donahue," a draw at liberal fund-raisers, and a pain in
the family's collective side. And this apparently went as much for the
family's starlet beside me as it did for Uncle Wolfy, the family fortunes, and my brother's budding political ambitions.

We rolled into the cemetery and soon the Lazzies formed a horse-
shoe around the flag-bedecked old monuments. I wished my father
could have been alive to see this, and Uncle Blitz, had he survived
that crash at Lime Rock, would have been all pumped up and boyish
at the sight of these great cars. He would get that way whenever
there was something he could be proud of that was not just the
possession of his competing brother Wolfgang.

Aunt Morgan, who was my oldest surviving aunt, was the first one
out of the cars, and she looked a little peaked. The contrast of her
pallor against the black padded shoulders of her suit was striking
enough to make several of the people who were waiting near my
grandmother's freshly dug grave move toward her with outstretched
arms. "I'm all right," she pronounced with typical bitchy steel, jaw
locked tight as a safe. And then Wolfy, somewhat sheepishly for him,
hauled himself out of the Lazzy.

"Jesus" was all he said, and my brother Edward walked up to him
and patted him on the back. Wolfy just stood there, blinking in the
sunlight, as people stepped out of their cars. The crowd that was
there edged toward him and then surrounded him, like musk-oxen
protecting the sick chieftain of their herd. He looked far older than
his fifty years, drink having done to his face what a long siege does

to a city. And though he was no longer drinking, the drinker's sadness lingered. And the former drinker's anger was never far from the surface.

"When are those women going to leave you alone?" said my ditzy Aunt Lizzie with a British nanny's chipperness superimposed upon our serious mood.

"When is Wolfy going to leave *them* alone?" asked my brother Edward with a nervous laugh, and his sycophancy made me sick. There was one thing above all else Edward had never understood, and it was why Wolfy and Blitz, hell the whole Daley family, had become such targets after Rose dissected the behavior of the male of our species with such bombast and shock value. Edward was now a major success on Wall Street, refined but somehow still ignorant, dating dumb, pretty rich girls who saw in him the war hero he most genuinely had been. His early fame as the head of Vietnam Vets for Victory had clung to him even now that he was celebrated for his stunning leveraged buy-outs. He continued to let loose these comments that made my sisters and me groan, but which made many of his girlfriends laugh and playfully punch him. With war wound for verisimilitude, he basked as near as he could to Wolfy's aura, while at the same time he was unable to pull off Wolfy's wit, his daredevil charm.

"They're never going to leave me alone, and we all just better goddamn well get used to it. Now let's get this thing on." Wolfy motioned with an abrupt gesture of his shoulder, and so we moved, dazed at all that had happened, dazed at being at yet another funeral so soon after the last one, and this time for the last human being who could possibly give our world its center.

So we moved past the camera platforms Elsie Grodinger, the family's longtime press agent, had long since set up. We couldn't track down any of the numerous priests who had said daily Mass over the years for my grandmother, but we made certain that reporters had telephones for filing their stories.

We moved down the little path to where some benches had been placed for my aunts and my uncles to sit. The rest of us all sat down where we could, on stumps, the more boorish of my cousins on gravestones, the lighter children on the hoods of cars, and we waited for the priest to say the final words, holding out hope they would be reverent and touching, evocative of the sweet old woman my grandmother had turned out to be as she settled, even slumbered, in her dotage. But when we were all ready, we looked around. The priest had yet to arrive.

"Oh, this is just great," announced Camille. "Typical family planning."

"I don't suppose, when you think of it, we ever had much use for *family planning*," I whispered back. Camille and I looked out at sixty-odd cousins farting, picking their noses, resisting the temptation to smoke dope, get drunk in the woods, or mate with the locals.

On the other hand, out by the cars, several other cousins, as well as my older sister, Betsy, in her pin-striped suit, stood laughing and smoking cigarettes, reflecting on the events of the day: the chartered flight from Teterboro, the inedible brunch at my grandmother's antebellum mansion, the eulogy, the strange demonstration. I liked the way they looked. I thought, looking at my aunts and uncles as they waited for the priest, looking at my dozens of cousins, looking at the assemblage of friends, servants, and family hangers-on, how when we had been growing up we thought we were *it*. The family was that large, and with our houses and our pools and our lakes and our stables, and our very own ski area it was easy to believe we were the center and all who came courting must play by our rules. And in or out of our own world, we usually would win.

But now the family was under siege and I did not know whether they were up to the business at hand. Now the houses were being sold off, being turned into condos or fancy country restaurants. And the auto business? Hah, hah, hah. What had once been fame had taken on a sort of seedy notoriety, chronicled by published reports of our arrests for drugs and public drunkenness, our barroom brawls, our publicized promiscuity and celebrity bed-crawling.

But now the priest was here to deliver his final words about my grandmother, who lay at a peace exponentially greater than that she had found by merely going gaga. We could see behind the police cars with their circular flash of red lights yo-yoing from one side of their roofs to the other. They held back the streams of demonstrators who, if they couldn't get a piece of us, by now wanted to tear into one another. It was time to get out of here.

My grandmother buried, our cheeks were dry. We began to drift toward the cars, the tiny first cousins, once removed, wondering what was the big deal, the teenage cousins wondering where the party was. For all of us, but it seemed especially for my sister and brother and me, these funerals were becoming a habit, and I didn't much like that. I'd almost gotten to the point where I wanted to complain, but *who if I cried would hear me among the order of the angels?* Today, strangely, was such a beautiful day, and after we had buried my grandma, as we walked toward the cars, all the old men and women came up to the grandchildren and said things like, "I worked for your grandfather for nineteen years," and they said it exclamatorily, with love, over and over, to the point where it was they, the old servants, who shamed us into tears, and not the hard-hearted members of the family who were all perfunctory and practical and worried about the travel arrangements.

## —— CHAPTER TWO ——

WE BATTENED DOWN THE hatches and the old prop plane took off. Carolina spread below us as we nosed into the north. It was Wolfy's idea that the plane take off at 5:04, as opposed to 5:00 or 5:15, "an old CIA trick good for gathering the strays." Never before had I heard that spooks used the Good Shepherd model.

And so we flew from South Carolina for perhaps the final time, but it did not really feel like a retreat. As my cousins' little children were free to roam the aisles, the reporters all in unison chanted for some grog. A number of us chatted in a hushed and smoky throng, planning the family's comeback.

"First things first," said Uncle Wolfy, leaning across my brother Edward to tug at the stewardess who was spaced-out in the aisle. "Would you mind keeping those gentlemen and the lady in the first two aisles happy until we get to Teterboro?" he asked with his suavest grin, which, given the weather-beaten contours of his rough-and-tumble face, made him look a little grotesque. "I mean happy as larks?" There was something scary about the extent of Wolf's decay, but it had its effect, and the stew shot off to the front of the cabin, a model of efficiency in the care and feeding of the press.

"Let me ask you a question, Edward. Are you really serious about this thing?" Uncle Wolfy asked this with an intimacy that was belied by the fact that peering over the backs of seats like Injuns over a bluff were my sister Betsy, a couple of my aunts, the gorgeous Camille, and several cousins; all of us so unalike, but with this family bond between us. What Wolfy was asking was whether it was true that Edward was going to run for the United States Senate.

"Wolfgang, I have never been so serious about anything in my life," Edward said with the kind of arched-brow charm that made him seem the Plexiglas persona of sincerity. Oh, Edward. My older brother. A bore, often a prick, or at least he had been when we were growing up. Yet there was something about Edward I really did admire, and I think it was his ability to attain no-nonsense size-ups in a world of commerce and clubs. What did I have against him? His philistinism, and especially the way he had treated our poor brother, Sam, when he had dodged the draft and gotten into trouble. But there was so much to be said for Edward, his being a genuine war hero, the way he played his one-armed game of tennis, and his ability to make money, great headline-grabbing gobs of it, in these rhythmic triumphs the newspaper I worked for usually followed and condemned.

"You're really going to challenge your *own uncle* for his Senate seat? You beast. Aren't uncles sacred?" asked Wolfy with mock hurt. And my pathetic Uncle Andrew sat there with a humorless, proud nod.

"What do you think of that, Charles?" Wolfy asked quickly in the challenging manner of a shrink, or the intrusive hucksterism of a daytime television host.

"How do you want me to answer? As his brother or as a reporter?" or maybe I should have asked, "As the nephew of Edward's opponent?" As a brother, my mind was quite divided, part of me saying, Yeah, Edward, go for the gusto, and the other part of me saying, Aw, Edward, would you quit this jag already? Whereas, as a reporter, even a quite unsung one for the *Downtown News,* I recognized that Edward had a shot at defeating, yeah, you get it now, our Uncle Nathaniel Stanton, hero of the Watergate hearings, champion of table-thumping moderation, a Republican who for years had been considered beatable in a primary, though the general had always proved a waltz. And as my Uncle Nate's nephew?

"As a reporter," Edward asked.

"Oh, the guy is vulnerable as hell," I said, knowing the rabid activism of New York Republican primary voters and the kind of right-wing candidate I had no doubt that Edward could become. "Nate's too liberal, too pompous by half . . ."

"But lovable, no?" asked one of my prettiest cousins. I remembered she had worked the summer before in Uncle Nate's Senate office as an intern, a position all the Daleys had held during one phase of adolescence or another. She'd probably graduated from Uncle Nate's office the way most Daleys had: with an almost complete contempt for government, for the people who worked in it, and for the Stantons, who had always been our rivals in Mingeboro, and with a certain guilty joy in our proximity to electoral fame. But for the most part, we left with a certain respect for the old coot, and I admired the class he showed in doting on the rest of the Daleys, even though only my sisters and brothers and I were blood relatives of his.

"Okay, I grant him his charms, but he borders on the cliché of the crotchety but principled Republican who culturally is just not one of them. A, pardon me, one-armed war hero who's made a fortune, has the same cultural background as Nate but is more down to earth by nature of having made his own money, created his own business, could give it a hell of a shot."

Edward looked at me as if these were the first nice words I had said about him in public in years, and I had to admit they could have been. We were not terribly close. Other than at funerals or our occasional overlapping retreats to Mingeboro, we seldom hung out together, and certainly never by choice. I cried when he went off to Vietnam and I cried when he came back wounded, but I just hadn't spent much time with him since. He was older and not very cool. We were both mutually repelled while at the same time fascinated by the other's world. When we were together, he was always pumping me for information about downtown nightclubs, the denizens of which he was none too convincingly dismissive. And in my turn, I was contemptuous of his money-grubbing friends, though I studied them every chance I got.

But now that my parents had died so close together—and I mean within the same weekend—Betsy and our little sister, Annie, who was away at boarding school and hadn't been able to get to today's funeral, well, we'd worked real hard to get along. And if contempt for the rest of the Daleys and the Stantons was one vehicle we used, that was fine. Now we tried as best we could to pretty much ignore our cousins when we were in Mingeboro. We banded together. There was great civility over our weekend breakfast table. As a political junkie, I had found myself drawn toward him during this testing-the-waters phase of his campaign. And so long as the subject never turned to by brother Sam, Edward and I had recently been more civil toward each other, though no one said we actually had to be friends.

"What about as his brother?" Wolfy coaxed.

"As his brother," I began, clearing my throat, but just then the plane hit a pocket of air that let us slip, and we went into a plummet that must have lasted ten seconds. Glasses and ice were spun toward shoes, stomachs found chests, and chests rose to necks, and shrieks could be heard throughout the slide. Then we began to even out, coming back up again with a near visible pull from God, and the chucklin' drawl of the pilot began to explain that we'd just hit a little ol' spot of rough air, heh heh heh, when suddenly the plane went into a flat-out free-fall.

"Charles," Betsy shouted and grabbed me around my neck, and in the split second between her doing that and the plane righting itself, I could see most of my tumbling cousins were almost expressionless, unless you count that fatalistic *O* each of their mouths was shaped in, while my strapped-in cousin Camille and Uncle Wolfy seemed to stare calmly at the clouds out the windows.

Then the plane was flying normally again and my cousins traveling with small children tried to stanch the caterwaul. We could see in the front of the plane that Arthur Begelman, that mesomorphic cynic from the *New York Post,* was choking on a lime rind, his glass hand having been caught atilt as we went into that very first drop. For Arthur the plane was still going down, but my Uncle Andrew rushed up and hit him a good one on the back, and moments later Arthur was doing what Arthur did best, which was to complain about the arrangements. And this one was a doozy. We would hear about this.

"God, wasn't that fun?" asked one of my bright-eyed cousins. He was known to be not averse to risk, having picked up where his father left off when he hit that wall at Lime Rock at 160 miles per hour. Another cousin whose name I barely remembered pretended to slap him, and the two went into this pivot-and-dodge routine, until Aunt Morgan grabbed them by the backs of their necks and settled them down, their eyes bulging like fish. She looked as if she rather enjoyed that.

"So, Edward, you're really going to do it, huh?" asked Aunt Lizzie, everything now back to quiet chaos. She had always been close to him, partially because she was only seven years older than he was, partially because, as my sister Betsy put it, they had always pimped for each other.

"Yeah, Liz. I'm going to do it."

"Why? I mean aside from the ordinary: you've made a fortune and you're bored."

"Well, Liz," Edward said with the quick reaction of the aspiring pol, "I just don't think Uncle Nate is a particularly good senator."

"Oh, Edward, for Chrissake," I said, "you better have a better reason for running than that you just don't think the guy's quality stuff, because that smacks of upper-crust particularity, and I guarantee he'll prove you wrong. If you're going to be running against your own uncle, and I mean in the primary of what is essentially a royalist party, you better be a bit more apocalyptic than that. I mean, 'The guy is a drunk. The man is a menace. When Nate Stanton gets on the Shuttle from Washington, it's time to lock up the silverware.' That kind of stuff."

"Yeah," said my eighteen-year-old cousin Owen Claydo, who was fresh from setting every high-school pitching record in his home state of Arkansas. "You gotta have an ad that, like, shows some old bum, you know, face down in the gutter with Nate's trademark Irish wool hat down right in front of the camera. And as this car pulls up behind him and you see him caught in the headlights, a voice-over goes on, saying, 'It's ten o'clock, do you know where your senator is?' And you have the whole thing wrapped in ten seconds. And you do that at one hundred gross rating points a week for three weeks, just that one ad every night at ten. Every channel. Whoo!" Owen whistled.

We looked at the floor and then at one another; we had never taken Owen all that seriously. He was just our smart southern cousin with the mean fork ball. He had recently received a little notoriety for refusing to provide his father, the disgraceful husband of our sainted late Aunt Mary, with an alibi for taking part in a Klan ambush of some Communist Party members over near Fayetteville. Owen was now exiled from his own home for his own safety and was staying with Andrew and Melissa. He had apparently traded the major leagues for an education. And he was on a roll, no doubt about it.

"And then what you gotta do, Ed, is you start this ad with a dark screen and someone whistling 'Sweet Georgia Brown' that breaks to a slow-mo' shot of a black basketball player doing these jump shots, right? And this voice, this voice comes over saying, 'Being a globe-trotter is a very good thing . . . if you're a basketball player.' " Owen paused and giggled. "And then you have this scroll of all the trips Nate's taken since 1960, whether they're junkets or not. I mean, slip his travel agent a fifty and you got the whole damn history. Don't pick on Taiwan, if he's been there, and Israel could be a dud. But anything else, anything in Europe, especially like southern France, or Asia, oh, man, it's all fair game."

And Edward sat there blinking at Owen, who was grinning underneath his baseball cap with the emblem of the Braves in the front, straws of blond hair spilling over the plastic strap in the back. Owen blinked a lot too, but he wasn't blinking now. And you should see him throw a slider.

Edward sat there as if realizing for the first time the kind of negative advertising you could concoct if you were going after a member of your own family. I mean, if the things we knew about the Stantons ever were to be used as weapons . . . How awful and mean and nasty it could be. I wasn't certain how I felt about that prospect. Betsy asked how old Uncle Nate was.

"I dunno, sixty-five or so?" I ventured.

"Oh, but the guy looks really old, doesn't he?" she said.

Now Betsy was by all measures the most levelheaded one among us. Hers was a clear drop of normalcy in an ocean of family neurosis. And that's not really fair; it wasn't as if she was normal in the banal sense. She was extraordinary, but seemingly without the family ration of demons. I mean, she had graduated Barnard near the top of her class, had set intercollegiate freestyle and butterfly records, dated nice, good-looking guys who treated her well and offered her challenges, and yet . . . And yet, Betsy had a nasty streak, the familial nasty streak, and we all looked at her as mischief clearly sent a shadow across her lovely, smooth-skinned face.

"I mean, he really looks *awful*, doesn't he?" she asked with her tongue making an exploratory swipe across her pink full upper lip.

I saw what she was getting at.

"From drink," I offered solicitously.

"Yeah," said Wolfy, who needed no probing. "Six years is a real long time."

"And a six-year Senate term is eternity for someone on death's doorstep," said Betsy.

"That guy looks like death warmed over," said Owen, getting into the flow.

"And that's a hell of a thing to say about death," said Edward with a grin that was nothing if not triumphant, with a slight twinge of guilt in its curl.

"Now you got it," Betsy said, and that's just about when as a family, without any of the consultants who soon were to flood Mingeboro, and completely against the ethics of my chosen profession, we settled down to plan the campaign.

## —•— CHAPTER THREE ——

AS THE PLANE SET down in Jersey, its tail winds swept up snow. And the view we'd promised the children just did not come to pass. There was no glimpse of lights off the Empire State Building. Manhattan lay in a stormy shroud. And as we all spilled off the plane onto the floodlit tarmac, a cold chill crept into the cabin.

The voices were a babble of tales we all would tell, some of my younger cousins already embellishing into mock heroic terms the dive the plane had taken, as if they'd seen fighters off the wingtips.

There we were, straggling off the runway, when rushing out to greet us was this unkempt charging herd, flashes popping, motor drives reeling, and there were angry shouted orders for us to be racked into a pose.

"What the hell is this?" asked Wolf with some annoyance.

"Don't worry, Wolfy," said Elsie Grodinger, the family's press agent. She had been in the front of the plane, quietly baby-sitting reporters. "Just a few photographs for the morning papers."

"Why? All we did was to go to Mama's funeral."

"Well, you see, I . . ."

"Elsie!"

"Well, I did have the pilots radio ahead about our, er, problems in the air."

"How did you get them to do that?" I asked.

"I wrote them a check," she said with not the least bit of embarrassment.

"Oh, God," said Wolfy. "Here it comes."

"Hey, Mr. Daley, over here. C'mon, smile with the broad."

Wolfy grimaced as my cutest cousin took a visible lunge away from him to get out of camera range. "That's my seventeen-year-old niece you're talking about, dog breath. Get out of my way."

Wolfy—after a long day, a day in which he'd fought the urge to drink the way children have to fight the urge to pee—Wolfy, I'm afraid, did take a swing at a photographer, and while he missed the man, his ring hit the camera's flash attachment with a huge gong, and they both let out a howl.

Children giggled; Aunt Morgan looked up to the sky with a gesture quite wasted when a snowflake hit a contact lens and she had to double up for a second to let the moisture stream away.

The photographers beat a quick retreat, covering one another with bursts of flash like the Daltons on the run. But that was not all, for just then Stanley, who for years had been the family's New York City driver, came rushing out toward us, and if Stanley was rushing, there was something major to worry about, like a world war or a subpoena.

Just as Stanley got to us and paused to catch his breath, Wolfy turned and said, "Hey, look here, Elsie, darlin', how much do we pay you to handle our press?"

"Not enough by half, Wolfgang."

"Look, whatever we pay you, can we please pay you the same amount to *not* get us press?" They stood there for a minute glaring at each other as the snow fell around them, and Stanley fought to get the words out.

"There are at least two camera crews and six re-re-reporters in there, Mr. Daley." Stanley was a retired cop who had no time for nonsense from kids, parking-lot attendants, doormen, and, most of all, reporters. His bulbous Polish nose often was aglow with drink, and he seemed to slump in an overweight coat from some TV crime show.

"What?" I asked. "Just 'cause the plane hit a little turbulence?" Even at the height of our wealth and fame years ago, something like that couldn't justify this kind of coverage.

"Well, not exactly," said Elsie.

We all whirled. The cousins who were holding their children seemed to sense that this was an excellent time to stay near the plane, cold as the air was, while these matters were resolved. Especially when they saw us look toward the Avjet terminal as if it were inhabited by some jungle beast that we had no nets to catch.

"What do you mean, Elsie?"

Elsie scrunched her freckled nose and smiled like a grandmother in an ad for chicken soup. "The AP guy radioed ahead that Edward was going to have an announcement to make."

"He what!" said Edward.

"Elsie, what do you have, a guerrilla radio operation in the front of the plane?" I asked.

"And where'd he get that from?" asked Uncle Wolfy. We looked over to Andrew, who had gone to talk with the reporters after our little dive.

"Oh, shit."

"Andrew," asked his older brother, and Andrew came forth with a grin that quickly left when he took a long look at our faces, "you didn't say anything about Edward and the Stanton seat did you?"

"What do you mean?" my handsome Uncle Andrew asked, quickly thinking what he should say to the older brother who all his life had predicated punches on the answers to such queries.

"You didn't happen to mention that Ed was thinking of running for the Senate," I offered.

"Oh, that. I didn't have to. They already knew, Charles. It's been speculated on."

"Yeah," I said, "speculated on. In columns." It was true. Edward's moves toward an open challenge to Uncle Nate had been written about in what appeared to be a carefully orchestrated press campaign. "They do that kind of thing. It becomes news when you confirm it."

"No, wait, Charles, they knew. That Samantha from the *Daily News* said, uh, 'So, Edward's going to challenge his own uncle.' And all I said was, 'Ain't that something?' What's wrong with that?"

"And did you say he'd made up his mind?"

"Uh, I said he could probably tell them for himself tonight. Why?"

Edward stood there mortified, and as soon as I had taken my hands off my face, I turned to him. No matter my ambivalence toward him, no matter my conflict as a reporter, this qualified as a family emergency. "Edward, we're going right into the lobby and let them throw whatever questions they have at you. And if they ask you any questions about whether or not you're going to run, just smile. And any questions you don't want to answer, laugh. Just be loose and laugh. Crack jokes. I don't mean stand there and say, 'Did you hear the one about the priest, the nun, and the BMW?' I mean saying things like, 'Hey, when I've made up my mind, I'll let you be the first to know.' And then ask for their home phone numbers."

A gust covered us with a spray of dry but chilling snow, and the women, who had dressed only in spring skirts and light jackets, were standing there miserably.

"How bad do you think it's going to be?" asked Camille, coming up to me and slipping her arm inside my own as she clung to me for warmth and attention. After years of ignoring each other, we'd become instantly chummy.

"Let's find out. Owen, just run up there and get an idea how much of a zoo we're talking about now."

He was back in a second and the news, well, the news about the news wasn't good. Apparently, in spite of the snow, we now had Channel 9 and Channel 5, as well as a couple of network affiliates, and there seemed to be a bunch of radio reporters with their ever-present need for drive-time sound bites. Wolfy put a brave face on things and turned to the family with a grin. "Head 'em up," he said. "Move 'em out." And with a number of cattle sounds rising in the chill airport air, we began to walk toward the door.

Steeped in the fluorescence was New York's Fourth Estate. The camera stands were mounted and were pointed at the door, so the moment we walked in, there was no place to go. At first there was a standoff; the reporters would not move, and yet the family could not slide inside the door. So Wolfy and Edward had to stand to the side and let our cousins and aunts and Uncle Andrew walk into the lobby one by one like hostages being released. That's when reporters started shouting out questions.

There was a whine from all the cameras as the auto rewinds ran, and the flashes that kept on popping were like a bad strobe in a club. "Mr. Daley, you going to run for the Senate against Senator Stanton?" was the question first pitched by Tony Echeveria, the political reporter from Channel 2, a smooth, cigar-chomping Cuban who wore white suits in March, as he was even now, with sclerotic slush clogging the arteries to Manhattan. He looked as if he was none too pleased to be out at Teterboro on an evening such as this and that he thought making an announcement of candidacy in a situation like this was truly bush-league, though he was much too classy a reporter to ever let that show on camera.

We could see there were eight reporters, not including camera crews and stills. It was what is known as a full hit. And they had struck the posture of vague hostility and utter contempt. And in return, what was the reaction from the seventy or so of my relatives who now were standing inside the lobby, beginning to thaw out? Fear. And more than a little corresponding contempt. Oh, and a great deal of excitement. It had been years since we'd been on the cover of *Life*. Things were happening once again.

"I'm thinking of it," said Edward almost inaudibly, standing up to the microphones that had been hastily slapped on top of a table.

"How strong a possibility would you say it is?" Tony asked with reasonableness. "On a one-to-ten scale."

Edward seemed to crane his neck to look to me for help, and as I was about to try to slow the answer with a soft shake of my head, he got this mischievous glint in his eye. And it was in the slow motion with which disaster strikes that I saw him smile, lean forward into the microphone nest, those snakes in front of him, and say, "Ten."

Pandemonium. Questions were lobbed in as if by mortar. Follow-ups came strafing across the deck. How did he feel about going after his own uncle? Did it have anything to do with Stanton coming out against the Vietnam War when Edward was running Vietnam Vets for Victory, the organization that made him famous ten years before? How much money of his own would he spend? From whom had he lined up support? Would he accept the nomination of the Conservative Party as well as the Republican Party, and had he already spoken to the Conservative Party leadership? Did he think his personal life would interfere?

"My what?" Edward asked a gloating Arthur Begelman.

Arthur sat there savoring the situation in which he—who by his own admission weighed 412 pounds, unless that was just to scare the kids who were getting on the plane with him—could make the attractive young hero squirm. Arthur looked a little like a bloated Burl

Ives, and he sat there puffing his pipe with self-satisfaction, having slowed down the responses that Edward had been making, completely against my advice, in a precise, ponderous, humorless, but admittedly faultless fashion.

"Your love life, kid."

Edward looked over to me helplessly. Hey, what could I do? As a reporter and all. But this was family, and though I thought for a second whether or not to let him hang, I guess I really didn't want to punish him, for I stood forward and said, sotto voce, "Yes, Edward, guys like Arthur *are* going to ask you questions like that when you make your formal announcement of candidacy, which, folks, this most definitively was not. We've got time for one more question."

And then we were saved by a softball from Honey Laab, the cute blond reporter Channel 5 had just brought up from Hartford. We had been watching her on weekends up in Mingeboro. "Mr. Daley, you and the Daleys are from Connecticut, and yet you're going to run for the Senate from New York," she asked. "Is that fair to the people of New York?"

Edward lunged and the ball went into the stands, a speech about his involvement in New York "for the eleven years since I returned from Vietnam," a period of time in which "Nate Stanton, who does not hail from New York, has spent more time in the country in Connecticut, on the shores of Dewey Beach, or on the links of Costa Brava than in the neighborhoods of Nassau or our cherished streets of Queens. He wouldn't know Horseheads from Hauppauge, Skaneateles from a hole in the ground. That's why we need to have a new senator from New York."

And with that the Daley kids broke into applause, and if I hadn't been so depressed by that gaucheness and breach of press-conference etiquette, I would have breathed a sigh of relief that Edward seemed to come out of what could have been a complete disaster with at least a point or two.

The shouted questions continued as we began to stream throughout the lobby, questions to Edward about whether the family's documented womanizing—and Wolfy's ex-wife's portrayal of them in her notorious book—would hurt him with the women's vote, questions about whether this was a blood match between two families, but Edward kept on walking toward the automatic doors to the buses Stanley had chartered. And I realized the flip side to how suffocating my family could be was just how physically protective the numbers were, as Edward strode through—above—the crowd, protected from reporters by my cousins.

Tony Echeveria, who had befriended me a year before when we were both staked out on the mayor's race, sidled over to me as I was about to make it out the door. "So, Charles, what role you playing here? Reporter or press secretary?"

"Oh, shit, Tone. Brother, I guess." I liked the hell out of the guy, not least because he was the most serious television reporter I had ever met.

"Yeah, well, how's that going to play with Hank and Rachel at the paper? Kind of tough to write about a race between your own brother and your uncle."

"Yeah, it all comes home, if you'll pardon the expression." I looked down at the floor, then out the windows to where the last of my cousins was clamoring up the snowy steps into a silvery bus. A diesel rev announced intentions.

"Well, you know the expression, 'All politics is local,'" he said, taking the cigar from his mouth and giving my hand a squeeze.

"Yeah, I guess I never realized how local. Thanks," I said, and stepped upon the magic pad that made a big door open. The engine was anxious. The bus seemed to huff. I took the step toward my family.

## —— CHAPTER FOUR ——

As I GOT ON the bus, I remembered that first night I was allowed to enter the dining room at my grandparents' unaccompanied by one of the nannies or the maids. I was allowed to march in so triumphantly to eat dessert with my grandparents, with my parents, and with some aunts and uncles. They sat around the table gesturing politely, as this was a family of polite gestures. They sat drinking their glasses of wine, wiping their fingers after immersing them in finger bowls adorned by lace doilies. I pushed open the door from the butler's pantry with the encouragement of the cook, and there they were, smiling, seemingly in expectation. They were all a little high from the wine. I looked across the table and saw my mother smiling at me. She was wearing a maroon suit and a shiny brooch. My grandmother sat tall and arch in her old wicker chair and she stared with obvious disapproval at my poor grandfather. He was so much smaller than she now, he'd shrunk somewhere along the way, and he sat being fed at the opposite end of the table. He'd been fed by a servant in the months since he lost the ability to so much as speak. They dressed him in his gray suit as if he were a doll, much the way they dressed me for these occasions. Though they all smiled at me as I ran quickly to mount a chair and kiss my grandmother's dust-covered cheek, I could tell that the smiles were compensation for the silence of the old man. For I knew also there was something wrong, and it had more to do with the two empty chairs than it did with the limp head of my grandfather.

His hand fell embarrassingly into the mashed potatoes, but my grandmother sighed as if he'd collapsed face first. Then everyone's attention was diverted by the roar of my missing uncles, late as usual, by the sound of their souped-up cars approaching. They made their living in those cars, and it seemed when they were not working on them, then my uncles were out playing in them. A least that was what my Aunt Rose would spit over scotch at my mother's poolside cock-tail hours when she stayed late into evening descending in layers of Black Velvet. And I could tell my uncles were racing recklessly this very minute. They were driving off the blacktop driveway onto the lawn that several of the maids' husbands were forever employed in manicuring. And they were racing the cars with the engines my father had built. I could tell that from the sound; it had come out of the factory so many evenings late into my mother's impatience. My uncles were driving through the flower gardens and accelerating around the house.

The roar was of cats locked in combat over land coveted but not needed so badly they cared they were destroying it. My uncles were sure to be ripping up the lawn and driving over the pale flowers that scented the air so delicately. I knew they might drive into the foun-tains or even down the tiers to the gardens that rolled toward the highway. And this was the first time I was allowed all by myself into a room with adults. I toddled over to my father, who now was throwing down his napkin. As he got up he spilled his wineglass and I watched him hurriedly throw some salt on the blotch it made on the linen.

"Charles, come here," my grandmother commanded, but my father had his hand held out to me, though briefly, warning me that it was now or never. There was no time for indecision; I could accompany him, but could not hold him back, for outside his brothers were testing engines he had spent so long perfecting. I followed my father as the roar of the cars kept getting closer, kept nearing the house. He limped out the door to the hallway, ducked before the low ceiling of the den, and clattered into the room we grandchildren had begun to call the Jungle Room. It was a huge old room with tile floors, the smell of dampness and Spanish moss; there were vines and a spiral staircase, twisted up like the horns of the kudu on the pink wall; further smell of mixed chlorophyll and water.

From the Jungle Room we could see them, those huge bubble-nosed and tail-finned test racers now heading away from us, heading across the lawn toward our neighbors that green mile away. "Fantastic," my father was saying, taking off his glasses and pinching the bridge of his nose, then putting the glasses back on while at sixty miles an hour the white car overtook the red car on the back lawn. As the cars turned and came flying past the small office my dad sometimes worked in, as they were propelled so ludicrously toward us, I could hear footsteps across the tile floor.

My grandmother was approaching, followed by my mother and my aunts and my Uncle Andrew, the only one of the Daley brothers disinclined to race autos. Bringing up the rear was one of the maids propping up my grandfather. A couple of cocker spaniels wondered what the fuss was all about, Uncle Andrew was chuckling, and so was my mother. But Rose, whose husband was out there proceeding so recklessly, was as thin-lipped and disapproving as my grandmother with her wide shoulders and big bosom and her shawl. Even then, I knew her complaint: that all their fun was edged by danger. And my uncles were still coming toward us across the field. We all paraded outdoors, the better to see and hear the antics unfolding before us. My father flashed his eyes across those cars and there was joy all over his face. Success was registered for every decibel by which the engines' roar grew greater. One car was overtaking the other as they came at us at more than fifty miles an hour. I could see it was Uncle Wolfy who was beating Uncle Blitz, and this was no surprise.

When they had surged so close to us that my grandmother shrieked, thinking they were going to drive right through the Jungle Room and over her rubber plants and wicker chairs, the cars suddenly turned—we could hear my uncles laugh as they whizzed by—and headed back into the open field. My father was in hysterics too. "Goddamn," he shouted ecstatically. "Christ on a Chris-Craft!" Uncle Andrew and my mother were still laughing. But my grandmother was horrified, and Rose, her daughter-in-law, looked disgusted. It may have been the first time they'd ever agreed on anything.

My father turned to me smiling and slapped at the artificial leg he'd acquired the very first time he'd competed in a professional auto race those many years ago. And then he smiled tenderly at my mother. Then the cars were coming toward us again and my grandmother was shrieking. Uncle Andrew tried to keep her calm, reaching up to pat those shoulders that were on a level with his head while shushing her with piercing, yet vacuous eyes.

Wolfy was still ahead of Blitz. He gunned his engine one last time and went past the huge elm that shaded the house, and once past it he had to start putting on his brakes. Only he was going so fast and the green grass was so perfectly soft that he sent up two huge plumes of mud in a comical wake that caught Uncle Blitz full in the windshield. And then Wolfy began to mire himself into the ground in two precise tracks.

Uncle Blitz was forced to stop similarly, only even more quickly, else his demonic testing end in the coupling of the autos and a hole in the side of the house. At the last possible second he averted a crash and, missing my grandmother by *inches*—"ah!"—nuzzled the car delicately against those big green bushes that were the last defense of the Jungle Room. At this point Blitz fell out the door with tears of laughter streaming down his cheeks. My father limped over to him with his arm around Uncle Wolfy, both of them unknowingly paying homage to the man who would die in precisely the fashion he had just avoided. And the three of them laughed and hugged and gestured wildly. By this time everyone was surrounding them, and the dogs were running after each other's tails in spirals that narrowed like the staircase inside the Jungle Room. Even my grandmother was forced to start a smile that grew until it was as robust as she was at her feistiest. Her laughter was forgiveness.

And my grandfather, who had started the whole thing, the automobiles, the beautiful grounds, who had conjured all this up from the nothingness of southern poverty, my grandfather just stood there propped up by the maid, who was more attentive to him than any of his progeny. So I went over to him, small child in front of the weak old man unable to so much as feed himself. That's what everyone thought. I reached up and held his hand. With a simple human touch, I wanted to make him feel he was part of the action. I guess I sensed his powerlessness. I didn't expect anything from the patriarch, though those weren't exactly terms I thought in when I was five years old. I just wanted him to feel included. I never expected what happened next. Never would have expected it in a million years. My grandfather winked.

## —— CHAPTER FIVE ——

IT WAS A LITTLE out of character that as we rolled into Manhattan no one in my family was heard to speak. Camille sat hunched beside me blowing desultory rings of smoke, her thick hair resting lightly against the frosted glass. A disinfectant stench stalked the aisle as I sat there dreamily trying to make sense of the day, or at least of my family, my goddamn family.

My parents died not long ago, which is why I sat there smarting; the death of my old grandma pulled the scabs off all my wounds. And an hour with my family, well, an hour with my family could be a lot more stressful than that feeling when our prop plane all but dropped out of the sky. My family has a tendency to overwhelm outsiders, and we do it with the unthinkingness of Zulus set to overrun the fort. We just pour increasing numbers at you, colorfully dressed but bent on victory, and finally you go down. "I give," you cry. "Uncle."

It was just as wearying to some of us on the inside. My family demanded a sort of quirky conformity. As eccentric as we were, with a grandfather who'd disappeared to go hunting for some flower in the Punjab, with aunts who wrote detailed sexual exposés about uncles, sometimes we exhibited conventionalism, which, more than the eccentricity, wore me down.

I'm talking about the rather newfound expectation of Yale, the Brooks Brothers dress code, the ethnocentrism we felt on our estate. More to the point, the prospect of Edward's candidacy was a threat, a truly terrible threat, to my newly won status as an adult in my own right, away from the family, semi-independent in my role as a reporter. And I was drawn to Edward's candidacy, because he was, after all, family, and I am a political junkie. Yet when I had stepped in to protect him this evening from reporters who bore in, I was directly violating the ethics of my profession. I sensed how vulnerable I was to being sucked into a campaign I would rather cover objectively from the outside. It's a problem when you want to be a reporter and your family's the news.

Camille sat smoking and the windshield wipers squeaked as we drove into snowflakes that dissolved upon their contact with the headlights. I was reminded of a childhood in the glare of photojournalistic scrutiny, of a family that looked as good in black 'n' white as in color.

My grandfather always claimed to hate being in the public eye, but he must have known that the story of an upstart taking on Ford and General Motors in the postwar era would sell as many cars as his extraordinary talents at mechanics and design. He was not a fool, though I suspect that after a time he was crazy as a loon. How else do you explain a car so far beyond the American public of the sixties as the Lazzy? It was later to become the ultimate American status symbol, the elite's version of the '65 Corvette, but at first it was viewed as an oddity almost antidemocratic in its European flair.

He *earned* all his coverage in *Fortune,* not to mention the cover story in *Time,* which I vaguely recall as the most celebrated moment of my childhood. So it lasts a week; we saw it as a marble arch. And when the news turned troublesome, shortly after he broke that strike and we began to be sent to nursery school accompanied by bodyguards with names like Vince and Gus, he strode triumphantly around the grounds in Mingeboro, utterly unaware of what it was like to be a four-year-old escorted to New York City school yards by those gentle serge-cloth giants. He had no idea that we were whisked into waiting cars each day, away from our ambulatory, laughing friends, away from photographers, toward this idealized false normalcy.

Since his death our fortunes had slid. But there were times when we still were caught in a glare as bright as Manhattan, now distantly visible through snow and the metal spires of the George Washington Bridge. As when my Uncle Wolfy won his first Indy 500 and had his own cover on *Sports Illustrated,* or when his wife made the rounds of talk shows for denouncing him. Or, in a limited fashion, like tonight, when the mere rumor that my brother Edward was going to challenge our Uncle Nate for his Senate seat brought the camera crews to Teterboro in the middle of a snowstorm.

The family exuded the confidence of the securely rich, but we weren't that secure, and we sure weren't that rich. We'd only arrived at this stage in the last generation, and it looked as if, having learned not to slurp with our soup spoons, we were going to be shown to the door. And the tradesmen's entrance at that.

I sat there dwelling on my family, and it was difficult not to. My answer to the family was to have something of my own, my own byline in the paper. My grandfather's answer years ago was simply to disappear.

It was as if that whole period of self-willed silence—four years by the time he left—was a storing of energy for some final effort. We had no idea of his whereabouts over six months of investigative reportage, detectives lounging around the house as anxious directors of Daley Motorworks drank lots and lots of booze; and finally, the oddly soothing conclusion reached by a number of us that anyplace he was—short of being held hostage in some distant dusty airstrip— was better than the deal he had at home.

We felt he was better off anywhere in the world, that Mombasa, Djakarta, even Newark, New Jersey, was better than sitting with my grandmother, mute and feuding. And then just as surprising as the discovery he had stuffed his bed with pillows and had slipped into the night was the postcard that arrived one morning from India, telling us not to worry. Laconic, sure, but it said more than he had for years.

When he returned—without fanfare—he was again quiet, though no longer silent, telling us of his trip in hushed tones. He returned tanned and looking healthy, dressed not in the pair of Peter Sellers pajamas we jokingly expected, but in a pin-striped suit he'd had fitted on the deck of a houseboat in Srinagar. He looked dapper and fit.

My grandmother wanted him committed, was adamant about not letting him in the house, and it was just as well we had to sneak him in, given the number of paparazzi who had staked out the driveway when word spread he was back. While my uncles greeted him with a little bemusement, I remember my father was the one who gave him a hug and quite seriously, quite sonorously welcomed him home.

His daughters were protective of his every effort, and made sure when they were around that he did not have to make a single wasted movement. So long as my aunts were in attendance, he was protected from reporters, snake-oil salesmen, and my grandmother, who took to his coming home by taking to her bed. You could mark her decline from the day he returned.

And so my grandfather, not such a weak old man as many of us had figured, was able to spend the last few years of his life floating through the house on currents separate from those of his wife of fifty years. His existence was now almost exclusively made up of the Jungle Room and the Orientalia with which he surrounded himself. He got very, very weird.

I remember when I was about eleven and staying as a houseguest while my parents wintered somewhere in the sun. Ed, Sam, and Betsy were off in boarding school and little Annie . . . I don't know where she would have been. At home with her nanny, I guess. I walked past the Jungle Room late one night to fetch myself a Coke, ritualistically looking in, for this wasn't a room a child could pass by lightly at night. If there were demons in the old house, you could bet this is where they hung out. But on this evening, as I looked in, I saw my grandfather sniffing flowers in the dark.

"Grandfather," I said with much surprise, and went over to him. He was tiny by now, I was gaining on him rapidly, and his breath was very bad. He was smiling, and it reminded me of that wink he had given me years before. It was so quiet in the house, but he moved with such assurance I gave up being scared. I knew my grandmother and the servants were asleep, because I had begun keeping track of their movements the way a prisoner knows the sweepings of the searchlight. I was about to talk, but my grandfather put his finger to his lips and, both eyes flashing, even the one on the side of his face that was paralyzed, he led me over to the corner of the Jungle Room underneath the huge windows.

It was totally dark on this side of the room and only squares of light from our distant neighbor's porch were visible nestled against the house. Here and there were vines and tables and huge columns of ivy hanging from the ceiling thirty-five feet above us.

My grandfather led me past the small Buddha Commanding His Family Not to Fight. He led me past the small couch covered with crochet work that had survived his Oriental eccentricities and past the bowls in which seemingly phosphorescent goldfish swam. Next to them, there was a beautiful papier-mâché table with nothing on it save a single pot with a single flower barely visible in the darkness. It was a black rose.

I knew that he had spent years trying to find one, and when his correspondence finally directed him to an Indian village where they grew, he disappeared. And now he was back, and was soon to die. And it seemed at that moment that having the black rose was one of the reasons why he would quite genuinely, if somewhat ridiculously, die happy.

He pulled me down beside him on the cool tile floor next to the table, and together we knelt. Our backs were supported by those copper pools that flashed orange each time the fish stirred. The old man was smiling a little vacantly at the flower he had so conspired to put before us. Every time I tried to say something he would hush me with a solitary finger raised with sanguine purpose to his lips. I knelt this way until I fell asleep, like an altar boy nodding off before Communion.

When I awoke it was lighter in the Jungle Room and the windows were all streaked with moisture produced overnight in this dank atmosphere. Outside the grass was sautéed with sunshine splattered on dew. My grandfather was beside me, kneeling exactly as he had been when I had fallen asleep, and I remember he referred to the black rose before us with the identical palms-up gesture with which the priest had greeted our family at my grandmother's funeral.

I have never known precisely why my grandfather had me wait up with him that night, have never sensed exactly what the purpose was, or what was the lesson my grandfather was passing on to me that morning as the rare flower opened so slowly, so sensuously, petal after petal, revealing its delicate organs only after following a process that had been handed down to it from forever.

But I do know this. As painful as my legs were as I kneeled with my grandfather, I wouldn't have traded this for anything in the world. And as suffocating as the family could be, there was a power to their energy as rare and as special as the black rose before us. I could never simply turn my back on this.

PART TWO

# CHAPTER ONE

IT WAS A VERY tense week for the front desk at the *Downtown News*. First, a disaffected member of some indeterminably threatening cult took offense at a photograph that had appeared in last week's issue, a photograph in which his face had been half cropped. He'd expressed his displeasure by browbeating poor Angela, the cute but smart-ass receptionist I had a crush on, until she began to whimper. Then, sensing his moment had quite arrived, he lit and tossed what everyone later expanded into a stick of dynamite, but which the police, when they carted away the remains of the garbage can it had blown up, stated was a mere M-80. It was loud, but lethal only if this asshole's luck really was bad.

Then, just as Angela was getting over the incident and was a little embarrassed by all the attention she was receiving, her week ended on a worse note. She was sitting at her desk looking out on Broadway and across it to the greasy spoon on the corner of Spring Street. She sat framed by more flowers than the widow of some Little Italy don when a burly-looking gent in an overcoat suspiciously warm for this April afternoon lumbered into the small entranceway that boxed off the warren of offices.

"Can I help you?" Angela stated with the perfect amount of cool for a pretty young college-educated punkette who held the privilege of a day job south of Houston.

"I wish to speak with your arts editor," the man said. His eyes, Angela later would say, were noticeably glazed, his hair greasy even by street-people standards, and his beard was flecked with what looked to be acrylic pink paint. For the neighborhood, he was normal.

"I believe the arts editor is in an editorial meeting. Did you have an appointment with him, Mr. . . . ?"

"Oh, yes," the man said as a delivery boy stepped in behind him looking anxiously at Angela to see if he could drop off his package and get back to his appointed rounds. "For now," said the visitor, "I'm afraid I'll have to leave my card."

Reaching into his overcoat, the man brought out a hatchet.

The delivery boy was out the door in the time it took Angela to shriek, and with that, the man laid out his hand by the telephone console and whacked his fingers off at the ridge of knuckles.

Needless to say, the subsequent, seemingly permanent bivouac of cops in the lobby made for a little tension just as we were heading for press. I don't think anyone that afternoon was able to get his mind off the image of those fingers twitching by poor little Angela's switchboard, or of the cop who so calmly scooped them up so they could be reunited with their rightful owner. Angela was in such a state of befuddlement that after weeks of politely turning down my offer of drinks or dinner she jumped at my suggestion to come to Mingeboro for the weekend, just as soon as we put the *News* to bed.

By midafternoon, the *New York Post* was reporting that while the madman's fingers had gone off to St. Vincent's Hospital, the man himself had calmly traveled by subway and bus up to Bellevue. The fingers were put into a cab for the journey to catch up with their owner.

It was in this charming mood that the editorial meeting was held to decide the fate of my article on the Liberal Party's efforts at fielding a candidate to run against Senator Nathaniel Stanton. The building itself would have needed a chiropractor to scrunch out the tension.

I was sitting at my desk in the large, cluttered loft that passed for a newsroom, telephone plugged into my ear, shoulder in its customary slump. I was rather guiltily talking with Jimmy Zion, a Republican media consultant whom my Uncle Nate had called as soon as he read in the papers that Edward was thinking of running. I knew that ethically I should be talking to Jimmy only if he was a source. He had once upon a time been pretty good, though now he was rather desperately over the hill. What Uncle Nate didn't know was that Jimmy had approached Edward months before, urging him to make the race. Now that it was inevitable Edward would do so—the announcement of his candidacy was scheduled for next week—Jimmy was trying to remind me, as Edward's brother, of his early support, and was being helpful in small ways, such as getting quoted saying nice things about Edward and his upside potential as a candidate. Today he was passing along information that reflected the way Nate was taking to the notion that his own nephew was going to challenge him.

"Oh, he's pissed, Charles. I mean *pissed.* Hurt. But pissed. He can't believe a goddamn Daley is going to do this to him."

"What, he said that?"

"Oh, shit, yes. And that's all your Uncle Ethan can talk about these days. 'Those fucking Daleys. That Irish scum.' Stuff like that. I like your Uncle Nate, but that brother of his is not a nice man."

I felt my cheeks burn just a little bit. Across the newsroom we were having ourselves a little fashion show, new skirts and tops being shown by a Soho designer who dreamed them up, or so she said, in an effort to get Louise Squeeze, the fashion editor, to do a photo spread. "These were made for the *Downtown News,*" I heard the woman say with ballsy certainty. Although we were supposed to be a community paper, it was accurate to think of the *News* as a window through which downtown life could be viewed by rich people on the Upper East Side, people who needed an up-to-the-minute hipster Baedeker before zipping down on weekends to unload buckets of credit-card receipts.

"Yeah, Charles, I would say whatever bad feeling is there, and I think it's plenty, it's being egged on by Ethan."

"He never much liked us to begin with," I said absently, staring at the pale downtown model, unconventionally stunning with her short mousy-brown hair and nuclear-powered cheekbones. Then, focusing on my pigsty of a desk, the black phone, the cord that curled to my ear, I said, "The thing I'm curious about, Jimmy, is whether or not Nate and Ethan are taking this thing seriously. Do they think they can shoot Edward like a fish in a barrel, or do they sense they may have a little problem?"

"Nate told me when that picture was in *People*—By the way, you get in any trouble for that?"

"I may still be getting in trouble for it." The photo showed me lunging forward to protect Edward at that airport press conference. Christ, when I had needed a break, a Luce publication had reverted to form, running its thousandth picture of us. I looked through the window into the room where my editors were going over the front-of-the-book pieces. Paddy Mack, my Marxist nemesis, was pointing right at me, and unless I was imagining it, spray seemed to be issuing from his lips.

"Well, your Uncle Nate told me, 'Give it to me straight, Jimmy.' So I said, 'Senator, you may have problems.' He goes, 'Jesus, that little pissant was head of one of those organizations that presented Nixon with resolutions urging him to stay in Vietnam and fight.' I'm not thinking. I'm trying to humor the guy, so I say, 'You got him there, Senator.' And he goes, 'Course I don't have him there, idiot, this is a *Republican* primary.' "

I bet Jimmy lost the account right there, hence the call.

"So I'd guess you have to say he knows what he's got coming. He did say one thing I really liked, though."

"Yeah, what's that?"

"I said to him, 'Senator, how much money did you spend the last time you got primaried?' And he goes, 'I remember exactly. A hundred and sixty thousand dollars. And against a kook. I had him when it came to fluoride.' " Jimmy began to laugh, and I did too, as I could see Nate saying it, sneering about the conspiracy theories of the right wing that he had successfully beaten up on the whole time he'd been in politics. And which we hoped had finally come home to roost.

"You can't help but like the guy," I said.

"Of course not, Charles. Let's face it, you got some great rogues in your family. Both sides. Why am I telling *you* this? You're the only guy I know could make money off his goddamn *dog,* so you're on your way too. Me, I gotta work to make a living, so I gotta go. But keep me in mind."

"I'm just a reporter here, Jimmy."

"Okay, I'll come down on my price."

"I mean it, Jimmy."

"Charles, you tell me that, I believe. Things change, you know where I am."

I thanked Jimmy for the call, and just as Jimmy knew I would, I immediately began to dial my brother Edward.

## —— CHAPTER TWO ————

MY EDITORS WERE A very long time in their deliberations and I began to get nervous. First I paced, checking in on chums. Then I went to Dave's for an egg cream. Finally I went over to my basket to check my mail.

Four notices about some band I'd never heard of that was about to play at CB's. About fourteen press releases from candidates for office, all of which I scooped under my arm. An invitation to a press party for which Generation X would be flown over from England and back the same day without any performances. What were they trying to hide? A letter complaining that I had song titles all wrong in my review of the Buzzcocks' new album. And a letter from my Uncle Nathaniel Stanton.

There was a ruckus near my desk where Roger Rabin was holding court. Roger was the paper's resident trendsetter, the man who could make or break a particular club in the space of a well-timed snort. He could determine whether people would be boasting about or hiding the fact they had gone to a particular party, opening, or event the evening before, could calibrate presence in precise social mileage. His level of approval was determined by his cocky air and his particular level of dishevelment as he wandered in these early afternoons. Sometimes writers trying to curry favor and guest passes to newly opened clubs could upon Roger's arrival be seen gleefully reaching for their phones to tip off the management of the lucky few that had made the grade. Today we were treated to words like "divine," "stunning," and "original." By the rapt look on the faces of the interns, typesetters, and receptionists, a club was born. Someone was going to get rich on the basis of Roger's henna-headed approval.

"Hey, Charles, there's a call for you on oh-seven," yelled Jeannie, the intern who covered newsroom phones.

"And it is?"

"It's your brother Edward returning your call," she yelled before picking up other lines. About six heads turned and I found myself looking over to the editorial meeting, which now seemed to have reached a heated peak.

I waited until Jeannie had sent a call elsewhere before asking her if I could call my brother back, and sat down at my desk to read the letter from Uncle Nate.

Only it wasn't from my Uncle Nate, though it was sent on his stationery. It was a handwritten letter, vaguely legible. It was from my Uncle Ethan.

It was short, and not very sweet. "Dear Charlie," it began, which since I was about seven had not been the form of address destined to get anyone but my grandmother on my good side. Ethan knew that. "I understand your protestations to the *Village Voice* that all you want is to be a good reporter for the *Downtown News,* and from what Nate tells me you're probably okay at it. But I also know you Daleys are a close-knit swarm, and there is no way you and Edward aren't talking from time to time about this folly he's set out on. If you do talk to Edward—I can't, I'm afraid I'd spit in his face, the punk—it would be excellent for you to mention this could get very ugly, very fast. Welcome to the reality of primary politics. Sometimes I don't think Edward realizes what he's letting himself in for, though I know he knows what it's like to be fragged by his own troops." I winced at that. "I'm just doing him—you—a public service by telling you what this thing could be like. Now, I would love to talk with you about this when I get back to New York, or else we could meet for a drink at All Odds or at your house in Mingeboro, though I'd prefer it if you came to All Odds. The view down on you Daleys from our mountain is very clear this time of year. Let me know. P.S. I was truly sorry to hear about your grandmother. You kids have had a rough year. No need to make it worse."

I wondered if he knew how rough it could be if a reporter, say me, printed his threatening letter. I wondered if he knew the maxim that you don't pick a fight with someone who buys ink by the barrel. Maybe I could teach him a thing or two, no matter what the Stantons' view down upon us from their estate at All Odds.

All my life the Stantons had presumed that because they had arrived in Mingeboro first, had carved out a duchy on the high plains of Mount Targa, then for obvious reasons they were superior to us. And they held on to that notion stubbornly, even as my paternal grandfather was being recognized as a genius for inventing the automatic transmission. As the Daleys became the larger family both in numbers and in visibility, the Stantons began to try to rub in their social superiority. And whether it was by inviting famous artists up to their estate, or through their touching all proper bases between Amagansett, Paradise Isle, and Fishers Island (while the Daleys became more and more entrenched in Mingeboro), the Stantons just never let up. Which used to drive my mother crazy, partially because she would have liked to have gone to Amagansett, but mostly because of how silly the rivalry became. There were times when it seemed because each could be so silly she was willing to give up on both her own family and the one she had married into.

The door opened from the editorial meeting and I could see Hank Nostrum, the editor, walking toward me.

"Hey, Hank," I said, straightening up and getting my feet off the desk, pronto. "What's up?" I asked with all innocence. But I had to catch my breath.

Hank was a tall, bearded man given to wearing sweaters even in the summer. He was a former Green Beret turned Pulitzer prize-winning investigative reporter for a number of papers in Texas. He'd been recruited the year before by the *News*'s absentee Brit owners, who thought he could bring an intellectual sheen to the paper, to toughen it up, make it a little less the tip sheet for aspiring hipsters and a little more the nonideological competitor to the *Village Voice*. He was a tough son of a bitch whose taciturn authority was a little intimidating to some of the paper's more creative types.

"Not too much, Charles. Your piece on Brian, um . . ."

"Eno."

"Yeah, Brian Eno is going to be the lead in 'Downtown Style.' "

"Hey, that's great," I said. It was. Besides being in the paper's most visible section, the lead story in "Downtown Style" got more artwork than any piece other than the cover story. "What about my piece on the Liberal Party?"

"We need to talk about that. C'mon in!" He motioned toward the conference room. I felt as if I'd just been called onto the stage of "The Price Is Right."

We clumped across the newsroom floor. The fashion show was scattered by Hank's Texas-sized gait. Inside the room were the members of the editorial board that each week elevated or broke the hearts of a dozen *News* writers.

A foot from the table with her head down was Katrina Smith, only the most beautiful woman south of 57th Street. That's all. She was intimidating in her frosty inability to be charmed, the absolute authority with which she would kill a story, and her legendary ability to have any rival somehow exiled to the Bowery beat. She was a mystery, because no one had ever seen her go out on a date, eat dinner out, be anywhere but here, though periodically she was spotted leaving the building. Instead, she would hang around the office chain-smoking, dressed in expensive blouses and blue jeans, looking just completely beautiful from Monday through Sunday.

Then there was Rachel, whose multifaceted roles included those of publisher, salesman, wife to Hank, and informal ally to all writers who had a gripe with the cavalier treatment their copy received, particularly at Katrina's hands. Rachel was the politician of the office, the one to whom appeals were laid, and often she would come up with the trick, the inclusion of the extra interview, the excision of the offending quote, the miracle insight that would provide enough of a consensus to allow a piece to run. She was a jolly, fleshy woman who drank stout, sometimes at work. Rachel and I were each other's favorite. Now she smiled with what I took to be sympathy as I darkened the editorial doorway.

And then there was Paddy Mack, our resident ideologue. Paddy always treated me with disdain. It wasn't so much he resented the fact that I wasn't a Marxist, though that probably would have been sin enough. It was that my mere presence on the staff was representative of the bourgeois materialism that so corrupted the paper. Paddy was unrelenting in his derisiveness about the hipster ethos that infused the place, and was unyielding in his dismissal of the paper's role as arbiter of fashion that paid all our salaries. His belief in the paper's mission had more to do with Lincoln Steffens than Andy Warhol. Paddy was the former campaign manager for dozens of liberal citywide candidates, and he was always trying to get the paper to go to the left of the *Voice*, preferably with as little humor as possible. Hirsute, built like a bottle of Guinness, his complexion suggested he lived underneath a rock. Although he had a monklike quality, all the while you sensed he wished to burn the clergy.

"How ya'll *doing?*" I asked with a cheerfulness that was wholly forced. I hardly recognized my voice.

While there were grunts of greeting, only Rachel even bothered a polite showing of teeth. Hank got right to the point. "Charles, I think what you've written is pretty good, even newsworthy. But, well, Paddy here has a few problems with the piece, not least of which being the fact that you are even *doing* a piece when you might, as has been argued, have a conflict of interest here."

"Fair enough," I allowed, trying to show my reasonableness.

Paddy was having nothing to do with reasonableness. "As Marx is my witness," he began with his lilt, "How do you think you can write about the Senate race with your own brother going to be a candidate in it?"

"Easy, Paddy. I won't write about the Republican primary, and I'll avoid the Senate race during the general. That seems clear enough. It's obvious."

"Right, Charles," Paddy said thoughtfully, as if what we were discussing were a matter of academic concern. "So instead now you feel you can take potshots at the Liberal Party."

"There isn't a cheap shot in that piece, Paddy. There is, however, reportage, if you can recognize it."

"Cool it," said Hank with firmness. He was stroking his beard with his right hand as he leaned back on his chair, spilling cigar ash on the table in front of him. With one smooth scoop, he levitated the ash and sent it over to the garbage can several feet away from him. "This isn't a closed book. I'm willing to listen to why you think you should be able to continue to write about politics here while you have a very clear-cut conflict of interest."

"Hank, I don't see how I have a conflict of interest right now."

"I suppose Paddy's argument would be that even if you're not writing about the Republican primary, you may have an interest in making the Democrat or the Liberal candidate look bad."

"Hank, that's a solid piece I wrote. I make one reference in there to the general election, where I say the usefulness of New York's Liberal Party, like the Conservative Party, is that of the tail wagging the dog, and that, in fact, the utility of both parties has to do with the way they influence the Democratic and the Republican primaries. Even Paddy has written approvingly in the same vein."

Paddy looked through his rimless glasses at me, eyes a little rheumy and theoretical. He became very calm, and I saw him catch Katrina's eyes for a second. "Why don't we go over the piece for a second, Charles? You have as your lead, 'The Liberal Party of New York is sometimes thought of as seven men looking for a job. This year it looks as if the seven are all going for the same job.'"

Paddy looked at me again and I back at him. "That is a cheap shot," he said with quiet triumph, as if divining from the text a magically subversive act of commission.

"That's a good lead, Paddy, and leave the guy alone," said Katrina to my utter surprise. "What he says is precisely the truth, that the Liberals are so badly squabbling right now, they probably *are* going to nominate some purist. He won't get the Democratic line, and whether or not Edward Daley beats his uncle in the Republican primary, the Liberals, once again, might defeat the Democrat. It's legitimate, it describes New York's particular political system, the guy wrote it well. I don't see a conflict."

Paddy glowered across the table, waiting for Hank to step in. I wanted to carry off Katrina and marry her. I'd always liked her. Her social habits were a little odd, but other than that she was a wonderful woman. Great editor, calm, reasoning . . .

Paddy chimed in right then, and my moment was lost. "How can we, though, pretend to be objective when there are pictures of you in *People* magazine, for Godsake, leading the press conference at which your brother announced his intention?" Paddy looked confidently at Hank. Hank was taking the judicious, rabbinical view of things, beard being stroked to a glossy point.

"That was a set of circumstances I had little to do with. We were coming back from burying my grandmother. We got sandbagged by all sorts of things. Christ," I said, and tried to find the right way to say what I had to get out. I felt I was on the edge of winning them over, but I knew their judgment on the ethics of things, the ethics of my trying to make my livelihood in the way I wanted to make it, still hung in the air. I could blow it as sure as I could save it.

"You can't expect me not to talk to my brother. Of course I'm going to. But I'm not going to be part of his campaign."

"How can we trust you on that, Daley?"

"Paddy! Maybe *you* can't. You've sat in on more campaign strategy sessions than the average media consultant. Newfield, over at the *Voice*, your great chum and rival, has practically been campaign manager to a dozen candidates. And you've tried to top him. But I mean it. I will voluntarily not write about Republican politics during the primary season or about the Senate race during the general."

Paddy turned to Hank. "We're going to be made a mockery, Hank. Stanton's going to say anything we do to him—and there is much to be done—is because we employ his opponent's brother."

"I'm also *his* nephew, Paddy."

"Don't remind me. Alexander Cockburn is going to have a field day with us. You know that."

That I did. He had a point there. Cockburn had already written in the *Voice* the mere fact that I, a union-busting Daley, was writing for the *News* was an affront to progressive culture.

"What do you say, Hank?" asked Rachel quietly, leaning over the table with a certain weariness we all shared. It had been a very long week.

"I think we ought to run the piece. I think Charles should continue to write about politics and rock 'n' roll. And if you are seen, Charles, at an event for your brother that is not so general as a parade or so specific as a family picnic, I'll take you off politics until after the election. Unless you want to ask right now for a leave of absence."

"No, no, no, no, no! Bless you, Hank," I said, getting up and planning on getting out of there before Hank changed his mind or anyone voiced stronger opinions as to why I should be cashiered. "Thank you very much," I said, edging to the door. "I won't let you down." And then with a wave I stepped back into the newsroom.

It was awfully quiet for a Friday night, but this week we were putting out a special issue on summertime fashion and entertainment, and most of the back of the book had long since gone to bed. Only a few stragglers getting in their copy, as well as those who made the newsroom their home, clustered in groups, talking about the scene at the clubs tonight.

Which was why Roger Rabin was still lingering. When he saw me he came rushing toward me with a deference he usually displayed only to new boys who had started work as interns or to mid-level rock stars in the Soho pantheon.

"Is it true?" he asked breathlessly.

I was tired, I was late for my little rendezvous with Angela, and I seldom paid too much attention to Rabin. "Is what true, Roger?"

"Your cousin is Camille?"

"Camille Daley?"

"She goes by 'Camille' now. So does her band."

"Yeah, she's my Uncle Wolfgang's little daughter."

"Little daughter? She's a star! She's going to be the biggest thing in Tribeca in a matter of days! I haven't stopped talking about her since I saw her at Mudd Club. She's incredible! What a voice, and that face . . . ahhhhhhhh!"

Roger was positively rapturous, grasping at his short, spiky hair as if for purchase, twisting in his slim Italian suit. "No shit," I said.

"And she's related to you Daleys."

"Only through birth, Roger. After that, she was on her own."

"Ahhhhhhh!" he moaned into the newsroom, and picking up my satchel, I made toward the entrance that had so recently seen fingers aflying and tossed-in bombs.

## ——— CHAPTER THREE ———

BY THE WAY SHE threw her bag into the backseat, I knew Angela was ready to roll. So we shot up the West Side Highway and were off into the night. Mingeboro beckoned like a steaming hot bath, like a tableful of food, like a comfortable bed, with no one there, no one at all, to bother us.

It was two hours over hill and dale, past speed traps and the gradual dropping off of juke joints and burger stands, until we began to hit the farmlands that slumbered in the highway's wake. Just five miles from Mingeboro, the road took its dip into Mills Corner, New York, a tough little town with fender shops and grain storage tanks, and the memory of a time when the railroad still cut through it. There was this one street I knew, a street with houses that sagged in Appalachian dishabille. Several of the houses had '62 Chevys planted nose down in the front yards, surrounded by tricycles, guarded by dogs. There was this one house whose particular level of decline sparked some chord of mischief within me, and I pulled right up in front.

"Honey, we're home."

"Nice try, Charles, but you don't live here."

So I put the old Bavaria in gear and we drove on up the street, turning back onto the road that would deliver us to my home, and I began to tell her about my dog, Fido, who was my major source of income.

"Wait till you see him. Boy, is he cool," I said with the reserve of a father talking of his firstborn. But where fathers have to take out baby photos to show what the kid looks like, with Fido no such act was necessary. For Fido was an icon. Fido was a star. Fido was a gold mine that for years had paid my bills.

When I was thirteen and a real brat, only marginally more interested in sex than in drugs, my mother surprised me one morning by giving me a blue tick hound in puppy form, a dog so pretty and well behaved just being near him made me mind my manners. I took him with me everywhere, and damn near balked at boarding school when the prospect arose that Fido would not be accepted, which truly was a surprise considering they accepted *me*.

Then, when I was away at school, my parents one weekend were visited by friends from the city, one of whom was the director of a large advertising agency that had Puppy Crunch for a client. Without telling me, my parents took Fido for a screen test, and within a month, my dog had jumped into television sets as the grumpy mutt whose demeanor changes only by constant hits on a proffered dog biscuit. He should have gotten an Academy Award, because Fido hated Puppy Crunch. But a lot of dog food had gone over the lawn since then.

Within five years, the merchandising was complete, with a Fido T-shirt, calender, and bumper sticker, and talk of a syndicated cartoon show based upon his life and times. His only rival was Morris the cat, but whereas there was only one Fido, Morris was generic. There were dozens of that goddamned cat. We all breathed a sigh of relief when they let Morris die.

My father early on insisted that since Fido was my dog, I was to be the beneficiary of his royalties. Which is how, given that my parents' estate was still in probate, I was able to live where I did on the Upper West Side on what they paid me at the *Downtown News*. But there was one problem. Over the years, Fido had taken on a peripatetic nature, and now he showed up at the family estate only to collect his mail and to see if his agent had called.

Everywhere he went, Fido was a hit, children oohing and aahing over him, families willing to hand over dinner to this stranger—well, Fido wasn't a *stranger* to anyone—but to this visitor who scratched on the screen door and came in and licked their faces. And now, after not having seen Fido for a month or more, since the last time I was home he was elsewhere, I was anxious to see him, hoping he would be there when Angela and I arrived.

The road slinked blue as hills wrapped the lakes, and there wasn't a car to be seen. We gently curved our way past the golf courses and estates, windows open to the fresh spring air that pulled New York away from us. I looked at Angela and she was all curiosity, nose sniffing that air for the clues it would bring. Up the hill past the crude ski area, then onto the gravel horse path, and within moments we were on the back end of my family's estate, headed for the small house my sisters and brothers and I had kept after selling off the big house we'd grown up in on the other side of the woods.

I jumped out of the car, toes set to greet the familiar gravel crunch, and threw out my arms to catch my little doggy, who by now weighed in at about one hundred pounds and was a hero to the canine geriatric set. Nothing. No dog, no noise, definitely no noise but the sound of Angela tentatively stepping onto the driveway and the solid chunk of a Germanic car door closing. The small gray house hung below the pines, through the trees we could see what stars there were, and then the sky was torn by the low honk of migratory geese heading to their summer home in Canada. I took Angela's hand and we walked around the house toward the cliff that over- looked the flat black lake. Across it the lights gleamed in a dispersed universe and there came the anticipatory thrashing of landing geese paddling even as they hit. As the wind picked up and hit the cliff, I took Angela in my arms, and gone was the thought of the afternoon's tensions, elsewhere was the sight of those fingers twitching, who cared where my fickle dog was, and it didn't matter that this place where we were alone was the exile my family had been sent into upon the deaths of my mother and father.

## —— CHAPTER FOUR ——

ANGELA SLID FROM THE dawn's early light as it crept toward her blond hair on the pillow. Neither of us could sleep anymore, awakened as we were by the sound of a howling dog, of cars in the driveway, of chuckles and the smash of glass. And so she listened to me tell tales about my uncles, and when I finished, she laughed. She lay on her stomach, and both of us hugged pillows and peered into each other's eyes.

We agreed we would keep our newfound friendship a secret in the office.

"I don't want people at the *News* to think I sleep around, though I don't want them to think I *don't* sleep around either, you know what I mean?" she confessed.

Did I know what she meant? Coming from perhaps the only family in history whose men were publicly brought to task for being sluts, I think I knew what she meant. I was far better behaved than I had been in college, when I took seriously my Uncle Blitz's directive that the duty of men was to always get laid. I guess I no longer believed the only reason one would turn down sex was for aesthetics. There weren't many other reasons, but there were some.

"It always comes as a shock to men that we talk about them the same way they talk about us," she continued with a chuckle, though since I had sisters, that wasn't news to me. Angela's sleepy lids made her green eyes older; a touch of freckles tumbled on her upper arms. "You should hear some of the things women at the *News* say about you, Charles," she teased.

"What do they say?" I said, looking up with eyebrows arched. But that was about when the door sprang open and Betsy fairly lunged into the room.

"Oh, God, Charles, I'm sorry. You didn't tell me you were coming up with anyone," she gasped.

Angela rolled over and languorously pulled up the comforter, and from the neck up faced my breathless sister. "That's because I hoped no one else would be here," I said a little indignantly. "Angela, this is Betsy, and Betsy, this is Angela." They nodded to each other, smiles in place. And then Betsy was all business.

"It's Wolfy. He's drunk. Well, to be more precise, it's Wolfy, Andrew, and Melissa, and all three of them are drunk and sitting on the porch." Oh, no. More of the family was here. "Wade and I just discovered them when we woke up, and, well, last night we saw your car."

"Wade?"

"You'll meet him. He's holding them at bay."

"What happened to Gordon?"

"Will you come down and help me, please?" She looked a little exasperated, which was the near-instant reaction we all had when Wolfy slipped off the wagon. It destroyed our newfound sense of equilibrium, a sense that as bad as things had gotten, they would not soon be getting worse. With Wolfy drinking, all bets were off.

Angela slid into a pair of blue jeans. I scraped khakis off the floor. "How bad does this figure to be?" she asked, looking up from her sneakers.

"Hard to say. With Wolfy, drinking is always a sordid adventure. At least it has been for the last few years."

The sun was shining through the skylight as we came to the head of the stairs. We had to wing low to avoid those horns of the kudu that had followed us from my grandparents' old house to this one. This place was what we third-generation Daleys had once used for parties, privacy, and assignations. It held memories of chemical nights when things had gotten out of hand, one night in particular when twenty-three of us had sat watching hurricanes of color on the walls while my brother Sam stared at a trout he had just cooked without benefit of butter, occasionally jabbing it with a fork and mouthing, "Wow."

Now it was overstuffed with artwork and the *objets* from the old house upon the distant hill we had moved from shortly after the death of our parents, it being the big ticket item in the disposition of my parents' Estate. It was stuffed like a refugees' museum, and my brother Edward and my sisters and I, I have to admit, were at times filled with irredentist dreams of retaking the mainland. We still held fantasies of storming our old house and upending the cozy breakfast nook the movie star and her architect husband had to our minds stolen from us, though they had given us more than a fair price. They had bought it months ago and they let us know right away just how much charm their presence would offer when they called the dogcatcher and had the wandering Fido thrown like a vagabond into the pound. For that, they would never be forgiven.

Angela and I hit the stone steps down into the living room, past the huge Picasso portrait of the Daley Lazarus Uncle Wolfy had long ago persuaded the master to paint. It had served as our corporate logo. Hanging over the fireplace, it showed the sports cars from several sides at once, with something like the Eucharist rising like the sun behind it. Across the room was the trademark steel grille of the Lazarus hanging over the bar, so it looked as if you were about to be run down even as you fetched yourself a drink. Perhaps given our history, that was the point.

The sliding glass door to the porch was open and frosty morning air poured in. I clutched Angela for just a second as we walked through the dining room and into the day.

"Ah, Charles! Our family's ink-stained wretch. And a friend! I was just telling your sister's boyfriend," Wolfy said, nodding toward the middle linebacker of a preppy who was crouching on his haunches, scratching the ear of Andrew's smelly hound, Alf. Then Wolfy looked as if he'd lost the thought. He looked truly grisly. "I think the Stantons are Jews," he said brightly.

"What makes you say such a pleasant, noncontroversial thing like that, Wolf?" I asked as Angela looked on horrified, and Melissa, my Uncle Andrew's wife, cracked up on the porch railing she was straddling. Below her was the rocky incline to the boathouse.

Betsy glanced toward me, then lowered her eyes. How many times would we be embarrassed in front of friends?

The lake was steaming and the geese were getting frisky. Uncle Andrew seemed to slump where he was, as if to sleep the day away. But Aunt Melissa, who was sixteen years younger than her husband, just shook her mane of curly brown hair and looked on bright-eyed, drunk but bright-eyed, ever amused at her brother-in-law and the whirl of partying he brought with him, though of late it had been punctuated by bouts of sobriety, which were no fun at all. But which I found to be a lot more fun than this.

"Well, Charles, my steady nephew, has it ever occurred to you who owns all this?" He motioned not just to the gray house behind me, but to the woods, the clear sky and lake and surrounding grounds that as far as we could see held homes and tennis courts and stables.

"Well, we own all but my parents' old house, a section or so of the Big House, and the back acres that are being developed into condos. As you well know."

"Wrong," said Wolfy with his finger straight up, as if to signify lesson number one was about to commence. "Banks own all this. There isn't a paid-off mortgage in the family. And you know who owns the banks?"

"Jews," pronounced Melissa. Which was particularly unbecoming, given the fact that until she married my Uncle Andrew and had gone on the New York–Mingeboro social circuit, she'd probably never met a Jew. Melissa still was no doyenne of New York's or even Mingeboro's social scene, though she would have liked to have been. She had been a very pretty teenager who had grown up in the pew ahead of Andrew's at St. Mary's. Hers was the most petty of small-town anti-Semitism and it reeked of that countrified air of ignorance that usually stemmed from rising land values and the advent of city folk.

I noticed that Andrew seemed particularly appalled. He seemed to perk up and glower, all at once.

"The Stantons," said Wolf triumphantly.

"I'm a Stanton, Wolfy. So's Betsy. You have a problem with the Stantons?" I had problems with the Stantons myself, but hell, that was my business.

I saw Betsy looking horrified, beginning to slink behind Wade, to put his considerable bulk between her and her uncle, who was sitting there drunkenly, oblivious to the pain his words were creating, the mortification we were suffering before our guests. Typical alcoholic selfishness. But Angela looked fascinated, as if she were at the best cage in the zoo.

"I have a problem when I am turned down for a mortgage on a house all the way down in Florida because of the credit report emanating from a certain bank in Hartford," Wolf continued. "And your brother Edward has a little problem when he has to wait fourteen days for a check to clear that was supposed to be the deposit on his New York City campaign headquarters. And we all have problems when Andrew can't make the payroll just as the contract on your late father's fuel-injection system is about to come through and we can't get a loan to tide us over. Yeah. I got a problem with those Stantons and their financial network."

"First and foremost, Wolf, you have a drinking problem," Betsy said softly, a little hesitantly, though Wolfy paid her no mind. Betsy had been light-footed in the way she said what she said, as if, after all we'd been through over the last few years, she felt our family problems were our own business. I saw her blink a little shamefacedly at the bland and horrified Wade.

"There are other banks, Wolfy," I said.

"It's the whole system, Charles. Somehow they've already begun to foul our credit rating, which is a very serious modern version of the age-old smear campaign."

"Yeah, and time is of essence," Andrew suddenly said, perking up, his bleary eyes holding a tiredness I had never seen in them before. Andrew was all dull sweetness and hardworking incompetence. "We can make the payroll for maybe another two months. But we don't start getting paid for the injection systems until November at the earliest. That's a few months late with us several million dollars short." The family was relying on Detroit buying a fuel-injection system my father had perfected just before he died. The survival of

Daley Motorworks, which Andrew now headed, depended on the injection system.

"And I suspect," said Wolfy, "that a factory closing in the middle of a primary election might attract a little notice, eh?" Wolfy looked mean, as if he was slipping into that notorious phase of his drunkenness that had hurtled him onto the front pages of so many small-town newspapers.

"Jesus," Betsy breathed, and Wade stroked her hair. Who was this guy?

"Yeah, it's bad," Wolfy said, as if suddenly sober. "The Stantons are out to get us, and they've found our weak spot: cash flow. They haven't made any overt threats yet . . ."

"Oh, yes they have," I said. "I got a letter from Ethan yesterday."

"That monster," Melissa said from her railing perch.

"That creep," agreed Betsy, who looked at me with surprise.

"You're kidding," said Wolfy.

"What did he say?" Andrew wanted to know. Even the dog seemed to pant heavier.

"He wants me to come to All Odds to talk about getting Edward out of the race. He put in some not-so-veiled threats that life could be made difficult for us if Edward didn't pull out. And he wrote it in this particularly crude fashion. I mean, all sharp elbows and head butts."

"He has never been known for his subtlety," Betsy said with a shudder. Uncle Ethan had always been an ogre, the brother whom even my mother had no time for. Long ago he had taken over the task of keeping the Stanton's money growing, and he was a man to be reckoned with, as he would often tell you, for aside from being Nate's political hatchet man, he was a lawyer to movie stars. Which was sometimes hard to figure, since Ethan was a big, creepy guy with a strange cast to one eye that usually spooked horses, children, and household pets. He wasn't known for having relationships that weren't predicated on money or power, and if I were a sheep on the farm behind All Odds, I would have been very, very nervous. But he clearly had a talent for preserving the Stantons' old wealth, which ought to have dwindled by now, there not exactly being a boom market for Connecticut iron ore. I of course had to like him for that on a certain level, though there was no way I could get my hands on any serious family money until I turned thirty-five or proved I didn't need it or both, such was my parents' will. Thank heaven for pretty dogs.

Ethan clearly had a talent for protecting dubious young instant millionaires from the scams that sought them out like groupies. He had an impressive roster of young stars, athletes, and other winners of life's lottery whom he took care of through a world weariness and an impressive knowledge of the tax code. It helped that his older brother was the ranking Republican on the Senate Finance Committee.

I had to admit I knew from our proximity he was a very canny operator. And now after years of feuding between the Stantons and the Daleys, between the two sides of my own family, we were about to head to war. In public, in the political arena. And in private, where the money lay. And looking at my inebriated uncles before me, one of them the remnant of fame that had turned to infamy, the other the guardian of a fortune that had never realized its promise, that in fact was slipping away, I wondered what kind of battle we were capable of. I mean, if the enemy came over the wall of the fort right now . . .

Wolfy stood wobbly on the wooden deck, seeming to come out of his stupor. "God," he declared, "that was absolutely no fun at all." It was as if his binge had left a visible bathtub ring around the day. "Why do I keep doing this to myself?" he asked the trees.

Andrew stood up and patted him on the back, patted on the back his brother who once upon a time had been an Indy champ, but whose fall from the perch of fame and glory was so visible, so tangible, that unfortunately it had taken on the air of being inevitable. It was as if the family were playing out some fate, and Wolfy simultaneously was our leading and our lagging indicator.

The hound nervously walked into Wolfy's knee, and both Wade and Angela looked as if they were more than a little embarrassed to be witnessing this. This continued unraveling of a family.

"What are you going to do about Ethan?" Andrew asked.

"That's right, *Ethan*," Wolfy said, his back to the trees. Melissa now swung her leg over the railing and alighted on the porch with an innate steadiness no amount of partying could obscure.

"I'm going to go see him," I said after a pause. It wasn't the way I had wanted to spend this weekend, but the family always did seem to intrude. I always needed a rest *after* my weekends in the country. "It's been a while since I've been up to All Odds. God, the last time had to have been to that infamous birthday party."

"The one where those girls from Harvard OD'd?"

"They didn't OD, Betsy, they just got a little panic-struck."

"Make sure you count your fingers and toes when you leave," Wolfy admonished. "You'll let me know what happens?"

"Sure. Where you staying?" Wolfy's fall on hard times had resulted in his selling his house, which was rather empty anyway, once Rose moved out. Now he mooched meals and cadged sleeping quarters from the family, usually from Andrew and Melissa. He tended to pay one back in sprees.

"I'm staying in the apartment by the pool."

"Okay, I'll call you tonight."

Then Betsy announced that Edward was going to be up, and Annie would be back from school for part of the weekend. There was no possible way we would be able to fit everyone into this small house, the first time so many would be here since my parents died.

"The place will be rocking. It'll be like old times," Melissa enthused. Boy, she really did like to party.

"Not exactly, Melissa," Betsy said. "Annie tends to throw a wet blanket on fun."

"I'll stop by," Wolfy said.

"Let me call you first," I told him.

"Anything you say, Charles." And with that, Wolfy lurched off through our heavily mortgaged backyard.

—— **CHAPTER FIVE** ——

OKAY, YOU SHOULD KNOW.

There are two things in life that make me weepy: disasters and good sportsmanship.

Like the linebacker who extends a hand to the quarterback he's just blitzed. The first baseman who gives the rookie the first baseball he hits. The "Nice shot" uttered by the pro who's just been aced. I mist.

And disasters, those squibs of muddy cliffs and Third World bus rides, the eighteen-point headlines of planes going boom in the night. Tears drop.

Combinations of disasters and good sportsmanship completely break me up. Like the story about Khrushchev going to the American embassy the night JFK was killed, himself blubbering a little bit. And he might have been the one who had JFK killed. *That's* good sportsmanship.

I believe golf would be interesting only were the loser under penalty of death, and if it were played under a time limit of, say, forty-five minutes per eighteen holes. Only then would it be a true spectator sport. I can see loudly dressed creatures running along the course clubbing each other in order to get to the next tee in the two minutes allotted per hole. Putting greens would be styled for a demolition derby. The first golfer to reach the eighteenth hole would have to stand under the shadow of a hooded brute with a scimitar sharpened and in hand.

But you can bet the commentator's voice would still be hushed.

The fact that I love football and hate golf doesn't contradict, since in games of savagery, which arguably football is, one of the humanizing factors is the order imposed upon it. While golf, which is ordered to the point of being anal—the commentator not wanting to disturb the golfer as he defecates Fabergé eggs—would be mostly improved if you could add an element of savagery to it, some tangible high stakes. Not just a giant facsimile of a check.

Which was sort of what I was thinking when Edward came home and immediately went off to the links with Betsy and Wade. And I thought Angela and I would have the house to ourselves.

Angela was curled on the rug with a book, and I had to admire her ability to concentrate. Though I would like to have joined her, to have relaxed, I kept thinking of the afternoon meeting I had reluctantly just scheduled with Uncle Ethan. For some reason, I kept coming back to Blitz's fiery crash two years ago, which is easily pinpointed as the moment when things for us began to go off the tracks.

Well, I guess you could say the torpedo amidships came when Rose left Wolfy and wrote her book. The publicity buildup was in some ways worse than the book itself, though that was vicious, and, I have to admit, pretty exciting stuff. Passages about my uncles and racing groupies occupied about a third of her little chronicle, and while it was written to produce revulsion for my uncles—successfully, I might add—it certainly was titillating for a nephew reading about his own.

But with all the notoriety those episodes received, nothing seemed to demoralize the family so much as the death of William "Blitz" Daley, combining as it did the precise elements of disaster and good sportsmanship. For while it is disputed to this day, it seemed very clear to those of us who were in the infield at Lime Rock that Blitz had tried to cut off that moron in the Mustang so Wolfy could slip by in the penultimate lap. Blitz gave up his life in his final gesture to his brother. Not that that gave me any ideas in regard to Edward.

I kept coming back to that, steeling my nerve for Ethan: it was then that the family began to unravel. And now we were obviously trying to re-create a sense of family through a political campaign. Not the easiest way, I know, but then my family always did like taking risks. Politics is at once savage and ordered and the stakes are very high. There are rules set by election commissions and there are boundaries of good taste always tested but nonetheless arbitrated by the memories of editorial boards and reporters and ultimately, I guess, by the voters themselves. Outside of that, it's a free-for-all. It sure ain't golf.

I have always found it interesting that political professionals talk of politics in the metaphor of combat. On both sides, troops hold down the ground with phone calls made and doorbells rung, while the real campaign is fought in the air. That's the real weapon of politics, its A-bomb: TV.

And that's something that Edward, whose name ID was very low, was going to have to begin using in a manner that was the functional equivalent of carpet bombing. And the ultimate target was our flesh-and-blood uncles, one of whom was splendidly situated up on the mountain at All Odds.

## ―― **CHAPTER SIX** ――――――

THE BAVARIA BOUNCED UP the bumpy dirt road as Angela and I slowly made our way toward the foundry. We were nearing All Odds, fortified with nothing so much as the peace of mind that a gorgeous spring day and a conscience that's clear can induce in the stout of heart. We had hoped Fido would join us, to be with us at least as a talisman, but the pup was just not to be found. My breath quickened a bit as we drove by the pound, tucked into a curve underneath a powerful waterfall. But there was no sign of Fido here in these wooded hills.

Mount Targa was where the original Mingeboro had lain, almost three thousand vertical feet above the site of the present town with its ski shops, its burned-down city hall, its purveyors of preppy clothing, knickknacks, Heineken. The town had been founded on the very top of the mountain so the horses would have a running start when they lugged down the bountiful iron ore. By the time the ore was loaded into carts, it had been forged in the foundry into cannon-balls that would sink British ships intent on continuing despotism. Thirty thousand people had lived on the mountain during those exciting times, ten times as many as today, and they had stoked the flames, sweated through the night, produced the material that had driven the Brits into the sea.

It was this industrial might amidst the beauty of these sunburst hills that had proved the decisive factor in the War of Independence. Far less importantly, it was the history of this mountain that had proved irresistible to my Grandfather Daley when he was searching for a place in which to raise his growing brood, back when he first had a buck or two. The mountain looked down on what was then a private lake and the estate my grandfather was to buy in the twenties. And so we had all grown up watching the sun as it sank into a crook in the not-so-distant hills.

My Grandfather Daley's first real friend when he moved into the area was the man whose daughter was to marry my father, former governor William Stanton. Which was a lucky break, as the Stantons were the first family of Mingeboro. They had settled here under cloudy circumstances a long time ago. And while they had long been prosperous, the Stantons had cloaked themselves in an aura of mystery. It was known for certain that they held a strange alliance with some of the mountain's other settlers, ones who were poor and relatively landless, and ignorant to a point of pride.

These other settlers seemed to worship indolence, inbreeding, and rust. The Targies, as they were known generically, made a living stealing apples from the orchards and game from the woods. They stole wood from the forests and peace from the nurseries of the city folk who commuted here on weekends. Yet they had long ago worked out an agreement with the Stantons that tacitly was understood to mean they could have all the game they poached so long as they scared off poachers from out of town, especially from the New York side of the Stantons' mountain. And they could eat the fruit from the orchards so long as they could be counted upon occasionally to mow the lawns, bring home the cows, and clear off the snow in a particularly contemptuous and desultory manner. Whereas the Stantons, my mother's family, claimed they could trace their ownership and presence here back to the heroes of the Revolution, there was also a pedigree, if that is the word, to the flotsam and the jetsam of the New World who had first been introduced to working in the foundry. It was said both the Stantons and their neighboring barnacles had proved their fierceness by occasionally sniping at the redcoats and nicking their kneecaps, exploding their balls, severing limbs with the precise pop.

Though the mountain was gradually being developed, the most closely guarded prize was at the very top. Up there were the frigid lakes that had long ago been exploited for their ore. And since there was no electricity, the rich folk who came up each July to their wooden houses on the banks of the lake or near the foundry did by certain standards rough it. Mercedeses and Cadillacs were all left behind, and dusty Jeeps were king. It would get quiet early in the evening once the kids were put to bed, and what nightlife there was was conducted in darkness, sometimes by ghosts, with the stars right there, the crickets throbbing to beat the band.

But only halfway up the mountain was a huge field that seemed to wind its way forever down toward our lake, toward the town, toward a Manhattan that beckoned ninety-some miles to the south. This was where the Stantons had made their home since the early nineteenth century. This was where my mother had grown up, and where my father had first picked her up for drives in the custom convertible designed by his dad.

Angela and I emerged from the woods and the serrated light that had tickled our vision. And there we were, face first with All Odds. The main house was painted white and had, over two hundred years, spread in a charmingly ramshackle fashion, as if feeling its way into its own eminent domain. Surrounding the house with fortress stolidity were the stone garages and the indoor athletic arena that held squash courts, pool tables, and a dank aura. The arena had been built in the thirties at a time when the rest of the town was foraging in the woodlands for berries to eat.

Behind the stone buildings and peeking from the woods were some of the small stone houses that had over the years seen the weekend presence of governors, senators, actors, and artists, the naming of whom would seem like showing off. Perhaps Wendell Willkie's 1940 testimonial should be mentioned: "I know of no place in these United States quite as beautiful as Bill Stanton's home in Mingeboro." He said that from the back of a railcar not twenty-five miles away about a month before FDR clobbered him.

Now the guesthouses were seldom put to use, since unlike the Daleys, who couldn't keep away from one another, most Stantons tended to try to put as much distance between themselves as their money would cover. I guess with the exception of my Uncle Ethan, who weekended in the same large home in which Uncle Nate and Aunt Evie lived, and in which the family had been brought up.

I had only six Stanton cousins, which is one reason why I identified elsewhere, for in spite of my complaints about the clannishness of the Daleys, I've always been attracted to the roar of the race cars, the splash of the pool, the abundance of tennis partners. And even though the Daleys could be stiff, the Stantons were just plain dull. Each family could go wrong in very different ways.

There were Nate's two girls, both of whom were married and living in Washington, and four dread Abbotts, children of my mother's elder sister. If Angela and I had any luck at all, none of them would be with us today. And if our luck really held, we wouldn't have to see my Uncle Chauncey Abbott. Most likely he was off browbeating alumni into forking out cash for Yale's athletic programs. He could be guaranteed to mention Yale within four sentences of meeting you. He has been computer ranked as the World's Third Most Boring Person.

Only the station wagon was visible as we drove up the driveway to the house, the old station wagon that smelled of Pepper, Uncle Nate's decrepit Irish wolfhound. I began to feel relieved. But no, it was not to be, for there, hidden like a camouflaged tank in the enemy woods, was the purple Porsche owned by my most despicable cousin, Blake Abbott. "Oh, no," I said to Angela, who was sitting with her sunglasses on, radiating a kind of seraphic calm.

"What's the matter?" she asked.

"Aside from having to deal with Uncle Ethan, there is a particularly odious relative of mine here."

"Charles, I swear, and you haven't heard me complain, but I really have never met anyone who placed such importance on his family. You read the world into them."

The car was idling and we could see that Pepper was lumbering out to greet us. I shut off the engine.

"Lighten up," she said. "You're allowed to have fun this weekend."

That's when the first shot ricocheted off the driveway. A second one was quick to follow. "Jesus," I shouted and pulled Angela down as low as we could get.

"Who did that?" she hissed, and I didn't have to think; I knew.

"That's the relative I was telling you about."

"Oh."

The car door was opened and standing there grinning with this beautifully engraved .22 in one arm was cousin Blake. He had a beer in the hand of the arm that was cradling the rifle.

"Why, it's Charlie! How ya doin', dude?" He was dressed in a collarless pin-striped shirt and pleated khakis, barefoot as usual, and behind the gun he seemed to be as solid as the mountain. My cousin had the kind of build that made you think he could pull apart industrial forklifts in his spare time. And given the fact that all Blake was doing these days was working as a kind of factotum to Ethan—he'd been kicked out of law school the year before for an incident that involved drugs, violence, and a girl throwing up, though the details were sketchy, if numerous—he had plenty of spare time on his hands. I had been avoiding him in the city, though I knew he was out there. His presence had been telegraphed to me by dozens of incidents of boorish behavior at the swankest locations, and almost all of them involved his identifying himself as a Stanton, you know, one of *the* Stantons.

"Hey," he said to Angela. "I didn't mean to scare you, ma'am.

Forgive me and my loutish ways. Charlie here will testify that I enjoy a practical joke."

"There's nothing practical about shooting at someone, you asshole," Angela said as she got out of the car and stretched to her full five feet three. Blake towered over her, but she stood her ground, and in a minute he took a swig of beer and moved around the car to my side.

"Always a pleasure," he said smartly, holding out his hand. I'd had mine crushed by his too many times, so I just nodded to him. I promised myself I'd remain civil.

Ethan came out of the kitchen door and began to walk toward us, his hand absently dangling where Pepper could lick it, though the dog quite rapidly trotted away from him.

"Charles!" he said with deep resonance. "I'm so glad you came. Hello!" he said to Angela, and looking from her to me with a twinkle in his cast eye, I knew he meant to signal approval, but in an obvious fashion that would not be lost on her.

"I see you've met Blake," he said with a perverse wink. "Out doing target practice, Blake?" Wink, wink.

"Trying to choose the right target, Uncle Ethan."

"Well, why don't you go shoot some rabbits or a Targy? Hah hah hah. Your cousin and his friend and I are going to talk some politics."

"I'll sit in," Blake said firmly.

"Better you didn't, hah hah hah," said Ethan, and putting his sweatered arm around Angela's shoulder, he began to steer her toward the house. Suddenly there was the heart-skipping report of the gun in action again. Right in front of us came the quick dropping of a squirrel from the tree closest to the house. The squirrel had been walking on a branch that reached out toward the window to the room which I knew was Uncle Ethan's, and the bullet had passed right through the hapless critter and imbedded itself in the house just an inch or so from the glass.

"Nice shot, Blake" was all Ethan said as he kept walking, though Angela was, for the second time today, quite visibly horrified, with none of the fascination she had shown toward Wolfy this morning. This wasn't just an anti-Semitic drunk. This was my nut cousin with a gun. Who thankfully was now walking off in his bare feet toward the fields.

Ethan explained that the servants were out and asked if we wanted some tea. So we stood there as he moved deftly around the kitchen, breaking out the silverware, rummaging for lumps of sugar, making the judicious decision as to the type of tea he would use. I winked at Angela, but she seemed a little rattled, as if she were beginning to see the jagged outline of the barbed-wire borders my family, Stantons as well as Daleys, strung up to keep out strangers. Ethan kept on knocking about the kitchen, making small talk, asking us whether we thought Dean and DeLuca's was better than Zabar's, and whether or not the Spring Street Bar still served real brioche with its eggs Benedict. We didn't know.

The house was compellingly musty as we followed the chatty Ethan into the living room. He held the tea service with the solemnity of a sacrament. I hadn't been in this room for a year or two; even when my parents died, all the activity had occurred on the Daley side, much of which the Stantons just avoided. The room was just as stunningly eclectic as I remembered it: tusks of elephant, bearskin rugs, paintings by Richard Dadd and Francis Bacon, and the unlikely mesh of Bauhaus and Biedermeier furniture, all topped off by a view that had Angela transfixed. Ethan was right, the view down on us Daleys this time of year was awfully clear.

We sat on the large sofa that was pressed against the picture window, and the bright day sent our shadows lunging halfway toward my uncle. Ethan sat there stirring sugar into his tea and looking as reflective as a man with the eyes of a murderer can look. Then he grinned and kicked his desert boots up on the coffee table and said, "Charles," as if my name were the easily arrived upon solution to the gulf that lay between us.

"One thing about you Daleys my father always used to say: you all have that smile and you all sure can drive. You have your father's smile."

"Yes, but Mother's eyes, I am forever being told."

"That's right," he said kindly. "Your mother . . ." He glanced into his teacup and seemed to find something interesting in it, because soon he was holding it closer to his eyes, as if inspecting it.

"Charles, are you sure your friend wants to hear all this, oh, family stuff we have to talk about?"

"I'm having a fascinating weekend, Mr. Stanton," Angela said. "Unless my presence . . ."

"Oh, good God, no," he said, and if he could have reached it, I'm sure he would have patted her knee. "It's only that Charles and I have some business to discuss that is, shall we say, delicate."

"The delicacy isn't lost upon me, Mr. Stanton."

"Right, right," Ethan said, and began to twist his black mustache. "You're a writer with the *Downtown News*, Angela?" he asked.

"No, not yet. I'm doing what I can to get my foot in the door," she said. "Right now I'm answering phones. You don't have to worry about me."

And neither, I hoped, did I, though by even being here I may have been violating the agreement I had worked out with Hank the day before. But he had said I could attend family picnics, as I recalled, and hadn't put any kind of restriction on what we could discuss. True, though, this was no picnic.

"I do know you, though, Mr. Stanton," Angela went on, which was a surprise to me.

"Oh?"

"Yes, you managed some investments for a friend of mine, Laurie Krieger."

"Ah."

"You bankrupted her, I seem to remember."

I don't know whose eyebrows were raised higher, Ethan's or my own, though because Ethan was balding, it appeared for a moment that his eyebrows might go right over the top of his head.

He quickly recovered, saying, "I sheltered her income. That only makes sense if you continue to produce income, which she didn't once she started snorting three grams of coke every afternoon."

Laurie Krieger was an actress who had begun to make it on Broadway two years previously, but then had fizzled quite publicly, her no-shows and tantrums well chronicled by the *New York Post*. Now she was attempting a comeback, though she was only twenty-three, and just the past week there had been a feature on her in the *Downtown News*. She had starting hanging out with a number of the paper's writers, which must have been how Angela had picked up this detail. It certainly was news to me that Ethan had managed her money, and Angela hadn't said one word about it on our way up here. And there had been ample opportunity for her to do so, what with me chatting away about the people my Uncle Ethan hung out with. I looked at Angela closely, which I noticed made my Uncle Ethan look at me closely, and there seemed to be a battle between the two of us to see who was the one least taken aback by Angela's statement. It was the first time ever I had seen Ethan defensive.

"I recall her saying you lost a *lot* of money," Angela said.

"The paranoia of cocaine psychosis. And speaking of psychosis, how's Edward?"

That was fast. "He's going to run, Ethan. What can I tell you?"

"Well, to begin with, why is he challenging Nate?" Ethan asked, shrugging his shoulders. "This is family."

"It's true." I smiled. "You've always made us feel a part of the family."

"You worked in Nate's office, Charles. You all have. You can't say we've shut you out."

I thought for a minute. That was true too: we were invited over for Thanksgiving dinner once in 1965. I remember because it was a big deal that completely unnerved my mother, thinking as she did about the fights that were bound to break out at the table between my dad and Uncle Nate (politics), or between my brother Sam and Uncle Chauncey (politics), or between Blake and myself (ordinary congenital hatred). And when Nate's daughters had been married on successive summers up here on the mountain, it is also true that we were invited. But it is true again that it was always made clear that with the exception of Nate and his saintly wife, Viviene, the Stantons felt about us the way we felt about them, which could most accurately be described as controlled loathing. "We probably should leave family out of this, Ethan. I don't think Ed's candidacy is meant as an attack on the Stantons."

This angered him. "How the hell else should we take it? Nate's been a senator for eighteen years. My father, your grandfather, was the governor of Connecticut. And now your prig of a brother wants to challenge my brother, your uncle, in a primary. And you don't think we should take this personally?"

"I think you should take it professionally. I mean, it is not unheard of that senators get challeged in party primaries."

"By their nephews?"

"What is it, embarrassment you most fear?"

"Well, it certainly isn't Edward's ability as a politician. The guy is about as warm as a fish."

"That's smart, Uncle Ethan, you really should underestimate him. That's an excellent thing for you to do."

We sat there glaring at each other. A shadow came across the room and then was gone. I could hear Angela breathing beside me.

"All right, Charles, let's not fight, okay?" Ethan took a breath to express that he was calming down, and then he quite forcefully sat back in his chair and took a sip of tea. "Let me tell you what Edward's running will do, as I see it. To begin with, it will get a lot of attention, make a good story for the national press. They'd do *a* story on Nate's running for reelection anyway, but this will really get their juices flowing, am I right?"

He was.

"And it will focus attention on what happened to Edward in Vietnam, because that's his only real distinguishing characteristic." He held out both hands to us as if to beat back any protest. "I grant you, he's successful on Wall Street, but so are thousands of other guys.

"Now, Edward's running will put Wolfgang back in the news. Wolf's literary ex-wife will undergo a brief renaissance. And I have no doubt that it will bring the Daley Motorworks, which I am told is losing money hand over fist, under a brand-new kind of scrutiny. And for what? Nate Stanton has a sixty percent approval rating statewide in New York. He is an institution in the Senate. And he has many, many friends who happen to do such trifling things as publish the *New York Times,* if you catch my drift. And, as the ranking minority member of the Senate Finance Committee, he will be able to raise quite a substantial war chest.

"Edward is unknown, except to those rabid activists who, like himself, were more warmongering than Richard Nixon, whom I recall your brother condemning for being too much of a squish. Edward has never been tested politically, and I would venture the money he's going to have to dig out from his own pocket—because for sure no one's going to contribute to so obvious a losing venture—would be better spent trying to get your family's financial affairs in order. Christ, he's the only one in your family who knows how to make any money. He shouldn't throw it away.

"In short," Ethan went on, "there is very little upside and quite a considerable downside to his getting into the race."

"Except if he wins," I said. "And I think that's a risk he's going to take."

"But it's crazy, Charles. Don't you understand how dirty this could get?"

"Knowing you, I bet it can become slime."

"Oh, Charles, that's very disappointing. I thought, knowing how sensible you were, that we could talk. I see we can't."

"Ethan, you haven't given me a single reason to go back to Edward and suggest he call this whole thing off. He wants to challenge Uncle

Nate because he thinks the guy is too liberal. You know Edward, he's a square. He believes everything he reads in *National Review,* so help me God. He campaigned for Ronald Reagan against Gerald Ford, and raised a ton of dough. The guy is a true believer.

"Maybe our getting together today was foolish, but nothing compels me to urge Edward to get out of the race. And besides, it's very much winnable. I mean this, Ethan, Nate can be taken."

"All right, all right, you're as pigheaded as the rest of your family. But I'm warning you, this thing could get ugly."

"What do you *mean* by that? You keep saying it."

"You're just going to have to find out for yourself."

And with that we could hear the distant whap-whap-whap of a helicopter as it forced its way toward us on the mountain. "Ah, the senator himself," said Ethan, getting up to look over us out the window.

Angela stood with a smile on her face. "I get to meet him?" she said with some excitement in her voice. For the second time this afternoon she surprised me.

"I think it can be arranged," Ethan said warmly. We put down our teacups and went out to the garden through a door in the living room. We could see the helicopter steadily skipping toward us, suspended as it was over the distant lake. There, near the edge of the woods, I could see Blake begin to walk toward us, and he had, indeed, killed a rabbit, which he was swinging by its ears. Angela shuddered beside me.

But then Ethan was sidling over and saying, "I was very sorry that Laurie fell apart, you know. And I'm happy that she's trying once again. She's wildly talented."

"She's wild, all right," Angela agreed.

The conversation ended because we could not be heard above the noise of the helicopter as it set down with a wind that blew leaves through the air and Angela's hair back off her face. Blake was moving toward us, holding the rabbit so the wind from the helicopter blew its oozing guts away.

Uncle Nate got out of the helicopter scowling. He appeared to strike at the aide who handed him his briefcase. He shouted something into the chopper, his words lost in the wind, and then he slowly forced his way toward us on the lawn.

"Hi, Uncle Nate," I shouted as cheerfully as possible, not knowing if he considered me the enemy. But his smile matched my own as the

helicopter lifted off and backed away. Nate was wearing his customary Irish hat pulled way down over his ears, and it was clear that he
needed a haircut. Though arguably his yellow paisley bow tie went
with his tweed suit, it definitely needed dry cleaning. Yet he smiled
warmly and shook my hand, and when I introduced Angela, he
kissed her hand with a real flair. He was a charmer, my Uncle Nate.
But it was strange to see her curtsy.

I was momentarily at a loss for words, not knowing whether I
should fess up my allegiance to the enemy camp or ignore the upcoming campaign. I did genuinely like him, reminding me as he did
of the traits I had so loved in my mother: warmth, a sense of irony,
the bearing of the socially secure. But before I had a chance to say
anything to him, Nate surprised us all by saying, "You tell Edward if
I have another week as bad as this past one, he won't have to challenge me, he'll have the race to himself."

# ── CHAPTER SEVEN ──

MY FAMILY REVERED AUTOMOBILES and visitors so much that a
crowded driveway always seemed to us as fulfilled as a church with
its pews packed. Our ostensible draw was always our personableness,
but really it was my father, my charming father, who brought home
the visitors. Which is what Angela and I found when we returned to
the mountain. Visitors, that is.

There in the driveway were a dozen or so sports cars, station
wagons, and the odd Lazzy thrown in for good measure. Many were
recognizable as cars belonging to my relatives, which meant Melissa
had been at least partially right about this being like old times. There
had been a time when a collection of cars in this particular driveway
signaled an all-nighter, replete with pranks and feats of derring-do,
and the midnight expulsion of younger cousins. Tonight I was just
not in the mood to contend with all the jockeying, the posing, the
coping one had to do to keep the conversation light enough so that

no one actually said anything of consequence. The ofttimes dazzling hallmark of my family's wit. Shallow, shallow, shallow.

On the ride back I naturally had asked Angela about that Laurie Krieger business. It turned out Laurie was not a new acquaintance, but an old friend from a girls' school in Manhattan. "Why didn't you say anything to me on the way there?" I asked, I thought, not unreasonably.

"You were nervous enough as it was." It was dusk at the only stoplight in Mingeboro. Angela had on dark glasses. The red light hung. We had gone from not knowing each other to knowing more than we'd expected in a very short period of time.

"I wasn't nervous."

"Then why did you give me that nonstop history lesson all the way up the mountain?"

She had me there. Yet Angela, whom I found out had been a journalism major at NYU, now wanted to write about my Uncle Ethan for the *News*, something to be avoided at all costs. It would not do, with my disputed presence at the paper, not to mention the sense of siege that Ethan was already reacting to, to have an exposé right now of my uncle's money management technique.

That proved right there Paddy's point about the conflict I was facing between being a journalist and having a family that was newsworthy. And why should I hold back this chum beside me who had a brainstorm for her first submission to the paper?

Well, for starters, there was no way that Angela would have met Ethan without my taking her up there. And that fact alone meant she couldn't write about it. There are times when you are a fool not to make up your own rules. Celebrity closes some doors as it flings them open elsewhere. I mean, if I was a reporter and we were news, yet I couldn't write about us, then it was only fair that my friends couldn't either. I felt rotten as she smiled in contemplation of her byline.

"He didn't mean it" was Betsy's greeting in the kitchen. She was standing in front of the oven with a mug of coffee in her hand. My aunts Lizzie and Morgan were sitting at the kitchen table; from the living room we could hear the loud laughter surrounding Edward's teasing of one of my innumerable pretty cousins, as if he were holding something *just* out of her reach. But there were others in the house. The house felt heavy. Heavy with unseen relatives.

"Didn't mean what?" I asked. "And who didn't mean it?"

"Uncle Nate. Ethan just called and said to tell you Nate didn't mean it. Now it's my turn. He didn't mean what?"

I took off my khaki shooting jacket and wrapped it around the back of the chair Aunt Lizzie was sitting in, and leaned over for a kiss. I merely nodded to Aunt Morgan, whose nostrils flared in contemplation of Angela. "Hi, Aunt Lizzie, darling, and have you met my friend, Angela? And this is Aunt Morgan von Swoboda." Morgan flashed the only truly humorless grin I have ever seen, before or since.

"Well?" Betsy asked, poised to like the news, a smile playing on her lips. She was relaxed, or as relaxed as she allows herself to get. Gone was the suit she wore in the city, replaced by a flannel work shirt, a pair of jeans, and the same L. L. Bean boots she had once, at four in the morning, ordered by phone, just to see if the preppy hot line really was open at that hour.

"We saw Nate for just a moment as he arrived by helicopter . . ."

"I told you that would be Nate choppering across the lake," Aunt Morgan said with dry triumph to Lizzie.

"Yeah, well he just dropped in, and he was in this foul mood, threatening to step down. To quit. Resign his office."

"You're kidding," said Lizzie, and her pretty face widened with shock.

"Apparently Nate was, if Ethan is to be believed."

"What did you think of Ethan, Angela?" Betsy asked kindly, reflecting her chin in her mug.

Angela paused, because she was on the spot; my family could at times be a tough audience, people thinking they really had to perform, and they were right. They did. Outsiders' opinions weren't solicited that often.

"I . . . thought he was sort of charming, in a despicable way. He was as . . . prepossessing as I had been led to believe he would be. But there's something about him . . ."

"That makes you think you have met the creature from the black lagoon," Morgan observed. "He makes your skin crawl."

Suddenly an arm came around my neck and I felt a gun pressed into the small of my back. Only it wasn't a gun, it was an artificial arm, and Edward had been doing this to me for so long I was surprised for only a second. But Angela, well, Angela had not met Edward, and she let out an audible gasp.

"Hey, I'm Edward Daley," he said, moving around me and extending his good right hand. Angela shook it, but you could tell she wasn't sure, as if she thought a trick might follow. Not a good sign about someone running for office. Edward noticed and plunged in. "I heard you were up here. It's nice to meet you. Well, Aunt Morgan, what's on the fun scene for this evening?"

"Books and scotch," she said evenly, honestly. Since her husband, the phony Baron von Swoboda, had absconded with the twenty-two-year-old "Deb of the Year" two years ago, she kept pretty much to herself. Which was fine, both because she was a tough old bird who could handle it and because no one really wanted to spend all that much time with her.

"I've got to put dinner in for the kids," announced Lizzie, setting her hand down firmly by the coffeepot in front of her. Lizzie's girls were home from boarding school, staying with her in their man-less condo at the Big House, as my grandparents' former home was known.

"Oh, you both should stick around. It's going to be fun," Edward said, as if convinced. "Wade's gone out to get some cases of Molson he lost to me on the links today." Edward made as if he were putting, his metal hand wrapped by the flesh one.

"You did pretty well today," Betsy allowed.

"I was brilliant," he said with a smile, and you could tell he really meant that.

My aunts made to leave as Wade forged in with the beer. He was a pleasant-looking fellow, eager to please, and he just grinned, as if losing the golf match to my one-armed brother was his lot in life. Especially if it meant he could still be with my sister. They mooned at each other in the vaguely embarrassing manner of the newly in love.

Then we heard the front door swinging open with its signature squeal and a cheer go up in the living room. The sound had always meant my father. I didn't want to look, I wanted to be alone. With Angela. Yeah, with Angela, because I admired the way she had carried herself today in the face of my intimidating family and their steamer trunk full of peccadilloes. And I liked the idea that she aspired to write of the financial shenanigans my Uncle Ethan had wrought on her friend's fortune. Though of course she could never actually write it. I mean, without my permission.

But what seemed more important was to talk with Betsy, my older sister. For I never got to see her. Though she lived in New York, our worlds crossed even less frequently than Edward's and mine did. On occasion we ran past each other jogging in the park, but that was about it. So when Angela announced she was going to take a bath, I felt relieved, my anxiety's plug pulled, and motioned with my head to try to get Betsy to wander toward the playroom, which I had noticed was not filled with any cousins, uncles, aunts, and other siblings. A miracle.

Betsy followed me into the empty room. We punched the lights and all the photographs rushed to life: my father with the prototype of the Lazarus; my uncles with Parnelli Jones and Dan Gurney leering at this blond girl with mammoth breasts who was cleaning off a car window; my mother and father's wedding at St. Mary's, with my mother's face more than a little fearful. It has been speculated that she was as frightened about the rites—having converted to Catholicism only shortly before—as about taking the vows.

Once upon a time in this room there were Ping-Pong tables and the bumper pool my parents' generation had provided as part of their program of good clean fun. But then again, they had also installed a stereo, and let us buy rock 'n' roll records, and you know where that leads. They had taken it upon themselves as a code of honor that this was the house for the children and we should have it for ourselves. If that seems strangely liberal for my clan, it fits right into the program of nannies, boarding school, and other barriers that kept children one step removed from their parents. Consequently, to the sounds of the Beatles, to the sounds of the Stones and the Kinks and the Airplane, this was a veritable safe haven for drug abuse and sexual experimentation.

And yes, it was in this house that a decade before, my brother Sam and his friends from the regional high school had dropped some windowpane and had gone off to bomb the principal's office, which resulted in an outstanding arrest warrant and such travails that Sam could not even attend the funeral of his parents last year.

The teenage cabal met here, underneath the childhood portrait of the four oldest ones among us, Edward with both arms crossed, Betsy with bangs and a faraway look, me in short pants, my hair still blond. But Sam, my brother Sam in the portrait looked as normal as the Little League pitcher and altar boy he was when the damn thing was painted. I had not seen Sam for years.

"Whew," Betsy whispered as she quickly went into and out of the laundry room to check on the status of her clothes. "This was some day," she said, sitting on the couch and sorting through her socks.

"Yeah, well, how did the golfing go?" I asked, sitting on a pillow near her feet. Just behind me was the compartment that once had enclosed the family's communal stereo and its collection of records from the sixties, a stack which, I have to admit, I had pillaged before we purchased the house from the family. Now light shimmered off the photos, the entire collection of photos we had brought over from our old house. There even were pictures there from my grandparents' house, the Big House, portions of which had recently been subdivided into condos and sold off to outsiders who could not have known the significance of this staircase, of that wall, or of the large walk-in closet that had once provided bliss to children of different ages, whether it was as a hiding place during sardines or as a secret place for making love after swimming in the pool.

"Edward really was fantastic," Betsy said, sorting. "It's so criminal he lost an arm, Charles, because aside from anything else he has going for him, he has a great golf stroke and I bet he could make the Olympics in polo, if he was confident on the horse."

"I know," I said a little distantly.

"You dislike golf."

"It isn't my favorite sport."

"You're just like Dad."

"Well, he hated golf because he couldn't clump along the course with his artificial leg."

"No, it's something more than that. I think he hated it because he hated country clubs. He liked places where men got together to shoot or places where they got together to race cars. I don't think the idea of chasing around little white balls appealed to him overmuch."

"You could be right, Bets," I said. "You know, we haven't talked about Dad—or Mother—for a long time."

She paused in her sorting. "It seems like a weakness, or special pleading, to even bring it up." She hung her head for a minute, her so pretty face calm, almost preternaturally calm, for Betsy was an emotional woman. I can't tell you the amount of times I had to dodge her long nails or the books she threw at me, and she had always been lithe and strong, adept at trapping brats between the tennis courts and the swimming pool. But here she slipped into the kind of even acceptance of our fate that was the opposite of panic, of my usual panic, and I couldn't tell if it was real. If it was, it seemed superhuman to me.

"So who's Wade?" I said in a venture to trod on cheerier ground.

"Wade," she said with a smile. "Just someone I met at work. After Gordon and I broke up." She paused. "But we *can* talk about them, you know, Charles," she said, and reaching down, she began to stroke my cheek, and it wasn't long before I began to sob like a blues band, to wail like a banshee. I sounded like the shriek of a funeral train, and sat crying for a couple of minutes or more, and Betsy just kept her hand there, tears flowing over it like a waterfall on Mount Targa.

Perhaps it is time to fess up. You see, my parents died so unexpectedly and so recently in such terrible circumstances. Well, my mother's death was quite natural, merely heeding a recall from God that didn't make me any closer to Him than I had to be. I mean, aren't parents supposed to have a warranty?

She had a heart attack, at our old home, one weekend at the end of last summer when Annie had just gone off to her senior year at boarding school. And my father, well, I guess my father knew he couldn't survive without her and so he killed himself in the afternoon, apologetically, according to his note, but with the same sense of orderliness and dispatch, with the same sense of planning, with which he executed orders at the factory.

It was an executive suicide and it worked. He set out to create something, and then he did it. Methodically, without mess. The pills were powerful and fast-acting, and with that, Betsy and I, Sam in Oregon, and Annie and my brother Edward had to stare at ourselves anew. Only we couldn't, 'cause Sam and his wife, Claire, couldn't come back, or so he felt, because of that lingering warrant for his arrest. Though something tells me that Mingeboro's one cop wouldn't have arrested him in the middle of the largest funeral this town ever saw.

And so we had spent months adjusting to it, the deaths of our parents, and the one common thread among us, I knew, was that we couldn't adjust to it, that the void was too large, the pain too powerful. The only surprise was how large, how unbelievably total was its effect, and hardly just the physical, materialistic manifestations as unfolded by the Will that Still Was in Probate, but much more this sense that the pain just would not go away, that each of us was forever condemned to this state.

Which is why the prospect of Edward's campaign had been such a diversion back when it was something abstract and theoretical. Now it was real and it was something else again. And in between had come the death of our grandmother, and we had plunged into the same grief zone we'd inhabited after the deaths of our parents. I do believe there is a zone in which all grief is considered, and it has no temporal axis, no statute of limitations, only the sense of immersion into a plane where you can simultaneously touch all the spirits that have ever haunted you, friends who died young, relatives who died of old age, parents who died tragically, suddenly, rather than lingering on. That's what we plunged into, headlong, after our grandmother died, though even that was so diversionary from our larger pain that it seemed almost a relief.

We emerged from the grief zone with denial. Another family trait. The trademark that was the biggest gripe I had.

"I'm better now," I told my sister.

"I know, baby," she said.

"I just get so pissed off that no one in this family can *say* anything, do you know what I mean? We're all so glib, so quick and charming, and we all perform so well. But there's this kind of blockage that settles in with the wisecracks, this dodging of tragedies, whether it was Aunt Mary's death, or Blitzy's, or Mother's and Father's. We just crack jokes and make lists and plans and everyone gets so phony and just drinks. I can't stand it sometimes. It makes me want to get as far from here as possible. Yet, I feel all this responsibility . . ."

"I know, baby," she said.

"Betsy, I cannot get involved in Edward's race. I have my life and work in New York and I just can't give that up, not for him. I don't owe him anything. If I get sucked into the family now, I will never be able to get back out again."

"That's not necessarily true, Charles."

"I feel it is. Look, I love our cousins, but there are some—maybe me included—who are professional members of the family. And to be in any position to the family other than distanced is to be trapped."

"I'm not certain things are as absolute as that," she said. "Sometimes you see things in black and white, lamb chop."

"That's another family trait," I said, and laughed, and we sat there laughing, and sometimes crying, until it was completely dark and a limo's lights shone in the driveway.

# —— CHAPTER EIGHT ——

WHEN THE LIMO WENT and lodged itself between a Lazzy and a tree, the entire goddamn family came to watch, to kibitz, to make snide remarks about the driver. They came poking out of the house like sarcastic church mice, and then they kept on coming, oh, so many of them, stepping into the evening air to greet my sister Annie, who was sitting there, the limo's lone charge.

She bounced out looking stunningly beautiful, her long blond hair up in a bun, mink covering this red silk thing and the blue jeans between herself and which nothing would be allowed to come. Of that, I was sure.

"Edward," she positively squealed, dancing around my brother as she kissed him again and again. He just stood there, letting himself be kissed, with a slightly bewildered look on his face. "Oh, Edward, darling," she murmured.

"Damn," said the driver, scratching his head. Wolfy was beside him, looking contemplative, trying to figure which part needed to move first, the Lazzy, the limo, or the tree. The tree wasn't moving of its own accord, but he sized it up anyway, slowly walking around that huge stretch mother that was gumming up the works. "What do ya think, mister?" the driver asked in a thick Boston accent. "I got it stuck for sure." Wolfy nodded.

But Annie would hear nothing of it. "Oh, c'mon, Uncle Wolfgang. It can't be that bad," she said, giggling, and then she pulled Edward toward her by the crook of her arm. She hadn't even said hello to me yet.

Pressed around the cars by now like New Yorkers at a street scene were cousins by the dozens, with the usual cast of characters: Andrew, Betsy, Melissa, as well as Wade and Angela. And Annie would turn to one of us, to one of our cousins, and shriek out a greeting, and then turn with bemusement to this limo in its individual gridlock, which was of no real concern to her now, now that she was home and safe in Mingeboro. But it was of concern to me. Who had paid for it to bring her here?

"Charles, there you are!" She came rushing toward me so fast I had to catch her in my arms before she flew through the plate-glass window and into the living room. "Ummm!" She kissed me.

"Hey, Annie," I said.

"My troublemaking brother," she said without amusement. The prep school she attended up in Massachusetts still had some kind of plaque in remembrance of me as the school's biggest troublemaker, with more suspensions and threats of expulsion than any of the mass murderers, Symbionese Liberation Army members, and Watergate conspirators the school actually had graduated. The biggest act of defiance Annie had expressed while there was probably smoking cigarettes in an undesignated area, though for some reason she clung to the notion that I was this charmingly terrible person, though not so very terrible, as even the faculty, she claimed, seemed to roll their eyes and chuckle when they found out she was my sister.

Wolfy now was standing there with his arm circling in the direction the driver should turn the wheel, and the chauffeur for his part was trying gently to nudge the car, his head out the window for guidance, neck straining as he twisted and tried to drive, all at the same time.

"That thing is stuck but good," said my cousin Owen, my fastball-pitching cousin Owen, who sort of clung with mirth to my Aunt Melissa. She looked bleary-eyed but lovely in an Icelandic sweater and a pair of cords.

"Do you think they can get it out, Bets?" I asked.

"Dunno. Fool's got it wedged in there but good. And look, none of the cars in the whole driveway can get out of there while it's stuck."

"Oh, man!" the driver was bellowing. Then he and Wolfy seemed to go into conference. Within a minute the engine was turned off, and the twenty-six or so of us who were standing there in darkness continued to contemplate the scene.

Wolfy came over to Andrew and the two of them seemed to be trying to size up the crowd. They were looking at us like cattle breeders assessing a herd. We could see Andrew slowly shake his head with more than a little disappointment, and I was cheered by that, as if he'd decided we'd all make lousy rump roast, so why not leave us be. But then he came toward us, dispatched, or so it seemed, on some kind of an errand.

"What is it, darling?" Melissa asked as he jumped up the stone steps, displacing one of my cousins and her blond-haired, freckle-skinned, hockey-stick-toting school chum from their perch upon the garden wall.

"Wolfy wants me to call out some of the men to help us lift, and I mean physically lift by hand, a couple of Lazzies out of harm's way so that this guy can move his car."

This was a bit much. "He wants you to call your workmen out at seven o'clock on a Saturday night to bodily move a couple of cars?" I asked.

"Yeah, well, it will only take a second," he said a little sheepishly.

"*Andrew.* Those poor bastards are just now sitting down to a dinner of porridge and mead. Leave them alone. We can move the goddamn cars." Never mind what this would do for our problems with the union, this was just absurd.

Andrew sort of hung his head a little. The light from indoors was yellowing his high cheekbones, and his old leather jacket softly crinkled in the glow. "Yeah, I tried telling that to Wolfy." We looked over to the limo where Wolfy and the driver seemed once again to be in conversation.

"Look, Andrew, how many able bodies do we have here?" I began to do a head count. There was Wolfy, Andrew, myself, and so long as Edward had a flipper, he could help out too. There were smart cousins, dumb cousins, and over there was Wade, who probably could lift the limo all by himself. The younger ones could more than lend a hand, and Wolfy's deadbeat son, Taylor, I was certain, could be roused from his customary slouch. Both Betsy and Melissa were jocks of a sort, thought I would not have wanted to entrust a Lazzy to the muscles Annie packed. There were pretty cousins, ugly cousins, cool cousins, square cousins. "And what's the use of having so many cousins if they all can't pitch in and help, right?" I was feeling good, like the hero of the factory in some Socialist Realist epic. But Wolfy would not hear of it.

He positively scowled. "What are you talking about? That's what we have workers for."

"They're not our workers, Wolf. They work for Daley Motorworks."

He was glaring in as mean a fashion as I have ever seen him look upon a member of the family. While he seemed a little more rested than he had this morning, and while he was wearing a rather natty summer silk sports coat too early in the season, his face had that blowfish skin quality that let you know he'd had a good one on not too long ago. "I for one, Charles, am not going to lift this goddamn Caddy up, nor a Lazzy. But you just go right ahead," he said with a magnanimous gesture, and he and the chauffeur left the cars and walked across the gravel driveway and into the garage.

"What are they doing in there?" Edward asked.

"I don't know, Edward, but here's your first chance at labor-management arbitration. Can you imagine what the unions could do to you over this? I don't think Wolfy understands politics." Betsy let out a little laugh at that one as Melissa just stared at her. Andrew was standing there, deferring to Edward, deferring to anyone who would get him off the hook.

Edward blinked, looked to the crowd of cousins, all of whom were looking back at him. Even Annie stood there, a little breathless to be sure, her small breasts heaving like the moon was out and she was waiting for Gary Cooper's kiss. Edward made a half motion, as if he were about to speak, and then stopped.

"C'mon, Edward, let's have everybody lend a hand," I urged him loudly.

He looked very indecisive.

"Oh, Charles, the men won't mind," said Melissa, and I thought meanly that she should know, since she had grown up with them. But then again, so had I, for I'd been an altar boy and played in the Little League with several of them, and my instincts told me they would feel about the same way I would at getting called into work on my boss's little personal project midway through my Saturday supper. "Or if they do," she went on, "I'm sure we can organize some Targies."

I didn't even bother to respond.

Edward strode through the cousins and rested his hand on the offending auto. He walked around it as Wolfy had done, headed up the driveway a bit, and looked back at us standing there in the darkness underneath the eaves of the house. Walking over to cousin Taylor's wedged-in pale-pink Lazzy, he put his artificial hand down between it and the old Ford station wagon in front of it. We just stood there watching him, and I in particular wondered what he had up his sleeve, other than metal. In a minute he called for Taylor to throw him his keys, and Taylor, plump and spoiled Taylor, grudgingly threw them to him, eyes just about exploding with fear.

As the engine started up, Wolfy came barreling out of the garage with the giggling chauffeur in tow, the two of them smiling and sniffling just a bit. "What the hell's he doing?" Wolfy demanded to know in a voice that could be heard all the way across the lake. But no one bothered to answer, watching as we were. Edward was gently rocking the car and twisting the wheel in an effort to get it un- plugged.

"Edward, that car's worth a fortune," Wolfy shouted. "There are only twelve of them left in the New York Lazarus Driving Club, and we don't even own three of them!" Seeing that Edward was ignoring him as he tried to get a feel for just how far the car would move, Wolfy let loose with, "Think of your father." Betsy and I began to scowl at him.

Edward just kept on rocking, his artificial limb on the wheel as his good arm worked the shift, and finally, bumpily, with a spray of gravel, he had twisted the car out of the jam it was in, and the long black limo behind it now was free. My cousins all broke into ap- plause. Even Wolfy came over, and with a flush of exhilaration across his puffy cheeks, he shook Edward's hand. Edward stood there blinking with good fortune, having resolved a political crisis.

But Annie seemed to fall into a sulk, and as Betsy nodded to me, I followed my little sister inside. I just managed to catch the eye of the freshly scrubbed Angela, and I noticed she was following Wolfy and the high-stepping chauffeur back out to the garage for whatever it was—and it was obvious what it was—they had going out there.

Annie threw her bag down on the kitchen table and reached up into a cabinet to check her mail. "Where's Fido?" she wanted to know, and she wanted an answer, quick.

"He's not here. He hasn't been around for a while, Ann."

"He's never here when I am."

"Nor I. I mean, I'm here when you are, but the dog, I'm afraid, spurns us both."

She looked up at me when I said that, and seemed to get her anger in check. "Well, where am I to stay?" she asked with an ever so slight pout on her smooth-skinned face.

"I think we've got you sleeping in the playroom, actually."

In her eyes was horror. "The playroom?"

"Well, you see, Betsy and Wade are in the room you used to share with her . . ."

"Who's Wade? What happened to Gordon?"

"You'll meet him," I said. "And I don't know what happened to Gordon. At any rate, they're in your room, and I don't suppose you'd want to stay with them, no?" I arched an eyebrow, but Annie was not in the mood for a teasing older brother. "Edward's in the master bedroom, but there's only one bed in there, however luxurious and reminiscent of a pleasure cruiser it may be. And I'm in the room upstairs at the end of the hall, and I have a guest, and you're not invited."

"Our parents no sooner die than you turn the house into a bordello."

"Oh, Annie, priggishness in eighteen-year-old boarding-school girls is so unbecoming. You know something? I can't think of *anything* less becoming."

She didn't quite get it. "You're talking about me?" she wanted to know, her eyes rolling back and forth like windshield wipers, her hands on her hips, the mink pushed above her elbows.

"And anyway," I said, "who sent you home in a limo?"

She paused and smiled a little. "Lazlo Fortescu," she said with a certain reverence. Fortescu was the notorious Boston-based Canadian-born industrialist whose forays into New York real estate were putting him in the news, and he was also a well-known admirer of young women. His name and arm were usually linked with some long-legged starlet with enough social background to be able to make it at everything from Hollywood soirees to the state dinners he was occasionally invited to now that he had become an American citizen and a financial angel to the Democratic Party. Would you want him going out with your eighteen-year-old sister?

"Annie," I said slowly, firmly, as close to being fatherlike as I could pull off, "Do you know what you're doing?"

"Charles, I've known what I was doing—or not doing—with men since I was fifteen."

"Big deal, that's only, what, three years ago. This guy is a professional skirt chaser, and he likes them . . ."

"Like Wolfy, right?" She looked me coldly in the eyes. "Is he like your hero, our Uncle Wolfgang, Charles?"

There was this underlying tone of anger I hadn't expected to find *here*. I wondered what the currency was of *Pit Stop: My Life with the Daleys* these days in the boarding schools of western Massachusetts. Not to mention, of course, Western Civ. "I'm sure I wouldn't know, Annie. But you haven't, er, slept with him, have you?"

"Of course not, and fuck you for asking," she said, looking as if she was going to cry. "He's nice to me." Now she looked as if she was going to hit me. "I met him at Cynthia Worthington's parents' house in Truro last summer, and we've gone out to dinner a couple of times in Boston and New York."

"Boston *and* New York?" I repeated.

"I happened to see him at a party in Boston last night. I was staying with the Worthingtons; you can check. And Lazlo graciously allowed Cynthia to go back to school in his car, and then he had it bring me here."

"You'd better be careful, Annie," Betsy said as she walked in from the dining room, and I wondered how long she'd been standing there.

Annie got a little dramatic. She began pacing in preparation for the Big Scene she'd been playing in my family's kitchen since she was about six years old. The only difference was that this time she paused to light a cigarette, which she had never been able to do in this house. "All I wanted to do," she said with deliberation, "was come home and see my lovely family, or at least what's left of it. But I walk in the door and I'm immediately attacked . . ."

"Oh, Annie," we both said.

". . . by my brother, who thinks he can control my social life, and my sister, who has always hated me."

"Oh, Annie," we repeated.

"And all I wanted to do was . . ."

"Was what, Ann-pan?" Edward asked as suddenly the whole crew, the cousins, and the sniffling and perky trio of Uncle Wolfy, Angela, and the giggling driver, began to pour into the house. "It's so great to see you," Edward said, hugging her, and once again she began to squeal with delight, which quickly ended when she burned Edward with her cigarette and he jumped away. From there we wandered into the living room where corks were soon popped, bottle tops were snapped, and the stereo began to crank. Soon there was dancing and serious drinking, and hours later, I remember taking a quick survey of the mess. I could see the smashed lamp, Annie passed out on the sofa, and could still hear in my mind the sounds of the cars being dented as various people left and arrived, their parallel parking so sloppy that they succeeded, after all our earlier pains, in denting the vehicles anyway. I stood there woozily, and I did not know much for certain other than that I wished to be away from all this, well, not this—this was home—but as least away from these people.

I was tired, and drunk, as I usually got when I spent too much time with my family at home, and it seemed that for as much fun as the family could sometimes be, it was, by its own sheer brute energy, crushing all the while. The family made tacit demands on all of us, the most important being the Big Trade-In, wherein it was stated that in return for being protected by the Daleys and blessed by their name, you must renounce your individuality to protect the organism if it should ever, either collectively or in pieces, come under attack. That didn't seem like much, but when your own family exhausts you, and when it is sufficiently large and famous that you can't escape it as you read something so banal as the gossip columns or the spring book touts of political handicappers, there can be in a sane man an urge to get away, and that's what I was feeling in the blue hours as evening pressed toward morning.

Betsy was, I was sure, sleeping her untroubled sleep, the family just one more thing she coped with effectively. My brother Sam, however, had had to go all the way to Oregon to establish a life of his own. Granted, he'd been exiled, but in exile he apparently had flourished. And Edward, well, Edward I was not sure about, though there were times when I felt he was unfeelingly at the Daley center, compelled to do what was expected of him even though no one expected anything of him. Edward, I was coming to appreciate, was but a good-hearted overachiever, a little humorless, it's true, yet there are those who can attest to his bravery in a foxhole and to the sacrifices he was willing to make for others. But when he had asked me tonight, and not for the first time, if I wanted to come work on his campaign—"Wouldn't it be a load of fun?" is how I think he put it—I had told him flatly, "No." As Angela and I crawled up the stairs for the final time that night, I had this vague sense of guilt, the origins of which I could not place. Though I knew I soon would. I always did.

·

PART THREE

# CHAPTER ONE

I SPENT A WEEK at City Hall where investigators had found a large bag of cash. The networks were there as the mayor hemmed and hawed, and the presumption was awful. It was a week of stakeouts, late-night briefings, of leads panning out as revelations unfolded all around me. It felt great to be back covering City Hall, especially at such a time as this, but what sources I had had a year before when I covered the mayor now clammed up entirely. None of the breaks were my own. The *Post* and the *Daily News* seemed to have it wired, until the *Times* stepped in with the Big One.

The indictments were imminent when I was bigfooted by Paddy Mack, who wanted to cover them himself. Whether that was to protect his buddies or simply for the joy of nailing the mayor, I couldn't much tell. But I didn't get upset because at least Hank asked me to cover the story, and I was too busy to be pestered by my brother, who was locked in the throes of his announcement of candidacy.

The same week that flowers came to life in Central Park, I pulled several all-nighters at the clubs. I admit I had fun, but I was out on assignment, sent there to check on the business operations of the hottest scenes in town. All in all, I think that compared to the dance clubs, I found less corruption in City Hall, though I didn't make any friends save perhaps for the mayor when I wrote that in my piece.

I was enjoying the hours at the *Downtown News,* and my generally good relations with Katrina. Hank and Rachel acted as if the run-in we had had over the piece on the Liberal Party was long ago and of little consequence. I spent time in bars with Angela, with the kids from Circulation, saw Richard Hell and the Voidoids play all my old faves at CBGB. I was busy, but it was peaceful, hanging out with my co-workers. I didn't want anything to screw that up.

## ⸻ CHAPTER TWO ⸻

IT WAS ON THE Number Two train as I was coming home from work that I first read the details of why Rupert Murdoch had to sell the *New York Post*. He hadn't owned it all that long, though he sure had given the city a stiff jolt in the time since he'd been here. I kind of liked the way the paper had changed since I was a child, liked the splash of the headlines, the creative coverage, and the right change in the politics. Most of all, I loved the story of how Old Rupe now had to sell the paper as a condition of his buying the *Washington Post*, the right to which he acquired after he found himself in a card game with Katharine Graham across the aisle of the Concorde.

So there I sat in express-train sway, reading the *Daily News* coverage of the change in the ownership of its blood rival. It seemed the *Post*'s new owners were some good ol' boys from Memphis who'd made a killing in leisure wear and Elvis promotions and now thought they'd try their hands at journalism in the big city. They promised "quality journalism," whatever that is, and you could see the *Daily News* reporter sneering as he wrote. Then again, the *Downtown News* was not all that far from the sin of sneering, and when word spread of the amazing card game (no one believed it, at least at the time I was leaving), there were already four people assigned to "The Strange Doings on South Street," and William Rittersporn, the paper's ace photographer, had already set up his camera on the Brooklyn Bridge, telephoto lens boring in on Murdoch's office on the fourth floor of the *Post*.

This was all vaguely unsettling to an inveterate New York newspaper freak, and I wondered what the political orientation of the new boys in town would be. The subway rattled and rolled, and I looked forward to meeting my cousin Camille as she came from band practice to have dinner with me on the West Side. Her band had rehearsal space in a rock 'n' roll tenement on Ninth Avenue, and of late we'd been trying to make a point of having dinner once a week, if for no other reason than because she needed to talk with someone about the embarrassment brought on by her mother's newfound, near-instant success as a television talk-show host.

Rose Daley was the talk of the town. In fact, she'd recently achieved that cultural milestone of being featured, flatteringly, in "The Talk of the Town." "I, Rose Daley" had catapulted her to the top of the local ratings in a matter of weeks, and the cover story on her in the *Downtown News* had certainly lent a hip patina and acceptability in certain circles to a show I can say with all due deference was of marginal interest at best. What I had first thought would be the fastest-disappearing program in New York television history quickly became a cult item.

We first found out about it when the teaser came on just after the news that Edward Daley had that day formally announced his candidacy for senator. I was sitting alone in my apartment, a fresh beer cracked, "Live at the Witch Trials" by the Fall spinning on my platter in the background, when there was unmistakably Rose walking out of this Broadway theater toward the camera, sewage-system steam rising all around her. Some young tuxedoed stud held on to her arm with oleaginous certainty. I sat up with a jolt, practically knocking over the turntable to get the music off, the sound of the television up. An elderly lady with a phony, kitschy tiara and an Instamatic camera goes, "Who are you, lady?" And the ad with its grimy, *cinema verité* quality focused in on Rose, a spotlight swirling around the marquee behind her, going, "Darling, that would take a half hour to explain, Monday through Friday, at eleven-thirty P.M. on Channel 9." And then came the slow crawl at the bottom of the screen going, "Rose Daley: You won't want to miss her."

After I got up off the floor, my phone began to ring and it kept on doing so for hours, with everyone from an apoplectic Wolfy sputtering about his ex-wife's treachery to a somewhat subdued brother of mine calling from upstate where he was wondering what this would do to his candidacy. There were some predictable phone calls from political reporter chums of mine whose imaginations were such that this dual emergence of Edward and his Aunt Rose provided for interesting cross-fertilization. It looked as if the news would result by morning in a competition for who could write the dumbest afternoon lead. But the most plaintive call I received that night was from Camille, who really didn't want to talk, she just wanted to sit there, the line between us open.

Rose spent her on-air time interviewing downtown celebrities, sports figures, and people who worked strange cons or had recently had dramatic religious experiences. In spite of this format, it was noticed that she had on neither her daughter, whose band was developing a cult following at Club 57 and CBGB, nor her former husband, who was a "has-been, and a pretty pathetic one at that." Or so she told "Page Six," which for the last several weeks had been as much a sounding board for Rose as her show was. Both the show and the *Post*, at least the "old" *Post*, allowed her to spill her particular flavor of bile all over my family. When it came to my brother, she seemed to delight in Boy Scout metaphors, though in raw invective she seemed to be saving herself for Wolfy.

I received another phone call from Wolfy, this time at midnight. He seemed distraught; sober, but distraught. He told me he had no recourse but to write his own book to answer Rose, and he claimed he needed to do it especially for the way she had tarnished his late brother Blitz's image. Wolfy didn't have a lot of money anymore, and a source of particular bitterness seemed to be his divorce settlement with Rose. She'd used her money and the independence it afforded her to pen her book. The book he now claimed had destroyed him. I tried to cheer him up, to encourage him toward scribbling down his pain as an alternative to drinking. But he seemed rather matter-or-fact about his fallen condition. His need to write a book was partially to earn a buck and partially to set the record straight. If the act of writing it helped him straighten out, so much the better.

For some reason, I seemed to have become the family's lost and found, in spite of my swearing I would concentrate on my job. Aunt Lizzie would call to cheerfully gossip about the family, and especially about Edward. I liked talking to her because she was fun, and relatively problem free. I had Camille coming over tonight to visit me for dinner, Wolfy calling me at all hours, and Edward telephoning so often that I demanded he use a code name, Willard Nash, if he insisted on reaching me at the paper.

And then there was Uncle Ethan, who from time to time had called me with one dodge or another, trying to get the message to Edward that in spite of the fact he had announced his candidacy, in spite of the fact he had raised enough dough to have started ads that introduced him to the voters—"Ed Daley: War Hero, Businessman, a New Senator from New York"—it wasn't too late to drop out. "He's got an excuse everyone will forgive, Charles," Ethan said in a nominally friendly manner one morning. "He can say he's come to his senses." This wasn't the answer, no matter what the question.

Still, as the train let me off at the 72nd Street station and I trudged up the stairs to Broadway, I was feeling a greater semblance of peace than I had known for quite some time. I was doing what I wanted to do in the city I loved. In Angela it seemed I had a girlfriend. Work was going well, and New York was at that special cusp of promise between perfumed spring and summer. And I was bemused over the news about the doings of the *New York Post,* which is why I had a smile on my face as I reflexively swept the newsstand on the center island between Broadway and Amsterdam Avenue to peer at the headline of the Wall Street Edition. But my smile quickly faded, my equanimity about the *New York Post* tumbled back down the stairs to the rat-strewn subway tracks, for there was this headline going: " 'EDDIE FRAGGED', UNC STANTON SAYS."

## ── CHAPTER THREE ──

CAMILLE CAME THROUGH THE front door in a slightly twisting frug, cheeks sucked in, nodding approval at the sounds of the Clash. She had on combat boots and what looked to be an evening gown half tucked into the back of black jeans. Her eyes were dark as a vamp's, and her hair was a nest, a caramel nest, wild enough to be its own ecostructure. And no, she hadn't seen the *Post.*

"I don't often look at newspapers, 'cept for the *Downtown News.* That should please you some, darling," she said as she brushed my cheek with her lips.

I smiled and went back to the phone, asking for Edward, though he had meanwhile put me on hold.

"What is it?" she asked.

"The first of the attacks by Uncle Ethan. I have to admit, he warned us. But I can't believe Nate let it get this dirty, this quickly. I thought he was too canny."

But I knew that Ethan's negotiating style was to lead with a nuclear bomb. So did Camille, who commented, "Nate goes along with Ethan when the nervousness sets in."

Camille was a smart woman, a graduate of the Rhode Island School of Design, but she was not someone whom I would ordinarily go to for advice in matters political. So why didn't I see this coming when it was so obvious to Camille? And why, with my equilibrium dependent upon not getting sucked in, was I immediately pitching in to help?

"Yes, Edward, I'm here. Yes, I'll continue to hold."

Camille was going through my records, pulling ones she liked. Her head nodded to the refrain of "Hate and War," which was coming out of the speakers with insufficient volume to interfere with my conversation with Edward, that is, if I were actually having a conversation with Edward. He seemed to be wrestling with a tag team of advisers, of which I was but one. God, and I didn't even *want* to be one.

"You have Joy Division's record?" she asked.

"Under *J*. So, how's the band?"

Camille looked up from where she knelt on the floor. She gave me a genuine smile. "Did you *see* that Lick in the *Voice?*"

"Of course I did. I keep trying to get Ruben to let me do a piece on you guys."

"Is he going to? I'm supposed to ask."

"I don't think even if they do run a piece on you that they're going to let me do it. I have enough problems at the paper and with relatives of mine, if you know what I mean. But in the meantime, Roger Rabin mentions you in every column."

"He's like our press agent."

Ah, but I wanted to warn her: Nobody hurts you like your friends.

"That's a piss-poor idea, Edward," I said after he'd come back on the line and told me he was being urged to quickly put a television spot on the air to explain what had happened in the jungle those many years ago. Yes, Edward was shot by one of his own soldiers on a grisly day near the Cambodian border, and by the time he was evacuated, it was too late to save the arm. And yes, the subspecies of life who shot him did so in a form of mutiny, refusing to go up a hill that all afternoon long had been the sight of unspeakable carnage. But Edward was doing his duty, and no matter what you feel about the Vietnam War, the truth of the matter is that after lying there shot by a very bad person whom Edward had the misfortune of commanding, when the NVA regulars began streaming down the hill, it was Edward, arm all but hanging off of him, who led his men back across the river, giving them enough time to be choppered back to safety. And back at the base, Earl "Swamphut" Mosely had been fingered by his fellows as the one who shot the Preppy, as Edward, without affection, was known to his men. Swamphut had gone on to a life of Army prisons, out of which, so far as we knew, he would not soon emerge.

"You are a war hero, Edward," I told him on the phone, "while Nate Stanton was leading the charge against the war. You don't have to be so defensive that you actually put an ad on the air. That's a little like holding a press conference to deny the charge that you're stupid."

"But the war was unpopular," he said in a blurt of sheer obviousness. Which was strange, for among all of us, it was Edward who didn't blurt. He was a more measured kind of guy. Until he saw himself attacked on the front page of the *New York Post,* I guess. Now he sounded as if he were on speed. There was a little brittleness to his usual intensity.

I had to chuckle a bit, but low enough so he wouldn't hear me. Edward got sensitive at moments like this. "This isn't the general election yet," I had to remind him. "This is a Republican primary. Remember: right-wing activists. That's your universe until September. Until then, I guarantee you, it's a lot more dangerous for Nate to be bringing up the war than it is for you. You don't need to defend yourself, in fact, you can turn this into a big plus. Politics for the underdog is like jujitsu: you use their own weight against your opponents. And in this case, Nate's weight is his ability to command headlines. He's got his headline, which offers you a chance that until today you didn't have, which is to counterpunch. But if you make a television spot, well, for one thing, no one knows you yet, in spite of your introductory spots being on so heavy. So if you were to go on now talking about how you were wounded, what, twelve, thirteen years ago, the first impression a lot of people will have is that of a guy who had to go on TV to say he wasn't shot by his own troops for any good reason. They will scratch their heads."

"Well, what do I do? Jimmy Zion says . . ."

"Edward, he's a nice guy, but he's a hack. Get rid of him. The world is crawling with better consultants." I had some in mind. But one of the prices I had to pay for keeping an arm's length away from my brother's campaign was that I hadn't been there when he had gone about the business of hiring staff. Consequently, from what I could tell, his headquarters was crawling with overpaid phonies whose blandishments Edward naively fell for.

"Here's what you do. Tomorrow hold a news conference at the Roosevelt Hotel, just down the hall from Nate's New York City office. Make sure there are plenty of rolls and Danish for the TV crews, so they start getting in the habit of being there early. Let's see, the *Post* will play it big, because they have an interest in keeping the story alive, though that's the reason the *Daily News* won't go near it unless they absolutely have to. By the way, d'you hear about Murdoch selling the *Post?*

"Anyway, the *Times* will send a reporter who will sit in the audience and sniff, but won't write anything, at least not anything the Metro Desk will let him run. And what you say is, well, you hang your head and say it's disappointing to you that a man of Senator Stanton's stature would dredge up such a painful story. You should be willing to allow it might have been an offhand remark—it was, by the way. Yeah, apparently Nate was walking out of a luncheon at the National Press Club, cutting it up with a couple of old cronies in the press corps, when he was overheard by the *Post*'s Washington reporter, and she got it on the front page by the Wall Street Edition.

"But then you say that even if it were an offhand remark, it's just, well, disappointing that while you were off in Vietnam doing your duty for your country, Senator Stanton, who was ranking minority member on the Armed Services Committee, kept referring to the war as a waste and a lost cause."

"Is that how he referred to it?"

"Jesus, I don't know. Don't you have someone doing opposition research?"

"Uhh, we're getting to that."

"All I'm trying to say is that with the right tone—I think manly hurtfulness ought to do it," I said, as if choosing the precise shade of lipstick, "no one in the room will miss the point. This could be the kickoff to reporters taking you seriously, which they don't yet, other than for the money you're spending already.

"But Nate deserves to be gutted for this, Edward," I continued. "Imagine, attacking someone known by such a statistically insignificant segment of the population that he doesn't even register in the opinion polls yet!"

Camille flung open a closet door behind me. "Yes, I'll hold," I said a little angrily. I turned to see Camille on strange appointed rounds. She was going through my closet and looking at my clothes, and in a minute, I half expected her to start going through my drawers. She had taken the tour of my little den and traced her finger along the spine of every book. I think she was doing some kind of inventory.

"Boy," she said in the accusative, "your dog definitely is your best friend if he provides for this." She waved her arm around the room, and pointed to my deck above West 78th Street. For a second there, I began to recapture some of the equanimity I had felt earlier in the day when I was riding home in the subway. Before I saw that headline. "But we have got to do something about your appearance, sweetheart."

"My appearance?" I asked with some incredulity, immediately turning to a mirror. Things looked all right to me. Maybe a couple extra pounds. And Camille, well she was and always had been beautiful, but she dressed as if she were auditioning for some role by Bertolt Brecht. She couldn't have been talking about my appearance. But she was.

"Baby, I insist you come over here and look—just look—at some of the ties you have in your closet. I have never seen such things." She sounded genuinely amazed.

"Leave me alone!" I laughed a little defensively, or at least so it sounded. "So I haven't thrown out some of the ties I had in high school."

"Oh, but it's the shirts too! They're un-be-lievable. You are just ten years away from madras pants and golfing shoes."

"But I hate golf." But that wasn't the point, I guess.

"Darling, I love you, but look at this!" She swirled out of my closet with a pair of yellow bell-bottoms and pounced toward me like a trial lawyer with his hands on a bag of dope.

"Oh, Charles, how could you!"

"Now that's not fair." It wasn't. "Those literally are from when I was in boarding school." I really hated the idea of Camille thinking I was so uncool, in this, the nascency of punk.

I heard Edward's tiny voice come over the telephone I had wedged into my shoulder. "What're you up to?" he said with what for him passed as bemusement.

"Cousin Camille and I were just discussing my sartorial splendor."

"Camille, huh?" he said. "You think she could be any trouble during the campaign?"

I suppressed a groan. "I think her endorsement might win you the general election. C'mon, Edward, what are you going to do?"

"Cut a spot and air it."

"Please don't. I implore you." How could he be so stupid? "How can you be so stupid?"

"Listen, my friend. I have asked you for your help. We've been through this. But if you aren't here to defend your ideas, it's going to be tough for me to take your advice over that of my campaign advisers."

He said this in such a measured fashion—especially compared to the way he had sounded earlier, which was like a Cape buffalo plunging through a thicket—that I began to suspect the reason he had put me on hold was that he had to rehearse that little speech. And I had the feeling that the decision on what he should do about Nate's blunder had long been made by both Edward and the bozos he had hired. It seemed regrettable, though perhaps unavoidable, that in going from business to politics, he was going to need an awful lot of good advice to counterbalance his readiness to act upon bad advice.

"If I were a stockbrocker, I'd unload buckets of cash. And so on," I said. He knew one part of me wanted to help, though he really didn't understand why I couldn't. "But take my advice on at least this. You need to get some heavyweights helping out. Because you can win this thing. This is not a lark, as you remind me from time to time. The fact that Nate Stanton has made a stupid move like this this early shows that they have reversed themselves, Nate and Ethan. They're beginning to take you seriously. And they are very tough people."

"What's your point, Charles?" he asked stiffly, and I hated him for a moment for that.

"My point is you really do need to go and talk to those guys at The Firm."

The Firm was a new sort of one-stop-shopping political consultancy in Manhattan. The partners had a reputation, and a track record to back it up, for just brutally blasting away at incumbents in Republican primaries and general elections. They were pretty savvy buccaneers, and this was not the first time I had suggested Edward go meet with them.

"We'll talk about it soon. Right now, Charles, I really do have to go. But thank you," he said. And then he seemed to catch himself in his falsity, the gooey phoniness of the pol. Good ones learn to lose it after a while, the patent insincerity in these throwaway "thank you's". But young politicians were apt to be steeped through with the muck, that hollowness of voice. "I mean it, Charles," he said, this time with some warmth. "We really gotta get you involved. Don't be mad about my cutting the spot."

"Sure," I said, but he'd already hung up. He had the business-man's rude habit of hanging up too quickly, as if he were making money elsewhere while you were still disengaging from the phone.

Camille loomed beside me, sizing up something.

## —— CHAPTER FOUR ——

BY THE TIME WE finally got there, we thought the club had closed. It soon would be, I'd like to say due as much to the write-up its opening received from Roger Rabin as for any other single reason. I'd seen Roger sink a nightclub before, but not the way he soon chose to pick on this one. But for now there was life and we waltzed past it, past a couple of Bridge-and-Tunnel types being held outside the rope, past a pair of obvious *Downtown News* subscribers in that week's evocation of hip, past some punks too cool to go in yet, though it was amazingly close to 2 A.M. Amazing, since I was due at work at nine.

Camille and I were on the list. Well, I was on the list and Camille was my Plus One. There was a joke making the rounds about this time to the effect that it took five punks to screw in a light bulb. One to do the work, four to get on the guest list. That was about right.

Because the club was new and doomed, I didn't know a single doorman, but forward we surged to inform them of our presence on the magical list. The light was too bright and made everyone's skin look terrible, mine most of all, I thought, as I caught sight of a mirror lining the entranceway. I towered over Camille with this ridiculous hairdo, this spiky conversation piece, this radical thing on the top of my head she had just forced on me. Its topography ranged from mange to tufted butte, and it was on my head!

"Hi, I'm Charles Daley of the *Downtown News*. I have a Plus One." I hated the voice I recognized as being one-half octave higher than the cool I wished to project.

But I hadn't even needed to have explained. As soon as the doormen recognized Camille, there seemed to be a competition for the right to kiss her cheek. One particularly Nordic, faggy-but-you-couldn't-tell model with a pierced nose went so far as to lift her off the ground, and she laughed like a little girl going for a ride.

The velvet gate was opened and up the stairs we went, emerging into a world of solid red, the one-chord orchestra of the Mekons' "Where Were You?" crashing down upon us. "Omigod," whispered Camille as she vaguely clung to me. Looking up above us, we could see the stage was projected above the crowd in a solid T shape. The place was packed.

"What's the matter, too crowded?"

"No, it's the stage. You'd never get me up there. I hate heights." She looked around her. "This place sucks. But let's have a ball." She turned to me and I saw on her face the faintest hint of vulnerability, an expression which always seemed to puzzle me. For even tonight, her half collecting my wardrobe and calling the Salvation Army for a pickup before I changed my mind, even with her cutting my hair into this, this . . . disguise, I still didn't know Camille all that well. I had always, as I said once, felt her to be sardonic, but that may have been because she was the only member of my family whom I absolutely had to concede was cooler than I was, and one of the ways she proved it was by totally staying away from us. Good move. For some time our only glimpses of her were the occasions when she deigned to show up at the pool in Mingeboro, utterly gorgeous, dismissive, politely unwilling to take part in any of the games even I consented to. No Red Rover, no Marco Polo, no Trash the Relative.

Then, when Rose, her mother, divorced Uncle Wolfy, I took it as a healthy sign that Camille was absolutely loyal to her father, choosing to stand behind him when several of her younger brothers and sisters went on their mom's book-pushing tours. But what goodwill I felt for her at that time was wiped out when she posed with more than just her legs apart for *Hustler*. It was just a tacky way of saying something we knew anyway.

Yet now that I was getting to know her, I was beginning to think that maybe underneath all that toughness was . . . more toughness. Though when she was intent upon fun, she could be delightful. And tonight she was intent upon fun. Still there was something that just didn't sit right.

The Contortions were set to play soon, to stand up there on that runway and rain a diddy-wah-diddy hostile funk down upon their crowd. I had once seen their lead singer, this tough little jerk by the name of James Chance, leap off the stage at Max's like some diver off the cliffs of Acapulco. He had bitten right through this skinny kid's leather jacket, until the kid had started screaming and pummeling him. But there was a long way to go if Chance decided to jump off the stage tonight—maybe twenty-five feet. And even his best friends wouldn't dream of trying to catch him.

The crowd was dancing to Wire, "Dot Dash, Dot Dash," their telegraphic order, and Camille turned and said, "Come on." I followed, pausing long enough to get myself a beer and Camille some mineral water. I had learned she didn't drink, which only proved that long ago she had set out to be different from the family.

We stepped through a room that looked like a den, replete with books, low ceilings, and dainty Swedish lamps. There were people talking, but not much happening, so we continued on our search. The small alleyway we walked through was throbbing with people and crawling with music, and then we hit the aquarium room. "Holy shit," said Camille, and I have to admit we were impressed.

There in this huge, dark back room, the walls were alive, alive with fish: big hammerhead sharks in a tank on one wall, another wall shimmering with piranhas, the other two walls reflecting each other with thousands of tropical guppies swiveling in their schools as bright spotlights made their tanks busy with swirls of color. People just stood there, not dancing, hardly moving at all, though the music boomed. They just stood there with slack in their jaws, as if they were watching TV.

"I bet these people would rather see the video of a band than the band itself," said Camille dismissively into my shoulder.

"Nah, now that clubs are back, nothing will replace live music," I said. It was true that in the last year we had begun to win the war on disco, and live bands were now being quickly launched out of dives like CBGB into swanker uptown scenes. Though there was considerable argument that this was at best a mixed blessing.

"Oh, Camille, darling," said Roger Rabin as he ran up to us in a rush. "And her Plus One, my colleague. Her cousin," he pronounced as an afterthought. "Very kinky. Oh! And what is with the new look, Charles? Coming out, are we?" He looked as if he wished it were true.

"Hardly," I said sort of menacingly. If I could have growled, I would have.

"You don't look like a frat bro' slumming it in Soho anymore," he said, I think, approvingly. Though I sure felt a lot more that I was slumming it than I had six hours before. I felt a little self-conscious about this goddamn haircut Camille had given me with scissors from my kitchen drawer, though when I shot Camille a look, she pretended she didn't see me. She was searching through the crowd for something or somebody.

"Now this is for posterity," Roger said, taking out a Polaroid and snapping us in a flash, this big hammerhead charging in its tank toward Camille. "Oh, this picture is going to be glorious," he said, waving a little piece of cardboard in the air. "Tell me really, Charles. What do you think of this place? Isn't it just awful?"

"I like the fish," I said as a school of tropicals went crazy over Roger's shoulder. But Camille only sniffed.

"Can I write that down? 'Camille was at the opening of Club Blech the other night, but when asked what she thought of it, she merely sniffed.' Can I write that, love?"

"What do you think?" she asked me deferentially. I quite liked that.

"It's okay. Sniffing is probably the image you want to project." But before Roger could ask us anything more, the DJ started playing "American Beat," and we just had to dance.

"Don't say I have a weakness for the Fleshtones," Camille told Roger Rabin. And with that we were dancing, my cousin and I, and it didn't feel strange, it felt rather good. The fish were in some sort of feeding frenzy as the dancers thrashed about the floor. Oh, yeah, the tropicals definitely were spooked.

Hammerheads pounding, little piranhas shooting off like malignant stars, we tore up that dance floor. The one thing that was a bore was that paparazzi had singled out Camille and now were shooting pictures of us as we danced. I thought it a little too much. I mean, part of the joy of clubs was the fact that while the BPs who showed up were given a wide berth, they were treated like anyone else. In an amateur movement like Punk, everyone has creative license, most especially people who shouldn't have it. The upside of that was that some kid with an extraordinary getup was as fun to look at as Mick Jagger was when he arrived with girls in tow. Well, maybe that's not true. But the photographers were definitely pissing me off.

I bought Camille another bottle of water and got myself another beer. Roger made a beeline toward us, and I really wished he would leave us alone. He latched on to Camille and drew her toward him a little conspiratorially, though she was quickly nodding no.

"What is it?" I didn't want to be left out of any plans.

"Oh, James and Anya are having a little preset party backstage and Roger wanted to know if I wanted to come. But I don't, my dear," she said with a smile.

It was immediately apparent why, because striding toward us with a backdrop of sharks was the renowned Carlisle Jones. He was dressed in a plain white T-shirt and the same black jeans Camille had on, and he looked like a million bucks. You remember him, the lead singer in the Mustangs back in the mid-sixties, when they had that string of garage classics, the sound all cheesy with Farfisa, but menacing with jangling Fender guitars. The voice was too gravelly to be that of a mere fifteen-year-old, but it was. That was Carlisle's first incarnation.

Then came the Footnotes, seemingly remembered now by rock critics alone, and as their records were all out of print, they existed more by being cited in reviews than by anyone actually listening to them. They had been obscure then, but they were important now, this band out of Charlotte, North Carolina, whose sound so presaged what was becoming a guitar-heavy New York pop genre. From the dB's to the Crackers, the Cyclones to the Student Teachers, there were little echoes of the Footnotes, as if homage were a required citation.

Jones for his part went out of his way not to cash in on the legend that surrounded him. He may have been one of the only real rockers in town who didn't do a cover of a Mustangs song, nor would he go near any of the haunted dirges that preceded his crack-up at the time the Footnotes went down. Instead he played rockabilly with pickup bands, covering chestnuts, cutting no new ground. Carlisle Jones was a fixture, and apparently there was something going on between him and my pretty cousin beside me.

You might have guessed that by the way they immediately started to make out. That was hot. People stopped to gape, many of them not even recognizing who the two were, though the cognoscenti sure got it. They just looked so good together, this couple making out, and I thought about a dozen of us were going to unabashedly moon at them until they broke it up.

Camille was kind of glowing when they finally came apart, and it was terrible trying to affect nonchalance. "Charles, this is . . ."

"I know exactly who it is," I said, and held out my hand. "It was the Footnotes that got me through high school."

"Hmmm," he said, and arched his brow, his aquiline nose leading up to these powerfully concentrated eyes that bore none of the wreckage of his legend. He was reported to no longer be a junkie or a drunk.

"I was the first kid on my hall to have one of your records," I gushed, and in my defense, the guy really had been one of the greats, someone who one day should be installed in the Gene Vincent Rock 'n' Roll Museum.

"You were probably the *last* kid on your hall to have one of my records, too. Never sold much," he said in a southern accent. "You write for the *Downtown News*."

"Yeah."

"Seen your stuff," he said, and within a minute he was out there on the dance floor with Camille, and they looked as good dancing together as they had when they were necking.

Carlisle Jones. And my cousin. I was shaking my head at the thought of it when Roger Rabin came up to me again. We spoke for a few minutes about some interesting *Downtown News* gossip, some of which directly concerned me. He told me things about my coworkers I just never would have believed, except he *was* the gossip columnist, so I figured he ought to know. I was just about to ask him something about Katrina, the icy editor I had a crush on, when some people came up and in gales of laughter led Roger away. I was left to go buy myself another beer.

I was standing with my back to the hammerhead sharks, toes tappin to the beat, watching Camille and Carlisle Jones dance to song after song, when suddenly this figure moved in front of me and I knew there was going to be trouble.

It was my cousin Blake Abbott, whom I had last seen with a gun and a dead rabbit in his arms. He was very drunk, and he seemed to be hitching himself up for meanness, these two wide-eyed, giggling preppy girls clinging to each other behind him.

"This is an unpleasant happenstance," he said loudly.

"I couldn't agree with you more," I replied.

"This is a truly ugly situation," he said, putting his drink down on one of the small tables that here and there adorned the room.

"Why don't we just pretend we haven't seen each other. That way maybe we can enjoy our evening." In the background I could hear the signature sound of George Scott III tuning his bass, and this was quickly matched by the sound of Pat Place's crazy slide guitar.

"Frightened of me, are we?" Blake asked in a loud voice, and around us people were beginning to notice that a ruckus just might occur. Only there was an added inducement for people to get out of this aquarium room and head for the stage as the Contortions were introduced and immediately plunged into a cover of James Brown's "I Can't Stand Myself."

"I'm disgusted by you, Blake, but I'm not frightened of you when you don't have a gun in your arms."

"Well, you'd be frightened if you were smart, boy," and with that he took this absurd lunge toward me, swinging all the while. It was like child's work tripping the guy, and he collapsed like a sack of jute at the base of the shark tank. Big hammerheads seemed to be trying to peer out to see what the fuss was about. They were parked, snout to the front, some agitation in their ugly eyes. We were that close.

Blake got up swinging, and this time he connected. I could only hear ringing in my ears, that and the screaming of a woman nearby who jumped to get out of our way. Blake was drunk, but he was so incredibly strong that even a bad shot, a punch like this last one that went awry, hurt like a bastard when it finally landed. So we grappled around and around and eventually I kicked him, I thought in the balls, though if I'd landed a shot there, he would have gone down, I promise you. He stood there grinning and then we began to circle each other and bouncers were called and the music played on. There were about twenty people around us now, and I could see Camille and Carlisle Jones rushing toward the corner where we were, Carlisle looking as if he was going to bust this up, which I really hoped someone would do, and quick. I knew I was no match for this demented cousin of mine.

But before anyone could get there, before the bouncers were even through the door, Blake had me cornered with my back to the shark tank. It's a cliché to say that things happened in slow motion, but as I remember it, I can see every move, every step of the way to Blake's picking up that table and raising it over his head to throw it at me. And this he did, and I rolled out of the way, horrified, as the table went into the glass.

There was a split second when we looked at each other, Blake and I, and I thought I heard him say, "Oh, shit," before suddenly the glass shattered and the water—and the sharks—came out in this humongous rush. I dove as far to the side as I could, and could just see the first of the big hammerheads as it went right out of the tank and slid across the dance floor on a crest of water toward Blake.

Things get a little confused here, though I remember Carlisle jumping over one of the sharks as it thrashed around, coming to the corner where I had retreated, asking if I was all right. There were screams everywhere, male and female voices, and the four big fish were out there on their bellies, flopping about, cutting a wide swath as the water rolled all the way to the bar. I could just see the first big shark tear into Blake—it was a horrible sight, for which I felt no joy —and he let out a bloodcurdling cry. Water was all over me, people were crying, and the place began to smell funny. But next door the music was still playing on. "You, you make me break out. Make me break out in a sweat." Bouncers were looking at one another in shock, with not the slightest idea what to do, and I remember thinking, surveying the dance floor and trying to find where Blake and the shark had slid, that this time we'd done it. Now it was war. And there was no way I could be uninvolved.

## ── CHAPTER FIVE ────

THERE IS ONLY ONE good reason to have a telephone answering machine, and it isn't to collect messages while you're out. It's so you can screen your calls when you're in. It was only by virtue of one of those dandy machines that I was able to sleep late the following morning. By the time I officially got out of bed, I had calls to return to the following people: Camille; Hank and Rachel at the paper; Aunt Lizzie; Aunt Rose, for Godsake; two reporters from the *New York Post;* some guy from the AP; Carlisle Jones; Lazlo Fortescu, the industrialist who wanted to get into my sister Annie's teenage knickers; and my Uncle Chauncey. I called him first.

"You son of a bitch," he said. I waited for more, but that seemed to be it.

"How is Blake?" I asked.

"Aside from the fact that he's minus a fairly large chunk of his ass, I'd say he's doing pretty goddamn well."

"Oh, Uncle Chauncey, I really am sorry. I didn't start it, you know."

"Who the fuck cares," he said, and I could hear him start crying, which made me feel worse than I did already. While I had always despised the guy, I never thought he'd start crying on the phone with me. And I always thought he did care. At least about Yale. I didn't have to endure it long, for he abruptly hung up.

I got up and made myself some coffee. It was almost noon and it seemed to be a beautiful day. I took my coffee and the phone out onto my deck and sat there in the sun trying my best not to think for a little while, but the evening replayed itself unmercifully.

I called Camille and got Carlisle Jones. "Hey, man, how you feeling?" he asked in a perky voice.

"Dunno. You tell me."

"I suppose you're feeling a little better than that other guy."

"Yeah, what's the story with him? I just talked to his father."

"Maybe I better get Camille on the line," he said, and I could hear him hand the phone over.

"Darling!" she said

"Uggh."

"Have you seen the newspapers?" she asked.

"Oh, no, what's in them?"

"We just got an edition of the *Post.* They're playing it pretty big. They found out that Blake's the nephew of Senator Stanton. Want me to read it to you?"

"I'm not sure." There were pigeons all around me and the sun warmed my shoulders. I felt my head and my hand come away with shock before I remembered the haircut I'd gotten the night before.

"The headline is 'Deep Sea Disaster on the Dance Floor.' "

"Oh, Christ. Front page?"

"You bet. It goes, 'There was a disaster on the dance floor of newly opened—and newly closed—Club Blech in Tribeca last night when one of the twenty-eight-hundred-pound sharks decorating the club's "Aquarium Room" ripped into a patron who had thrown a table through the shark's glass tank.

" 'Blake Abbott of 778 Park Avenue, a nephew of Senator Nathaniel Stanton, is in fair condition in Roosevelt Hospital today, where doctors say there is an eighty percent certainty they will be able to make Abbott's shark-eaten posterior "right as rain" within a matter of weeks.' Shall I continue?"

"Why not?" I said wearily. A pigeon shit two inches from my coffee mug. It was going to be a glorious day.

" 'According to witnesses, Mr. Abbott was involved in a brawl with his cousin, Charles Daley of West Seventy-eighth Street, a reporter from the *Downtown News*. Daley is also the brother of Edward Daley, the recently announced challenger to Senator Stanton in the Republican Party's September twenty-third primary.

" 'Political observers throughout New York today were speculating that . . .' "

"All right, enough. No more."

"I'm sorry, Charles."

"Oh, it's not your fault." There was a click on my phone. "Is that you?" I asked her, but it wasn't. "Hold on," I told her, and pressed down for the other call. It was Betsy. "How are you, baby? I just heard."

"Oh, Bets, I'm okay, can I call you right back? I'm talking to Camille."

"Yeah, I'm at work. Are you sure you're okay?"

"I'm fine." And then I clicked back to Camille.

"What I want to know is how Blake got away with the shark just cutting him a new asshole . . . to coin a phrase."

"Oh, one of the bouncers had a pistol and shot the shark right between the eyes."

"Jesus. I really want to thank you and Carlisle for getting me out of there before the cops arrived. I imagine it was quite a scene."

"Well, it would have been worse if it hadn't been for Annie and that guy Fortescu."

"What do you mean?" What did Annie have to do with it? And, come to think of it, why did I have a message from Fortescu to call him?

"Oh, they were there."

"What?" What was my little sister doing at 3 A.M. in a punk club in Tribeca with a forty-five-year-old man?

"Yeah, he's the guy who took care of the cops, and I think he cut some deal with the club owner, because after Fortescu went to talk with the guy, he stopped weeping."

"What?" This is going to be some day for surprises.

The phone clicked again. "Hold on. Yeah?" I said.

"Charles, it's Annie. How are you?"

"How the fuck do you think I am? What were you doing there last night?"

"For one thing, I was helping to keep your ass out of jail."

"Why aren't you at school?"

"School's out, Charles. Forever. I'm a high-school graduate as of two days ago. Thanks a lot for coming."

"Oh, yeah. Well, I guess I should apologize."

"You don't have to do that. I'm staying at Edward's. That was amazing what happened last night."

"Can I come over?"

"Yeah, that would be nice. Can you bring me a cheeseburger from the Hollywood Coffee Shop and lots of newspapers? Tell Tony, the counterman, the burger's for me."

"Okay, I'll walk across the park, so it should be about forty-five minutes."

"Fine," I said and clicked back to Camille. "That was Annie. All is forgiven. She's staying with Edward, so she can't be up to too much mischief."

"I was up to mischief when I was her age, and so were you. Though we didn't like each other in those days, as I recall."

"Yeah, but she's my little sister and there's no one to look after her."

"I don't think she needs all that much looking after. She struck me last night as being awfully mature."

"True," I said, and for some reason I began to get depressed. The phone clicked yet again. I was beginning to curse Call Waiting. "Let me go," I said to Camille. "Anything else I need to know?"

"Only that you have to make a statement at Manhattan South sometime today. We promised this Lieutenant O'Neal you'd come down."

"All right. Gotta run," I said, and clicked the phone again. It was Rachel, calling from the office.

"Hi, Rachel."

"Well, this is one time I can't prescribe chicken soup for what ails you."

"Oh, no, I'm really okay. My ear hurts from where the bastard hit me, but I'm okay. You should see the other guy."

"I have. Roger Rabin has been showing off his Polaroids."

"You're kidding."

"Oh, no, I am not. Let's see. Right now we have a little photo spread of you dancing with Camille, no last name, just Camille."

"She's got a band . . ." I offered.

"I know who she is. So, we have this picture of you two dancing, and then we go to this monster of a guy cuffing you a good one. Then we have this photo of the guy lying in a puddle with this massive shark dead beside him. It's gruesome, but we're going with it."

"Thanks a lot. You're some friend."

"Hey, this is the talk of the newsroom today. More people are claiming they were there than possibly could have been. Are you sure you're okay?"

"I promise."

"Well, hang on for Hank."

"Oh, shit."

Hank came on the line. "Ho, ho, ho. This is the funniest thing I have ever heard of, Charles."

"Really, Hank, you mean I'm not in trouble?"

"Not for this. This is hilarious. I don't care what this has to do with the Senate race. Though you should know that everybody, including the *Times*, is calling asking questions about you."

"Oh, no," I groaned.

"Don't worry about it. This is great for the paper. Look, take all the time you need before you come into the office. In fact, I would specifically recommend you not to come in today. No one would get any work done." He started to laugh again. "Enjoy your fifteen minutes of fame."

I was suspicious, but I didn't say anything. Why was he so equanimous about all this when even mentioning me and the Stantons had not so long ago nearly elicited my walking papers? Couldn't say. I hung up and was just sitting there for a minute when the phone rang.

It was Angela.

"Charles, how are you?"

"Oh, God, Angela, am I glad you called."

"I just heard. Are you okay?"

"I'm fine, I'm fine, I'm fine." I was getting a little weary of having to reassure people that it was Blake, and not me, who suffered most today.

"What happened?" she asked.

"I'm not sure, exactly. Suffice to say I think it will be a while before Blake Abbott throws tables at people. I want to see you. How have you been?"

"Busy."

"Yeah, I haven't seen you at work. I've tried calling a bunch of times."

"I'm working on a piece."

"That's great, Angela. What on?" After talking with Roger Rabin the night before, I had a strong suspicion.

"Can I tell you when I see you?"

"Sure. When will that be?"

"Can you do dinner on Tuesday?" she asked.

"Not until then? But okay."

"I'll meet you downtown someplace?"

"I'll call you, unless I see you at the *News*."

"Great." She hung up and I sat there shivering a bit as a cloud went in front of the sun. At the end of the street, the Gothic spires of the Museum of Natural History seemed to be holding up the sky. I remembered I had to call Betsy.

I was just about to dial her number at work when, yet again, the phone rang. And as I was telling some guy named Colin Snidely of the *New York Post* that I didn't really want to talk about what had happened the night before at Club Blech, the line clicked, and I went to it only to find it was Aubron Powell of the *New York Times*, the dean of New York political reporters. I got rid of the guy from the *Post* and was about to settle in for a distinctly off-the-record discussion of Edward's chances against Uncle Nate when the phone clicked again. "Jesus," I howled, and when I found it was Tony Echeveria, my chum from CBS, I told him I'd have to get back to him. So, I returned to the conversation with Aubron Powell when the phone clicked one more time. "Aubron, I hate to do this to you, but will you forgive me?" He said he would, but he was a snooty sort and I wondered, I truly wondered.

"Hello," I said with real exasperation in my voice.

I couldn't hear what the person said.

"Goddamn it, will you speak up." I said, my equilibrium shot.

"Charles, it's Sam. How are you?"

And so it was, my brother Sam from Oregon, with whom I had not spoken for some weeks. "Sam, forgive me, but hold on just one second."

I got back on the line and begged Aubron's forgiveness, which was ostensibly tendered, and then went back to my brother. What a time to call.

"So," he said in his cheerful voice, full of the innocence he had never outgrown, "what's going on?"

"Oh, not too much," I said. "And how are the wife and kids?" And so we settled in, the phone clicking every couple of minutes or so, and I got to talk for a while with my sane brother in his sane world, far, far away from this sunny day in New York. I didn't tell him about the shark. I don't think he would have believed me.

## ⏤ CHAPTER SIX ⏤

ANGELA WAS SIPPING expensive white wine. Her mood was festive and she was chatty. Which was unusual, for I had found that after dinner she would normally sip coffee, or else Rolling Rock, and have to be stirred from a peaceful air of quietude.

We were sitting at a table at the back of Fanelli's, this seedy bar with awful food that was being coaxed out of easy desuetude and into a *Downtown News* hangout. The unwritten rule was that it was to be unwritten about. There needed to be one place near the office we did not celebrate publicly so as not to lose it permanently to hordes of uptown invaders. Like civic boosters, we had helped provide road maps and safe passage to our neighborhood in the hopes of building up revenues, but who in this conquering army of accountants, dentists, and would-be hipsters needed road maps?

Now the place was filled with painters, both real and imagined, a few of the old neighborhood boozers, and a couple of members of the Only Ones, a British band, being interviewed by a reporter I knew from *New York Rocker*, the city's preeminent fanzine. And Angela had a head of steam, a celebratory manner that was frank in its joy that tomorrow it would be her story that graced part of the front page of the paper, though coy about precisely what it was she had been writing during the past two weeks of secrecy.

"C'mon, Anglea, you wouldn't tell me over dinner, but you can't hide it from me, because I will continue to ply you with wine until you cough it up. What have you been working on?"

She looked at me, a little pixieish in this cotton miniskirt. Her strawberry-blond punk cut kept getting into her eyes as Fanelli's strong fan swept around the paint-flecked red room, seemingly as much to blow the flies away as to keep the place cool. "Oh, I might as well," she said with resignation, and at that moment the festive air snapped and I braced myself for the answer. Because I knew the answer, or at least part of the answer, from what Roger Rabin had told me at Club Blech. And it was clear during the last week at the paper that people were keeping things from me. Apparently Angela had been working on that piece on the Stantons, and while I was not too thrilled over it, given the circumstances of the last week, to have the Stantons raked over the coals would not exactly send me into a funk. But I wasn't prepared for what she now leaned into the candle-light and said.

"I think you better brace yourself, Charles," she said with the solemnity of a police officer sent to break the news to the squashed child's parents.

"For what?" I asked with innocence, with insouciance, thinking she meant an article that traced how sleazy was my Uncle Ethan, perhaps even how he had profited from his connections with my Uncle Nate. Boy, was I smug.

"Tomorrow there are going to be six articles in the paper on your family."

"On the Daleys? Not the Stantons?"

"Both. And you made the cover."

"I understand," I said with a little bit of panic welling up within me. There was no way they could run that many stories and not have one be the cover story. There wasn't enough room in the front of the book even in an advertising boom, which was something not occurring at the moment. "What happened to the cover on Rupert Murdoch's card game with Mrs. Graham?"

"It turned out to be a true story, so they're holding off on a big piece until they see what the new publishers do. But I don't think you understand. *You*, Charles Daley, are on the cover of the *News* tomorrow."

"What?" Hank wouldn't do that to me. He wouldn't go out of his way to embarrass me. He wouldn't pull a trick like that. "What's the picture of?"

She giggled. "Oh, it's a great picture. It's a Polaroid by Roger of you standing in the background being held back by Carlisle Jones while your cousin is lying there screaming, this big fucking shark dead beside him."

"Oh, no."

By the way I said it, she knew how bad I thought it was, so she wiped the grin off her face as best she could and began to stroke my hands. "I'm sorry," she said.

"So, what's *your* piece on?" I asked angrily, and signaled the waiter for the check. There was someplace we had to go.

"Oh, on the Stantons."

"Find out anything?"

"A lot. Your brother will definitely be helped by my piece."

"But not by the others?"

"Uh . . ." she started, and I didn't like this, didn't like this at all, either Angela's writing about us or the fact that we were the cover, but most especially the way this had been kept from me by Hank and Rachel, and everybody else who knew about it. I felt that I'd been taken for a fool, first and foremost, and that was before I even considered the family, of course.

When it came to publicity, good or bad, there were some members of the family who couldn't get enough. But I thought of Wolfy, of Betsy, of some of the others, who were just plumb wearied by this constant onslaught of media attention we had gotten all our lives, really, for my grandfather had been controversial in success and in eccentricity, and my father had had the lights turned on him for a while when the Lazarus was hailed as a triumph of American design and entrepreneurship. But when things turned sour, when the company had its first troubles and my grandfather had begun to seem weird and a political anachronism, the other side, the more troubling side of seeing your family attacked on the front pages of dingy rags, the negative side of notoriety had begun to wear and tear. And when the focus had switched to Wolfy's philandering, his hurtfulness and destructiveness toward his family, the whole thing had begun to resonate like a bad joke. Though there were some in the family—no names—who had begun to thrive on any little tidbit of attention, so long as the name was spelled right. And when that happened, the name was everything.

But *my* name was up on a headline, not a byline now, in the paper that tomorrow was set to rip off any and all scar tissue that had either settled in organically or had since been grafted on.

"Where are we going?" Angela asked as I abruptly paid the check and we headed for the street.

"To the loading station."

It was a beautiful, lightly cloudy night, the moon out full above the massive World Trade Center that loomed above us, dwarfing the old manufacturing buildings that were now cut into expensive lofts. We walked past garbage, art, and galleries, a poster for Laurie Krieger's performance in a new Sam Shepard play. We headed around the corner onto Broadway and found there was no night watchman at the *Downtown News*.

"Let's go around the back. They're usually loading at this time," I said, for there had been times when I was so excited about the prospect of an article of mine finding its way in print that I would wait outside in the winter air until the trucks began to load.

But for some reason, by the time we got back there, the last of the trucks was grinding away, and there was no one who would let us in. I rang and rang, but it was the end of the work week for the printers and the guards and the people at the loading dock. So we stood there a minute, trying to figure what to do. It was almost eleven, still too early for the paper to have been delivered anywhere except maybe the 14th Street subway stations, and I was in no mood for that.

Angela came up to me and put her little arms around my neck, and we stood there on Lafayette Street holding each other. What on earth had Hank and Rachel done? Back in the dingy glare of Broadway we hailed a cab and headed to her loft on Harrison Street. It suddenly, almost inexplicably, showered for a minute or two, though by the time we got to Hudson the moon was out again.

Angela was wearing a top made from starch and cotton Indian wind, and in the cab, as we began to kiss, my hand made small waves of her miniskirt. And when the cab pulled up beneath the awning of the gallery on the first floor of her little building, I paid the cabbie and got out of the cab, Angela standing a little sodden and dreamy-eyed at the door to her building. As I got to the curb, I put my hand on the fender to maneuver around a car, and I felt my finger touch a puddle of rain and Angela dissolved.

—— **CHAPTER SEVEN** ——

IT WAS A TEN-MINUTE walk from Angela's to the Canal Street station where I could catch the express train, but a cab was right there, and since uptown traffic this early in the morning was light, I grabbed it and was soon on my way.

Manhattan was magnificent as I rode the crest of the West Side Highway up from 59th Street. The sun gleamed gold behind the buildings. I felt pretty good, and then I remembered I shouldn't, and I asked the cabbie to drop me off at the newsstand on West 72nd.

The *Downtown News* had yet to arrive, which was typical of some kind of law the name of which I do not know, so let's call it Daley's Law. It states that the newspaper you absolutely must get your hands on will always hit the newsstands after you've been there. When there were articles of mine in the paper and I just had to see what they looked like, the issue would invariably straggle into the neighborhood like a bag lady. It would come in slow, but then sit around for a week. And when there was nothing whatsoever in the *News* I cared to see on Wednesday mornings, there it would be, piled chest high in front of every numbers-running magazine stand, every reefer-selling candy shop from Prince Street to the Westchester line.

I walked up Broadway with the *Times* and the *Post* in hand, refusing to read the *Voice* until I'd read its rival, saving the *Daily News* and the *Journal* for rides on the subway. I stopped in for eggs at Burger

Joint, and settled on a stool with an ocean of newspapers lapping at its base.

I tried not to notice the old woman with the beard who was sitting next to me dipping a Danish into a large pool of ketchup. Such was my concentration that I passed the sugar to the man with the blue eye shadow with hardly a human contact between us. One of the things I liked best about the Catholic Church's new liturgy was having to shake the hand of the person beside you before you accepted Communion. I liked it because I was usually next to my brother or one of my sisters and sometimes that would be the nicest gesture between us of the day. And I had even advocated that this ritualistic shaking of hands should be mandatory as well in the New York City subway system. Looking up from my papers for a moment, I began to rethink that notion. Sometimes my company in New York coffee shops forced me to qualify permanently that little piece of party patter.

By the time I got to 79th Street, the *Downtown News* was on the stand in living color. I have to admit the front-page photo was good. I mean, from an aesthetic standpoint, Roger really had lucked out. The black walls had a reddish tint, the shark was gray and so was I, and there was carnage from Blake's unfortunate rear sort of washed around the shark's mouth. Blake's face loomed in the foreground, constricted with pain. There would be those who would insist this was a setup, or at least a re-creation, but I could testify it was real. Oh, brother, was it ever.

What bothered me, I guess, as I walked down the hill to Riverside Park, was the garish headline. It read, "FAMILY FEUD," in hot-pink letters against the sea-green page, which nicely set off the darkness of the photo. Then there was a subhead: "The Stantons and the Daleys: Our Aristocratic Hatfields and McCoys. And We Get to Watch!" Someone had gone and turned my family into sport.

I went and sat on the wall along the roadway in the shade of tired old trees as runners loped by and the West Side Highway got busy. The listing of the contents on the cover was not very promising.

Let's see. There was an article entitled "Two Oleaginous Families," by the renowned Paddy Mack. Then Angela weighed in with "The Mystery of Ethan Stanton's Disappearing Shelter." Gee, that should be fun. What else? Well, there was a compilation by one of the paper's interns or shoeshine boys or men's room attendants entitled

"The Daleys and the Stantons: A Dossier." One of the paper's better political reporters had an article that attempted to chart on a taxonomic scale precisely what kinds of birds Edward and Uncle Nate were politically, as well as to assess their chances. One of my rivals had a typically fawning article on "The Democratic Hopeful," a transfixed lawyer from Queens who'd settled some public-housing dispute a few years back and then had cast about for a job, any job, at successive Democratic conventions. And last, but certainly not least, my Aunt Rose Daley was given the final word in what promised to be a chatty little essay entitled "A World of Their Own." It was supposed to be the inside scoop on the doings up in Mingeboro.

Where should we begin? How about with Paddy Mack's charming "analysis." He wrote complimentarily about our table manners, which wasn't such a bad place to start, but then he began to toss around words like "antediluvian", and "unctuous." And those referred to Uncle Nate, against whom Edward was running from the *right*. How would Edward be described? As a "twerp in a uniform who all but insisted on the slaughter of his men," someone who drove poor Mr. Earl "Swamphut" Mosely into an action which, while extreme, "was as finely etched in grand rebellion as in the attempted murder with which he later was charged." Hmmmm. That was one way of looking at it.

Grandfather Daley was said to have "bankrolled the rise of computerized right-wing nabobs." His achievements were cited in a backhand fashion, to wit: "Edward Daley's grandfather was able to carve a niche out of the increasingly monolithic world of the major American auto manufacturers." But then came the punch line. "To do so, he had to produce one of those screamingly puerile hot rods with a falsified European cachet that appeals to the hyperthyroid sex drive of horny fraternity brothers as well as to those whose entire lives lie in showing off their material possessions. Its apogee was the Daley Lazarus, created by Edward Daley, Sr., a car that has been shown to guzzle gas even as it nurtures the small-town dreams of would-be Lotharios, affordable only to those whose trust funds bulge commensurate to their blue jeans."

That's how he got on the subject of Uncle Wolfy, and you would have thought he was in the room with Wolfy and Rose on their wedding night, so much did he claim to know about the dynamics of their relationship. "After the death of William 'Blitz' Daley, the Daley family might have evolved into the relative obscurity of the protected rich were it not for the compulsion to seduce women that possessed the family's primary celebrity, four-time Indianapolis 500 champion, Wolfgang Daley. He was in the early sixties the Casanova of the race-car circuit, the Romeo of the racetrack, his insatiability part of the legend. But then he met his comeuppance in the daughter of a North Carolina judge. She was a beauty queen, Rose Boykin, and she thought she was marrying the most charming man she ever met, though in 'Pit Stop: My Life with the Daleys,' she described a life of male dominance that bordered on rape; of intimidation and mental cruelty, not to mention philandering." This was getting to be a bit much.

Just when I thought it was unsafe to read any further, Paddy turned his harpoon on the Stantons, and this part was a little more fun. "Few can forget the great harrumph that was sounded in Nate Stanton's great harangues against the war in Vietnam, though fewer remember the way he voted to appropriate, if not authorize, funds for just about any project the Secretary of Defense sent up to the Hill. And while he has long seemed to seek eventual canonization, while he has cast himself as a champion of the disadvantaged, it is disturbing to watch Nate Stanton these days, as he table-hops the lobbyist palaces, as he flies on the jets of corporate America, always explaining, explaining, explaining, how *hard* it is to fight for justice, how *deep* is the burden to which he subjected himself when he took on the public's trust.

"And then there's Ethan Stanton, the city's preeminent sleazeball (see 'The Mystery of Ethan Stanton's Disappearing Shelter' in this issue). While his brother Nate was portraying himself as something above politics, or for whom at the very worst politics was an evil that should be tolerated to do good, Ethan Stanton has simply put his nose in the bag and kept it there. And while enriching himself on the money he weasels out of his entertainer clients, Ethan does what he has always wanted to do, which is to control the patronage Republicans can get from Washington, usually by targeting the agencies from which graft is most availing." This was not very gentle, and cumulatively the Stantons came off no better than the Daleys. But that was a very small comfort indeed. And what would the rest of the paper do to us?

Well, first let's take the photographs. Some of them were highly complimentary. A few showed the Daleys as we looked at the end of World War II, all these smiling young people so gloriously happy!

My father and Uncle Wolfy were standing there in the uniforms of the Navy and the Army, respectively, and Uncle Blitzy and little Uncle Andrew were looking at them admiringly, while aunts Morgan and Lizzie bracketed my late Aunt Mary, the three of them looking so pretty and cheerful. And my grandfather, well, he was a head taller here than he was when he died, and you could tell the picture was taken at a time of great joy, because he and my grandmother were seen holding hands, something I can never remember seeing them do in real life. There were dogs scampering in front, and in the background was a truncated version of the estate in Mingeboro. It had yet to ramble into the behemoth that it became.

Not so happy were the Stanton faces in the photo on the other side of the page, showing my grandfather William Stanton and his tiny wife, with Uncle Nathan looking like something out of *Hellcats of the Navy* right beside him. I hadn't realized, or hadn't remembered, quite how handsome Nate was, at least when he was younger and cared about his weight and appearance. Uncle Ethan, who had only barely missed serving in the war, looked (in his cast-eyed way) just a trifle jealous of his brother, whose career in the Navy was, if I recall correctly, distinguished if perhaps unspectacular. But my mother and her sister Anne looked up at him as if he were the hero of the Pacific, as if it were he who had personally shot down Admiral Yamamoto.

My Grandfather Stanton glowed with pride, and he had much to be proud of, for behind him was All Odds; he'd been governor of Connecticut at a time when war had brought unprecedented growth; and just weeks before, he had handed away Anne in marriage. She stood next to her husband, the outrageously stylish Chauncey Abbott, who was wearing pleated khakis and a white sweater with a bulldog sewn on the front. He looked as if he was about to lead a cheer. But somehow it was only my blond and pretty mother who set the photograph off and made the Stantons seem as joyous as the Daleys, only my mother who looked clearly with eyes bright and teeth white right into the camera, offsetting the brooding Ethan as he stared from different angles off across All Odds. Grandmother Stanton, who died before I was born, sort of glowed there too, like a very warm ember.

There were photos of Wolfy winning his first Indy, the huge car in the picture bearing very little resemblance to the sleek monsters they were driving today. There was a photograph of Wolfy and Blitz with their arms around some pretty jet-setters, not their wives. I would have guessed 1965. One famous shot showed Uncle Nate staring down the table at what was quite obviously a Leadership Meeting at the White House with President Nixon, and the tension in the air was palpable, the moral dimensions to Nate's body language absolute. Once again, I had to admire Nate. The photograph showed him at his senatorial best.

And then, on the page that was titled "The Daleys and the Stantons: A Dossier," there was a huge centerpiece of a photo of the Daley kids, and I mean all of us, fifty-some little grandchildren, assorted parents, dogs, nannies, and servants. Naturally the most photogenic one among us was Fido, who had half the front row of four-year-olds in rapture. All the grandchildren looked so well scrubbed and well behaved, many of the boys in shorts (not me, I graduated from shorts when I was six), and there was my grandmother in the middle of us, almost swallowed by joy and the crowd. It was a cute picture, and other than the sheer volume and concomitant Catholicism, I couldn't see the average *Downtown News* subscriber condemning us for this.

But there was one thing in the accompanying dossier that I found particularly troubling. The twit who had written it had assembled a number of items that were more or less right ("Of the seven Daley children, four were born in foreign countries"), if irrelevant, and a number of "facts" that were repetitions of previously published nontruths, the most egregious of which was the statement once again that when my Grandfather Daley died, he was worth $211 million. Would that this were true. Even at the rate I spend money, the family would probably still be solvent had it been left such an endowment.

But the most troubling fact was one I had so forgotten that it took me a minute to recognize what the writer was talking about. He was talking about the Lost Tribe.

When Aunt Mary married Owen's dad, Quentin Claydo, in a small church in Washington-on-the-Brazos, Texas—in a ceremony my grandparents at first refused to attend, though Grandfather finally chartered a plane and arrived in the middle of it—she married a really first-class eccentric. I mean, even by our standards. Claydo was in those days toying with the idea of moving to Mexico to begin a life of lay work in Catholic missions, and that didn't sit right even with my religious grandmother. Mary had always been a dreamer, an idealist, toying with the idea of becoming a nun, then falling for the rotund Texas-born Claydo and his plans for evangelizing a country

that was already 98.6 percent Catholic. He was weird, but he had this
sort of William Jennings Bryan mellifluousness to his speech, and in
Mingeboro, frequently one of my uncles, sometimes even my father,
would try to belt him in order to shut him up.

Rather than go to Mexico, Aunt Mary and Uncle Quentin em-
barked on a journey that took them to Rhodesia, where he was out-
spoken in support of the Smith government's secession from the
Commonwealth. They came back to the States in the mid-sixties with
their African-born child, Owen. Then Uncle Quentin heard that
Protestant missionaries were helping Puerto Rican flood victims,
fiendishly working to proselytize them all the while. This he couldn't
tolerate, and within a week, he and Aunt Mary had taken in eleven
Puerto Rican orphans and started adoption proceedings.

Uncle Quentin next got involved in the nascent presidential campaign of Governor George Wallace of Alabama. Quentin was tolerated because of his obvious brilliance and articulation, though it was
understood that Wallace sneered at the way he tried to graft Catholic
evangelism onto Wallace's doctrine of ersatz white supremacy.

But then, tragically, Aunt Mary died of a cerebral hemorrhage,
and Claydo was a broken man. For a solid year he was inconsolable,
and it fell to the eight-year-old Owen to take care of his eleven little
adopted brothers and sisters in a squalid house near Little Rock.
This was too much for the family, and for once they acted, going
down to the farm in Arkansas where Claydo had settled and bringing
the orphans up to Mingeboro, where, for about a year, they stayed
with various members of the family. Owen refused to desert his
father, and so was left with him in a home whose dilapidation soon
became family legend.

I remember for a few months having to take care of Rudy and
Gabriella, who clung to each other, as lost in our family as they would
have been in the streets of New York. We nicknamed the brood the
"Lost Tribe," and when, after a year, it became obvious that they
hated the cold and the North and, especially, my family, we took the
offer of an old friend to have them placed with good families back
in Puerto Rico.

And so we forgot about them, as well as Quentin Claydo, though
every few summers Owen would come north and impress us with his
wit and ability to throw a baseball. Then, last year, the story broke
that Claydo had taken part in an ambush of Communist Party demonstrators just outside Fayetteville, and that Owen had refused to

provide him with an alibi. This was a gutsy thing to do, or else it was just the outgrowth of eighteen years of living with his nutty old man. Owen had been destined for Yale in the fall, but now his life was in danger, as the alibis of some of Uncle Quentin's accomplices hung on what Owen was supposed to provide for his father. This was why Owen was living in family protection, up the hill in Mingeboro in Andrew and Melissa's guesthouse. Though I understood he was spending most of his time at Edward's campaign headquarters in New York, sometimes sleeping there on the floor.

It was odd to read about the Lost Tribe in the *Downtown News*. I had to admit it added to the family's overall image of being bizarre. And it was odd to read that little Rudy was right now in the band of pubescent Puerto Rican hearthrobs, Menudo. I sort of vaguely re-membered him singing in a high-pitched voice when he and Ga-briella were in a sudsy tub together, but I never would have expected this.

There weren't many other fun facts in the dossier that enlightened me about my family. I think most of the readers who waded through it would have been pretty confused by the sum total of the entries. How do you reconcile, "The Daleys have been active in raising more than $2 million for the Archdiocese of New York," with, "In her book, Rose Daley estimated her husband had been unfaithful more than a thousand times"? Unless, of course, that was the point.

I was tired of the dossier, so I read Angela's article on Uncle Ethan. It was well researched, well written, and illustrated with the most awful picture of Ethan whispering into Nate's ear as if he were some shabby colonel telling the junta leader of the next six people to be executed. The article included not only the Laurie Krieger story but several other examples of people who had hired Ethan to shelter their income, only to watch it dwindle due to one unforeseen "natu-ral" calamity or another. There was a pattern she had unearthed and documented well. It suggested that those people who exuded strength and longevity had in Ethan a pretty fair investment coun-selor. But those people who, like Laurie Krieger, appeared self-de-structive, or weak, or not long for their millions anyway, often watched Ethan arrive at the hospital bed holding open an empty sack.

Less effective was her attempt to show collaboration between Ethan and Uncle Nate. There just wasn't any evidence that the brothers used Nate's position on the Finance Committee or the Armed Services Committee to enrich anyone in particular. I found it plausible that Ethan could take advantage of the appearance of having access to his brother's power without actually using the power itself to make him and his clients grow rich. But there was no hard evidence of inside information, of Ethan actually being the beneficiary of some inside track, some distant-early-warning system about changes in the tax code. Ethan was skillful enough to play people like a pinball machine. It's probable, however, he could ring up business with a nudge, lacking the element of actual corruption that could set the bells clanging.

It is true we had always marveled at the fresh infusion of wealth the Stantons seemed to have realized around 1964. It took my mother pleasantly by surprise, as she had thought her late father's estate was relatively modest. She didn't ask any questions of Ethan, since to be quite honest, she didn't really care to talk with him unless she had to. And she considered a windfall not worthy of mention; whereas if she had felt the pinch of declining fortunes, of course she would have been on the phone in a minute. She just took the money and spent it, on clothes for herself and us, on decorations for the house, on ski vacations for us in Aspen, or on spring vacations at The Breakers. But we'd never had the belief there was anything suspicious about the Stanton's somewhat stingy New England fortune suddenly blossoming in the go-go sixties just as the last of the Daley Lazaruses were selling and Father had begun to redirect the company into making specialty parts for the big companies in Detroit. Due to labor costs—and the long, ugly fight with the UAW—it just wasn't feasible to continue trying to make an independent sports car as expensive as the Lazzy when the muscle cars of the sixties were suddenly within reach of less affluent youth.

But I found the most troubling thing in Angela's article to be the reference to Ethan's refusing to be interviewed, while she detailed every item in the living room where we had sat that day up at All Odds. There was only one way she had been able to do that, and I didn't like being used, though I suppose that had I been in her shoes, I would have done it in a minute. I have, however, few enough opportunities to invoke high moral dudgeon, and I chose to do so now. In fact, I cataloged this as a betrayal. Oh, for sure, this wasn't nearly so dramatic as, say, Rose's screwing over of Wolfy, which was complicated by the fact that the betrayal was initially his. But the details, the minutiae, the evidence of how sharp Angela's eye was, how much she was studying us, bothered me. Because from an anthropological sense, I liked to know when my actions were being viewed under glass, I think especially by someone with whom I have just made love.

Angela's article saddened me because I realized from that moment on I would be unable to pull off the trick of working at the *Downtown News* without feeling uncomfortable about my brother running for the United States Senate. And while I was by no means in love with Angela, I really did like her and the time I had spent with her; found her funny and smarter than I would have expected that first night we drove up to Mingeboro.

I skimmed Rose's piece, which seemed less vituperative and a little more charming than usual. Her description of Nate as "a man who test markets his affections," I thought, cut close to the bone. But the blown-up blurb at the top of the page made for a little fresh bother. It said, "If the voters in the Republican primary have but a choice between these two turkeys, maybe I'll have to run." That would be an ugly sight to watch, as beautiful as Rose still was.

The morning traffic was getting busier as the sun got warmer, and I sat on the edge of the park planning my next move. I hadn't the slightest idea what it would be. I wasn't going to work today, that was for sure. Tomorrow we'd just have to see. I was certain that the sense of equilibrium I had created for myself at the paper, my home away from home, was gone. I began to feel sorry for myself. There was something inevitable about what I had to do next.

## —— CHAPTER EIGHT ——

I HAVE A FRIEND who makes the point that 'ere you go accept a job you're not really sure you want, you should make at least one unreasonable demand. I had that in mind as I waited in the forty-fourth-floor lobby of Edward's brokerage firm. This would be the last day he would put in any time there at all before formally taking a leave for the duration of the campaign.

It wasn't such a long wait in the lobby, though the seconds ticked by slowly as I sat there outraging some of Edward's partners by being jacketless, by reading the *New York Post*, while they were all well-tailored exemplars of their ordered world, striding purposefully by with the *Journal* tucked like an underarm bib.

"My little brother," Edward pronounced with precision from the doorway. I measured a quarter tone of warmth in his voice. "Come," he gestured, and I followed him in past the brightly lit conference room where gentlemen were discussing the market, in past the Xerox room where yobs were slaving over a hot machine, in past the collection of hot young typists who wore garish clothes and spoke in these unspeakable accents from the outer boroughs or worse. Maybe from Pluto.

We strode into Edward's unlit office, and from the huge window you could see the Port of New York in all its commercial bustle. The Brooklyn Bridge was touchable, and out over those small buildings was the beginning of that suburban stretch to Montauk. If I pressed my face close to the window and looked out of the corner of my eye, I could see the offices of the *New York Post*, which this morning for the first time was being published under the auspices of its new, Memphis-based owners. Whereas a headline yesterday might have gone, "MUM SAYS: HE TOOK ME PURSE," today there were pictures of an ordinary slum blaze with this headline going, "GOODNESS GRACIOUS: GREAT BALLS OF FIRE!" There was something going on over there. And what would this mean to Edward's—to *our* (there, I said it)—campaign?

"I've been trying to reach you for days," Edward said as he slid behind the desk that was not so much a desk as a full-fledged aircraft carrier. A B-1 bomber could have landed on it and stopped without a screech. Edward was for the B-1, incidentally, and any other weapons systems that came down the pike. He liked technology, though he could be an unmerciful critic of the brass.

"You have?" I'd been wondering when he would get to me, given the fact that since I had spoken with him last, he'd aired a spot that was roundly denounced, and I'd been both in the *Post* and now on the cover of the *Downtown News*.

"I have," he said a little defensively. "Good move on Blake. I hear he's going to be okay, though it took about six hours of surgery to make sure he can walk without a limp." Edward was pleased with life, that was for sure. He was practically bouncing in his leather-backed seat, his starched white shirt glistening in the sunlight that broke through the clouds behind him. "I, um, have to say," he said, clearing his throat, "that you were right about putting the ad on the air. I've gotten a disastrous response from people. You know. Ordinary people."

Well I did. I knew ordinary people. But he sure didn't.

"What's the response been?" I asked as his secretary smoothly marched in and presented me with a cup of coffee on this petite silver tray. Edward was having a glass of grapefruit juice.

"Bafflement. The market is nonplussed. People just can't understand what I was doing."

"Yeah," I said as neutrally as possible. This wasn't the time to say something like, "No shit, Sherlock." "So what are you going to do now?"

"We're going on heavy with the ID spot again."

"Shoulda been doing it all along," I allowed sadly.

"I realize that. I told you you were right, all right? Oh, and that was, uh, some issue of your paper. You think the club-hoppers and shoppers who read it were ready for all that?"

In the time I had worked at the *Downtown News,* Edward had never acknowledged that it might be something more than some college-town handout that you picked up in head shops. And once Edward found a preconceived notion he could get away with, a fuddy-duddyism that held up in our living-room court, he generally stuck with it. "I don't know," I said. "I do know this. I don't think I can work there anymore. And that's what I came to talk with you about."

He downed the rest of his grapefruit juice in one gulp with the clouds gathering in a bunch above his shoulders. "Shoot," he said, as he held up his metallic arm like a machine gun.

"Remember that offer you made me out in Mingeboro that night?"

He looked cagey, as if I could have been referring to any evening in the twenty-three years I had known him.

"Does your offer about hiring me for your campaign still hold?"

"Absolutely," he said without emotion. His eyes clicked, as thought the account was closed.

"In what capacity?"

"Well, Charles, what do you want to do?" He said that as if he were asking his little brother, and not an adult with some insight into things. I began to have second thoughts about doing this. Edward can take your confidence away just by the way he presents himself, so level and calm, the ordinary terrors secluded. All that was worn on his sleeve was cloth wrapping steel. But it was I who had for years explained to him the behaviorism of the electorate, and I could honestly say I don't think he could do this race without me. I'd known it all along, but before, it was hubris. Now it was an imperative.

"If I get in there," I said a little tentatively, "I don't want to be answering to those idiots who persuaded you to put on an ad like that."

"You want to run it, don't you?" he asked evenly, as if he'd divined intentions even I wasn't aware of yet.

"Yeah." I nodded my head, as if for the first time convinced.

"Well, all right. Good. I've been waiting for a long time for you to show a little entrepreneurial spirit. You're hired. And if you need to, you can clean shop. That's your decision. Only one thing, all right?" He pointed a flesh finger at me and cocked his head. This chestnut-brown forelock settled on his bushy brow. I nodded and he went on. "I handle the money, okay? That's one thing I do well."

I didn't doubt that for a second. "I can live with that."

"Good," he said, and stood up as if to come shake my hand. Edward was a busy guy and he didn't let you forget it for a minute. That was one thing he was going to have to shed in his transition from citizen to politician.

"Wait one minute," I said as I stood up. "I want, well, I want to be paid well for this, Ed."

"Sure."

"I mean, I want a lot of money if I'm going to run this thing."

"We'll work it out. And you'll earn it. I need someone I can trust, and there's much to be done," he said with a rare tone of magnanimousness.

Now for the the unreasonable request. "I want a corner office." It was a start . . .

"Done."

"And a secretary."

"Of course."

Well, that was easy. I racked my brain. "And a car and driver."

"I'm sure that can be arranged, Charles," he said as he began to shoo me out the door.

What else was there? "And an hour off to jog every day," I continued, but Edward only muttered something about joining me as he began to move me, his new hireling, out the door. Oh, he was so sure of the purchase of my services, and the ease with which he could promise me things made the result seem foreordained. I was halfway down the elevator's plummet before I realized I had forgotten the one truly reasonable request I had needed to extract from him. I wanted to run the thing without having to deal with the family.

## ⸺ CHAPTER NINE ⸺

RACHEL AND HANK WERE shocked when I told them, and I walked in and out without ceremony. I just entered the main red door and nodded to my friends, picked up my mail, and barged in.

"I'm quitting," I said.

"Why?" asked Rachel, instinctively getting up from the desk in the office they shared, a desk that was covered with newspapers, posters, cartons of Chinese food, and Styrofoam cups that sometime in recent weeks had housed coffee.

But Hank wasn't really surprised. "I wish you wouldn't."

"Gotta," I said, maintaining composure. I wanted to say, "You son of a bitch, why'd you go louse up everything?" But I knew why. My family sells papers. That's why.

For a year or more Hank and Rachel had been the center of the *Downtown News* crowd, a family I wanted to be closer to than the one I knew at home. Yet in the last week they had so disrupted things with this cover story that I felt as if I'd been picked up by the nape of the neck and dropped out onto the front porch. The worst thing was that any step I took seemed to lead in the direction of my family, my real family. And that was as disruptive to my dream of an ordered life as having a buzz saw started inches from my face while I dreamed of chasing gazelles through soft, piny woods.

We talked for a few minutes, it was actually kind of pleasant, and at the end I wrote a note for Angela telling her maybe I'd see her in a few months or so. I liked her, a lot, but it would be difficult to spend time with her. I would worry whether every conversation, every intimate act, would become grist for a future article. I left the note with Rachel. And with that, I was gone.

PART FOUR

# CHAPTER ONE

WHEN MY GRANDFATHER LEFT us to go hit the road, there were some who worried more about our money than about his safety. He was rich, that much was clear, but he had gone out of his way to make the estate so complicated that revenuers and takeover artists never would fully be able to grasp the extent of our family holdings. He held the key to it all, and when he was missing, there was a rush among us to try to pin down just exactly what was where. The tally was disappointing to say the least.

"Two million six hundred thousand and change? That's it?" It was my father asking the question over the phone one morning in Mingeboro. Apparently the search for clear deed and title to stock and other liquid assets had been only partially successful. "That can't be right," my father said, taking off the pince-nez he affected at the time in order to squeeze the bridge of his nose. "I'll be right down," he said, and then called our driver to take him to the train station. This was serious. You could tell by the way he clumped to the car.

On that trip and others, my dad had to dredge through the muck of paperwork that was organized like a protective swamp. And though an awful lot more that $2.6 million eventually was found, it was hard for anyone, us included, to get his hands on it. It seemed we were safe from infidels unless they were prepared to don waders.

It soon became clear that my grandfather's true genius wasn't in finding segments of the auto industry that an independent from the hills of Connecticut could slide into without actually being crushed by the giants. If my grandfather possessed actual genius, it was in the creation of dummy corporations that made our wealth an amorphous entity, more difficult to nail down than mercury. It lay in dispersing what wealth there was into enough nooks and crannies that no crooks or nannies ever could get their hands on it. But neither, it turned out, could we.

I thought of this one morning in June when we were sitting in the Jungle Room for a family business meeting. It was to be followed by a briefing on how things progressed for Edward in the campaign. I leaned back in the cast-iron rocking couch I shared with Betsy and stared up at the glass roof. It was broken into sections and outlined with lead, and etched against the blue sky were the reflections of the twenty or so of us who were sitting in sunlight. We were in a world overwhelmed by the smell of ferns. We all sat so attentively because we were listening to one of the young business advisers hired by Uncle Andrew to try to make more sense of our family fortune than, well, Andrew ever could have. I just kept staring at my family's reflections as the young man droned on about how "Aftermath, Inc., a Netherland Antilles corporation, owns eighty-nine percent of Duino Ventures, which in turn owns ninety-two percent of the Parnell Holding Company, okay?"

None of us was sure it was okay unless when he came to the bottom line it meant we had some money.

"Parnell," he continued a little nervously, "owes a one sixty-fourth overriding royalty on anything produced by the trust that originally was known as the Easter Trust, but which Mr. Daley, Sr., had changed to the Lazarus Trust the week before he died. Now, the Daley Family Trust, through its stock in the wholly owned Agenbite Corporation, is in complete control of Aftermath, yet due to the anchovy harvest in Peru, not to mention sunspot activity in the previous quarter . . ."

"Ahem," said Aunt Morgan, as she sat straight up in the cast-iron rocking couch that faced me. All you could hear was the gurgling of the indoor pools in which California golden trout still swam. "We've heard this tortured relationship described a dozen or so times over the years," Morgan continued. "I daresay Andrew may even understand it. At least I hope he does. But would you skip forward to the part about the revenue?"

"Revenue?" the young man asked, his voice rising as if he'd never heard the word before.

"You know," said Morgan as evenly as she could. "Income? Cash? Checks?" she asked with wiggling eyebrows.

He'd heard of it. "Well . . ." he began, and then stopped. "There of course is the Bayer Trust, and . . ."

Wolfy, who among his other creeping infirmities was a trifle deaf, his ears shot from engine roar, turned to Uncle Andrew and said in a stage whisper, "Which trust?"

"Bayer," said Andrew.

"As in 'the cupboard is bare,' " I said to Betsy, and she sat there giggling as quietly as she could, the couch we were on rocking a little against the floor.

"Yes," the adviser said with pronounced earnestness, "the Bayer Trust, which administers the income produced by one of the real estate ventures that Mr. Daley acquired thirty years ago, finally had some significant advances. Uh," he said, putting on his half-frame glasses and staring at his clipboard, "there were five units sold on Mount Targa, which produced for the Bayer Trust a total of two hundred and sixteen thousand dollars. Not bad," he said with a smile. "Not bad at all."

"Until you have to split it seven ways," said Aunt Lizzie with a fatalistic laugh, her eyes wandering over each of us. "And then, of course, live on it."

Uncle Wolfy looked glum. He was doing the math.

"And what of Daley Motorworks?" asked Betsy, speaking to Uncle Andrew. Betsy and I were in the meeting only because of the political meeting to follow. Otherwise I would not voluntarily have spent this much time with them, even with money at stake. Otherwise, only Edward, as the oldest son, would have sat in with the second-generation members as they got the cheery news about our fortunes. Now Andrew was looking at Betsy as if it were very poor form indeed for her to put to him the one question he wished least to answer.

The young financial adviser looked to Andrew for his cue, trying to see if he was expected to step in and deliver the news or if Andrew would do the dirty work himself. A hallmark of my family, of course, is a tendency not to do the dirty work anyone we'd hired could do for us. And especially when the news was as bad as it was. There were times when I wondered whether Andrew simply was inept, or if he worked at losing money for us. For a minute it appeared that Andrew was going to pretend he just never heard the question.

But then he sat straight up in his chair and let out a breath. He was dressed in this bright madras shirt and he looked a little tired, and of late he always looked tired, his handsome face very much under strain. Maybe it was the responsibility of running a company caught in the classic position of expecting revenues imminently but owing money now. Or else it was Melissa. That was what Betsy thought. She thought it was his wife who caused his face to be so taut.

"We're in a heap of trouble," he finally allowed. "There isn't a bank I've tried who'll loan us a dime until we pay off the Connecticut Bank and Trust, so Ethan Stanton's done what he set out to do in terms of cutting off our lines of provision." I could have heard the whoosh of a winter wind, though it was so damn sunny outside.

He shrugged and I had to feel for him. It was clear the family long ago would have preferred Edward to have run the Motorworks, but Edward was too smart for that. I looked over to the chair on which he perched and found him cringing, as if acknowledging some responsibility for the dismal state of affairs that Andrew was about to lay out.

"Which means," Andrew went on, "that the only place to go is the investment banking community. But, um, those I've gone to don't see the possibility that Daley Motorworks is going to recover anytime in the near . . ."

"I can raise the money," Edward said quietly, and all heads turned to him. He just sat there basking in the glow, and I couldn't tell if that look on Andrew's face was relief or if he suddenly hated Edward for taking on the responsibility Andrew in his formerly carefree way would have been happy to yield.

"Where you going to do that, Ed?" asked my Uncle Wolfy, who was now so attentive it seemed as if Edward was going to describe the road map to a town full of coeds.

"Oh, I can raise the money," Edward said modestly. "Think about it for a minute. Daley Motorworks is a prestige institution in an age demanding one word above all else: quality. Now Daley Motorworks Limited is an elite institution at a time when elite products have become the passion of young people. It doesn't matter how much we owe right now. If we market my dad's injector system right, we can make it the hottest thing in Detroit. People won't just buy that Trans Am or this Mustang; they'll buy the Trans Am with the Daley Injector, the Daley Injector Mustang. Or maybe we could even revive the name Lazarus. Oh, yeah," he said, getting this excited look in his eyes that, I have to admit, had us riveted, "try to sell a car on the basis of its sex appeal because it has a connection to the Lazzy and we'll do just fine. Man, young people will eat it up," he said, and I was convinced. Edward was very persuasive. "We forget that the Lazarus is still considered by the congnoscenti to be an American Lamborghini."

"Yes, but we have maybe another sixty days that we can keep the factory going, Edward," was Andrew's sad reminder. As inept as he was, he did know the math.

Edward turned on him, and you could tell that though he'd been making this up as he went along, he accepted the challenge he'd created for himself. "If we make a presentation to some of the houses on the Street based on survey research that shows what kind of name ID the Lazzy still has, and if we can get some good PR for Wolfy here as the national spokesman for the Daley Injector, the money will drop from the sky."

Wolfy was sitting there pointing to himself, a question mark before him in the air, but all eyes were focused on Edward. He was continuing matter-of-factly, offering the only promise we had that Daley Motorworks would not just fold up and die, leaving one hundred sixty families without a breadwinner, and this in the middle of a campaign. Oh, yes, we were riveted, perhaps Andrew most of all. "I can go to the Street," Edward went on. "I can help out."

I hated to be the one to have to bring my family back to earth, but this wasn't just my brother Edward who was talking, this was Candidate Daley, and I was his campaign manager, had been so for a month. "Hey, Edward, before you go on, I have to say I don't think going to the Street to raise money for the company is as effective a use of your time as going there to raise money for the campaign."

Well, you would have thought I had proposed to give what money remained to the Little Sisters of the Poor. I don't think anyone hissed outright—we were a very polite family at times like this—but I was face-to-face with this basilisk army. Edward shrugged, as if he would yield to a consensus, though it was pretty clear that the consensus here was for raising money for the company. But on the realistic side of things, if Edward didn't raise enough money for the campaign, he couldn't win. And I have to venture that in some ways Edward's being elected to the Senate had much long-range potential for the family. Other doors would open, and I mean that in the least venal of ways. I mean that in terms of press, which was as good as oxygen, for the family company.

We still had some assets that could bring in money. If only we could find them. The good news was we had an interest in the largest tin field in the universe. The bad news was that it was on the Planet Krypton. But we weren't completely broke.

The problem was that if Edward's attention was diverted, if he had to divide his time between raising money for himself and raising money for the family, not enough of either would be raised. We could end up in November with no company and no Senate seat, and a scenario could be concocted that after that we would be swept away like tumbleweed.

The only other person in the room who looked as if she understood this was Aunt Morgan. For all her lack of humor, for all her unpleasantness, she was the only one who you could say was on familiar terms with reality. Aunt Lizzie likes to say that the twin themes of our family are myth and fantasy, but even she right now was nodding along, though Aunt Morgan's countenance was firm. And ultimately she was the one who backed me up. "Charles is right, you know," she said. "Edward can't go into this campaign trying to set things right at Daley Motorworks."

But then Edward stepped in. "Oh, sure I can," he said. "Look, I can set things up with four or five phone calls, and Andrew—and Uncle Wolfy—can do the rest."

Wolfy was sitting there with his nose scrunched up. I think his reaction to Edward's suggestion about his involvement in this scheme was to question his nephew's political acumen. But when Wolfy looked at us, we smiled back at him, and instantly he puffed himself up to his former sense of self. Yeah, he guessed he liked that, spokesman for the Lazarus as we attempted to bring it back from the dead.

The thing was settled; we would try to regain our corporate self. This was one of those moments when being part of such a family, in no matter what stage of breakdown we found ourselves, could have its blood-calming sense of reward. And when the young man who managed our money began to speak again, the attention was still so riveted on our newfound sense of hope that after a minute or so his voice just trailed away.

# ⸻ CHAPTER TWO ⸻

I THINK MY GRANDMOTHER would have rolled in her grave had she known that when we broke for lunch we did so for burgers. She had always resisted her family's urge toward such victuals. Once, when my Uncle Wolfy was heard to praise the charms of the french fries served by the nearby Dairy Queen, my grandmother observed that that was fitting. "After all," she told him maliciously, "you're only two generations away from potatoes."

So as we wandered out of the Jungle Room amidst backslapping and good-to-see-yas, we made our way up the steps toward the pool. There our old servants who, despite our setbacks, still worked for Aunt Lizzie and Aunt Morgan, had been working on a barbecue. A soccer ball came bouncing over the bushes and Andrew tapped it back with skill. We could hear the squeals of little children as they splashed about in the shallow end, and over yonder, where so long ago I had seen Uncle Wolfy and Uncle Blitz race those test cars, there was some kind of game occurring. Several of my cousins and their chums, from I guess by now it would be college, were engaged in this Frisbee-laden, t'ai-chi-like ritual, punctuated by passes and manic gallops.

"Red Rover, Red Rover, I want purple to come over" was the call from one cousin, and you could see she had singled out Wolfy's fat son, Taylor, in his purple bathing trunks. Now, in typical hapless fashion, he'd have to run from the edge of the tennis courts and try to make it across the pool with this human chain of little Daleys set to dive as deep as they could to tag him before he touched the wall. His eyes bulged.

Bikinis were everywhere in evidence, and it had always been tough living on an estate that crawled with these long-limbed beauties, all of whom were cousins, or the wives of cousins. Although sometimes friends of cousins . . .

I saw Melissa in this outrageous little thing reading the same book she had first brought to the pool six years before when she was still dating Andrew. There were those in my family, most especially Betsy, who didn't like her. They didn't trust her because she was fun, though none too bright, and looking at her body, it was just too obvious what Uncle Andrew saw in her. What every man saw in her. Betsy at times could be a ferocious snob, and she saw Melissa as being beneath Andrew, though the truth be told, I don't think *Andrew* could have finished *War and Peace* in seven years. And it was *War and Peace* that Melissa had pursued every summer I'd known her, and I sort of admired her for that. Not so much that she was doggedly trying to read the book—and it's not as if the rest of my cousins sat there plowing through *Ulysses*—but that she would continue to do it so slowly in front of us, the most judgmental collection I have ever known. For that she earned my highest accolade. She was *sin vergüenza:* without shame.

Surrounding Melissa were some of her friends from town, mostly well-tanned, tennis-playing wives of men who made their livings in New York. And a sight for bloodshot eyes they were, cooing as first Andrew came to kiss his wife and then my one-armed brother Edward came to revel in their midst. Someone went off the diving board in a cannonball, and the rainbow spray chilled the women as they sat there in the sun.

Julius, the Count Basie look-alike who still lived on the estate employed by Aunt Morgan long after most of the other servants had moved back to South Carolina, chucklingly put his considerable barbecuing talents to work on the burgers, his white chef's cap rippling in the slight breeze that swept across the perfect day. On a tennis court Annie was beating back cousin Owen, who utterly lacked the finesse he showed on the pitcher's mound. His natural coordination still enabled him somehow to lob junk balls back over the net, the better to set up slams that showed no mercy. Luckily for her, Annie had been taught to play by Edward, whose awkward manner of throwing up the ball with the same hand that held his racket had never diminished his absolute control.

I stood on the gray stones that surrounded the pool and for a minute watched the tennis, a minute the Frisbee, several seconds eyeing the two boys kicking the soccer ball, and looking up above the tennis courts, I could see my cousin Norfolk patch out in a little 2002. He quickly curved around the gardens and bounced up the dirt road to the other side of the estate as if he were taking the same esses at Lime Rock that had killed his old man.

But now Melissa had put down her book and was holding forth.

"I have sex in all my dreams," she said conspiratorially. Tractors crawled the distant hills, and I knew that an animal was down, because there were hawks circling a mile away. They soared over Melissa's shoulder.

"Every single one?" asked her friend Mary Joy. Mary Joy was slathering suntan lotion over her legs, and since it had been several weeks since I had last gone out with Angela—or practically any other woman for that matter—I was tempted to make an offer to help her out.

"Every one I remember," Melissa said with a shake of her curly brown hair over those lovely shoulders, which, if you knew her as I knew her, if you had studied her progress in *War and Peace* summer upon summer as I had, you would have known were steeped in her late-June coloration. By August she would be absolutely black. You could set your calendar by it with the same grim assurance you had that she always got her second service in.

"Why do you think that is?"' she asked me, and she, Mary Joy, and their two pretty, married friends stared at me intently. Edward just sat there with this grin on his face. Me, women always want to hear talk; Edward can get away with merely grinning.

But I was staring off past the Frisbee players, past the little office that my father used as his own for many years. I was staring at this movement I detected in the woods at the edge of our square mile of lawn. Omigod. It couldn't be. But it was! It was Fido, my little doggy, returned to visit home!

I took off in a sprint and was glad I was wearing sneakers, 'cause I made that dirt fly. And there he was, sniffing at this flower, chasing that butterfly, my bluetick hound whose muzzle these days was getting awfully gray. When he saw me run toward him, I could see his tail awagging, and he ran right through the Frisbee match in a bee-line for the pool.

"Come here, boy," I shouted and then dove onto my knees as he ran into my arms. He was licking my face unmercifully as we rolled around on the grass. I caught a glimpse of a couple of my cousins' friends looking at me as if they thought I was the queerest thing imaginable. But as we wrestled, as I scratched his chest, the rest of the family left the pool and the courts to come to see our unfaithful little Fido. For in the absence of my grandmother, in the absence of my father, he was the only sign of untainted continuity that we had.

And he was fickle, that much was for sure; he hadn't actually spent an evening at home since we'd vacated the old house and moved into the one on the other side of the estate.

There were dozens now oohing over the mutt, children running up and reaching out their hands to touch him. Even Wolfy unselfconsciously threw his arms around the dog. It may have been the greatest spontaneous celebration we'd had in years, certainly greater than when we'd managed to sneak my grandfather past the paparazzi (and my grandmother) when he returned from his long trek.

But then Betsy wandered out from the house, and giving Fido a polite petting on the top of his spotted head, she announced that we better eat our burgers. For those of us in the political meeting, the outside consultants had finally arrived.

## —— CHAPTER THREE ——

IT WAS ALREADY THAT stage of the campaign where we had to take to the mattresses. That is, on the deck of Aunt Lizzie's condo overlooking the pool. Simon Ford, the consultant who had recently overseen Edward's impressive show on the floor of the Republican State Convention, insisted on sitting in the sun and getting a tan while the meeting went on, so the Jungle Room was out. Now we lay sprawled on the deck above the newly shingled guest quarters, the sun direct upon us, swimming-pool sound occasionally interrupting the serious discussion.

Sitting on the floor with his back to the pool was Mitch Sheedy, our sometimes gruff, phlegmatic pollster. Boy, did he look foolish in shorts. Edward sat upright on the floor next to him, nose at forty degrees to the sun, and afterward it would cause Harry Fox, our media consultant, more than a little chagrin to find Edward had a deep tan on precisely one half of his face. There was this clear line down the center of his nose as if he were divided into two.

Fox was an excitable type. You could tell by the way he strode along the edge of the deck, though the slightest slip and he'd splatter on the gray stone that surrounded the pool. Simon Ford, in contrast, lay on an air mattress with these reflecting glasses on, and had he not occasionally interjected an opinion, you might have thought he was asleep.

I called upon him to make a report on the events at the convention the week before. Now the group crowded around to hear how Edward had surprised everyone, us included, when he walked out with 41 percent of the delegates. All he needed in order to get on the September primary ballot was 25 percent, but the Stanton operatives had been telling reporters and delegates alike there was no way Edward would cross the enchanted threshold.

"We certainly won the expectations game," said Simon to the sky, staring straight up as the sun tanned his long, skinny frame. "You had Jim Surrette, swine that he is, Nate Stanton's chief political operative, laughing at Edward's chances. He was telling reporters right up until the first ballot how the Stantonites were going to remember who all got on the Daley bandwagon."

But that night it was magic. "All we needed to pull this thing off was one or two of the big downstate counties going along with our merry band of stalwart upstate souls. If that happened, we had 'em. Okay, so then Suffolk and Nassau both switch to Edward, with Uncle Nick Polenta, Nassau's perennial boss, coming up and cutting the deal in a dumbwaiter. That was great. That clinched it, but more significantly, I think it showed reporters that in the final analysis, Nate Stanton ain't even loved by the party regulars."

"What's the significance of Suffolk and Nassau?" Betsy wanted to know. She was a little more discreet about trying to get a tan than Simon Ford was; at least she had the common courtesy to be lying on her stomach, staring at the circle of fifteen or so of us here on the broad rooftop deck.

Simon pushed his shades farther up his nose and lay his arms against the deck in a complete posture of repose. "They're your archetypal machine Republican counties, okay? Rely on patronage and organization, and not incidentally, they actually have some patronage to dole out. But they don't like primaries. It upsets the order. If you go against the leadership, you are an outcast, a traitor. You will never again be a sewer commissioner. Now, they should be firmly in, uh, your Uncle Nate's corner. He's been a senator a very long time. And yet they're willing to risk something on a political unknown. Why? Well, it tells you something. There's a real softness to the senator's support, and at its base."

"Plus," I interjected, "these are the counties that actually vote on primary day."

"Yeah," Simon jumped back in, this time deigning to sit up and look at us. "That's where you harvest your votes."

"Thirty-three percent in a general election," said Mitch Sheedy from his perch in the shade next to Edward, who was just sitting there listening. For all his pretending that he knew what he was doing in the race, when he was with the consultants he was smart enough to listen. A big question I had was how long this would continue. In politics a little bit of knowledge is a very dangerous thing indeed.

"In a primary election, though," Mitch sort of grunted, "they can turn out up to fifty percent of a Republican total."

"And it's all one media market, see," said Harry Fox, who now was sitting on the edge of the wall, his feet tapping to some unheard beat, his day's growth of beard making him look, well, if not exactly shady, at least a little seedy. He looked like the kind of guy you saw at the tables at Vegas at eight in the morning.

"It's all New York media, see," he continued. "Lotta overspill into Jersey, Connecticut. But lotta bang for your buck on the Island." I wondered if he'd taken off gold chains before coming up to Mingeboro.

"So how come we didn't get more upstate counties?" I asked Simon. It had bothered me that night, though in the general revelry that followed the vote, in the slow appreciation that we were going to go over the top with some strength, questions as to why we didn't do even better seemed out of place.

"Because they still don't know who the hell he is. And that change in spots, you know, when Edward went on the air to talk about how he lost his arm, well, that one was a dud."

Edward sat there looking a little foolish, but Harry Fox jumped in again. "Before my time, kids." And it was. Harry, Mitch, and Simon had been brought in after I walked into the campaign headquarters and fired half the staff. "Now everything's going to change. Harry's on the case."

It was going to be a long campaign. Harry sat there on the edge of the deck pumping to that beat, lighting cigarettes and throwing them over his shoulder when they were done, just flicking them indiscriminately. I thought I could hear the sound of them hissing as they hit the pool where my little cousins swam.

"What I want to know," I said to Mitch Sheedy, "is what the benchmark shows." At midnight the night before, Mitch had come out of the field with the first postconvention survey of voter attitudes about Nate Stanton, about Edward, about our possibilities. "How bad or good is it?"

"It's good. It's basically good, I'd say. Among likely Republican primary voters, Nate has an eighty-nine percent recognition factor, but his negatives are high, roughly one to one."

"You're kidding," said Simon Ford. He was impressed.

"Yeah," said Mitch with a smile. "Forty-three to forty."

I whispered to Betsy that an incumbent was expected to have roughly two times as many people who thought of him favorably as thought of him unfavorably, especially within his own party. Otherwise he was to be considered vulnerable.

"The candidate profile is pretty good," Sheedy went on. He was awfully chunky, but he had an impressive demeanor, like that of an intelligent bouncer at a first-class bar. His handlebar mustache was the only affectation on an otherwise meat-and-potatoes face. "What your typical Republican primary voter would prefer is a younger senator, not part of the Washington Establishment, though still able to deliver the goods. In particular, they want someone who will lower their taxes and keep down inflation, at the same time helping to rebuild the military and cutting down on the general size and cost of government. I'm finding this everywhere, by the way. The tax issue in particular runs well this year among primary voters.

"Anyway, Edward," he went on, "the numbers for you seem pretty good. At least about where they should be. Okay, fewer people know you than live in Mingeboro. Those who do know you have a pretty hazy feeling about you. I guess the good news is that those who know both you and Nate—the activists—like you. But that is, so far, a pretty small number indeed."

"So what's the bottom line?" asked Edward, who was forever in search of it.

"Media" was the answer from Harry Fox, Simon Ford, and myself. Even Fido, so quietly sitting by me, seemed to thump his tail at that one.

"And lots of it," said Simon Ford.

"Kid, we are going to have to create you anew," said Harry Fox with what passed for him as rapture. "Just think of yourself as going in for a personality tuck. A little cutting here, a little fleshing out there. A whole new person."

Edward looked intrigued, if a little put out. I don't think he liked the idea of being turned over to packagers. I tried to make it easier on him by explaining to him the way things were.

"Edward, you lost a great opportunity by going on the air with a serviceable ID spot that introduced you to the voters but then pulling it. As everyone has told you by now, you confused things by letting your staff panic over Nate's charges about your war record. Now, what these gentlemen need to do is come up with a consistent theme and stick with that while enough people begin to have a better understanding of who you are."

"How much money do we have on hand?" Simon asked. By now he was sitting up lotus-positioned on the mattress, looking very serious—and ominous—in his reflecting shades.

"We've raised a little over three hundred thousand dollars and Edward's kicked in another seven hundred thousand of his own. Cash on hand is probably about eight hundred grand," I allowed.

"We need lots more," said Simon.

"Lots and lots more," said Harry.

"Well, you should know that Uncle Nate has raised only about two hundred thousand so far," I said.

"You have to be kidding," said Mitch. "He shouldn't be having any trouble raising money. He sits on the Finance Committee, for Chrissake. That's a license to print money."

"The fact is he hasn't really tried yet, though it looks as if he's going to have some kind of major fund-raiser in the city two weeks from last night. He's bringing up a bunch of his Senate buddies."

"Like who?" asked Uncle Andrew. He was just curious, sitting over there in a corner of the deck. Like his sisters, he loved observing political machinations. It was Wolfy who wanted to be consulted on points of strategy. But Wolfy was otherwise engaged right now, off in Mills Corner picking up his new girlfriend at the train. Wolfy was in love, which meant he was preoccupied. In addition to working on his book, his being in love made him altogether a happier sort to deal with.

"I hear he's bringing up Howard Baker," I answered.

"Baker?" said Simon Ford. "He's going to run for President. Why would he get in the middle of a primary?"

"Because the word in Washington is that Edward's going to get squashed like a fly," said Mitch Sheedy. "But I can't believe the Stantons think that. Not after the convention. Nate should have raised a million by now. You think they aren't taking this seriously? I mean, with numbers like this?"

"Did you do a head-to-head?" I asked.

"Yeah, but it doesn't matter. It's so early."

"But what are the numbers?" I mean, after all, we'd paid for them.

"They are pretty bad," he said with the nonchalance of a doctor reflecting on your count of corpuscles without trying to scare you.

"But what are they?"

"Fifty-five to ten."

Edward seemed to gulp at that. Sheedy leaned over and gently patted him on the knee. "Hey," he said, "don't worry, kid. Primaries break late, and right now you are known by next to no one. Those numbers might not change for a while, but that's insignificant. What matters is the curve by which you're getting known rising together with the curve of people liking you."

"Is that how it works?" Edward asked a little hopefully, as if the one thing he hadn't yet pieced together was how he would actually win. It had certainly been a gamble to challenge Uncle Nate for his Senate seat, but I had assumed that Edward had figured out how he'd do it. The bottom line to this, as I figured Edward had well calculated, was spending a bunch of money. But it seemed he feared whether even that would work.

"Yeah, something like that," said Harry Fox. "Now we need to get moving on new spots. I like this background. Yeah, this is good. I want kids in the ads, lotsa kids."

"Oh, sure," said Mitch Sheedy with a smile. "Kids will be perfect for when he talks about the Panama Canal, Kemp-Roth tax cuts, and outlawing inflation."

Then cousin Owen, who was one of the few members of the family I really wanted working on the campaign, decided to speak up. "I got an idea," he said. "Is your polling showing people don't like regulations by the government?"

Sheedy nodded at him.

"Then how 'bout this shot of a farmer, okay, on a tractor, right, with this voice goin' on about the noble farmer, blah, blah, blah. Then you see that because of government regulations, he has to have a portable john strapped on the back." Owen grinned.

"I like it," said Simon Ford. He too grinned, though Harry Fox looked a little malevolent. But Edward just sat there, trying to figure the significance of a farmer with a Port-o-san joined to his tractor.

## ⎯⎯ CHAPTER FOUR ⎯⎯

AS FIDO SCAMPERED UP the long dirt road that neatly bisected our forest, my friend Simon Ford beside me was heard to huff and puff. It was a beautiful day for running, and so we had set forth, leaving Harry Fox at the pool to ogle my cousins, with Mitch Sheedy heading for the phones to check the cross tabs from our poll. Sunlight streamed in swirling, speckled funnels, and the only sounds to be heard were our breathing, the occasional snap of a twig in the woods, and the noises of Fido routing rabbits.

I was glad to have been able to slip away and run with our principal consultant. I had called on Simon when I went over to the campaign with the authority to hire and to fire. Out, sadly, went Jimmy Zion and some of his cohorts from a different age, a different world. One, alas, without television and its concomitant ability to foster the swift accretion of negatives. In, of course, were the new consultants we'd assembled today on the deck. They added credibility as much as strategy. With this group, we were a serious campaign. The only one among the new trio of whom I was not sure was Harry Fox.

"I just don't know about that guy," I said, gulping air as we panted up the hill. At this rate, in another couple of miles, we'd be climbing up the trails that led to our private ski area, which came with T-bars and rope tows. As in so many other areas of my life, the pitch to the road sometimes made me wonder what I was doing this for.

"Oh, no, he's really good," Simon said as sweat streamed down his forehead and cascaded off his nose. Nearby came the gurgle of a stream. "He's a jerk, but he's a genius at negative advertising."

We had long ago agreed that going negative, flying over Nate's house and unloading a ton of shit, was something that was just plain inevitable.

"You can take some slick Madison Avenue type, and in the final analysis he might be aesthetically pleasing," Simon went on as we forged up the hill, "be able to dress well enough to comfortably sit still up here. He may even [huff] be able to keep [puff] from slurping with his soup spoon, but he can probably only tell you why you want to drink Coke. He can't make you think of Pepsi as poison. And Harry can make you think of Pepsi as poison."

That was true. I'd seen his spots. This guy could popularize botulism.

Ahead of us my pup was dancing on his hind legs, his forepaws thrown open wide, as if he were about to burst into song with his back to the darkening forest. We were on the road to the House of Lazarus, to which I held a key. Or at least the combination.

"How's business?" I asked as we bounced on. While I could often talk for hours about politics, on a day like today enough was enough.

We were passing through the most beautiful section of the woods. Down the hill a ways was where we had often shot grouse and the occasional pheasants. Within a mile we would come to the huge old garage that once upon a time had been my grandfather's private workshop, and where now eleven of the family's remaining Lazaruses were stored.

One of them was mine, and every so often I would go to visit it. The last time I'd been out here it had started on the second try—the engines were marvelously resilient—but I seldom drove it on the roads. In fact, so far as I knew, only a few of the cars were registered, either with the state of Connecticut or with the New York Lazarus Driving Club. So when *Road & Track* did its official tallies of how many of these prizes were left, they did not take into account our eleven Lazzies, which were off the market, though, in the condition they were in, they could probably fetch ninety thousand dollars each. If we truly wished to raise capital, one place we could start was here. If we wanted to push things that far.

"Business is good," said Simon. "Our foreign clients are where the real money lies, though we have a bunch of Republican primaries coming up."

Simon worked for that consulting group known as The Firm. It was a consortium of political operatives, all of whom were good, and

especially because they were mean. One of the reasons I had wanted
them to work for Edward was because I knew he needed help coun-
terbalancing Ethan's vicious streak. I could be as mean and nasty as
the next guy, but I hadn't brought it to the level of an art form, and
these guys had. Simon was the one among the six partners whom I
knew best, so I had turned to him to get the campaign on track.

We began a bumpy descent down a slow, winding hill. Fido slipped
over the edge only to reappear moments later down the road, tail
wagging, waiting for us slowpokes to catch up. When we did, he
jumped for my hand, and I had to cuff him a little to get him to tag
along. Soon he was following us, his nose to the road.

"I'd venture this will be about the best-covered primary in the
country this year," I said after a while. Because other than politics,
there wasn't too much else to talk about with Simon, I guess.

"Oh, no doubt. It's New York, there are family histories that in
themselves make copy, it's the New Right against the old moderate
wing of the Republican Party. Plus you got me involved." You see,
Simon was kind of controversial. "Better buckle up," he said.

Now Fido fell into step with us and banged against my leg. Within
a matter of minutes we would be standing in front of the House of
Lazarus. Fido had always loved to be there, especially when my father and my uncles were tinkering with the Lazzies. The hard work,
the real work, was still being done at Daley Motorworks at the base
of Mount Targa, and would continue to be, we hoped. Out here,
though, the work had been special, for love; for my father and my
uncles it had involved simply toying with the cars that were their
lives.

"I'll tell you, though," Simon was saying, "I think it's the foreign
campaigns that make you appreciate a good old-fashioned American
primary. At least we have primaries! And at least the losers don't get
thrown in the dungeon after the general."

While I don't think he really appreciated his irony, I wasn't really
listening, I was thinking of my family. But Simon went on. "I'm
having fun in the Italian election, I always do. Free trips to Rome,
it's great. Colombia's election is fine, though we're siding with the
leftists there. In foreign elections it doesn't matter what side you're
on as long as you get paid, right? Anyway, my partners say there's
only one thing to do in the Dominican Republic, it looks so bad."

"Yeah," I said. "What's that?"

"We definitely have to stage a coup."

I looked at him for a second, but we were nearing the House of Lazarus and Fido just went nuts. Fido loved to ride in fast cars, a Lazzy most of all.

We came around a corner and there, tucked into a particularly dingy bend, was the huge old garage we call the House of Lazarus. It seemed to be supporting a nest of sycamores on a ledge. It just hung there, this huge old thing, like wet moss in bright sun.

The House of Lazarus exuded rafters and spiders and the smell of oilcans. We stopped and tried to catch our breaths, drops of sweat splattering with a dark finality against the sandy road. Fido immediately went up and scratched the door.

I hadn't been here for, oh, I guess a year? Not since I last drove my Lazzy, which would have been the summer before, though I couldn't remember precisely what was the occasion. My Lazzy meant a lot to me, so much that I had been able to resist the temptation to drive it, even though it would have set me apart at college without even having to try. The Bavaria had fit right in with the Porsches and the Saabs and the Volvos, but I had taken a secret pride in knowing that the Lazzy could have blown them all away. The Lazzy was the essence of my family, and not driving it was the only delayed compensation I had ever sat still for. This was my srongest expression of maturity. Right now I wanted to get my hands on it, though, and take it for a spin.

My father had always said he wanted each of his children to have a Lazzy, and so we did. Only Sam actually used his, however, having driven off in it in the middle of the night. He reported it was doing well in Oregon, where now it was showcased in the lobby of the foreign-car dealership cum repair lot he had founded. Edward kept his Lazzy out on Long Island, at his lawyer's mansion in East Hampton where he had stayed one summer, just never bothering to bring it back to Mingeboro, since the journey would have taken more hours than Edward had to give to such frivolity. And having someone else drive it was unthinkable. Betsy had sold hers for a not inconsiderable sum, and had invested her money wisely. But we had little Annie's set aside for when we were sure she wouldn't loan it to some boyfriend. I guess our greatest fear, even more so than Lazlo Fortescu, was Annie one day driving up with some guy in a blue Camaro.

Uncle Wolfy on occasion took his Lazzy for a spin, though he seemed to be settling into the comfort of a big old Mercedes for his daily drives, preferring his Jeep for when he went out fishing. But up here was the mother lode, the greatest gathering of Lazzies still kept in one place. Though we heard rumors of vast California collections owned by rock stars with habits, the truth was that none of the cars up here had been driven more than five thousand miles. They were in a time warp. For the cars it was still the summer of 1964.

We could get in only if I remembered the combination to the front-door lock. "What's in here?" Simon Ford wanted to know, pressing his face against the smoky glass at the entrance to the office. You had to enter there to get to the garage, though each work bay had its own roll-up door.

"This is where we keep the cars."

"All the way out here? We must've run five miles already. You people really are eccentric."

But I didn't say a word since he would find out soon enough. And besides, I was having trouble with the combination. My father had set it, and I think if you took the date of his birthday and divided that by the date of his wedding anniversary . . . Yep, there it went, and we were in the door, Fido first, his tail wagging against the table in the center of the room. I thought for a minute that the lock was pretty flimsy, but crime wasn't something you had to reflect on too much in Mingeboro, Connecticut.

The day was still sunny, but the damp office was dark, and cool, as if it were underground. The last person who had been here, perhaps the autumn before, had left a coffee cup on the table. The cup was green with mildew; the coffee had long since evaporated. My heart beat fast when I remembered that in reconstructing the weekend that my parents had died, I was told my father had paid one last trip to see the Lazzies, which at the time had struck us as making perfect sense. He didn't call any of us, didn't warn us about what was coming, but he *would* go to face the more beautiful of the creations he had brought into the world. I doubt he came to ask their forgiveness. Yes, it would make sense for that particular forgotten cup to have been left by my father.

I wanted to be out of there. Either out of there or alone there, but certainly not there with Simon Ford, who was standing next to photographs of the glory days of Daley Motorworks, with his elbow rubbing off the dust to see the faces.

This was the office in which my grandfather had first labored after his initial success in making cars had allowed him to buy the estate.

There were still files and files of charts and designs, as well as cardboard boxes stacked to the ceiling with records of transactions from the days when my father and grandfather ran the business side of the company. This was a monument to clutter, to creative disorder, to the freewheeling days of precomputer accumulation. Would that our accountant had had the acumen of a Chinaman with an abacus.

We walked through the door and into the garage, and though it was almost entirely dark save for the light streaming through scatter-shot holes in the walls, you could sense the presence of great cars, as if they were purring, as if they were waiting to rise and zoom away, to head straight for the highway, where they would take on all comers.

Even Fido seemed to sense the importance of the room, as he kept hushed and stuck close to me, wanting to feel me next to him. Simon Ford was as reverent as if we'd entered a cathedral, and there was that chiaroscuro transition from a hot summer street to the stillness of a sacristy.

I found a light switch and turned it on, and there they were, eleven beautiful Lazaruses, shiny and bright as new, save for the cushioning coat of dust upon them.

"Holy shit," said Simon Ford, and he let out this shrill little whistle. They were lined up in order of brightness, from a canary yellow to a grape-colored one at the end of the garage, and in between I could see my little honey dressed in violet. "I had no idea," he said, impressed.

We walked across the floor, admiring this collection for its individuality, yes, but for its presence as a whole, somewhat the way one admires a large family with distinctive characteristics. These were American cars built when we were showing the world how to do it. The gull-wing doors unlocked, as I now showed Simon, with a solidity wholly European in its sound. The leather smell enveloped the car as soon as you opened the door. As I wandered over to a drawer in which I knew to fumble for the keys and a clip-on license plate, I was hoping that my car would start with the first try, every-time assurance that had once been the hallmark of quality.

Simon was moving with his back to the garage doors, trying to take in the scale of these eleven beauties stretched before him. The room was still without being stuffy in the least; the stone and the cars seemed to create their own air, inflated as it was with the large molecules of oxygen that seemed to lurk here in these woods, so close to streams and game birds, here in the cultivated damp. "Hey, would you mind flicking that switch beside you?" I said, and in a daze Simon responded, pausing for a moment before following my order. Within a minute the engine that worked the door in front of my Lazzy had done its thing, and behind Simon was the dirt road and the beginning of the wall of evergreens.

"This oughta do it," I said, and I got behind the wheel of my Lazarus, just breathing in its leather air, marveling at the complexity of its dash design some fifteen years before the Europeans would try to overwhelm our market with myriad expressions of neatly crafted gadgets. Gentleman, I said to myself, start your engine. And it did.

## —·— CHAPTER FIVE ——————

WHEN THE CHECKERED FLAG was dropped at Indy, my Uncle Wolfy hit the gas, and I was shot back into his chest with a thud. It was a stunt, Wolfy's driving a qualifying lap with his little nephew in his lap, and the only reason why the Speedway authorities allowed it was because my family was a fixture, and because Wolfy had already qualified with a record-breaking time the day before.

He headed right for that first corner where the pace car would veer off. It felt as if we were on some kind of sideways roller coaster as he nearly flipped me over to get the car through the corner. "Ahhhhh!" I cried, and I really did, all semblance of my previous bravery done with, all sense of fun a thing of the past, like looking forward to swimming underwater, but not realizing you were going to be held down as wave after wave crashed above you.

By the time I peered back at the road in front of us, we were hurtling, or so it seemed, right over the top of this wall. But Wolfy pulled us from the edge, and we seemed to slide across the road to steal an angle on the corners.

I was wailing and trying to make myself small, so if we crashed, I might be so inconsequential as to be lost in the attending commotion.

Like the theory that if you jump a split second before the dropping elevator crashes into the basement, somehow you might survive the fall.

But then we were on this straightaway and I could feel Wolfy accelerate so fast I thought we were going to the moon, for at that speed, there was nowhere else to go. Then the car ceased to accelerate, and we went through some kind of populated area and glided to a halt.

When the door was opened I leaned out and neatly vomited. I was seven, and it was rather a big day. This crowd of adults came rushing up to us with smiles on their faces, and Wolfy was swinging me up into the air and raising me aloft as if I were a trophy. Either the metal kind or a big fish, it was hard to tell at the moment.

Photographers were rushing up, since Wolfy was expected to win the Indy and this whole stunt was to go out over the wires as a homey expression of race-car intergenerationalism. And of late the Daleys were in the news, whether it was for the success of those newfangled Lazzies or for the rivalry between Wolfgang and William "Blitz" Daley, the Preppies of the Racetrack who were making such good copy.

"How'd the little rascal do?" my father said as he clumped up on his metal leg and was quickly shepherded into the picture.

I reached out my hand to him in panic, but was immediately told that such a gesture wasn't needed in this particular shot. Instead, I was to giggle, which in my condition, I could barely feign.

"Better than we thought," Wolfy said, smiling vacantly to the camera, his jaw set with his jaunty love of life.

"He cry?" my father asked, eyes straight ahead, and at that moment I really began to feel bad, because I had promised everyone I could handle it, the speed, the excitement, the photo op at the end.

"Not as much as we thought," replied Wolfy, "and he showed some real strength of character."

"Oh?" said my father, with an unlit—forbidden—trackside cigarette between his lips. He was staring down at me. I didn't know whether to squirm or puff my chest.

"Oh, yeah," said Wolfy, "he didn't puke until the door was opened. A chip off the old block."

—— **CHAPTER SIX** ————

THE ENGINE SURGED AND we charged through the door, patching out onto the old dirt road. Fido stood backwards with his snout to the vent. I had to admonish Simon not to drip on the leather seat, but he was too much in awe of the car to take offense. We tore up the road we had just jogged on, as the fine old engine roared.

We went into the first corner high and with some power, already pushing fifty where twenty would do. I wasn't a big fan of auto racing —my little jaunt around the track at Indy was my lone journey of that kind—and I have a tendency to drive my Bavaria like a slug. But anytime you get me behind the wheel of a Lazzy, well, I just can't help myself. A familial love of speed, of risks, of the need for sensation, gripped the wheel just as tightly as my hands did.

My family's athleticism was transformed in cars, where good eyes, good reflexes, and a skill at sensing the openings were all that were needed to excel. Now I was in my jogging clothes with teeth clenched and feet dancing between clutch, brake pedal, and gas. In any taxonomy of fun, this was of a higher order.

I looked over at Simon Ford, and for the first time today his equilibrium seemed to totter. He had held up better than most, but I could tell he literally was shaken by the way his sunglasses seemed to rattle on his nose. Fido leaned forward and gave him a big lick on the back of his ear, and that threw him. It was if the Death he had imagined hurtling toward him had instead turned out to have a wet tongue. And it attacked from behind.

We skidded around a corner and began our decline. It was a straight shot from here to the edge of the woods. "How fast are you planning on driving this thing?" Simon shouted, but I paid him no mind and placed my foot to the floor.

We were out of the woods and heading back to the house, and we went over a bump, with the wheels several inches from the ground. But the Lazzy set down with a reassuring ease and our trailing cloud of dust puffed forth. There was one little turn I guess I should have made, though it all turned out fine in the end. We found ourselves going through some bushes and then a tree suddenly flew in the way, and though we pulled away in the nick of time, we found we were heading for the pool.

"Oh, Jesus!" Simon shouted and, the weenie, he put his hands over his eyes. When he looked up again I was honking the horn and the children in the pool were cheering us on. We were by them in a flash, this supercharged Lazzy, with my dog's tail waving out the back vent like some anarchist's flag.

It didn't take long till we were out on the road again, and it just felt so good to be driving. After a while Simon moaned and slumped there as I took curve after curve, back roads and highway, gradually circling Mingeboro till there was nothing left to do but motor home. The Lazzy seemed to sense that, but then so did I. It was days before I could get Simon to offer up advice.

## — CHAPTER SEVEN —

MY INITIAL INSTANCE OF political action occurred at my first Holy Communion. The archbishop was there in a frisky mood and decided to grill the communicants. "Who," he asked as we sat in the front pews, the twenty-four of us who would taste that day for the first time the Body and the Blood of Christ, "is the enemy?"

Well, without missing a beat, as they say, I raised my hand and answered, "The Russians."

Now, it was a devilish answer, but it wasn't the one he was looking for, and I still remember the groan the archbishop let out. Today, however, I gratefully intoned, "Thanks be to God," when Father Liebman freed the communicants.

This particular day was a beautiful East Mingeboro scorcher with high cumulus clouds blowing down off the top of Mount Targa, and I was attending Mass with a slightly hung-over sister Betsy. She was hung over because the night before, before Mitch Sheedy and Harry Fox had driven off with Simon to go back to New York, we had a cookout at Uncle Andrew's that had gotten out of hand. Suffice to say that there were no broken lamps, no dented cars, though we had had a somewhat delicate time getting the Lazzy back to the house my siblings and I now shared on the cliff above the lake.

Though it was some miles out of our way, we liked going to Mass said by Father Liebman, for he was the only Catholic convert I knew who preached tolerance as his first order of business. You got the sense when you went into the confessional that he merely shrugged at your sins, or was on the verge of saying, "Is that all?" From time to time, he told a hilarious sermon, and he told it in this delightful New York accent that sent most of the townies to Mass in Mingeboro proper and attracted New Yorkers from four towns away. I liked the sense of peace I got when Father Liebman said his Mass, and often I would sit there and take my brain out of gear for a half hour or so, the only time in the week when my mind could wander with no hope of conclusion. Of course, I often ended up sitting there thinking about nothing but sex.

Now we meandered out of the church, and there was something a trifle wrong, a tad discordant, though the clouds were puffy and the organ was on key. And that's when we heard the insistent beat of Lou Reed's "Leave Me Alone" from a nearby car stereo, and I just had an inkling, just a sense, that I knew something was up.

We walked down the steps of the church and looked down the hill into East Mingeboro, the road to which whined with Ferraris and Porsches up for the races at nearby Lime Rock. "Leave me, leave me, leave me, leave me, *leave* me alone," intoned Lou Reed, with the low saxophone and these crunching guitars seeming to punctuate the movements of parishioners as they split into groups and headed to their cars.

"Where are they?" I whispered to Betsy, who was fumbling in her shoulder bag for her sunglasses. She looked like a wreck, though not so bad as the time some years ago when she came to Mass, after a night spent suspiciously, with a "Mick Is Sex" button pinned to her dress. As I recall it, Father Liebman had smiled.

"Where is who?" she asked somewhat absently.

Then we saw them, Blake and Ethan, and they were sitting in Blake's Porsche, and to make matters worse, Ethan was holding an obviously uncomfortable Fido in his lap. The dog began to struggle when he saw me.

"Hello, Ethan. How are you getting around, Blake?" I asked as smoothly as I could, as Betsy beside me shivered. The day was warm, the sun was bright, but Betsy seemed suddenly to have gone cold.

"Hey, fine, Charles," Ethan said magnanimously before his nephew could speak. Ethan's lips were stretched in a semblance of a smile obscured only by the evil downturn of his black mustache. His head was sufficiently obscured by the roof of the car that you couldn't see either his cast eye or his balding pate, but he looked nasty enough anyway. "Will you turn down this dreck," he commanded Blake, and I saw my cousin reluctantly do so. Fido was stuggling. I wondered how they had been able to get him into the car.

"Oh," said Ethan, as if reading my thoughts, "we just saw Fido wandering around so we thought we would do you the courtesy of bringing him to you before, hah hah hah, he ended up in the pound and was, well, you know, destroyed."

There had been problems with Fido and the dogcatcher that had received some attention in the gossip columns. And particularly in *Ad Age,* which revered the old pup like he was Bob Hope or someone.

"Well, we appreciate it, Uncle Ethan. Can I have my dog back now?" The campaign had reached the stage where I didn't have all that much to say that was polite. He let go and Fido clamored to get out through the window, though it was not a graceful sight at this stage in the dog's old age. He sort of panted by me, a little embarrassed.

"So, uh, Charles, you all certainly put on a good show at the convention," Ethan said with what was supposed to pass for a grin.

"Things went well, didn't they?" I said.

"Oh, sure, sure. So now we have a primary."

"Yep, amazing place, America."

Betsy was looking as if she wanted to be out of there, and Blake just stared at me from the car. It was the first time I'd seen him since that night at the disco those weeks before. He seemed none the worse for wear.

The last of the parishioners had wandered to his vehicle. Now we just stood there as car after car breezed by, the monster Ferraris letting their throats rattle as they downshifted for the ride from this old white church down the hill into East Mingeboro.

Ethan paused before starting to speak. He seemed to be choosing his works carefully. He opened his mouth, closed it, began again.

Finally, in a voice that was so soft we hardly recognized it, he said, "Just don't say we didn't warn you."

"About what, Uncle Ethan?" I said as evenly as I could.

But Ethan had nothing more to say. He just sat in the car shaking his head, and it was he who leaned over and turned up the rude chugging sound of Lou Reed.

Blake had something more to say, however. He got out of the Porsche and slowly straightened up. We could see that he needed a cane to brace himself. He was fatter than he had been, and looked awful in this billowing white shirt and cutoff blue jeans.

"You'll see what Ethan meant, Charles. Take care of your sister, Charles," he said contemptuously, and then he laughed. "Take care of your dog," he said and laughed, and I stood there as he got back into the Porsche with a little difficulty and started the engine with an electronic boom.

"You too, Blake," Betsy shouted after them as they patched out in the dirt before hitting the road. But I was in no mood for such a gesture. I was trying to imagine how far they would go.

## —— CHAPTER EIGHT ——

IN THE MORNINGS WHEN my driver came to pick me up, I would rejoice for a minute at the prospect of hard work. I was arriving at the campaign headquarters very early these days, sometimes before seven, and it was a rare day indeed that I left before artificial light took over the streets, the sky suffused with darkening blue. In between those moments occurred a million phone calls, a half-dozen or so crises, and at least one plaintive note from the road with Edward complaining about the size of the crowds or his handlers complaining about Edward. And with all that nerve jangling, with all the logistical nightmares of having to be in two places at the same time in overcrowded Manhattan, with all the headaches, heart attacks, and moments of despair, I would from time to time have to pinch myself with the excitement of it all, and especially with the blood-calming satisfaction that adrenaline inspires. In a paradoxical way, overwork creates its own order.

I was beginning to find that any problem I had with yielding to the family's embrace could be subordinated to my love of a good old-fashioned political brawl. And this one promised to be a beaut.

No longer did I have much time to be downtown, unless it was to head to Wall Street, either with or without my brother, in search of funds. Sometimes we would motor down midday for Edward to lunch, or I should say to talk, while I lunched with a half-dozen or so nonplussed investors who demanded to know the answer to one critical question: Could he win? Could this formerly sane buddy of theirs, who had never been known to place too much at margin, could this chum of theirs from the courts, from Skull and Bones, from the Street, actually defeat a sitting senator with whom they'd all grown comfortable a long time ago? For in spite of voting for every income-tax hike that had come along, Nate Stanton had always been helpful to business, whether it was fighting for a capital-gains differential or targeting specified industries for breaks. He was a known commodity, whereas Edward, infused with rhetoric about cutting taxes for individuals, talking at a fast clip about what could be done for the entrepreneur, could wax positively rapturous about "the special interests who for too long have had their noses in the trough." This scared particularly the young guys. They'd yet to get their noses in.

These trips downtown were fruitful, and we were beginning to raise big bucks. If money is the mother's milk of politics, this baby was ready to grow.

The closest I got to the *Downtown News* these days was when we did a fund-raising dinner at this restaurant on Greene Street. Though of course I still read the paper, and though I talked on occasion to my friends there, my contacts with the *News* grew slight. Angela had some weeks before ceased calling, exasperated by the efficiency of our receptionists, who wouldn't "just tell him it's Angela." They all but demanded name, rank, and serial number.

The receptionists were on strict orders to protect me from the forty or fifty good Republicans around the state who called every day to give unsolicited advice, not to mention the vendors, scam artists, and seekers of political welfare checks who had heard there was money in the Daley campaign, who had sniffed out our good fortune. And it was good fortune that Edward had tapped into a vein of entrepreneurial investment. We were buying thousands of gross rating points in each of New York's nine major media markets.

Downtown began to seem like a different world from the suit-and-tie existence I now lead. I no longer thought I could afford to let Camille dress me. I was glad that at last my haircut was beginning to grow out. And the ties she picked were just too outrageous.

I missed being downtown, seeing bands at all hours of the morning, partaking of a life predicated on the necessity that you didn't have to show up for work at the uncivilized hour of nine with, horror of horrors, your face shaved, the bleariness coaxed from your eyes.

I did sneak down periodically on weekends to see Camille, who, amidst much public name-calling from her old band, had now formed a new band with Carlisle Jones. Carlisle had returned from a trip to L.A. with an idea for music that was at once very hard punk, but saturated in the roots of early rock and roll. They were playing it only at the likes of Tier III down on West Broadway, but it was potent, and could not for long go undiscovered. Already Christgau was giving them a Pick in the *Voice, New York Rocker* exulted and swiftly slapped them on the cover, and Roger Rabin was going wild.

On this particular morning, as we drove down sleepy Columbus Avenue, the papers spread on my lap while Carmine, my driver, bore down on garbage trucks and taxis, I was feeling pretty good about things. I was chipper, because the day before, we had committed the sin of news, and if news is a sin, in politics you can never be too virtuous.

Edward's attack on Nate for having voted for seven specific tax increases in the previous four years was carried in the *Post* and the *Daily News* and got such a feeble response from a Stanton spokesman that we were clearly awarded the round. When Edward called Nate "the tax collector for the welfare state," all Nate's spokesman could come up with was something lame about trying to balance the budget. What a weak argument.

The *Post* was covering the campaign with far more interest than the *News*, perhaps covering it more closely than it would have even in the Murdoch days. We were due soon to sit down with the new editors, and I rather looked forward to it, just as I looked forward to the rest of the campaign. I was quickly becoming a junkie to the euphoria of seeing a positive piece show up in the papers, or a good thirty-second sound bite of Edward on the evening news. It was tough to break into the New York City media market, but Edward's forays upstate were seemingly successful as he returned with passels of good tiding: clips, videotapes, endorsements. And we of course recycled these immediately and sent them to the downstate reporters, so they would get this train-leaving-the-station sensation about the campaign.

Edward had taken headquarters in a dingy old brownstone off Fifth Avenue at West 54th Street, a location that was central enough so that meetings were easy to arrange, yet sufficiently upscale that it had yet to be a magnet for kooks out to offer their dubious services. Every campaign needs to have a Deputy Campaign Manager in Charge of Kooks, ideally someone of phlegmatic nature but good appearance who can listen to these people with a demeanor of satisfying impressiveness. The nuts were always there, always ready to disrupt the campaign. I have to admit, I was having a little trouble controlling everything.

I had never met our communications director because thus far he communicated only by notes slipped out from under the door he was locked behind. Either by those or by terrifyingly lucid and brilliant phone conversations on the office intercom. On the phone he seemed like a regular guy who simply had an IQ of about 210. No one knew where he came from, and when I arrived no one could tell me how Rick Morgan had ever been hired. I would have hired him, probably on the spot, if I had ever met him, because the memos he cranked out, as well as his multitudinous position papers, were miracles of clarity and insight, with a shrewdness of analysis of how Edward could score points with a particular action. But he was just so odd; behind his door could have been Prince Charming or the Elephant Man. What was most important was that he was tremendously effective, even if a campaign strategy meeting had to be conducted with his presence felt only through the speaker box. And his laugh over the box could send a chill up your spine. It had this metallic quality that sounded like a pen just touching the spokes of a fan set on high.

Rick's eccentricities were benign when compared to those of our Rommel-worshiping field director. Tim Verkhovensky saw everything in the context of desert warfare. Putting on a television spot sent him into raptures about "air cover." Volunteers in the upstairs loft who stuffed envelopes were "loading bullets." Bad press was hailed as "incoming rounds." And he was certain we were going to win the primary because we would "turn out the troops" if only we could husband our "petrol," which in this case was money. His use of the word "petrol" was interesting, considering he was born and raised on Long Island. He was a maniacal little bastard who could get on your nerves, but press him and he could tell you what vote we needed throughout New York's sixty-two counties in order to beat Nate Stanton. And he was a right-wing nut who had been laying in wait for Nate for years.

There were dozens of other eccentrics who somehow became involved in this thing, from a filthy millionaire who rode herd over the volunteers to the neurotic scheduler who carried a stopwatch with her and forced meetings to run according to precise minutes she had had her staff work out. Even Carmine, my driver, a veteran of several Conservative Party campaigns, was obsessive about Brooklyn politics to the point where he viewed Truman's dropping the bomb on Hiroshima as the end result of something put into motion in a Bay Ridge school-board meeting.

But it was great working with these people, and they had already taken on a group cohesion, had already exhibited an esprit de corps that I sensed would serve us well in the months ahead. There still were some things to work out—little things like having the receptionists not answer the phone with this "Daley for Senate, what's it to ya" tone to their voices, and our launching the targeted direct mail from houses we'd contracted with in Chinatown. But here we were nearing the Fourth of July and Edward's candidacy was bustling along, getting good press upstate where the Republican base was massive, raising money here in the city, and with Edward's ease as a candidate growing every day. Yes, there was a certain magnanimity, a secureness in my sense of equilibrium as I stepped out of the car and, thanking Carmine, began to walk up the steps to our headquarters.

And of course that's when an ashen-faced cousin Owen came tripping down the steps, blurting out, "Oh, Charles, you've gotta call home. I think they murdered Fido."

## ⸺ CHAPTER NINE ⸺

EDWARD'S EULOGY OF FIDO was sweet and sad, and several of those present were moved to weep. We did not know where else to gather in remembrance of my little pup, so that night we headed for the Daley Motorworks town house on 36th off Park. All the Daleys who worked in New York, as well as several members of the campaign staff, gathered to mourn the famous doggy who had met such a tragic end.

He had been found on the lawn of our house. Our own lawn. He was found there by gardeners who'd traveled over the dirt road from the main part of the estate, intent upon mowing around the bushes. What they found was an assassinated Fido, his throat cut, dead, they guessed, for a day. The description was grisly. Three days previous to this, I had seen him held against his will in a car that was owned by my cousin Blake, my Uncle Ethan reluctant to let him go.

It was obvious who'd done it, unfortunately for me. I say unfortunately, for on the morning he was found, I had by previous arrangement agreed to meet a reporter I knew from the *New York Post,* and we were supposed to have breakfast in my office. When Owen told me that Fido had been killed, I had blurted out a curse at Blake, vowing that I would avenge my graying puppy's murder. By noon, the *New York Post* had headlined, "STANTON WILL PAY, VOWS DALEY BROTHER," with the subhead going, "Accuses Sen. of Bizarre Dog Star Death." This brought an unfortunate gathering of camera crews staked out on the front steps of our campaign headquarters as I rehearsed what I had to say, periodically sending out emissaries to see if the reporters didn't just want to go away. I was not at my best. I was bereaved.

A strange rumor reached Edward where he was campaigning at a county fair near Skaneateles. He caught me before I went outside to face the cameras. "What the hell is going on?" he asked, phoning me from where the car had stopped in Index. He sounded really pissed, like my big brother or something.

"They killed Fido," I said.

"Oh." His voice was softer. Then he said, "I heard you'd accused Nate of trying to murder me."

"Who told you that?"

"The county chairman. He heard it on the radio."

"Oops." So I told him what happened and went out to face the cameras, and in front of them, I reverted to the aw-shucksin' altar boy who'd wriggled out of trouble all his life. I never exactly denied I'd accused the Stantons, though I did say I was certain Senator Stanton had nothing to do with it. And you'd have to say I got away with it, because all the five-o'clock news shows used clips of me essentially repudiating the headline in the *Post* without ever actually contradicting what I had said earlier. These fine lines are borders, and if you cross them, reporters will shoot your credibility on sight.

During the day we received something like three hundred telegrams of condolences from the strangest group of people. Corporate execs who'd grown up watching Fido on television, now completely distraught as word of his death spread. His producers in Hollywood called up shocked, with descriptions of the treatment they were working on. They had had plans for a movie with Fido playing the wizened mutt who teaches a ghetto pup the joy of life in the great outdoors. They actually had plans to have Fido film in the Tetons with a backpack and sunglasses on.

*Ad Age* sent over the most obnoxious reporter, and I mean *the* most obnoxious reporter, trying to be Woodward and Bernstein on what appeared to be his very first assignment. We finally had Owen somewhat indiscreetly threaten to punch him out until ultimately he fled.

It was about four in the afternoon when the networks got on the case, and a researcher from CBS had me go over the Life and Times of My Dog Fido until she had the story right. It was maddening. But she had a sexy voice.

I wanted to be left alone to mourn for my dog, but I had to work to make sure the right spin was on the story in case they played it that night as news. I spoke with Betsy, who was hurried, and didn't have much of an opportunity to talk. She'd never cared all that much for Fido, but she knew he was important to me, so she let out a comforting "Ohhhhh" that was more help to me than I can possibly tell you. Annie was a champ about the whole thing. She found out early in the day when she came into the campaign headquarters. Her first reaction was "I'm going to kill the son of a bitch," meaning cousin Blake, and somewhere I think my parents smiled down upon us.

Then came the call that sent my hard-hearted assistant aflutter. I was numb, and had been walking from office to office to find out what was going on in the campaign's respective divisions, people having been warned to stay out of my way. How could anyone have done that to my dog? But I jerked to attention when Gloria, my disrespectful assistant, walked in and reverentially said, "It, it, it . . ."

"It what, Gloria?"

"It's, it's, it's . . ."

"Well, that's an improvement, Gloria. Who is it?"

"They said it was Walter Cronkite for you!" she gasped, and I forgave her for her uncharacteristic flap.

"Hello," I said into the receiver. "This is Charles Daley."

"Hold for Mr. Cronkite," said a whiny, tiny voice.

"Mr. Daley," came the familiar voice, and I could picture him, white mustache against the mouthpiece, eyes twinkling in an avuncular manner, "allow me to say I was a big fan of Fido."

"Aw, thank you, Walt . . . er, Mr. Cronkite. That means a great deal to me. Call me Charles."

"But I have to ask you one question." There was mirth in his voice.

"Okay."

"We're going to do a somewhat whimsical look at Fido tonight, a remembrance."

"Uh huh."

"I have to ask you if you are accusing your uncle, Senator Stanton, of having your dog killed?"

He said it with this edge at the end of the sentence that was filled with the indignant wonder he reserved for war criminals, incompetent politicians, or NASA officials standing next to the exploded Apollo, with soot all over their faces.

But he was Uncle Walter, and how could I flat out lie? So I did the much worse thing. I told the truth. "I'm certain Uncle Nate knows nothing about it. Jeez, that's not his style at all. But I'm also certain that some mutual relatives—well, I have this sicko cousin who may have had something to do with it."

"Why?" he asked, and, boy, you could hear that voice resonate around Manhattan. It hit peak levels on the telephone.

"Maybe to scare Edward. Maybe out of spite. Maybe to try to get him out of the race."

"It's a serious charge."

"Oh, but don't get me wrong. I'm not making a charge. I want to forget the whole thing," I said, and I did. "But you asked, and I can't lie to you."

He seemed to chuckle a bit at that. "He was a great dog," he said kindly, if noncommittally.

"Yes, sir, he was."

And with that, Cronkite got off the phone and I was left wondering what he was going to say on the evening news, whether he was going to take the ugly details of our little family feud public for the entire country to see.

I got Simon Ford on the phone. He was not a happy man. "How could you accuse Nate of killing your dog, and accuse him through the *New York Post,* for Chrissake?"

"Wait," I said. "It's worse. I think I just accused him to Walter Cronkite."

"What?"

"Well, he called me, I kid you not. And he asked if I was accusing Nate of killing Fido."

"What did you say?"

"Well, I told him I wasn't accusing Nate, though I had a cousin who might have done it in order to help Nate."

"Aw, you're going to get fucked, Charles. Oh, man, we're going to hear about this."

And he was correct. At seven o'clock we dutifully piled into the green television room where five televisions were stacked on a console, each of them turned to one of New York's major stations. Pressed around the room were Tim Verkhovensky, who knew enough to stay out of my way this particular evening; Gloria, my assistant; the Countess, as we had taken to calling the somewhat tattered aristocrat who ruled the volunteers with an iron fist; my sister Annie, who stood next to me, her arm making windmill motions across my back; and several of the office aides who made of the headquarters more of a home than their apartments would be this summer.

Owen was sulking on a couch underneath the window that looked down on the Museum of Modern Art. He was mad at me because he thought I blew it. Not by accusing Nate of killing Fido. Hardly. He was mad because we hadn't done it through paid television. Owen wished we'd saved our ammo for a spot that said something like,

"What would you say if you were told your United States senator murdered a national hero?" By going public, I had ruined the element of surprise.

Now we had the news on, and after a report that there was trouble in Central America, that the Soviets were humiliating us at the UN, that Iranians were beginning to get uppity, and that the President had called for a "new moral vision" for America, Walter Cronkite got this sad look on his face and announced that "a venerable American institution is dead tonight at the age of ten." As a photo of my dog in action loomed behind him, he announced it was "Fido, the dog that graced American screens longer than any other canine spokesman for dog food." Cronkite allowed that Fido was found with his throat cut on the lawn of the Daley family, his owners, in northwestern Connecticut. The campaign manager and brother of Edward Daley, who was challenging Senator Nathaniel Stanton of New York in the Republican primary, accused the Stanton family of having Fido killed. Cronkite continued, "The Stantons and the Daleys are related through marriage. Police said an investigation is under way." Cronkite put down the papers he held in his hand and the television screen abruptly filled with a clip of Fido in his prime, running across a lawn full speed with a dog bowl between his teeth. He would be missed.

The phones started ringing and the buttons on the switchboard began to light up like a fleet of bombers appearing on a radar screen.

With very little talk we vacated the premises, the insistent ringing of phones hastening us elsewhere. Some of us had already agreed to meet later at the Daley Motorworks building for a toast to old Fido, so we split up, a trio walking down Fifth in the muggy evening air, the rest heading for taxis. It was I who headed downtown on foot, joined by Owen and Annie, as taxis honked and jostled, and clusters of people moved down the sidewalks on their way home, to fun, to anywhere but a service for a dog who had been murdered.

I was calculating in my mind what the effect of Cronkite's announcement would be, wondering what the percentage of calls coming in at the headquarters was from reporters trying to get more news, when I stopped myself and thought: My God, here I am acting exactly like a Daley—thinking more about the news of the death than of the death itself. When my mother died and my father soon joined her, the first reaction of the family as a whole had been how we would contain the news. And when my grandmother died this past spring, the first reaction of the family had concerned logistics and management, if not of the press then certainly of the tone of the information. And here my dog had died and I was walking to a family service for him trying to figure the best way of controlling the reports of his demise. And it was worse than that, for I was trying to figure out how to use his death to our advantage.

"What's up, Charles?" said Annie as we walked past the brightly lit windows of Saks, the beautiful mannequins posed in anorexic splendor. I've always thought you could tell a lot about a society by the quality of its mannequins, and here in the late 1970s these were pinched and artificially slim. Annie, on the other hand, was filling out. She had put on a pound or two, and it was not unbecoming.

"I was just thinking about Fido."

"Ohhh. Poor baby. We'll get you a new dog."

"It's not the same thing, Ann."

"I know," she clucked. "I know."

She had been working on the campaign for a few weeks, largely helping to involve teenagers in the grunt work, and a disproportionate number of handsome young men seemed to have a newfound interest in politics. They were willing to work all sorts of odd hours so long as Annie was among them. She did not seem to be spending too much time with Lazlo Fortescu. And contrary to the indolence of her previous summers, now that she was a high-school grad with no intention of going to college, she seemed to be willing to work her pretty little tail off.

"I've been thinkin', you know, Charles," Owen now said as we cut down 47th Street and headed toward Madison.

"What's up?" I asked.

"This may not be such a bad thing, your spilling the beans to Cronkite."

"Well that sure makes me feel better. I thought you were getting ready to fire me," I said as jauntily as I could. For the thing other than blood that connected Owen to the family was his intellectual judgmentalism. He let it be known that he would not tolerate stupidity, especially from his elders. And right now, because of my fessing up to Cronkite, I was in the doghouse. And I no longer had a dog, so there was plenty of room.

"I did want you to save that episode for a spot later in the race, but this thing might work out fine. Let Nate explain he didn't kill the most pop'lar dog since Rin Tin Tin," he said, and started laughing, and we joined him, Annie and I, standing there on the verge of Madison as the evening began to quicken with the humid threat of rain. We could picture Uncle Nate in exasperation clutching the podium as he denied he killed our dog. "I did not kill the dog," he would say. "I am not a dog killer!"

No, he would never say that. He was too slick for that. Somehow he would turn it to his advantage, maybe throw it back at us. "Ed Daley will stop at nothing to take my Senate seat, including killing his own brother's dog, then blaming it on me." But that had a "nah-nah-nahnah-nah" quality to it that he no doubt would, with the dignity he'd displayed since 1960, avoid at all costs. Oh, boy, could he turn on that sense of righteousness at the drop of a hat.

We stopped for a quick slice of mediocre pizza near Grand Central and walked the remaining distance to our town house. Mr. Greco, the mustachioed building manager who'd taken care of every little Daley who'd ever passed through New York, was standing in the doorway, welcoming us with glee expressed by his bushy eyebrows raised to the height of a normal person's hairline. How did he keep those monsters up so high? He and Annie made a big fuss over each other, and then he ushered us from the steamy, gray evening into the chill of the air-conditioned house.

"Where is everyone, Mr. Greco?" I asked.

"They're getting a head start on you in the library," he said, pointed his finger and crooking it upward, as if his arm could reach all the way in a curl up the stairway to the building's fourth floor.

It was too hot to squeeze into the little elevator, even with the air-conditioning on full, so we set out to walk up the grandly appointed staircase that corkscrewed through the center of the house. We had briefly considered making this building Edward's campaign headquarters, since it was no longer exactly overburdened with activity from our auto company. And in spite of our juggling the tax code, it was not depreciating. In fact, when Andrew, six months before, had worked out his austerity plan for saving the company, one of the few romanticisms he allowed himself was keeping the building, and on top of that, keeping on the Grecos to clean it. Otherwise, given the low volume of family traffic, the building would have been draped in dust, from the boardroom on the second floor to the tiny offices on the sixth in which no one had labored for years.

This was a building whose quiet class had served as a metaphor for how we saw ourselves. It had been a tastefully reassuring first step for emissaries from Detroit who came east to find out what these damn Daleys had to offer. I am told they came at first reluctantly, though of necessity, because my grandfather was in the 1940s hailed in the popular press as a genius at engine design. And when the senior vice presidents from Ford and Chevrolet politely, but wisely, presented themselves, they were to find hospitality offered on silver trays while they sat on antique furniture. And this from a family "two generations away from potatoes."

We crept up the carpeted stairs, and on the landing we could hear the hushed commingling of serious drinkers with a perfect excuse. In a family like mine, mourning brings a reward as certain as daylight.

"This place always gives me the spooks," said Owen, and that could not be discounted. When Owen was a boy and would come to visit, my father and sometimes Uncle Wolfy would play a game with him. They'd tell him that he should go hide, and if they found him, they'd kill him. Owen was very literal-minded, another family trait, and so at the age of six he'd been brought back to us by a police officer who caught him trying to get a taxi to take him home to Arkansas.

Now we stepped out onto the fourth-floor landing and padded across the maroon carpet to the library. It had once been my grandfather's domain. Even in shrunken old age, he had sat behind a huge library table in a chair that was fit for a king. Now we could see the same table set up as a bar, with a polite young man, temporarily hired, serving what seemed to be straight shots to the fifteen or so people already there, including Edward, whose only humanizing quality it sometimes seemed was the fact that he enjoyed a drink. Yes, for although there were times when he wasn't quite human, he was forever a Daley. And he was forever a Daley drinker.

"Charles," he said, and put down his drink and walked over to hug me. He squeezed me so tight I thought his metal arm would puncture something. He stepped back so I had his full regard, and I felt part sheepish and part dead, as if something had ascended with Fido's spirit.

"Hey, babe," said Betsy as she walked over and gave me a hug. She was still dressed for work, with her hair in this severe bun, but in the soft light of the library she looked like sympathy personified.

A low rumble of thunder rolled across the roof and a blast of wind hit the large windows that overlooked East 36th Street.

"Boy," I said with an attempt at levity, "does this seem familiar or what?"

"Oh, yes," said Edward distractedly, "mourning's become our set condition. It's mourning again in the Daley family." He was looking a little gaunt, and I noticed his suit seemed to hang from him. There were black bags underneath his eyes I had never seen before, not even when he first came back from that army hospital in Hawaii. I'd been meaning for a couple of weeks to find out, at a greater depth than our thrice-a-week morning conversations would allow, just how burdensome was the strain of his being a candidate. But here in his appearance I thought I had the answer. At this point in the campaign, he was already a perpetual-motion machine. Always on, with no privacy and no real rest.

"It's time you said hello to me, Charles Daley," said my Aunt Morgan, who, surprisingly, came up and gave me a maternal hug. She was not one whom I would have suspected would drive to New York for a wake for a dog, but who knows what Irish genes will make someone do.

"Hi, Aunt Morgan. Thanks for coming."

"I saw Walter Cronkite," she said. "Let's let Ethan Stanton try to get out of this one." She and Ethan had loathed each other for about forty years. She was looking at me through her faintly tinted glasses and for a minute I loved her resolve. Aunt Morgan was tough, there was no doubt about it, and I began to feel good about extending the feud into the realm of, oh, the thirty million people who watched the news.

"Ummm, I was going to talk to you about that," Edward said. He looked stern and a little shell-shocked, but he seemed to be clutching a certain equilibrium, as if he could live with what press would follow. After all, someone had now attacked our family. They had killed our dog! What would they do next?

"But this isn't the time, right?" I murmured, looking around at Stanley, our driver, eyeing me with watery eyes of sympathy, too choked up to come over and talk. And there was Uncle Wolfy nuzzling his blond flight-attendant girlfriend in the corner. Uncle Andrew had by now taken the bottle of scotch out of the bartender's hand and was pouring himself a more liberal dollop than even the bartender, on instructions to pour stiff ones, was willing to allow.

"Right," said Edward. "Now is the time to celebrate our family and mourn our many dead."

We gravitated toward him and Wolfy attentively came forward. Edward was the family's spokesman now, had become so by dint of having put up his head to be knocked off in this, his first season of real public challenge. And as the town house was suddenly rocked by the sound of summer thunder, and as the windows were suddenly splattered by a rain so violent as to suggest a squall at sea, Edward gripped his gin and tonic by the top of the glass and let it dangle at the end of his one good arm.

I saw Camille and the renowned Carlisle Jones arrive at just that moment, and as they were a little disheveled but perfectly dry, I knew they had hurried ahead of the storm. I waved with my finger and Camille smiled across the room. Now, as he stood underneath the portrait of our grandfather sitting in a white suit, looking pensive, now as the rain tore down around the town house, Edward began his eulogy of Fido.

"Fido was the most unfaithful mascot any family relied on for its sense of self," he began, and we murmured in recognition. "He was also the biggest money machine my little brother Charles will ever be the beneficiary of," he said, raising his glass to me. "He was a special dog who brought joy to millions of boys and girls who saw him on TV, and he brought great joy to our family."

We were silent now, with no one squirming. We just listened, a few of us with heads cocked to one side, as the thunder boomed and the smell of rain began to fight through the air-conditioning.

"This is a family that has had great privilege, great joy. But this is a family that has had great sadness and great loss. For all the advantages we've had handed to us, there has been a tremendous amount of work, and a certain amount of sacrifice. Most importantly, though, is that for all that God has smiled upon us, we've lost too many of our family members at too young an age, at too high a cost, to not appreciate the simple joy that a being like Fido could bring to us."

I looked around at Camille, a daughter who had not spoken to her mother in perhaps five years; at Owen, a motherless son whose father was in some jail in Arkansas; at Betsy and Annie, who had only Edward and me, pathetic as we were, to give them a sense of family; and I thought of Sam, so far away in exile, in Oregon, who by now was a grown man but would remain a disembodied telephone voice attached to a picture of the sensitive little boy whom Edward always picked on. And I looked at Aunt Morgan, at Uncle Wolfy, and Uncle Andrew as he steadily sipped from his glass, and thought of their loss, of brothers, sister, the natural disruptions of their lives. Tears rolled down the cheeks, however, not of any of my relatives, but of Stanley, and of the bartender, who didn't even know us. Mr. and Mrs. Greco were peering around the corner and they both looked ashen. Even at a time for expressing the hurt that welled within us, my family stood dry-eyed and drinking as Edward went on.

I missed some of what he said, but I tuned in again when he got to the part about how Fido had met his end. "It is clear that Fido was killed by someone who wished to hurt us, and they succeeded in their task. But we will not give in to those who wish to hurt us, or even to the forces of the market that, with no malevolence intended, nonetheless persist in thwarting our business endeavors. I am proud to be a member of this family, though there are some times when it hurts an awful lot. Let's remember the dog that made us happy, that made us a family, and let's not let this family break down in the face of the loss of our parents and our siblings and our business and our luck, eh?" And he just stood there for a minute, and while the lightning was outside, the electricity rippled across the carpet. Then Uncle Wolfy softly said, "Here, here," and the bar was reopened. Within two minutes we were making small talk, because the object was to never let on. We might pretend that it was to never give in. But the object truly was never to let on.

## —— CHAPTER TEN ——

SUNLIGHT BOUNDED TO THE edge of the bed, and I was not quite prepared for it. I stood in front of my mirror, trying to whip my face into shape. After last night's mournful carousing, the mug just would not cooperate. It would not get with the program, no matter what I promised it. And if I could have given my face an ambassadorship, I would have.

The good news, as I made faces in the mirror, "We're so pretty, oh, so pretty," blasting out of the speakers, was that a cool front had followed the violent storm and New York was in for a day of delicious air. "We're pretty; pretty vacant" went the Sex Pistols, and I sang along, reaching for a tie from my new wardrobe from Barneys, which I had allowed Camille to help pick out for me soon after Edward had hired me. I had not asked the cost of things, I just spent. Edward was paying me very well indeed, and before this time, I thought my dog would pay for the excess. Though royalties would continue for a while, and while he was heavily insured, the days of Fido's ads for Gravy Train providing same for me were irrevocably behind us.

My hair had grown out from that pineapple I had gotten from Camille, and now I paid someone a lot of money for a more moderate version. It was less drastic and far more malleable, but today it was determined to do its own thing, and coupled with the bags under my eyes, the office pallor to my skin, and this brand-new, slick Italian double-breasted suit, I looked too debauched to be heading to midtown. If I were a cabbie looking at me, I'd probably think, Little Italy.

The stereo was on a trifle loud for eight-thirty in the morning, especially given that all my neighbors worked the irregular hours of alternative New York. I had the Pistols blaring because I was trying to get blood to circulate. Once my landlady had knocked on my door when I was playing the Ramones or Richard Hell and the Voidoids —I forget—and when I answered the door, she was standing there, insolent though a little out of breath, having walked up from her basement apartment. "I have only one question," she asked, and I said, "Shoot." "How is it that someone who plays this kind of music can afford to live in this apartment?" I wasn't certain whether she was railing against the market or the age, but I guess her question was rhetorical, since she didn't wait for an answer; she just trudged on up to the next floor, perhaps to harass someone else.

I wiped the suds from my ears, tied my tie, and looked around the room for forgotten objects I would need at work: fountain pen, pocketknife, credit cards, eye drops. Each night when I arrived home, and no matter what the hour, I would try to clean up my apartment, try to bring some order to it. And in the morning, I would find tides of records, books, magazines sweeping across the floor, and sometimes empty bottles of beer arranged like a platoon of little toy soldiers. Soon the process would begin again, quotidian rhythms of attempted order.

I switched off the stereo and, still whistling, prepared to leave, when there was this knock on the door. Oh, shit, I said to myself, for I was late, though a forgivable offense given the antics of the night before. I walked over to the door and flung it open, all the while attempting to put on that suit jacket Camille had picked out for me with the seductive incantation that I should trust her. It was Mrs. Basil, my landlady.

"Hello, Mrs. Basil, what a delight," I lied. She stood in front of me in her dressing gown with her beer belly protruding, her hair the color of Corona Extra, laying in unwashed loops around her ears, as if she were still a German schoolgirl. To top it off she had this mole, no, I won't describe that mole under any circumstance.

"You haven't been around lately," she said in what can only be described as the accusative.

"No, ma'am, I've been busy. What can I do for you? You see," I said with my most charming smile smeared across my less charming than usual puss, "I'm late for work."

"This arrived yesterday," she said, handing over a registered letter.

Red sentry lights began to go off around my eyes when I saw that registered letter, and though Mrs. Basil stood there waiting for me to open it, I thanked her and gently closed the door.

It was from my cousin Charlotte Childs, née Abbott, whose apartment this was by lease. My claim on it was subordinate to hers. I had lucked into the sublease when she moved to Washington to marry Uncle Nate's administrative assistant. The letter read, "Charles, I've tried reaching you by phone for days, but you haven't been leaving your machine on and I don't know where else to reach you. Call me at once. It's important."

So I took my jacket off again, for I feared the news was lousy, and I went over to the phone and punched out numbers. If the reason for her getting in touch with me was what I suspected it might be, I would want to punch out more than numbers.

The phone rang once, twice, then Charlotte picked up.

"Charlotte, it's your cousin Charles."

"Yeah, Charles, how are you?" In the background a baby began to cry.

"I'm fine, a little hung over. How are you? I got your letter."

"I'm rotten. I'm leaving Kingsley. Actually, I've already kicked him out of the house. I'm leaving Washington, and I'm going to move back to New York."

Oh, great, I said to myself. I looked around at my bookshelves and records, my paintings on the walls. Everything looked very solid, as if it liked being here. As if it belonged.

"I'm sorry to hear that, Charlotte. Not that you're leaving Kingsley, that part's overdue. But that your marriage is breaking up and all."

"And that I need my apartment back."

"And that you need your apartment back," I repeated. "How long do I have?" I felt as if I were asking that of the doctor who'd just confirmed malignancy. And I could have lived with her saying, "Six months, maybe less, maybe more."

But no. "I need it by the end of the month. I'm sorry, Charles, but I warned you I might need it on short notice when I rented it to you."

It was true, but when someone is offering to let you rent a glorious apartment on the Upper West Side with hardly a security deposit put down, you don't listen to the threats of later inconvenience. And brother, this couldn't be coming at a worse time.

"End of the month?" I asked, just to make sure.

"August one. I can stay with friends, or at Dad's apartment on Sixty-fifth Street. I refuse to stay with my sister and the nerd she's married to, and I won't subject myself to staying with Blake."

"What do you hear out of him?" I asked.

"That's like asking how the Hell's Angels are doing. He sits up at All Odds, smoking dope, drinking lots of beer, maybe doing worse stuff, and plotting how to get at you all. Have you seen him lately?"

"Yeah, I have." I didn't say anything about my dog.

"I heard about Fido. It's Blake, isn't it?"

"I don't know, Charlotte." I was beginning to sag at the prospect of having to find a new apartment in the middle of a campaign. My energy level would take no kidding and was beginning to meet up with my evening before.

"Well, you should know. He is obsessed with getting back at you."

"I kind of had that figured."

"You don't hate me, Charles, do you?" From Charlotte, that was as familiar a refrain as her pleadingly asking you if you thought she was fat. Lying, I always provided the answer she wanted. Charlotte, last I saw her, had become a tub.

"Of course not. I understand. You need to get away from Kingsley. I'm surprised you could last this long with that prissy fuck. What are you going to do?"

"I'm going to tear a page from your Aunt Rose," she said brightly.

"Beg pardon," I said.

"I'm going to write a book about Kingsley and the way he typifies men in Washington. I mean, he was doing it with seventeen-year-old interns. Of both sexes. No, that's not true. He *was* chasing every skirt in town, near as I can figure."

She wished me luck with Blake, and I wished her luck with the move, though the truth be told, if the trucks with her furniture took the wrong turn at Wilmington, I would not start keening.

## —— CHAPTER ELEVEN ——

WE COLLECTIVELY DECIDED THAT my place was on the road. Whether that was to keep Edward out of trouble or me out of trouble, I had no time for reflection. One evening we were having a strategy session with our consultants, the next day I was out at Teterboro, nose in a bag of doughnuts, as the little King Air taxied down the runway for some upstate destination. We were headed for the land of the mighty Republicans. I was in charge from the road.

This change was not a coup, I was assured, merely an adjustment. In the meantime, Simon Ford, the crack consultant, would be spending more time in the office. Quite a buzz followed our news on Walter Cronkite. There were several requests for candidate schedules from such faraway papers as the *Baltimore Sun* and the *Chicago Tribune*. When I met someone at a party or a bar, now they clutched me with glad-handing curiosity.

The news generally was good. The Conservative Party of New York, which Edward had been courting during the three years his Senate bid had been percolating in his brain, had given him its nomination. There wasn't much fanfare, they just up and gave it to him.

They practically threw it at him. They had been waiting forever for Nate Stanton to have a respectable primary challenge, in particular a challenge from the right. In Edward they had it, but the endorsement was still something of a gutsy move. It meant they could kiss good-bye whatever little senatorial patronage and courtesies they had, unless of course he won. Unless of course he won.

The endorsement had gone underremarked at the time, even though it meant that Edward would be on the ballot in the general election whether he won or lost the primary against Uncle Nate. There was, of course, an escape hatch in case he didn't want to go through with such a campaign, though such a campaign might not be so foolish as it looked at first blush. Uncle Nate and the Democratic nominee, Hamlet O. Cattanasio, both appealed to a certain stripe of liberal, their positions on a variety of issues identical. In a three-way race, Edward could sneak around the right flank and cling to 35 percent for a victory. It was not unheard of. There were precedents.

But Edward was a party man, he really was, and so privately there was some discussion as to what he would do should he lose the Republican primary to Nate. Publicly, however, there was none of that. Whenever reporters asked him whether he intended to stay on the Conservative line should he lose the primary, his answer was invariably, "I'm not going into this race intending to lose. So, you see, I can't answer that question."

It was a pretty good answer, holding out the sense of mystery, some would say blackmail, to those Republicans wondering who would be the best candidate to hold off Cattanasio: Stanton on the Republican line hampered by the brash young millionaire on the Conservative line, or Edward with a consolidated hold on both. And sometimes when Edward was asked the question of his intention, if he sensed he was in front of a right-wing crowd, he would turn it into a little lecture on "those bureaucrats at the Pentagon, not to mention those cynics in the U.S. Senate, who got us into the Vietnam War with absolutely no intention of winning. I would never get into something I wasn't determined to win." It was a surefire applause line. He was beginning to sense his chance. He was adhering to the maxim of that great New Yorker George Washington Plunkitt— Edward seen his opportunities and he took 'em.

Whether or not he was the Republican nominee in the fall, if Edward stayed on the ballot, he would be going up against this guy

Cattanasio. Hamlet Cattanasio was a heavy-lidded, athletically built lawyer with a great sense of humor but a bizarre way of doing business. He kept referring to Edward and Uncle Nate's competition as "the battle of the barons," and he once suggested to the *New York Times* that the two Republicans should fight it out by dueling with silver spoons. He was deft, he was smart, and he did not enjoy the fact that all the fun was being had by Republicans. He couldn't help but inject himself into our race, and he did so with these vicious asides that had a tendency to find their way into print. These depth charges of his were always, significantly, sunk with an understanding of our fight as a family squabble.

Perhaps it's not unusual he saw things this way, the primary taking on the air of a massive family fight; after all, he was a New York Democrat. It's interesting that it was a theme he couldn't leave alone. And he had this tendency to communicate it in an unusual fashion. Rather than respond directly to a reporter's question, old Hamlet would answer the question with questions of his own. Then, the next day, his press secretary would release a Xeroxed page from Hamlet's daily diary, in which he would spell out an answer with great eloquence. He was mercurial, impulsive, but he held himself in check sometimes so he could meticulously sculpt his straw man, his hilarious riposte, his unintentionally obvious obfuscation. Had I been still a reporter, I would have loved to have studied him, for Cattanasio was a fascinating animal. He was a demagogue, an orator of the old school, complex in a way that made Nate look like an eggplant. As it was, I had plenty to attend to on my own side of the aisle.

We flew to Binghamton, Elmira, Plattsburgh, Poughkeepsie, Middletown, Schenectady, and Rome; from Syracuse to Hauppauge, back to Oneonta, from Albany to Buffalo and back by way of Rome. Actually it only felt as if we had made it to Rome, though our statewide treks were constant. And in spite of the distances, clutching morning coffee as we peered down on the V of Westchester, squeezed as it is between the Hudson and the Sound, or clutching frothy cans of beer as we flew back into the city over the sprawling estates of Tuxedo Park, the topography of New York was soothing. A simple reward for the kind of life in the air we were leading was the sensation of choppering above Manhattan, seeing which buildings had pools, and how precise was the order of the grid that physically kept the city in check. And seeing the spray of water-skiers on the Finger Lakes, the lights at night from county fairs, the carpet of green fields from Dutchess to Allegheny gave us a sense of peace. In this plane, we were in control, and no matter what news was spreading from the city to Buffalo, from Albany to Binghamton, up here there was nothing that could go wrong other than our falling from the sky. And in our little King Air, we never had that feeling.

My link to the campaign by now was by the phone. It was with my back to the booth, my eyes wandering over the sight of Edward greeting local pols come to greet him at the airport, that I learned of Wolfy's excerpt from his book appearing in the August *Esquire*. He hadn't shown it to me, but the rumor was that it would take on Rose with a steel glove of humor. And it was on the phone that I found out Wolfy and Andrew had been only partially successful at raising company money from some of the young entrepreneurs on Wall Street to whom Edward had introduced them. And over the phone that I heard about all the writers who were preparing to do feature stories on the campaign and the family.

We went to editorial boards for Edward to lay out his case. These usually degenerated into thinly veiled class wars. Going to editorial boards is like engaging in group therapy with a roomful of cynics, most of whom hold heavy grudges before they ever meet you. It's usually a study in their inarticulation, not the candidate's. Edward's jokes would go over like bombs, and I always felt overdressed.

We were more successful at radio stations. Edward would fill the airtime with the sonorous voice he inherited from our father, jiving with the interviewer, making little jokes, but setting out his campaign themes no matter what direction the conversation went. He was getting good. He would walk out of the dark studios generally in an up mood, reflecting upon the lines that worked and the ones that didn't. His tone was always respectful of Uncle Nate, but filled with disappointment that Nate was so at odds with the Republican electorate.

We kept finding the one thing that seemed to spark the imagination of interviewers was Edward's support of those Kemp-Roth tax cuts. What about the deficit? the interviewers would ask. What about inflation? But Edward was ready for them with a little of the old supply-side religion, and we found that not only did that make for great applause lines, it neatly underscored the differences between Uncle Nate and Edward. Uncle Nate rejected supply-side economics as being "irresponsible." But you could see the gleam in people's eyes when it was explained to them, and New Yorkers in particular thirsted for some relief from their high taxes. This was a positive answer that for once didn't cost them money.

We went from Utica to Ithaca, where a member of the local Teamsters union allowed as how he thought their endorsement might be forthcoming if Edward would make an investment in a luxury retirement village in Key West. But when Edward asked him, "Key West? Is that where you buried Jimmy Hoffa?" the deal swiftly was off.

"Nice move, bonehead," I said as we walked out of the hotel room.

"Oh, you think I should have taken the endorsement, huh? How many FBI agents do you think were in the next room, Charles?"

He was probably right. Nate Stanton had long been a friend of the FBI. That could have been a setup, and I felt like a dummy.

The campaign on the road was punctuated by press conferences where Edward stood surrounded by those brave Republican officials who in each locality were willing to buck their U.S. senator in order to endorse his primary rival. Some of them smiled proudly at the cameras and looked confident. Others slouched and had to hide their hands under their armpits to keep them from shaking. Some of them seemed relieved that the party at last had a conservative alternative to Nate. Others seemed to appreciate Edward as nothing more than a vehicle by which they could exact their revenge on Nate for some long-ago slight, some petty insult, some vote on an appropriations bill or a nomination to a service academy.

One way or another, as we traveled across the state, a line on the Republican primary ballot settled, the Conservative line in the general election secure, reporters were beginning to take Edward a little bit more seriously. The didn't want to know about Fido and my Club Blech brawl with Blake; they wanted to know about specific issues relevant to their area. Would he support the expansion of Fort Drum, the building of the Shoreham nuclear power plant? On each of these issues Edward was briefed by a county-by-county memo he received the morning of every trip.

It was usually very early in the morning when we went across the George Washington on the way to Teterboro; there was fog still on the Hudson and people driving in from Jersey had their headlights on. And it was early evening or night by the time we returned from the road. Which was why I was looking forward to the break that was coming as we returned home on the Fourth of July. I was going to head downtown to meet Camille and go with her and Carlisle Jones to some party in the Bowery. It promised to be fun.

## —— CHAPTER TWELVE ——

"EVERYBODY HAVE A GOOD time," shouted Peter Zaremba as the Fleshtones thrashed about the makeshift stage at the front end of the loft. With that, the guitarist stepped onto an amplifier to let loose an assault on his twang bar, and reverb rocked the room. This was closer to a frat party than it was to the hipster ethos. It was, after all, an American holiday, with roots more permanent than those seen on the heads of the many newly blond punk rockers.

"I feel guilty about liking the Fleshtones so," said the flush-faced Camille. But it was okay, because there on the dance floor was her boyfriend, Carlisle Jones. We were somewhere in the Bowery, it was early in the evening, and fireworks were set to go off. Over there were the members of Suicide, looking awful peppy. I saw Lydia Lunch eat an hors d'oeuvre; a couple of Necessaries, and a Tuff Dart. About half the staff of *New York Rocker* had somehow found the loft, and now the Fleshtones bit into a Lee Dorsey chestnut and some of the dancers chanted along. "Ride your pony," they sang at the tops of their lungs.

"This beats working, doesn't it, Charles?" Camille sort of breathed into my arm. Then she reached up and messed up my hair and playfully tugged me out onto the floor. For a childhood we'd feuded; now when she saw me she was positively kittenish. Though she could slay you with her gorgeous sardonicism.

As we danced, I noticed that the singer, this guy Zaremba, moved from his Farfisa organ to his microphone and back again like a klutzy host trying to make an omelet in the kitchen while everyone crowds in to watch.

A while later, a little breathless from the dancing, from the beer, I stood on the rooftop deck, which by now had begun to fill with fireworks watchers. The sun was descending on Jersey City and I was standing against a railing, a little woozy, but happy. The crowd looked as if it had been a long Fourth of July. Everyone was loose and a little tattered. Most were tattered all the time, but there was a gaminess about tonight that made the crowd as funky as its surroundings.

Nearby in Chinatown things were getting out of hand. Firecracker assaults by different gangs made the city seem like Beirut on a Christian holy night. Everything seemed normal enough until Camille came out of the stairwell wearing this pout.

"*Que pasa,* Camille?" I said.

"Oh, Carlisle has admirers."

"Of course he has admirers."

"Does he have to use his tongue when he meets them?" she asked, I thought, not unreasonably.

"Look, baby," I said, "you have admirers too."

"Sure," she said, whirling around so her back was to Brooklyn, the air whizzing with bottle rockets and erupting in M-80 assaults. "These guys at the clubs . . ." She said it so forlornly. Then she went, "I was telling Blake . . ."

"Blake?" I said, standing as tall as I could and beginning to loom over Camille. "Wherever did you see him?" Was he here? I got a little jumpy, and then a big sucker exploded nearby and I practically jumped into her arms, cartoon style.

"He came by Club 57," she said with a little exasperation. The door to the stairwell opened just then as more people walked out onto the rooftop, and in the second it took the door to slam against the wedge of yellow light, the sound of laughter from the loft below blew up like a comedy track, traces of dance music ringing around the edge.

"So what did you tell him?"

"I told him he was an asshole and that you were going to kick his butt."

"Oh, great."

"Yup. And you have plans to tear him apart from limb to limb."

"Excellent," I said.

She let a smile play at the corner of her lips. She could see I was a little freaked out. "You know what I told him really, Charles? I told him it was ridiculous, his behaving this way, and that things were getting out of hand."

"Good." I was genuinely relieved to hear this.

"I mean it. This is so stupid, the Stantons and the Daleys killing each other's dogs."

"*We* haven't killed *their* dogs!" I shouted, and some people on the deck, especially those of the hipper-than-thou, heroin-shooting variety, looked up with bemusement. "We haven't killed *their* dogs, Camille," I whispered.

Her tone had been so reproachful, false though it was. This is how moral relativism gets started. And by relatives.

"I mean it just the same. It's stupid, behaving like that. Leave that stuff to our parents." I grimaced at that. "Oh, I'm sorry . . ." she sputtered, and I knew she was, so I let it pass.

"I'm for fighting as hard as the next girl," she went on. "In fact, if Carlisle isn't up here in about ten seconds . . ."

I was hovering over her, and she was so lovely, with the sunset spreading all around her left shoulder, there was no way, if I were her boyfriend, I would linger in that loft.

Behind her the low Bowery rooftops were platforms for a dozen stages, each of which seemed to be unfolding as a separate family drama. Soon, bouquets of color would light up the evening sky. But it was hard not to get lost in Camille's enchanting Daley eyes, her uncharacteristically large breasts—uncharacteristic of a Daley, that is—and these above the flattest stomach you ever saw. You probably *had* seen it, if not in *Hustler,* then elsewhere. That midriff was her signature now in the photos that were taken with Carlisle Jones.

"So what else did you say to Blake?" I asked her gently.

"I told him he should apologize to you."

"Did you tell him he could do this through a letter, or maybe over the phone?"

"I told him he should come here tonight and do it in person."

She wasn't kidding. Panic loomed within my heart. I couldn't feel my legs beneath my knees. *Where's the rest of me?* Or to put it more bluntly, where could I get the necessary weaponry to deal with my maniac cousin? The man who had killed my dog.

The door burst open and we pivoted. No Blake, but no fun either. I mean, just the *possibility* that he could show up was adding a little edge to the evening. Instead, coming through the door was Roger Rabin, who after a minute of insulting the way I looked ("What ever are you dressed for, Charles? A bowling tournament?") was anxious to tell us about the *Downtown News*'s annual lists of who was In and who was Out. He would tell us whether we wanted to hear it or not.

"I'm going to put Rupert Murdoch on the In list," he said. "After all, Murdoch's *Washington Post* is a distinct improvement. It has WINGO instead of editorials."

I wasn't really listening. I was combing the crowd nervously. I heard Roger say something about Edward being In, but then, so was Stupidity. And speaking of stupidity, I was certain Blake would be here before too long. Roger was going on about how Wolfy had made his In list, while Wolfy's ex-wife, whose show just weeks before had been considered cool, was for some reason on the skids. Rose was O-U-T.

But then I was staring at this woman with blond tied-back hair who stepped out of the doorway and hesitated, a tentative look on her face. I'd seen her someplace before. She was quite pretty, with a wide forehead and an intelligent countenance, and wearing this colorful peasant skirt, she looked utterly out of place.

"Laurie," called Camille, and the woman half smiled for a nano-second and purposefully strode toward us. Of course. It was Laurie Krieger, the actress. Camille introduced us, but I wasn't much fun. Pretty as she was, I could but mumble a greeting. For over on a roof across First Avenue there was this guy standing, seeming to adjust some kind of tubing. I couldn't see his face, but in the distance he seemed familiar. Who was that guy? "Hey, Camille, isn't that . . ."

Camille looked over with squinted eyes. "It's Blake," she said utterly without alarm.

"What's it look to you like he's doing over there?" I asked worriedly. Behind us now the first volley of the city's fireworks floated into the air, exploding with a disappointing absence of snap, crackle, and pop. Laurie Krieger stood there with this smile flashing on and off her face, not certain whether this was some kind of family routine. She was affable enough, if a little hesitant about what she was doing with us, though we seemed to be the only people on deck she knew, or whom she would care to. Fear crossed her face when I turned to Camille and said, "Omigod."

Blake looked up from what he was doing and intently glared at us. In one motion, he lit a match and, as it flared up, touched it to this string that flared like a sparkler. Only it wasn't a sparkler, it was a fuse to some kind of rocket, and it appeared to be pointed straight at us.

*A screaming comes across the sky.* The missile shot by us with a blue flame that came *that* close to singeing Camille's dark hair. Under the circumstances, it's kind of understandable that she shrieked.

A second barrage of fireworks was sent aloft behind us, breaking into a cluster of unusual coloration. People on the deck were heard to ooh and ah. The only ones appropriately concerned with these fireworks moving laterally were a Spanish family on the roof across the street who were standing and pointing expressively at my crazy cousin across First Avenue.

Camille and I grabbed Laurie Krieger by the hands and began to try to make it to the stairwell. In the rush, we tripped over one another's feet, which is why we were still there when Blake took his cigar out of his mouth and touched the glowing end to the fuse of a second rocket. "Cheeeeyou!" This one shot through the night so close to me I had to dive face first onto the deck. "Charles!" screamed Camille, and then she was down on her knees attending to me like a medic.

"Let's get the hell out of here!" I gasped and rolled to the stairwell. But as I stumbled to my feet, and as we were about to duck down the stairs, there was Blake, calmly using the cigar to light a third fuse. "Whooooosh!"

This one took off and changed course the second it was over the street. It curved up on a trajectory that would have taken it to Mars if there hadn't been something solid in the way. I looked up as the Goodyear blimp floated serenely out of harm's way. The rocket, however, had hit our building's water tower with this temendous *gong!* Just as the third bright explosion of fireworks was sent aloft by the side of the Statue of Liberty, the rocket landed on the roof and began whizzing around like a dog chasing its own tail. For the first time, the people on the deck stopped to notice what was going on, though across the street, the Spanish family now were jumping up and down with fear, shouting to relatives and clutching one another. We could see through the red glare that Blake was scuttling like a crab back into the darkness, and as he scurried, the rocket that had been spinning on the rooftop burst into flames.

That got everyone's attention. And then there was a rush for the stairwell, with Camille, Laurie Krieger, and me leading the way. The party was in full gear on the floor below, but even the dancers could smell smoke. We spotted Carlisle, and with surprising calmness, we thundered down the stairs. By the time we could hear sirens, the party was safely spilling into the street. I wondered what Blake accomplished by burning down the building. This was over an election. This was Democracy in action.

## ——— CHAPTER THIRTEEN ———

I THOUGHT MY FAMILY was weird until I met Laurie Krieger. We were sitting in a Blarney Stone on East 14th Street that was getting set to close for the night. Carlisle and Camille had left, but not before we'd made a pact that we wouldn't tell the police what we knew about the building that had burned down in the Bowery. We wouldn't let on that it was my cousin who had gone awry, and not just some reckless Roman candle. Another headline would be bad for the campaign.

Now Laurie and I sat talking as she drank water and I nursed a beer while old regulars slept facedown at the bar. I was having a wonderful time listening to her life story.

And I thought *my* family was weird! So I had a one-armed brother who had made a fortune in the market and was running for the United States Senate. That was normal enough. So we were trying to make certain my eighteen-year-old sister wasn't carried away by an amorous forty-five-year-old industrialist. Humdrum. That I had a fugitive brother who hadn't been home since the night he set out with a headful of acid and plans to blow up the regional high was simply a tale of the epoch. And so my uncles were exposed in a bestselling tract shortly before one of them was blown to bits in a race-car crash that to this day was used by ABC Sports for its "Agony of Defeat" segment. So what. And what if I did have a dog that made a fortune for me and for the dog-food industry before he was murdered by a cousin who'd just burned down a fucking building in the Bowery because he was trying to nail us with a ground-to-Daley missile. I'm telling you, compared to her family, mine was normal. Maybe even bland.

I lose track of which of her siblings languished in jail, which one had married into royalty, and which one had married a thrill killer. One of her brothers had sold secrets to the Russians and a sister kept snakes in New Orleans. Chemical dependency ran through her family like rickets among the Hottentots. "People assume my love of theater must be a family trait. I tell them, 'No, the only traits my family has are neurosis and alcoholism.' "

She came from a show-biz family of sorts. Her father was a theme-park developer from Clifton, New Jersey, who missed the skate-boarding boom on the early side, but who otherwise caught trends too late, which was why the family still was in possession of approximately one hundred and sixteen thousand Hula-Hoops—Hula Land closed after only six weeks—and dump trucks full of molding Davy Crockett caps with their furry tails intact. Mom was a singer when the theme parks were in business, but she sang rather more like Imelda Marcos than Tammy Wynette, whom she physically resembled. While Space World may have been a hit in the 1960s, it was of late a certified dud and destined for closure. Woodstock Nation, in Ashley Falls, Massachusetts, was successful, though increasingly litigious. Strewn with an era's sea wrack, it was thought not to be long for this world. Now Dad sat out in the back of the house drinking Rob Roys and praying for casino gambling to hit just about any beach town between Portsmouth, New Hampshire, and Ocean City, Maryland. She called home every Sunday.

All things considered, I supposed we could have competed with the Kriegers for sheer strangeness. My basis for comparison was a little suspect, considering just having two parents alive struck me as exotic. We sat across the table and tried to top the other with family tales of eccentricity. I led with the story of Quentin Claydo, the Lost Tribe, and the Ku Klux Klan. I figured that ought to impress her. I was holding my grandfather's disappearance and his search for the black rose in case I got into a jam. Her single best story was rendered better by the delivery than it was by the plot summary. She was, after all, an actress. It had to do with all the Kriegers going to Las Vegas one Christmas a long time ago, with her six siblings leading a full-scale breakout of the kiddie dorm in the MGM Grand, resulting in the Nevada National Guard being summoned on Christmas Eve by

Governor Paul Laxalt, helicopters searching city streets while her parents gambled obliviously.

"You know," she said, leaning over the table with a sly smile, "I'm friends with your friend Angela Moranis."

"And also my uncle Ethan Stanton, if I'm not mistaken."

"He owes me money and a whole lot more. He ripped me off when I was too messed up to do anything about it. I have a deal with a lawyer, but the suits are still in rehearsal." Her face became a little flushed at the mention of Ethan's name, and her nostrils flared discernibly.

"What exactly did he do, Laurie? Angela's article told some, but I'm a little vague."

"You want the pretty version or the ugly version?" It was clear she didn't want to gloss over her feelings for Ethan, who was, after all, Blake's boss. Blake, who'd tried to kill us earlier in the evening.

"As you like it," I said.

"Okay, I was in this comedy on Broadway called *Souls of Your Feet*. There were a few dance numbers, but mostly it was one big expedition into pop psychology. It was awful."

"I remember it. You were supposed to be terrific in it."

"I was good," she said, nodding, "at first. Then I stopped eating because I thought I was too fat for the part. I started doing white crosses to lose weight. Then after the show I wouldn't be able to sleep, so I'd have a few glasses of wine and, maybe, a lude. Then lots of wine and a few ludes, and so on. Eventually I was scarfing up mounds of coke. It's the usual story, and not a pretty one.

"I was making good money, and I wanted to protect it. From me. 'Cause I didn't trust myself as far as I could throw me, which might have been pretty far by then, because I was so thin, except I was so weak from lack of sleep and doing all those drugs. I made what at least five people told me was a no-lose move: I asked Ethan Stanton to take care of my money. Three months later, I was fired from the show. I was, ugggh, I was in awful shape, and I was trying to check into the Payne Whitney Clinic up at New York Hospital . . ."

"Yeah, I know it," I said, "my family keeps a suite there."

"And I had to call up Ethan to get my money back so I could pay for the hospital. It took me three days to reach him by phone, and in those three days . . ." Her lips trembled just perceptibly, though she kept herself in check. "In those three days the *New York Post* had a running commentary on why I was fired from *Souls* and where I was going to check into. I finally got Ethan on the phone and he told me the money wasn't available. I said, 'What do you mean, it isn't *available?*' And he just calmly said, 'It isn't there.' He didn't even bother to lie. I would have liked that at that point, I would have liked to have been lied to, do you know what I mean? He just said he'd invested in an oil syndication that hit nothing but dry wells, though he though eventually some money could be recouped."

"He must have been operating under the assumption you wanted your money sheltered, and you were thinking he was investing it for profits."

"It doesn't matter what the understanding was, does it? He lost— or stole—every penny I earned when I needed it to save my life." She said it like "Save my *life*." "And I'm not being dramatic," she continued. "I'm a poster child for rehabilitation." She waved her hand in the air as if it were a tambourine. "But I feel he took my money and just threw it away. Although there are some pretty big names who swear by him. He didn't take care of me because I wasn't important enough and he knew I was in rough shape."

"I've heard that about him," I allowed.

She leaned across the table with a smile. All she had before her was this glass of water, and she'd mentioned earlier that she hadn't had anything stonger than a cup of coffee in almost a year. She looked older than she was. I would have said twenty-six or -seven, though she said twenty-three. "So what happened between you and my friend Angela?" she asked with an eyebrow raised coquettishly.

"Nothing all that much," I mumbled. Something dumb like that.

"What do you mean? She liked you, she told me so. She had fun up at your house."

"And then she went and wrote about it!" Boy, did I sound defensive.

"It was her break!" She said it more with humor than with anger, as if making fun of the fact that I couldn't understand that.

"Fine," I said. "That was the choice she made."

"Oh, come on. You truly are protective of your family, aren't you?"

"Well, in this case, I was being protective of me."

"Ah," she said, "but you are. You don't even want to be critical of Ethan, do you? You just defended him to me. To me."

It didn't make me happy that the Daleys were in the trenches, coughing on the mustard gas of the Stantons. And it wasn't just terror at Blake going bonkers, and the reckless bloody turmoil that followed in his wake. Strange as this may seem, I enjoyed the way the Daleys were congealing as a family, and there was no way we could do that without the Stantons as a cause. But the price of our order was the disorder from without, and the Stantons were, after all, family as well. It would get worse, I could see that now, could tell that tonight by Blake's emulation of Wernher von Braun. We Daleys had the unity of Londoners under attack. As familiar as we were, we were ultimately strangers, yet also brave together.

Laurie spoke up kindly, as I seemed stumped for words. "Your brother is running against your . . . uncle?"

"Aye."

"Your uncle's the senator, right?"

"That's it."

She scrunched up her nose. "And you're a Republican?"

"Hey," I said, "there was enough in my family to rebel against without bringing politics into it."

"Mate, we're trying to close up here, you mind?" said the balding lump of a bartender who rolled over to the table. He was somewhat out of breath and glistening like a boiled new potato.

"No, of course not," I said and we slowly rose from the table. Laurie was living in an apartment just off Gramercy Park, and I walked her there, just enjoying being with her on these late-night holiday streets. We collected phone numbers and schedules, coolly, as if it were information each needed for our daily duties, and I promised to come see her performance and to take her out for dinner afterwards. She allowed that she'd like that. Oh boy, oh boy, oh boy, I said to myself as I wended my way to Park Avenue South, where, among throngs of hookers, I landed a cab like a water-skier among fishermen. What a wonderful night! And then I remembered Blake and I frowned the whole way home.

# ⸻ CHAPTER FOURTEEN ⸻

ADVICE SQUAWKED OVER THE speaker box from someone I had never laid eyes on, and it all made perfect sense. Rick Morgan, the campaign's communications director, was here, of course, in the morning. He was never anyplace but here. It was he who, over the metallic locks of the aural canal that linked us, advised me to go to the police —advice I politely refused—and failing that, to go to Ethan Stanton to see if he couldn't shut down that crazed nephew of his. Not Edward, Blake.

"Tell him what Blake's done," Rick said in this weird, hipster accent rendered all the stranger by virtue of its disembodiedness. "Make him administer justice. But for sure, make him get Blake under wraps." There was a *puff!* sound that came from the speaker box as if this were all so obvious.

"That's really a very good idea," I said, but when I began to ask him another question, the line that connected us was dead.

Rick's voice would float in and out at whim, like a genie's. Sometimes you'd be in the middle of questioning him on something and it would just disappear. If he was in a particularly bad mood, he would rattle his files and bang on the radiator, and you'd jump back from the phone rubbing your ear. There were other times when his voice was so steady, his advice so sound, I would sit in my office with my feet on the desk as if I were in the midst of long-distance therapy, though his office was the one just at the end of the hall with the skull and crossbones taped to it, "Do Not Disturb" and "Toxic Material" painted on it in orange Day-Glo. It was a curiosity all the volunteers showed their friends, replete with whispered imaginings of what was inside.

So I reported in to Edward and told him the whole story. He listened as I described the scene complete with sound effects. I'd like to say his response was "To hell with the campaign, justice must be done." But he just whistled, went "Whew!" and asked if I thought the newspapers were on to Blake. He was worried, as was I, that getting Blake arrested, while a service to every woman, child, and small furry animal in northwestern Connecticut, would, in the eyes of the public, reduce the campaign to a farce. Edward was enough of a politician, and had a vague enough understanding of the law, that at the end of the conversation he put in, "You realize, don't you, that if you think Blake is responsible for a near death, you have an absolute obligation to the police to turn him in."

This was terrible, this was awful, here I was being cavalier about my own near demise, but I admit, I burst out laughing when Edward said that, because his posturing was so correct. "Yeah, I realize that, Edward," I said. And then I could hear a woman murmuring in the background, and I knew I had not caught him at his apartment alone. Edward's love life, historically excellent, came of late in dribs and drabs. In fairness, he spent all of his time running around the state, so this was a nice development. A Cheshire-cat smile hovered over the receiver.

I finally reached a horrified Camille. She was adamant that we go to the police "and nail that sucker's balls to the wall." I felt sleazy having to explain to her that it wasn't the expedient thing to do. It would be our word against Blake's that he was on the roof that night, and it would be hard to prove he'd tried to kill us even if we could make positive identification. There was no real point in going to the police.

"Except it would be right, baby."

"You got me there." I was beginning to soften, so I figured to shore up my resolve I better get in touch with Uncle Ethan. I wanted to see him squirm.

He was gracious, as if he were expecting my call. I told him I had to speak with him, in person, preferably this morning.

I walked the seven blocks from the campaign headquarters to his small law office and investment firm high above Park Avenue. The day was troubled with the potential for rain, and it would be difficult to say who looked more sheepish, those people carrying umbrellas or those who were not. Ethan's receptionist was lanky Sheena the Punk Rocker, kinkily made up today in a girls' school outfit and a little bow tie, and she urged me to sit down in the waiting room, which was a tableau of plushness. Typically for a Stanton, it was a picture-book expression of eclectic interior decoration, with Bauhaus furniture, Navajo rugs, an elaborate IBM Selectric at the reception-ist's console, and subscriptions on the coffee table not only to the *Wall Street Journal* and the *New York Times,* but to the *New Republic, National Review, Billboard, Variety, Cahiers du Cinema, Art News,* and

*New York Rocker*. I looked for *Easyriders*, *Red-Hot Mamas*, and *Guns &*
*Ammo*, but for some reason Ethan didn't have these exotic offerings.

This may have been the only law office in Manhattan that had
nothing but Warhols hung along the hallway. Right in front of me
was a huge Mick Jagger, and as Sheena came back with a surly
gesture of her head began to lead me down the hall, we passed Mao,
Castro, Elvis, Muhammad Ali, and Truman Capote. Were there any
women? Ah, here stood Marilyn Monroe.

"Uncle Ethan?"

"Charles," he said in the warm, triumphant tone he reserved for
entrances and exits, and telephone conversations with those people
whose calls were, for particular reasons, only episodic.

I was ushered to a couch that was cluttered with papers and con-
tracts and blueprints for what appeared to be a house of some great
scale. I noticed the architect's name, a Mingeboro celeb.

"What's this?" I asked with genuine curiosity.

Ethan was getting organized for our little meeting, picking up his
coffee cup and putting his half-frame glasses on the desk as he came
to sit in the easy chair next to the couch. "Ah," he said, "the new
house." He plunked down on the leather seat a little awkwardly.
"Your Aunt Vivi decided, not without some justification, that it was
strange that I continue to live in the house with her and Nate now
that both of them are in their seventh decade. Did you know Vivi
just turned sixty? Did you send her a card?"

"I'm sure the campaign sent her some direct mail," I said, but
Ethan paid that no attention, his eyes seemingly caught by the blueprints of his house. That thing was going to be a monster, maybe the
same size or bigger than the main house up at All Odds. Hmm. So
Vivi and Nate are kicking Ethan out of the house they'd shared
forever.

"And so I'm going to build," said Ethan, "down the field a little bit
from the main house."

"So you can have a closer view of the Daleys."

"Hah hah hah hah hah, that's rich, Charles, that's good." He was
dressed in a linen glen-plaid suit, with these new Bally shoes on, a
bright-red tie tucked into his vest. His mustache was its usual evil
self, though his face looked a little pale and puffy for this time of
year. The eyes were malignantly intelligent, though his cheeks didn't
have their usual courtroom glow. Maybe the campaign and what I

always suspected was a viciously debauched life-style were finally catching up to him.

"So what brings you here, Charles, other than to visit your tired old uncle?"

"I wondered if Blake might be around."

"Blake?"

"Your nephew. Big guy, not too smart."

"He doesn't work for me anymore. He's probably in Mingeboro. Yeah, in fact I think he's out there running his new business. You know he's going into the wholesale orchard fruit business."

"My," I said. Ethan had said all this a little too calmly, and sipping his coffee, he was just a tad to slick to be real.

"I was kind of hoping he'd be here," I lied. "You see, he tried to kill me last night, not to mention also trying to kill my cousin Camille, oh, and your old friend Laurie Krieger."

He got nervous at the mention of her name. "And how could Blake have done a thing like that?"

I reached over to the *New York Times* on the couch beside me and opened it to the Metro Section, which had reported on the building that burned down in a mishap involving fireworks. I handed it over to him to read the small article. As he did so, I stood up and wandered around his tidily impressive office. There were pictures on the walls of Ethan with such disparate characters as Steve Lawrence and Eydie Gorme, Rod Stewart, Vitas Gerulaitis, Ed Sullivan, Cheryl Tiegs, and a recent one with him at what appeared to be Studio 54 with a tableful of Kennedys, everyone looking hyper but wasted.

"So," Ethan said, and I came over and sat down again.

"That fire was Blake's doing. He tried to kill us with fireworks aimed right at us. Fortunately they missed, but they burned the building to the ground."

"That's ridiculous. What proof do you have?" There was a barely perceptible twitch that tugged at the skin immediately below his left eye.

"Not only our own eyewitness account, but there was a family—a nice Hispanic family with a grandfather, in-laws, we're talking dozens of good, hardworking possessors of green cards—all of whom say they can identify Blake. And if they can put him there, we can qualify his actions as attempted murder. No doubt about it. And there's one more thing."

"Yeah?"

"It hasn't made the papers yet, but I'm told there was someone in that building, one Aurelio Rodriguez, who was asleep when it burned down. And you know what that means: Blake's not guilty of *attempted* murder, he *is* a murderer."

"I don't believe you. Have you gone to the police?"

"About to," I calmly said.

"If you were serious about this, you would have gone to the police already. This is ridiculous, and I don't have time for such an amateur shakedown."

"Well, you're going to have to make time for it when they come and take Blake away in manacles, and I tell the police that Blake had to have been working on your orders. It might not stick, but in the context of the Senate race, don't you think it might get a little press?"

He stared at me with utter impassivity, his eyes just barely blinking. We faced off against each other, me on the couch, Ethan in his chair, relatives in a standoff. How had we ever gotten here?

Ethan leaned over and picked up the phone on the table beside the couch. "Sheena, get me Captain Veryser in Manhattan South. Thank you." And with the same impassivity with which we had been looking at each other, he replaced the modern phone in what passed for its cradle.

"What are you calling him for?" I asked a little nervously. I doubted he was going to turn himself in.

"Oh, he's an old friend of mine. I'm going to ask him what happened at that fire, because I have reason to believe some of my kin were attending a party at that building. Oh, and I want to ask him about that murder."

"Okay, so Aurelio Rodriguez lives." Hey, it was worth a try.

He picked up the phone. "Cancel the call." He paused. "I don't care if they're finding him, just hang up."

"But the rest of it's the truth," I said, getting back my courage a little. Jesus, the guy could intimidate me. "And let me tell you this, Uncle Ethan, if you don't get that nut sent off to summer at the foot of Mount McKinley, he *is* going to kill someone, and it will be dumped on your doorstep." I began to talk myself back into boldness. "That son of a bitch was trying to throw a table at me when he had his unfortunate appointment with the shark, and I saw the two of you with Fido three days before he was found dead."

"I had nothing to do with that!" He seemed outraged at the suggestion. That seemed right then to break his defense of Blake.

"I'm not saying you did. It was Blake, I know. And it was Blake last night who set off rockets pointed at Camille and me. Look," I said, and I leaned forward to speak with my uncle whom I had never liked, partially because my mother didn't like him and so I didn't have to, but at least I'd always gotten along with him. I leaned forward as if there were some familial understanding between us, in spite of the fact that we were trying to raid his power base, his brother's Senate seat, and he was fighting back financially and through the medium of his deranged Abbott nephew. In spite of all that, Ethan looked at me calmly.

"This thing has gotten out of hand," I said. "This is not a joke, and there is no way we can keep this in the family, if you will, with all the scrutiny we're going to come under. So we're trying to beat Nate. So what?" He started, but I raised my hand as a gesture of an unfinished thought. "We can survive this thing, whether Edward beats Nate or not. We'll still have money—what's left of it," I said with a smile, "and we'll still have a certain, oh, position. But if Blake keeps this shit up, someone is going to get hurt, and it could be you. He could bring this whole thing down on you, Ethan. He could."

Ethan stood up and went over to the big silver bullet of coffee he kept on his desk. He poured himself a fresh one and brought me a cup. "I was telling you the truth when I said Blake no longer works for me. He doesn't. He's staying at my apartment right now, scared half to death. I didn't know about what, but he seemed to think it was pretty bad. He's going to go away for a few weeks, not just at my request, but at Nate's. Do you know that Nate controls the trust? Of course, you do; you get your checks the same as we all do." No, I didn't, unfortunately. They were tied up in the estate.

"Well, Blake, not having the inclination or ability to handle honest work, is particularly susceptible to doing what he's told to do by the guy who can shut off his income. And that goes double for your Uncle Chauncey. He's getting ready to take in his little boy, who's all grown up and all gone bad. No matter what happened last night, it was already decided by Nate and by me that young Blake was going to have a pleasant summer at the beach—in Maine, not the Hamptons. And as of tomorrow, he's gone. I promise you."

He was looking at me with such sincerity I didn't quite have the heart to ask him to put it in writing. If Blake were exiled until the end of the primary, it would make life a little easier. It might turn this thing into a regular campaign, which was dirty enough, but would be slightly more pleasant if the prospect of losing your life weren't a part of it. Even though I thought golf would be more interesting if the players were under penalty of death, politics was by definition more exciting, and didn't need that extra bit of tension. And since I had four siblings and a slew of cousins to worry about, the prospect that the campaign would be free of terrorism was welcome. I grinned.

"I was hoping you'd say that."

"I mean it," said my Uncle Ethan. So he stole money, so he was a real sleazy power broker, he was *our* sleazy power broker, and in this instance he wasn't so bad.

"Let me ask you a question," I said.

"Sure."

"You guys really think you have this thing locked up?"

He squinted for a second to decide what he should say. Pulling a cigarette out of his pocket and leaning into a match, he said, "Barring something unforeseen, there's no way we can lose. The numbers just aren't there for Edward. We're going to crush him."

I smiled. He was deluding himself. Which was good.

"Let me ask *you* a question," he said. I nodded. "Why are you at all involved in this? I thought you wanted to be a writer."

I laughed. "Maybe I still will be. Maybe you'll be my subject matter. Maybe I'll write about how you got rich."

"Hah! How I got rich! That's good, Charles."

"What's so funny?"

"Can't tell. I gave my word a long time ago."

"To who?"

"To whom," he corrected. "And it doesn't matter. But I must say one thing. If by some miracle Edward pulls this off, it'll be that sawed-off arm of his that does it. People perceive him as a hero. If he wins, it'll be because of his artificial arm."

"Oh, no way, Uncle Ethan. It'll be because of the truth."

"Fuck you."

## —•— **CHAPTER FIFTEEN** ————

WHEN THE GATE SWUNG shut at the Abbotts' farm on the cliffs above Cape Elizabeth, Blake stood behind it with a beer in his hand. This was told to me by his mother, who was standing at her kitchen sink, doing the play-by-play. "He's inside," she said dryly, and then I could hear Uncle Chauncey take the phone from her with a little bit of a struggle. "Charles, that you? Listen, you son of a bitch. When I was at New Haven we had a name for people like you," he growled, but then the phone was back in Aunt Anne's hand and she was speaking in the clipped voice that was so similar to my late mother's. I could hear a screen door slam in the background. "I'll tell Nate that everything's under control. So you can call the dogs off now." It was a curious turn of phrase under the circumstances.

Blake was in for a regimen of sun and sand, of fresh Maine lobster and corn, and few are the exiles who have it so good. And few are the communities that feel such relief when the bully has been sent up the river. His removal made July more enjoyable in New York, and anything would have helped, for this was a July whose heat was stifling.

With Blake not lurking out there, we were free to concentrate on politics. These were, if you will kindly pardon the expression, the dog days of the campaign. Coverage by the newspapers was slight, partially because they were getting a little bored with Edward's message, but mostly because July is a month when people are thinking about their tans, about love, about whether the Mets will recover and the Yankees will quit squabbling. The important things. There isn't an awful lot of time left, even with the extra sunlight, for the posturing of candidates in a primary fight.

We made up for this with heavy purchases of television time, and our ads had more episodes than "The Honeymooners." This gave the illusion of activity, since if Edward wasn't going to automatically get news coverage by, say, standing in front of the capitol in Albany talking about the absurdly high taxes New Yorkers pay, it nevertheless made a nice backdrop for a commercial. And whether Edward was crotch-deep in the Love Canal, gesturing behind him to the

Statue of Liberty, or dwarfed by the construction of the World Trade Center, Harry Fox's spots did the trick of projecting Edward as vigorous, inconoclastic yet respectful of traditions, a patriot who could eat the Soviets for breakfast, provide prosperity for all, and still be a regular guy.

The worst press we got out of our entire cycle of July ads was when, in order to soften the harshness of Edward's image from an earlier batch (he had promised to personally witness the first execution should New York ever reenact a death penalty), we'd gone on the air calling him "compassionate." The picture showed Edward playing with several of my little cousins in an Edenic corner of the estate in Mingeboro. There were dappled meadows. One thought of ewe. Then Murray Kempton pronounced in a column, "When a Republican calls himself 'compassionate,' he knows he's going to lose."

There were yucks in the Stanton camp following that one, yucks we heard for days. And it was dumb to have put on the ad, because all our data showed Republican primary voters this year didn't give a rat's ass for compassion as compared to their interest in inflation, the general state of the economy, and a feeling that the nation somehow was weakening. Though we needed to soften Edward's image in the general, during the primary campaign we needed to consistently portray him as having the answer to the problems of concern to Republican activists who voted in primaries. Another wasted ad.

Though nominally I still was in charge, the fallout from the Walter Cronkite incident, as it now was called euphemistically by our campaign strategists, allowed them to rather tactfully ease me out of the leadership role. There were decisions now made by them, with Edward and my finding out what was planned after Harry Fox had already begun storyboards on spots. This bothered me, especially when it resulted in the mistaken touchy-feely spot they had rushed on the air when the first small rise came in Edward's negatives. But I bit my tongue for now. For undeniably, my being on the road with Edward was a help, and slowly, inexorably, I could feel the campaign's upward surge.

For some reason, Nate had yet to go on the air, and it would have been the ideal time for him to do so. He was stuck a good deal on the floor of the Senate, and Edward was the beneficiary of a number of Uncle Nate's cancellations. In our weekly staff meeting—the obsessive scheduler timing each argument with a stopwatch—Simon

Ford would glance at those invitations including Senator Stanton, and looking at the legislative calendar, he would recommend which ones Edward would attend. "The chance that Nate will cancel is high. Christ, the guy *likes* to vote. And who are they going to send as a surrogate? Ethan?" All would laugh at the suggestion, yet since my meeting with him, I wasn't so gleeful about cutting him down. He had shown the good sense to pack Blake off to summer camp in Maine. That was something.

It was only where Nate and Edward came into direct confrontation that the news that would define this campaign was created. And that just wasn't happening. Yet in the absence of having ads of his own, I would have to say we were turning Nate into a video punching bag. Edward was constantly on the attack, about Nate being a big spender, about his wanting to keep taxes high, about his support for the Panama Canal treaties and his seeming delight in SALT II. And in defense came nary a peep, though there was an onslaught of leaked promises that Nate would soon take the gloves off, his avuncular image to be shed and the battle-wizened old pro to emerge. But no forum for doing so materialized. We worried about our good fortune. Were they hoarding their money to blow Edward out in the last thirty days?

Of all the invitations to debate thus far offered, Uncle Nate had accepted only one. It was from the new owners of the *New York Post*. These guys showed why they'd been able to turn a minor empire in leisure clothes and Elvis souvenirs into the bucks that bought them the *Post*. Without any mincing they came right out and said that if either campaign chickened out on the debate, fine: they'd just turn over the editorial *and* news pages to the opposition. Not even Nate thought he was above that. So there we were with a debate scheduled for the first week of August, which was fast approaching.

It was during a meeting with the new owners of the *Post* that Edward and I got an inkling of what they were like, and we rather admired them. We arrived at the South Street entrance one sunny morning as cars whizzed above us on the FDR Drive. As we were standing at the entrance, workmen were still clearing away debris from the redecoration that was going on. I raised my eyebrow for a minute when I saw them walk out with this stuffed kangaroo and throw him into a Dumpster. What struck me was that he was stuffed in a crouch with these boxing gloves on, bright red ones that lit up the morning. Without thinking twice, Edward and I both rushed into the street and quickly hustled the thing into our waiting car, the driver looking spooked as we put the kangaroo next to him in the driver's seat. He kept casting sideways glances at us as we stepped back away from the car, admiring our handiwork. After that, meeting with the new owners was a breeze.

## ── CHAPTER SIXTEEN ──

NEW YORK THIS JULY was abuzz with talk of Wolfy's article in *Esquire*. When I read it, I was reminded of leaving the church and heading for the cemetery where my grandmother was to be buried, those women holding up signs with messages like, "Have You Stopped Beating Your Wife, Mr. Daley?" Wolfy's answer now was "Not quite," rendered in an acceptable fashion, as his literary pummeling of his ex-wife began in earnest.

The excerpt painted a picture of a sad, put-upon Wolfy, whose single immature goal was to make it back alive from the racetrack each week in order to play with his little children, only to find Rose with a swami, two blond homosexual hippies, and an unctuous little chemist apportioning the dollops of strong LSD, the cooking and the cleaning, natch, not done. And he told it in a style that admittedly was a little macho and conventionally upper-class, but wholly sympathetic because he was so damn funny. He told the story made famous in *Pit Stop* of his lunging at Rose at an awards banquet in Monaco, and pointed out one little item Rose had neglected to mention: that just before dinner, he had caught Rose and her Tyrolean paramour offering a reefer to his ten-year-old boy, the bed inside all torn up from their afternoon merriment.

Now of course it would have been better if he'd merely squeezed a grapefruit in her face. Instead he decked her, and lost the war right away. But he told his quite horrible story with such verve and self-deprecation that his innate conservatism seemed supportable, if not precisely hip. Maybe the times were achanging.

There were promises of more revelations about Rose and her life-style, not to mention the history of his own and Blitz's heroic careers at the racetrack. The book was to be published in the spring. In preparation, Wolfy went on "Donahue," where within a matter of minutes he had turned Donahue's terrier mannerisms against him and won the audience to his side. "He's so cute!" gushed one six-foot, two-twenty housewife when her turn came at the mike, and she was backed by applause.

Suddenly offers were pouring in for Wolfy to do "Live at Five" and New York radio, and rather than having to hide him in the back room anymore, he became a draw at Edward's fund-raising events. There he was in the Hamptons at a five-hundred-dollar-a-head cock-tail party for Edward, holding court on the deck with the constant Perrier in his hand and his fabulous girlfriend, Abby, at his side. And there he was again, much slimmer and positively clear-eyed at our campaign staff meetings, holding himself in check, and doing so with a great deal more confidence than he had expressed (as bra-vura) in his drinking, philandering, loudmouthed days.

There was one nightmarish weekend in Mingeboro when Wolfy went off the wagon and was not so much fun to deal with. Some-where in the night he put a big dent in his own son's Lazzy. The next day at Mass he looked so gray and remorseful there seemed no point in chiding him: his guilt was palpable. Mostly, he seemed reconciled to his occasional slipping, but his constant yearning for something was something.

He was proud of his writing—he'd written the bulk of his memoir in under one hundred days. And it showed. But while it was re-ported by those who had read it in its entirety to have utterly roman-ticized life among the Daleys, my opinion was it had a gritty touch of reality when it came to his domestic life, his recognition of himself as an alcoholic, a fallen man, with a sense of utter purpose only when behind the wheel of a very fast car. He went on offense when it came to Rose's portrait of him, though he owned up to some very clear faults and excesses. The inherent conflict between his best and his worst was handled with brutal honesty. And at 140 miles per hour, in overdrive, well, one slip and . . .

But Wolfy's newfound acceptability, while terrific for him and a relief for the family, presented some problems for me. The biggest one was that he chronicled in that article his life as a party animal, and invariably, as I went to real-estate offices to talk about the apartment I just had to have by August 1, brokers would look at my credit statement with an approving nod, ask me if I were related to the Daleys, you know, *the* Daleys, and when I said yes, a little grin would cross their faces. "You're kidding." "No ma'am," I would say. And immediately they would go into a little speech about how the particular building I was interested in was "a quiet building," with "no loud parties." And what did I do for a living? When I told them politics, they would roll their eyes, the security deposit would head skyward, and for what? A broom closet with fold-out couch and its very own subspecies of *Blatta germanica*? I kept looking, and if worse came to worse, I was prepared to move into temporary lodging at the Daley Motorworks building on East 36th. So much for my independence. I wasn't about to take to the grates, but it was a little unnerving just the same.

I was, on the whole, pleased with Wolfy and his nearly invariable fitness, and especially pleased that entire restaurants didn't clear upon his entrance. There was a sudden Wolfy chic, or at least I thought I detected it when one of the fashion shows in the pages of the *Downtown News* was done in a race-car motif. I don't know whether that was a direct reference to Wolfy or if it was just an expression of the zeitgeist. Either way, as a leading indicator as to how his celebrity options were being traded, it was a healthy sign.

## —— CHAPTER SEVENTEEN ——

IT WAS AROUND THIS time that a number of Big Name writers began to huff into our lives. They would show up at the headquarters or at a press conference, and some of them literally would sniff. I'm not talking about the major political reporters. Oh, those guys flew in, spent a pleasant day with us, took a quick read of the situation, and flew off to write what was largely the same story. Family feud. New Right agenda. Slim chance for the challenger, though money would be the equalizer. That sort of thing. Differences were expressed by minor stylistic flourishes disguised as interpretation.

But these Big Name literary types would circle us like cats before the fight, not saying anything overmuch, trying to let on how classy they were, how clearly superior, and while they found it undignified to have to cover a family such as ours, they would buckle down and do so for the sake of their professional responsibilities. They wanted to be treated either on socially equal terms or as reckoning creatures who could size us up in a fashion they were reluctant to admit we deserved. They implied we weren't worth their clever insights, their glorious prose. And while we may have been their equivalent at Mortimer's, perhaps being able to get even a better table than they could without having to make a fuss for it, we clearly were a shabby example of how rank was the American dream. But one thing they had to admit if they came out to Mingeboro—we did live fine! And that drove them crazy.

A constant theme was the family money. It was variously reported that my grandfather had left $178 million dollars, or else he had left nothing, having cleverly dispersed the money as his statement of distaste for the progressive income tax. The latter was closer to the truth, though even it assumed there was actual cash to be dispensed to the crevices.

It was one of the Big Names who, writing a piece for the *New Republic*—they called Edward "an arriviste right-wing wog who happens to have a Yale degree"—had a version of family history that struck us as a revelation. Our powers of familial self-delusion, our need for the family's twin themes of myth and fantasy so absolute, none of us ever put together the following assemblage of circumstantial evidence, though once it was pointed out to us, it was like looking at the clouds with the shape of the ducky delineated, never to see the simple gray again.

This Big Name wrote that in the late 1950s, before Nate was a freshman senator and the Daley Lazarus became a sought-after object of sporty Americana, my grandfathers Daley and Stanton went into business together and lost their shirts. This much we knew.

It went on to state that former governor William Stanton, who was referred to in the *New Yorker* as "The Great WASP," in 1960 had committed suicide following his business failure. That was a matter of supposition. It could have been a hunting accident. There was a shotgun, a fence, he was old and had always been a little sloppy about the conventions of upland game-bird safety, or so my father said.

But then putting together something so obvious that we had always shied from talking about it, the Big Name wrote that my Grandfather Daley's deaf-and-dumb act and, finally, his disappearance were his means of not having to speak about his best friend's death. A death he had played a role in, insofar as going broke had broken the governor. That was the revelation. We'd simply never made that connection before.

Now, given the family's stilted nonchalance, the general reaction to the piece among the second generation was "Do ya think? Naaah. Let's play tennis. You mix the Bloodies." But among the members of my generation, the reaction was "Heeeyyy!" We wanted to get to the bottom of this.

My cousin Owen had far too many other talents to waste them on research, though he was good at it, especially opposition research. There was no one else as good as he to turn to. We had him organize some of the brighter young cousins to start prowling through the files in Mingeboro and New York to see what there was of interest, especially with regard to joint Daley/Stanton finances. And though they were looking for the real story about my Grandfather Daley and my Grandfather Stanton's relationship, there were some interesting things they came across, and it bore directly upon my mother and our family.

Let's see. Four weeks before Grandfather Stanton was found dead in his woods, the joint venture he and Grandfather Daley had entered into—it was to develop a Formula One race-car track near Columbia, South Carolina—went belly up, stinking up every other entity on his family's beach. Grandfather Stanton lost almost three million dollars, all of it his own, while my Grandfather Daley, it appeared, had quite typically lost nothing of his own. Yet, from looking at the records of my mother's tax returns, something rather dramatic changed in the years following her father's death.

After years of minuscule disbursements, suddenly by 1964 the Stanton trust was vigorous, with spectacular profitability. And what was interesting from a political standpoint was that the money was invested in companies that all were involved in the same endeavor: making munitions for the war in Vietnam.

When Owen came into my office, most apologetically, and nervously ran through what he had found, he pieced together a tale of surface impropriety that was a little breathtaking. At the end of his presentation, the sound of Rick Morgan whistling tinnily came across the squawk box. What Owen had discovered was that over a two-year period in the mid-sixties, the two years during which Nate Stanton later said he had "agonized" about the war, the Stanton Trust was making a bundle on the war effort. And the head trustee was at that time serving not only on the Finance Committee but on the Armed Services Committee of the U.S. Senate.

"I can't believe he thought he'd get away with this," said Owen, as he sat there in my office scratching the Atlanta Braves cap on his head.

"Well, he did get away with it," I said. "That was years ago. There wasn't even an ethics report for senators in those days, so in the absence of someone really digging into things—and in the absence of Nate's having a real opponent in the last two elections—it just sat there."

"That was real decent of you and Edward to let us go through your mother's files and all," Owen said in a gentlemanly fashion, but it was hard to think of the material in front of me as anything that had to do with me.

It was Edward who was outraged. He couldn't believe that our uncle had not only criticized the war but made money on it. People forget it was Nate whom antiwar students had urged to challenge President Nixon in the 1972 New Hampshire primary, and in reality he was a war profiteer. During that time when his name was mentioned as a possible presidential challenger, albeit a quixotic one, Nate had puffed up with celebrity and spewed on about morality. Then, sizing up his chances, he'd declared victory and gotten out. Now it appeared he'd been shrewd enough—actually, venal is the word—to have gotten rich on the war his opposition to which had made him a national figure. Though locally it was still giving him problems. His war-hero nephew was challenging him. And whereas before, the challenge had been ideological to the point of being theoretical, now it was based on a hardened anger.

At first Edward's anger was hard to fathom. Not the cause, but the depth. There was a strategic decision not to go off half-cocked, not to use the information we had until the perfect moment. But there was an underlying anger to his energy that was a little scary. I worried that Edward might explode in public the way he had sometimes as a young man when Sam and I would piss him off while he was trying to woo some local high-school girl. These days he kept his anger under lock and key and projected controlled affability.

But the riveting anger that was there did not go totally unnoticed. Beth Fallon wrote in the *Daily News* that, far from the unemotional corporate exec Edward appeared at first blush to be, "he tends toward the volcanic. He believes most passionately in things, and of course the thing he believes most passionately is that his uncle Nate Stanton should no longer be a senator. It promises to be an old-fashioned bruiser of a fight, because seldom have there been two Republicans so at odds, with such a peculiar intensity by one to unseat the other."

Toward the end of the month Edward began to get good press, in the form of rather flattering feature stories, complete with war photos, charts of profits in the stocks he had touted, and long, lightly edited interviews in which he'd been able to spew forth his world-view. But going into that debate with Nate, the first real opportunity to engage him, I'd have to say Edward had one thing on his side, and it was the same thing that could do him in. It wasn't money, though it now looked as if Nate was so overconfident that he was saving his bucks for the campaign against Democrat Cattanasio. It wasn't the sympathy of the press, for each of Edward's attacks on Uncle Nate enabled reporters to depict Nate as the embattled public servant, the victim of a grudge match by a New Right automaton. No, what Edward had going for him, and what I feared the most, was that anger, that bristling energy. I was worried what would happen when he got into the ring with that crafty old man, our Uncle Nate.

## ── CHAPTER EIGHTEEN ───

WE HAD A CASSETTE of *Rubber Soul* and "Drive My Car" was playing. This as Wolfy, Laurie Krieger, and I made our fourth trip in his Mercedes to move me into my temporary digs. They were here for me on this cloudy Saturday because I had to vacate Charlotte's apartment and had no place to go but to the building on East 36th Street.

They were surprisingly good-natured about moving me, Wolfy because he didn't really have anything better to do, Laurie because it gave us a chance to see each other.

Given her performance schedule and my hours on the road, this was not an easy thing to arrange. I had seen her play and marveled at her grace on the catwalk. She had a comfortable presence, made for the tank-top shirts and jeans she wore, made for sandaled feet, for her hair tied back, for mirrored glasses that reflected light around the Public Theater. Okay, I'm holding something back. We'd been, um, seeing each other. We'd sweated through sheets. I'd kissed her *there*. I was in love, and it had happened very fast, though for once it wasn't at all ambiguous.

Wolfy was unbelievably good-humored and efficient in his efforts to help me move to the Motorworks building with everything that would fit into the back of his spacious town car. Down steps we now carried boxes containing one thousand seven hundred fourteen albums, from Willy Alexander and the Boom Boom Band to XTC's first record. There were three hundred pounds of books, eleven boxes of cassette tapes, and a silver-framed portrait of Fido. The cassette player was pumping out *December's Children* as Mick Jagger sang "Route 66" and Wolfy wheeled us up 36th Street. I looked over to him, always more comfortable behind the wheel of a car than anywhere else. I looked at Laurie in the middle and marveled at how handsome they were together, my uncle and my new girlfriend. I was just sort of glad to be with them.

"Head 'em up, move 'em out." That magical rallying call Wolfy had used since I was a child still worked now. His face was weather-beaten, but not defeated at all. There even was a rested look about it now, the deep tides of alcohol having long since washed away and left the rugged contours of a bluff. And he was strong, Wolf was, fake wheezing "Jesus" as he picked up a box of records and then barreled past a singularly useless Mr. Greco, the caretaker, as he carried them up the marble stairs.

I had taken the old apartment on the third floor that once upon a time the family's accountant had called his own. There still were dusty remnants of tenants past, newspapers from the fifties lining the shelves, wire hangers that were as solid as bicycle frames hanging in the echoing closet. But the ancient air-conditioning still rumbled, and it was without too much work for someone acclimated to the thrice yearly exodus from home to school and back again that we moved everything upstairs. And quickly the most important ritual, the assemblage of the stereo, was accomplished. "My Generation" came booming from the speakers as Wolfy stood there panting a little bit, looking somehow out of place with a can of Pepsi in his hand.

Later, after Wolfy had gone to meet his girlfriend down in Soho, after Laurie had gone to change for her performance, I began to explore the building. There was so much dust and so many photographs. It was dark and I put on few lights so as not to disturb the Grecos in their permanent encampment on the first floor. There were rooms of dusty maps of Mingeboro, anachronistic office furniture, leather-bound desks, and the framed schemata of engine plans from long ago when eight cylinders was king. I discovered a secret stash of Montrachet, framed prints that were worth a fortune, but most of all there were files, miles of files, more so than in the House of Lazarus. Yellowed crinkling paper, tiny perfect type. And they got me to thinking. We were a note-taking lot. We kept records, like civilized beasts. If there was a story to be told about the Stantons and the Daleys, it was in here someplace, probably in triplicate. I didn't look. I cleaned up and went off in search of Laurie, hoping to woo her back here after her performance. Hoping to woo her back here to my marble-floored digs, to my ancient air conditioner, to my repository of family records that had to hold some kernel of news that would save us.

## ⸺ **CHAPTER NINETEEN** ⸺

WITH OUR TV ADS out blazing, it was time for the debate. We did not
know what tricks, if any, Uncle Nate had up his sleeve. Edward was
ready, or so he kept claiming, but the suspicion remained that this
was not the case. The suspicion remained that he simply wanted the
murder boards called off. For we'd taken to sitting around the green
room at headquarters, a collection of us encircling him in a sadistic
ring of preparation that seemed to know no bounds.

"Why would your own troops frag you?" was the low point of our
day. I was the one who asked it, and Edward looked as if he wanted
me to wither up and die. There was a point to our nasty questions,
they were to prepare him for the fray. And after two afternoons of
this, we did not know whether he was ready for my uncle or ready
to retire from the fight.

There was one surprise for Edward cooked up by Simon Ford. We
had set up a phone call from one of Edward's idols, and he would
receive it moments before the debate. The intention was to give him
a last-minute boost, because no matter how you looked at it, it was
this debate that would start the stretch drive of the primary campaign.

The day was miserably hot as we arrived at the Sheraton Centre.
Tim Verkhovensky was playing advance man, and he led us past the
throng of cameras and down to our holding room. The Sheraton
was unbelievably tacky, with rude red carpeting and mirrors everywhere, but it was the perfect place for this debate, for this assemblage
of the city's power brokers. There was something not just outer
borough, but otherworldly, about it. It had the garish backdrop that
always seemed to turn up in videotaped evidence of an FBI sting.

It spooked Edward a little, and the moment we walked in, the
noisy whir of cameras capturing his purposeful gait, he tightened up
and grimaced. He barely saw the "DAY OF RECKONING" headline
that graced the *New York Post,* barely laughed at my wisecracks. And
if he wasn't going to laugh at my wisecracks, I was useless.

"Here's the drill," said Tim Verkhovensky, all business now, like a
fight promoter who knows the fix is in, and how it's supposed to

look. "Edward comes out at eight-forty-five and mingles with his crowd on the way to the stage. Nate should already be here then. At nine they'll call the two o' youse up to the stage where youse park it in one o' the chairs. The format is opening statement, then question to A, two-minute response, question to B. A and B are determined by the flip. Okay, B responds two minutes, A gets to rebut one minute, as does B. They do that five times. Then, like youse wanted, youse get to ask one question o' the senator and he gets to ask one o' youse. Three-minute close by each, do a little impromptu press to declare yourself the victor, and we're outta here."

But Edward hardly listened. He knew all this stuff anyway, and boy, was he ever nervous. I knew Edward well enough to sense when he needed company and when he did not. Right now he was tighter than a vise and there were only two things to do: keep him from coffee and somehow find Wolfy. I made some remark about checking things out and left him in the holding room distractedly leafing through papers.

The hundreds of people who streamed through the portals were seemingly chanting, "Food! Blood!" They had the same expectations as denizens of the auto racetrack, most of whom came less for the whir and the whine than the wreck and the sirens.

There had been several of these events during Rupert Murdoch's reign at the *Post*, and under him they had been classy, well-stocked affairs, with overcooked eggs and petrified bacon. But this had been at a time when Rupe's largess was part of his grace. Now there were these dudes from Dixie and austerity was the watchword. People looked at this sorry breakfast before them, and they nibbled at the biscuits and tapped their spoons gently against the grits, trying to determine what kind of victual this could possibly be. "The least they could have done was serve some bagels," said a white-haired gentleman with a snowstorm of dandruff on his polyester shoulders.

It was relative pandemonium. I saw reporters lined up around the camera platform that must have been seventy feet long. A string of cameras was set up on top like a flight of vultures alighting on a fence. There was the mayor, his first appearance since the indictments of his aides, and he was backslapping a notorious right-wing state senator from Rockland County. There seemed to be some joke that was keeping the mayor quite characteristically amused. Maybe it was the same joke at every occasion.

My Aunt Rose was hovering around the lights in front of the press section. Once she had been referred to as a social butterfly. Now she bore a strong resemblance to the creature known as Mothra. She was dressed in this embarrassing outfit that made rather too much of her endowments that had seen better days and far too much sunlight.

Over there was our little cheering section, looking glum and out of place. We'd bused in housewives from Brooklyn, geeky students from parochial schools, and hard-line old men who smelled of cigars and would bore you with tales of Conservative Party campaigns of yore. They were a small group, for we were allowed to smuggle in only this minimum. It was supposed to be a rigorously nonpartisan crowd.

To a certain extent, it *was* a nonpartisan crowd, in the sense that since probably 80 percent of it was Democratic, they hated Nate and Edward equally. There were politicians from Queens clustered in a gaggle, and I heard one silver-haired, paunchy assemblyman say to the Queens County Democratic chairman, "Hey, I wouldn't vote for either of these guys if you paid me a million bucks." Then he paused and said, "Weeeeeeel, maybe!" And they all cracked up, slapping each other's backs, exhaling great clouds of cigar smoke.

Over there was a table filled with some of the national reporters who had swept through once already. They were back for what promised to be one of the defining events of the campaign. They looked vaguely excited, though a little inured to the season's pivotal event, having seen it all so many times before.

Bald and puffing waiters were squabbling with diners who demanded something edible, something recognizable, something other than this southern junk. They simply came back and poured coffee in big mean glops that rocked up the sides of the cups and onto the white tablecloths.

The stage was awsome, the big green banner of the *Post* dwarfing the twin podiums set up there. Lighting engineers were twirling knobs, and the podiums came in and out of focus. The room was filling up, and there was a din rising and taking on life. I saw Jim Surrette, Nate's good ol' boy press secretary, cutting up with some of his chums in the press corps. Surrette was a good guy, but he was just *such* a Republican. There were lime-green pants in his closet for sure, though he exuded a sort of boozy jadedness. He was no doubt predicting the particular manner of Edward's quite likely demise. But I thought we had 'em.

Clutching my arm now was a guy who looked familiar. Yes, it was

Lazlo Fortescu, and he was all solicitude about Edward's condition. "Is he loose, Charles? Is he feeling up to this?" he whispered confidentially. He addressed me so familiarly that I had to remind myself I had never met him. I knew there had been some kind of spat last week between him and Annie. She had gone to his house for dinner but had been back moping at Edward's at a surprisingly early hour. So long as she lived in Edward's extra bedroom, we had no real worries about her and this handsome lecher. Edward kept tabs.

Lazlo had a broad, cruel, confident face. He had started raising money for Edward, though we saw the gesture as being something he was doing to get in good with Annie. Or maybe something more. Uh oh. I was beginning to recognize the symptoms. Yeah, you could see it in the uncustomary deference, the sudden softening of confidence. It wasn't just a hard-on for my sister that he had, it was a crush on the Daley family. My uncles used to call them Jock Sniffers, these admirers who would hang out with them on the racing circuit, picking up tabs as the price for being in on the glow. Later we more politely pegged the species, dubbing them Daleyophiles. It was cruel to make fun of people who simply liked your family, even if at times it was tough to see which of the family's myths they had bought into. But it was surprising to find the disease in this feared developer.

"Edward's feeling fine," I said to Lazlo. "It's nice meeting you," I added politely, my eyes sweeping the room for Wolfy.

"And Annie, is she here?" He asked this in a matter-of-fact manner that somehow offended me.

"Yessir, but she's with her boyfriend and a chaperone." I wanted to add, "And a contingent of Marines and Immigration officers." No reason to encourage him.

A paparazzi's flash went off, and I knew instinctively that it had to be Fred MacDonnough from the *Village Voice,* since his shtick was to photograph people talking to each other at public events, the better to later illustrate muckraking tales of venality.

It was getting time for the show to go on and still no sign of Wolfy, so I gently made my way through the late-arriving surge to get back to the holding room. I saw a couple of young women whom I recognized as Stanton aides, and they, for some reason, looked panic-stricken. They were talking to each other as if in great fear, though they paused long enough to send hateful glares my way. I walked out through the hideous foyer, which was as crowded as the ballroom inside.

I couldn't find Wolfy, and finding him was important, because
there was no one else who could loosen Edward up. Perhaps we had
overdone the debate preparation, for while Edward had reluctantly
sat down in the green room for something he had termed "silly," it
was a confident candidate who had submitted to it. And two days
later, after going through worst-case questioning, it was a husk, a
humorless, snappish, shaken man who emerged.

The worst thing that could happen on the stage this morning was
for Edward to bristle or get angry. But when I left him to go on my
search, he was utterly uptight. So I needed to find Wolfy, because
Wolf could make him giggle. And Wolfy had gone through enough
competitive situations in his heroic career to know how to get Edward up for this moment. He could get Edward into a charming,
confident frame of mind where he could roll with the punches and
pummel Nate Stanton.

As I was about to step back into the holding room, I saw Tony
Echeveria, from WCBS, whom I had been promising for some weeks
we would allow to film an entire day-in-the-life segment for his Sun-
day-night broadcast. But since this meant keeping the entire staff on
good behavior and faking mock strategy sessions, I had been putting
it off. "It's now or never, Charles," he said with some firmness. His
voice suggested a friendship was about to suffer. He was dapper in
this pale-yellow double-breasted linen suit, and on the ends of his
bushy mustache was the slightest crust of grits. Someone had eaten
that glop, and I was a little surprised it was Tony. I promised him
his day would come soon.

I darkened the doorway to the holding room and was buoyed by
the giggles that crept out from inside. That was a good sign. Inside I
found Wolfy, Annie, and Simon Ford, and they were convulsed with
amusement as Edward stood nervously, his face somewhat flushed,
holding the telephone receiver to his ear.

"What's going on?" I asked. Wolfy looked at me with this deli-
ciously mirthful expression. Simon Ford looked as if he were about
to burst into laughter again, and Annie looked helplessly from Edward to Simon to Wolfy and then back at me. She let out this husky
chortle. Oh, she was getting to be a big girl.

"It's the phone call," Wolfy said as if that were the most obvious
thing in the world. And then I remembered the surprise we'd arranged for Edward. Two weeks previously, former President Nixon
had approached Simon Ford to see if Edward might be interested in

some debating tips, and Simon had jumped at the chance. Nixon had asked Simon because he had not wanted to be rebuffed directly by the candidate who in earlier days had denounced Nixon for being too liberal.

We had thought such a call would give Edward a much-needed lift, and would loosen him up a little. Plus the old man did know the ropes. Instead, as Edward waited for the call to come through, there seemed to be added tension. His teeth were grinding. His face was part flushed, part white with fear. I'd seen kids like this in psychedelic furies at high school, but I never thought I'd see Edward look like that. He glanced over at Wolfy and Wolfy cracked up, and Edward, suddenly near giggles, went, "Cut that out!" And Wolfy did.

Then we heard, "Yes, Mr. President," as Edward snapped to and began to speak to the man who once had been his hero, though he'd been awfully mad at him when he stopped bombing Haiphong. We were utterly silent now, listening to Edward listen. Edward turned to me and gave me a wink, then pointed over to the other side of this garish room where a phone was on a silver table, and taking his suggestion, I went over and gently uncradled the receiver, holding it to my ear.

"Well, sir, I feel all right," Edward said in answer to a question I came in late on. "A little nervous."

"Uh, well let me say, it's okay to be nervous," said the familiar voice over the line. "The other guy's nervous too. Though with Nate Stanton, he's probably overconfident. Probably thinks since he's known as a silver-tongued orator and you look too young to be a senator, he has the upper hand. He doesn't though," Nixon said, and I swear to God he chuckled. Sort of a resigned, knowing chuckle. "But you're not feeling sick or anything."

"No, sir, I'm fine."

"Because that shows. I was sick when I debated Jack Kennedy. I had a fever and a banged-up knee, lost fifteen pounds. And it showed. It matters more how you look, Edward, than what you say."

"Oh, yes, sir."

"Those people who heard that first debate of ours on the radio thought I won it. And I did. But those people who saw it on television said I lost. And I did. Because I looked sick. And I was, you know."

"Yes, sir."

"Terrible temperature. And my knee, banged it on a car door.

That hurt. Hurt like hell. The doctors wanted me to delay the debate, but I never listen to doctors."

"I see," Edward said, and then he turned to Wolfy and Simon and gave them a shrug, like, What is this guy talking about?

"We had Nate Stanton by the balls, you know."

"Sir?"

"During . . . Watergate. We had Nate Stanton. He sat there on the Judiciary Committee like some deacon of the Eastern Establishment. And all that time we knew about his stock trading. John Mitchell wanted to use it, but I said no. Some of the candy-asses on my staff still thought Stanton would vote against impeachment."

"Huh," said Edward.

"You do know about the stock trading, don't you?" Nixon asked with a little frostiness, as if the least we could do is have a campaign organized well enough to have found these sorts of things out.

"Oh, no, we do, Mr. President."

And then Nixon rattled them off. "McDonnell Douglas, Pratt and Whitney, Dow Chemical. And yet he could hold peace vigils with the Reverend Mr. Coffin." Hey, what a memory.

"We're planning on bringing it up later in the campaign, sir."

"Let's think about that for a minute," Nixon said, and he sounded almost joyful, happy to be back in a strategy session over something as important as a primary election.

A head peeked through the door. "Five minutes," it said, and then disappeared.

"Primaries are decided in the final days," Nixon grumped. "But those Republicans who vote in primaries, well, many of them are bluenoses, goo-goo types. And they hate stealing. Normally that would receive the majority of the press. But let me say, this primary seems to be special. And it must be Wolfy Daley. I can see the Punch Sulzbergers and the Kay Grahams, the beautiful people, trying to protect their pal Stanton and planning to screw a real American hero like Wolfy Daley. I saw him win the Indy in 1967. The Indiana primary was pretty dull in 1968. But '67 was a great sports year. The Cards beating the Red Sox. Green Bay in the Super Bowl. Great year, 1967. But the campaign is already being covered like a general election, and the press is fawning all over Stanton. That's the way they are. The beautiful people. They never liked me. I didn't go to a fancy Eastern school and wouldn't go to their Georgetown cocktail parties. Yes, I'd think about going with the attack on this stock business."

"You mean in the debate?" Edward was surprised, and I could see Simon Ford looking over at us, trying to find out what Nixon was saying.

"In the debate," said the former President. "You'll never have better press coverage. Even the national boys will be there. But you have to make sure you look calm when you're on the attack. And above all, Edward, don't be dull. The only thing worse in politics than being wrong is being dull. And . . . that would be a [expletive deleted] mistake."

"Yes, sir, I know that."

"And smile, Edward. Have you shaved?"

"Yes, sir, I have," said Edward with a smile.

"Shave again, and don't let them use that beardstick on you. It makes you look dead. I mean it. Well, good luck to you. I'll be rooting for you, so feel free to call."

And with that Edward placed the phone back into its cradle and, grinning wildly, relaxed as a weekend in Mingeboro, he went to shave again before the debate.

## —— CHAPTER TWENTY ——

So WE FILED OUT of the holding room and made for the great hall. And there was not a single human face in the crowded path up to the stage. Edward raised his arm in victory for a debate that had yet to begin, and while it was in the air, the only part of him people had to grasp on to was his other arm. That arm. The metal arm that protruded from his sleeve.

Such was the magic of the moment, they did not seem offended in the least. For here was the winner, oh, not yet, of the debate. That hadn't happened yet. But without doubt, Edward was the bright young personality of the summer. Edward's ads were on television as heavily as the latest offering from McDonald's, and from this he momentarily had the power of some revered young hotshot jock, some anchorman or Broadway find. And clinging to a wide-eyed Annie, we could but jostle, Wolfy and I, pushing Edward before us to the front of what was by now a very large crowd of people.

But Nate Stanton was a genius, that was clear by now, for he waited until the crowd had gone through its cheer for his challenging nephew, waited until some had said all they wished to say, waited until there was tension again in the room after the cathartic greeting for Edward. Nate waited until we began to wonder if he would even be there, and still he did not come out.

I saw Jim Surrette looking frantically at his watch and then browbeating the two female aides, who clearly didn't have a clue. And as we stood there, in the front of the room, our air of triumph quite palpably being sucked out the door, a rumor began to spread. People began saying that Nate Stanton, the lovable old coot, had just plumb forgotten the debate. He wasn't ducking it; he had simply spent the morning prowling around the garden on the fourth floor of his Gracie Square co-op trying to find the perfect carnation to put in his lapel.

"This is a fucking insult," Simon Ford whispered to Surrette when he wandered nearby with what publicly was a look of chagrin but which up close came across as a smug play at evoking a triumph.

"You're just jealous," Surrette said. "I think you better keep an eye on your candidate."

And it was true. There was Edward at the publisher's table, drinking coffee and, quite clearly, beginning to wilt.

"That son of a bitch," I whispered, and Annie, who was standing next to me, the eyes of Lazlo Fortescu burning from three tables away, said, "Who? Who's a son of a bitch, Charles?"

"Your Uncle Nate."

"*My* Uncle Nate? What, you've disowned him?" she asked with the same good humor she had been displaying during the months she'd been on the campaign. She was still a bit too prissy, but then so was Edward. "I couldn't disown anyone who could pull off *this*," she said.

The crowd began to whimper, to moan, to offer its perplexity to neighbors—"Where the hell is he?"—and then the doors at the back of the hall burst open, and walking backwards, struggling with a busboy or a loony who had grabbed him, backwards through the door came my Uncle Nate Stanton, the senior senator from the great state of New York. He turned, blinked, a pink carnation peeking out from the eyelet of his blue seersucker lapel, his polka-dot bow tie holding up his fleshy double chin, and he went into a quick dip and crunch, as if he were about to break into a frug. Holding both fists in the air, he posed for just a second in the triumph of the fighter who's arrived. And our moment was lost right then. The cameras converged and he walked up the aisle to the cheers of, well, everybody. Us included. 'Cause how could you not cheer such a classy arrival, such a well-timed gesture, such a calculated ploy to increase your opponent's tension. In one master gesture, he had shown himself to be the wily old fox, no matter how much glamour had settled on his challenger. I knew we'd been had when I saw Jim Surrette standing there with his cigarette between his lips, clapping without a single bit of the usual phoniness spread on his Pillsbury dough-boy face.

Nate walked to the stage with applause from every corner. He held his arms in the air when he wasn't shaking the dozens of hands that grasped him. He dipped every few yards in a rhythm that probably had "The Great WASP" rolling in his troubled grave. Here was the sixty-some-year-old senator doing this move like a black cornerback who's just returned an interception forty-seven yards. There was suddenly nothing old about this man, and his seediness, manifest in the wrinkles of his suit, somehow this morning was stylish. So stylish, I wondered how we ever imagined we could challenge him. And if I was thinking that, what was happening to Edward?

What was happening to Edward was that he was rising to the occasion, and in this instance that meant standing there with wholly unforced joy on his mug, clapping his good hand against his pant leg while Nate slowly made his way, almost like a victory lap, toward the publisher's table. When Nate got there and stood in front of Edward, Edward went and did the perfect thing. He took his uncle in his flesh and silver arms and hugged him, and the two rocked with a professional lingering that allowed the still cameras time to break from their pen and move in for the shot. And with that little bit of down-home drama enacted, the crowd went wild. It seemed almost anticlimactic when the two of them, helping each other up the steps, were herded by the panelists onto the stage.

My Uncle Nate stood up there nervously and fiddled with his mike. He looked as if he had never stood before a crowd like this.

My brother Edward rocked on his feet until he found a comfortable spot, and as the crowd quieted down, the *Post*'s new editor in chief, who was moderator for the Main Event, welcomed the audience and the guest debaters. He softly drawled what a pleasure it was to welcome everyone there, most especially "the two most interestin' Republicans in the state," as he went on to introduce the panel.

The three reporters who'd been picked to hurl questions were seated side by side behind a tacky card table, knees underneath a green-and-white tablecloth with the boldly stated logo: "The Post— Are You Getting It Every Day?" There was, first of all, fat Arthur Begelman whom we had the pleasure of taking with us to South Carolina for the funeral of my grandmother not so many months ago. Arthur sat there puffing on his pipe, occasionally remembering to smooth down the sleek little otter of a beard that wrapped his chin.

Next to him was Jane Ross, the pretty and diminutive scourge of City Hall. She was pleasant enough, but she was tough, and a terror near deadline. I'd had phones slammed in my ear, and when I was a reporter at City Hall, I'd suspected she'd stolen my notes once after I was given an exclusive by the mayor. Yet she was charming when she wasn't on a story, and few could hold grudges about her on-deadline fiendishness. I was actually glad she was on the panel, because I had this sneaking suspicion that she had a soft spot for Edward. She seemed to get uncharacteristically enthusiastic at his press conferences, covering his proposals with a rare lack of cynicism.

The third was Steve Athole, the Albany bureau chief and a politician's nightmare. You can guess what his nickname was. He was a skinny, pumped-up terror with thick glasses, a long, angular nose, and a mastery of New York political history that was a marvel of the arcane. I always suspected amphetamines to have aided his productivity. I mean, this guy wrote so many stories a day, whether by himself or in tandem with others I would not have been surprised to one day see a byline, "By Steve Athole and Steve Athole." Besides, when *he* was on deadline, he was more than a little schizzy. He wore Chemistry Club skinny ties and, invariably, the nerd's plastic pencil shield tucked into his polyester shirt. Like Arthur and Jane, he looked eager to get into the questions, though his nervousness made me nervous, and there was this malicious twinkle in his eyes that made me fear what could happen to my brother, to my tiger, to my one-armed candidate who was standing at his podium waiting to go on.

The moderator went over the rules, complete with instructions on the little miner's lighting system that turned from green to yellow when your time was expiring. We half expected sirens to go off when the red light signaled you'd worn out your welcome. Upon the coin toss, with Nate looking for divine assistance and hastily calling "Heads"—which it was—the crowd went silent and waited for the debate of the summer to begin. There weren't any other debates formally scheduled; this might be the only opportunity, other than waving at each other through newspapers and dumping money on ads, for the candidates to give the voters a chance to see them in direct confrontation.

They were supposed to make a three-minute opening statement and then step back, let the other reply, rebut each other quickly, and then yield to the questioners. No sparks were expected from the opener. It was in the next round that the fur would fly.

Nate stood there for a minute and collected his thoughts. The thing I knew we had going for us was the way he looked down his nose when he began to approach the audience. He *literally* would look down his nose. He *pursed his lips*. His pink face looked ghastly, despite the vigor of his entrance.

This was the first time Edward and Uncle Nate had come face-to-face since the previous Thanksgiving when, long after word had surfaced that Edward might challenge him, Nate had been an utter snot at a Mingeboro touch football game. Nate's behavior was all the more boorish in light of his not attending the funeral of our parents, since he was all the way beneath us on a junket to the People's Republic at the time. There he was toasted like a giant of world affairs. Sort of like Nixon. Was that when Edward tipped over the edge and decided to challenge him? When Nate couldn't come back from hobnobbing with the Chicoms in order to attend his own sister's funeral? When Commies treated him like a brother and he couldn't even bury his sister?

Standing up there waiting for the first round, Edward looked utterly benign. He looked like a priest just about ready to consecrate the Body and the Blood. He looked like a steady, if stiff, man of clear accomplishment. You could have told he was a Dewar's doer just by looking at the way he stood there, gazing down at the podium, waiting for the old man who'd won the coin toss to quit futzing around and begin this thing.

Nate looked up with a stern expression, quickly patted down a flyaway orchestra of gray hair he seemed to sense was waving above his brow, and he said in this clipped, Yankee manner, this weird voice and pronunciation scheme that was part Mingeboro, part Jerry Lewis at Oxford, "I'd like to thank the *New York Post* for their hospitality this morning, and to welcome the new owners to New York. A free and vigorous press," he continued, pronouncing "vigorous" as if it rhymed with Toys "R" Us, "is essential to our soul as a society. I invoke the word 'soul' because I fear for our souls when there are those who would by artifice construct an image that somehow they, who have not proved themselves in government, nonetheless are the more serious pro-duct for the voters to pur-chase on election day.

"This goes to the nature of what sort of society we are and, frankly, I submit there are broad questions that must be addressed by the good voters in the Republican Party of New York in the September primary.

"For eighteen years I have served the people of New York in the greatest deliberative body civilization has ever known. When you look back on the nation's history, when you look back two hundred years, the fact that we are at this civilized juncture inspires one's faith in one's Maker. It has been pointed out by those far more learned than am I that two hundred years ago France was a monarchy, Germany a but loosely connected federation of duchies, Russia was ruled by an empress, and Britain had but the barest semblance of nascent democratic institutions. Japan was ruled by a shogun; China, an emperor. Only the United States, with its splendid constitution and bicameral legislature, has survived in the same form of government as it had two centuries ago.

"I mention this for, in spite of our abiding institutions, we're a brash, informal, iconoclastic lot, and sometimes there is a tendency to move impulsively in the democratic equivalent of revolution to whisk some momentarily attractive, glib, and sometimes even dangerous person into office. I trust, ladies and gentlemen, you will look very closely today, in person every bit as much as through the magic prism of your television set, to decide who of the two men in front of you you would choose as your next senator.

"Impulse is actually unhealthy in a situation such as this. The impulse of the electorate is why we have the system of checks and balances that we have, why we have four-year terms for Presidents and six-year terms for senators. Now, it would take very little balance among each of us to determine why my opponent, who I can without the usual euphuistic blather state up front is someone whom I love, is not the person who could best represent our state in the Senate or even our party in the general election. He is someone who, in the forgivable ignorance of youth, does not understand the nuance of keeping world peace, nor the complexity of how our society cares for itself."

He paused for just that instant and looked over at Edward, who was pawing with his left foot ever so slightly at the waxy floor, as if all he wanted was a chance to start punching. As if all he wanted was to trample his opponent.

By now the timekeeper was signaling red. We could see its pink reflection under Nate's chin like a buttercup at sunset. The moderator was looking around him a little helplessly, inveighing with the panelists at this breach of etiquette. He leaned forward and said softly, with this annoyed look on his face, as if someone had dribbled party dip, "Tahm, Senator."

But Nate ignored him and kept on at the mike. "I've been proud to represent the people of this great state because I'm proud of the people of New York. The people of New York have wished to take care of the poor and the elderly, even people in wheelchairs. This is something on which we reached consensus a long time ago. The people of New York, the men and women in this room, long ago recognized the military's tendency toward giantism, and while preserving the jobs of this state, I've tried my best to keep perspective by being certain the generals in the Pentagon had no free hand at the checkout counter."

When he said that I looked across the table at Wolfy, and he was raising his eyebrows too. Up there on the podium, Edward was suddenly furiously writing notes.

"The people of New York have benefited from the federal government I'm afraid my opponent would shut down in some libertarian rush to install his theoretical absolutes as the national doctrine." Nate looked up, as if he thought he had Edward there. "My opponent would put in place his radical plans that are downright scary to hundreds of thousands of Democrats who have, frankly, voted for me in the past, voters whom we need to vote for the Republican candidate if we are not to turn things over to the Democratic demagogue as far to the Left as my opponent in the primary is to the Right.

"I look forward to the debate, and wish in advance to thank the *New York Post* for this generous opportunity for our views to be delineated in a fashion deserving of the electorate."

With that, Uncle Nate stepped back from his lectern, a little pink-faced, but pleased, quite obviously pleased, for he allowed himself the luxury of a smile. And then, when it came time for Edward to step up to his microphone and there was gentle applause rippling from the crowd, Uncle Nate applauded for him too, in the outlandishly wide swipe of a bear ringing some unfortunate hunter's ears.

Boy, these guys sure were polite. But it had never been lost on us what kind of negative advertising we could concoct against our own relative.

Edward stood up there looking more than a little nervous, but he nodded at the panelists, at the moderator, and, a little hesitantly, he leaned into the microphone and gauging its force field, modulating his opening remarks to find its range, he said, "I too would like to thank the *New York Post* for this opportunity. Where else for free could you eat breakfast and get to see a letter-perfect imitation of a Harvard professor lecturing a bunch of recalcitrant freshmen?"

Staggered chuckles swept across the crowd. "I want to thank my Uncle Nate Stanton, our senior senator, for the opportunity he has given me in this debate, and to thank him for the very interesting version of history—and my positions—he just rendered. It's very true that two hundred years ago France was a monarchy. I'm more interested, however, in the fact that only twenty years ago Cuba was, if not a Jeffersonian democracy, at least not a floating aircraft carrier for the Soviet Union with troops fanning across Africa trying to impose Marxism-Leninism. I'm fascinated by the fact that only four months ago the Panama Canal was rightly acknowledged to be in the vital interests of the United States of America and Nate Stanton voted to give that away."

When I saw Edward pointing with his real hand at Uncle Nate, I was suddenly glad that we had put Edward at the podium to Nate's left, because otherwise it would have been Edward's metal arm pointing, and it looked rather too much like a machine-gun barrel for comfort.

"It's true," Edward went on, seemingly taking on confidence, loose as a goose, the model of the comportment that Harry Fox, through incessant coaching with the video monitor, had hoped Edward would become. "The United States is the only country for two hundred years that has had the same form of government. But it's not true that our philosophy of government has remained the same. For in the last few decades, men such as Nate Stanton have forgotten the lesson of the Boston Tea Party. They've forgotten that the great revolution that forged our nation was a fight for freedom, yes. But it was also a fight against unfair taxation, the arrogance of power, a distant capital invoking its will on our people. And, ladies and gentlemen, our relationship to Washington under this President is not unlike our relationship to London under King George III."

Edward paused and looked around the room. "Now I'm not going to subject you to a long history lesson. And I'm even going to stay within the confines of the time that's been allotted, unlike my opponent. But I must tell you what this primary fight is all about. If you believe that Tweedledum is just as good as Tweedledee, then by all means vote for Nate Stanton. But if you believe as I do that this economy can perform without stagflation, and that cutting marginal tax rates will get this economy moving again; if you believe the position of our nation in the world will increase by revitalizing—not scuttling—our navy, our strategic forces, our conventional forces; if you believe that it's time the status quo in Washington was changed, then vote for me. I thank you for your patience at sitting through these history lessons and listening to the senator and me this morning."

He was rewarded with a light sprinkle of applause that swept from back to front, our ringers in the corner whooping and hollering as though they were watching the Rangers stomp the Islanders. And while the moderator was looking at his notes to see what he was supposed to say next, Nate just went right back to his microphone like he'd bought it, he'd paid for it, and he was going to use it. "Let me say that if I were a Harvard professor, Edward, I would give you high marks for style, but I'd probably flunk you for not having learned anything."

There was a sudden wince on the face of the panelists, and they looked at each other as if they smelled something awful. I saw reporters scribble, and the wall of cameras seemed to lean in toward the stage. And as a groan was heard here and there, Uncle Nate, oblivious, went on. "For you actually think the national consensus we've arrived at isn't good enough for your radical band of merry men who would, what, turn over the government to those who think we should spend more on missiles while the poor get crumbs? I've seen your ads; they're slick, and I would probably say e-ffec-tive, if people don't see through the gaping hole in your argument. It's social Darwinism you want. You want to turn the clock back, I must assume, to the glorious days of Herbert Hoover. I fear, maybe I shouldn't use the word 'fear,' no, what the hell, I fear your campaign portends poorly for the party and the system. There's a Luddism to your beliefs, an urge to simplicity I acknowledge is attractive, or would be if you were running for the Senate from Utah. But this is New York, young man, and in a society as complex as this, your oversimplified *laissez-faire* plans for stripping the government will be, I trust, rejected by the voters in the Republican primary, as they most certainly would be in the general election."

Once again, Uncle Nate stepped back from the mike. By this time it was clear that whatever Nate pitched, Edward would hit. A smile played at the ends of Edward's lips, and looking around me, I knew that if it was political theater we were after, we had it, for there was a roomful of people engrossed in the debate, and the panelists hadn't even gotten to the first question.

"I'm glad," said Edward, "that Senator Stanton invoked the Luddites. For those of you who didn't go to Harvard—and I would suspect you are the majority—the Luddites were nineteenth-century Britons who hated progress so much they went around smashing factories and machines. This would be today's equivalent of bombing computer plants in Rochester or in the Silicon Valley. Now, the interesting thing, at least as I see it, is that of the two of us, the one who fears progress is the senator. Of the two of us, the one who wants the status quo to remain is my esteemed opponent, Senator Stanton. Of the two of us, I am not the one who fears the future.

"Senator Stanton says that all our problems are so unimaginably complex only the priesthood currently in place in Washington can run things. They're the only ones sufficiently up on the arcane technicalities to run the country. Bunk. This is a country that was founded on certain self-evident truths. A sixteen-hundred-page tax code, complete with dozens of provisions to help those companies that have jetted Senator Stanton around the country, is not the mark of an advanced civilization. It's the mark of a society that has forgotten some of the simple truths that made us great.

"Senator Stanton would have you believe the complexities of government, which he, of course, has mastered, are necessary for New York's survival. That's bunk too. What New York needs is jobs, jobs, jobs, and Nate Stanton has no more idea how jobs are created than does the man in the moon. And one way to create new jobs is to unshackle the entrepreneurial spirit to encourage new investment. To give an incentive. *Yes,* the notion that New Yorkers need protection from the type of taxes Nate Stanton thinks are the hallmark of an advanced society is a simple notion. But you would have to ask the senator why he thinks the system should stay the same. It ain't working, ladies and gentlemen, and our senator certainly has no solutions to fix it. What is to be done? Not something even more complex, that's for certain. Not just more wealth redistribution, but something simple and obvious like wealth creation. And reducing the share that the government takes of our earnings—the government Nate Stanton is so satisfied with—is the right first step."

And that seemed to be the end of Edward's argument. I thought that other than rambling a little bit, he'd scored the points he needed. The message I heard was that Nate was part of the past, and I wondered what Nate would do to counteract that. But I never expected what came next, never would have expected it in a million years.

"Mr. Moderator, point of per-so-nal privilege!" said Nate thumping his lectern in the way people remembered from those televised Watergate hearings. This was the old Nate Stanton whom America knew, the one who turned absolutely red as he screwed up his sense of outrage before withering some foolhardy witness. But this time he was turning his wrath on my brother, who was standing there nonchalantly, as if he could take it, as if he'd slipped the cookie from the cookie jar into a pocket where it would never be found.

"Point-of-per-so-nal-priv-i-lege! My opponent just stated that the tax code is riddled with exemptions for companies that do what, young man? That jet me all around the country?"

Nate turned to the audience and looked at us for a minute as if he was disappointed in human nature. As if he'd just been mugged by a cherished friend. Then he looked down at the floor and slowly turned toward my brother. "Edward, I have reported every trip on every jet I've taken. In addition to which, I helped write the so-called ethics report we in the Senate must fill out every year. So I resent your outrageous statement, and I demand an apology."

Edward looked at him for a long five seconds.

"You have to be kidding, Nate."

The cameras were panning from one to the other as if this were the finals in the U.S. Open.

"I most certainly am not kidding, Edward."

I saw Jim Surrette look nervous, biting a tiny wedge of nail all the while he kept on with his cigarette. Wolfy was riveted, with a big grin on his face. On the stage, all three panelists had circles for mouths, like fish. Then Edward had this grin on his face and I thought, Oh, oh. I'd seen that look before, and it was when we were in the terminal at Teterboro long ago in the snowstorm, when I'd urged him to be coy and he'd all but announced his candidacy. It was his special what-the-hell look. Geronimo!

"You may have helped write the so-called ethics report, but before you wrote it, you would not have been able truthfully to fill one out. My understanding of the ethics report, Nate, is that you have to list all the stock transactions you make, and that it is frowned upon to make a massive profit on stock whose value has been raised by business with the government. Especially when one's position on a Senate committee would provide inside knowledge of how that stock should trade."

Edward was talking soothingly, intimately, as if there were just the two of them. When of course not only was there a live audience in the hall, there were something like a hundred reporters.

"It's incredible that you would stand there and bring up the ethics report when I know you made hundreds of thousands of dollars in stock in Pratt and Whitney, Dow Chemical, and McDonnell Douglas back in the sixties . . ."

"No!" Nate barked like the most alert guard dog this side of Hell. Behind him, Jane Ross actually did jump up from where she had been mesmerized by Edward. "You, sir . . ." Nate said, as if about to begin a long sentence. But then he moved over to stand about an inch from where Edward stood protecting his ground, calm, almost slack, leaning against his lectern as Nate stood beside him, challenging his space. Nate looked as if he were about to hit him, and this was too much for the still photographers. They broke from their pen in a herd, and in a second, the single second that Nate continued to stand there, a little taller than Edward but now seemingly to tower over him, they lit up the world in a blitzkrieg of flashes. Nate stood there as Edward began to have to fight to keep from grinning. Oh, but you could see he was pleased. "It matters more how you look,"

Nixon had told him, "than what you say." And Edward knew enough by now to know he had just won the debate. And they hadn't even gotten to the first question.

Uncle Nate must've sensed he'd blown it. He visibly shrugged as he made his way back to his lectern and said, "I deny his allegations." Then he was quite saved by the moderater going to the panelists, and the first question from Steve Athole was about revenue sharing or some such thing. You could tell Athole was going to stick to his script.

But throughout the rest of the debate, though they clashed on point after point, all we could think of was the way Nate's losing it would show up on television, in the newspapers, and most especially on the cover of the afternoon's *Post*. Edward was the underdog, Edward was the challenger. But we'd sure scored this morning. Gotcha!

PART FIVE

# ─── CHAPTER ONE ───

"POINT OF PERSONAL PRIVILEGE" resonated from the speakers as multiple images of Nate flashed before my eyes. We were in a television studio near Times Square, standing in front of a bank of monitors as dozens upon dozens of the video Nate loomed in threat against Edward. It was nearly midnight, the week following the debate, and this was a collaborative effort, making the ad that would capitalize on Edward's success when Uncle Nate lost it in public.

Sitting around the studio were the consultants to our campaign, as well as the senior staff. Laurie Krieger was there and so was Uncle Wolfy, but Edward had long ago been invited to leave. We were frightened he would want to tone down the ad that we had planned to be particularly vicious.

We'd taken off, the campaign had taken off, even the polls reflected it. From the interest in the media alone, from the sheer volume of reporters who wanted to travel with us the next day, we knew we were hot, we knew we were viable, and we took to the feeling as if there had never been doubt.

It still would not be easy. You still would have to call Edward a long shot. But as we sat looking at the images of Nate's going out of control, again and again and again, the tape rewinding so we could go back to the precise second when he had begun to lose his cool, there was a good feeling about what we could make of Nate's rare on-air mistake. Now that he had given us the opportunity, it was easy to go for Nate's gut.

"Okay, hit the audio," commanded Harry Fox, his hair wreathed by cigarette smoke.

"Nate Stanton's been a senator for a generation now," said the folksy voice we'd chosen. It had stood out from all the others for the precise gentle wisdom it expressed, for its easy resonance, its familiar tone. The picture on the screen that Harry Fox called up was of a classic Nate Stanton, smiling as he marched in the Saint Patrick's Day parade. The picture froze. Harry spoke into the protruding microphone that rose from the bank of knobs in front of him, and with the high-speed whir of the tape rewinding, we went back to the beginning. I was standing a few feet away, my hand resting in Laurie's. It seemed we had been here a very long time.

"That picture doesn't do it," said Harry. "That's what's wrong. It's too sympathetic."

"Nate Stanton's been a senator for a generation now," the voice a minute later said again as a more serious portrait of Nate, his official portrait, was replicated on the bank of televisions. "A generation in which we've continued to hold the same high ethical standards, the same values," the voice went on in its friendly, utterly benign fashion. Then, with a flick of a switch, Harry made Nate's face suddenly melt, as if a candle had come too close to the videotape.

Immediately the image cut to the debate at the Sheraton with Nate looking indignantly at Edward and pronouncing, "I helped write the so-called ethics report we in the Senate must fill out every year."

The frame froze on Nate and then suddenly cut to Edward's reply. "You may have helped write the so-called ethics report, but before you wrote it, you would not have been able truthfully to fill one out."

Then, in a flash, with the guillotine sound of a paper cutter laying waste to a hundred pages of bond, there was a blowup of the stock-market pages from the *Wall Street Journal* and on the screen was a scroll in white letters of all the stocks Nate had traded for the Stanton Trust, their closing prices, and the profits he'd made. "McDonnell Douglas, Pratt and Whitney, and dozens of other companies that did business with the Defense Department while Nate Stanton sat on the Armed Services Committee were among the stocks that made Nate Stanton rich," said the voice.

"And how does Nate Stanton react when this point is raised?" On the screen once again was the *New York Post* debate, and the wall of videos was frozen on a truly frightening close-up of Nate's face as he leaned in over Edward. The particular camera angle made him look sickly, arrogant, and most of all, guilty. Harry must have combed through an awful lot of footage to find this exact shot. And then came the tag line.

"Isn't it time we had a new generation of leadership?" And with that there was a picture of Edward standing at his lectern all alone as the sound was turned up full to the applause he received at the end of the debate. And Edward stood there with the look of a winner, an honest man, a leader. With the look of the next senator from New York. A different voice, Edward's in fact, said quickly, "Paid for by Edward Daley for the U.S. Senate. A new senator for New York." Cut.

Wolfy sat there nodding. "It's terrific," he said. "Perhaps a little too easy on Nate."

"I like it," said Simon Ford. "It's still rough, but we're on the right track."

Harry Fox lit a cigarette and looked toward me. "You think he'll go for it, Charles?"

"Yeah. I think he probably will," I said, and I stood up. We were on the road in the morning, leaving from Teterboro bright and early, and I had few enough nights with Laurie. And Laurie and I had plans. We were a five-minute taxi ride from the Daley Motorworks town house. "It's a little complicated, a little busy, but I agree with Simon. It's good."

Harry leaned back in the studio chair, pleased with himself. A puff of smoke rose toward the low ceiling of the control room. "I think just maybe we got the bastard."

As Laurie and I made our way toward the studio door, we heard the squeal of the tape rewinding. They were ready to take things once more from the top.

## —— CHAPTER TWO ——

WE LANDED AT ONE of those homely airports that isn't much more than a strip of tar and a little shack, with funny old pay phones and stacked cases of soda pop propping up the porch. The cars were lined up on the runway with their doors open toward the plane, late models borrowed from a dealer, denoting good advance work. Tim Verkhovensky stood grimly with aviator shades reflecting the mid-

August day that whined with insects and the occasional sound of trucks downshifting around the bend on the road that would lead us to the prison.

It was one of those sunny upstate days where the good news was that I wasn't in the city, and the bad news was that I still was hard at work. The heat made the runway swim, and corn prospered in the fields that surrounded the airport. It sure felt like God's country. We were here to see the electric chair.

"You okay?" Verkhovensky whispered in a rare act of solicitousness as I stepped out onto the runway and gave him a high five. Since I was on his case constantly, always wanting reassurance that things in the field—the mechanics of voter turnout—were working half as well as our ads on the air and the coverage in the news, this was either a genuine act of kindness or a willingness to escalate our feud.

"I'm fine," I answered dreamily, distractedly, and then I stepped back into the plane to collect our ragtag band of reporters, who didn't know where we were or much care so long as there was some news that would come out of this upstate sojourn. They had the rootless cosmopolitan's contempt for country living, and the cynic's weariness with political campaigns, though some had begged, *one* had actually begged, for the chance to go out on the road with us. Now that it looked as if Edward might win, the competition for a King Air seat provided us just that tiny bit of leverage.

"Jimmy," said the emerging Edward in the sonorous voice that was so much like our father's it spooked me. He was stepping off the plane, his jacket over his shoulder, tie dangling in the air behind him, as Jimmy Fish slowly made his way toward him in this awful old sports coat, shyly holding out his hand. This was the liberal assemblyman who at the convention had said to Tim Verkhovensky, "Listen, you little right-wing bastard, I'll break your balls!" And now here he was, with his photographer in tow, saying hello to Edward, his new political ally. There was going to be a press conference at the front gate of the prison during which the two would endorse each other in the upcoming primary, now just three weeks away.

Even with our newfound respect, the handwriting on the wall said nicer things about us than some of the reporters on the plane. A Gannett newspaper poll released over the weekend showed Edward trailing Uncle Nate by only six percentage points, with 30 percent of the electorate undecided. Edward had jumped something like eighteen points in the two weeks since the debate. But we kept on hearing all this rubbish about how he was "too conservative."

And so we had taken to the road to collect the endorsements that earlier in the campaign we had publicly discounted as worthless. We went out on the road to the Republican heartland, determined to press the advantage we'd gotten when Uncle Nate was publicly reprimanded for being rattled, to say the least, in the debate.

When the *Village Voice* came out calling Nate a crook, I think it actually helped his campaign. But most of the voters we now talked to remembered the sight of Nate on the stage, looking as if he were about to hit his younger, war-hero nephew. Nate was suddenly caught in a frenzy of explanation. It was a sight to behold. And Edward hadn't yet decided whether or not to put the "ethics" ad on the air.

The cars were ready, a sleek little line of shiny black Oldsmobiles with velveteen seat covers and factory air. We herded the reporters into their van and sped off into the cornfields. Seven miles later we could see the looming wall of the prison set back on a hill. As we got closer, we made out the cluster of local reporters, dispatched from Poughkeepsie, here to see Assemblyman James Rensselaer Fish IV publicly recant his earlier invective against Edward and endorse him for the United States Senate.

They were waiting for us just outside the undramatic gates of the prison—it looked like the entrance to the high school I went to—with their mikes displaying their station's call letters. I was a little disappointed we hadn't been able to draw any of the television stations from faraway Albany, but that had always been a long shot.

The cars pulled up and we all jumped out. Jimmy Fish took a long time hiking up his khaki fishing trousers and smoothing down his grayish hair before smilingly greeting reporters. "Hello, sports fans," he attempted as he walked, a little awkwardly, toward them. But they stood their ground in the shade of the prison wall with hardly a pleasantry among them.

"Edward, a word with you if I may," said Jimmy Fish. He jerked his skinny, angular face to motion Edward to the other side of the car. So while our reporters, the four who were traveling with us, filtered out and blinked up at the prison, Edward and Jimmy Fish were already into a huddle.

"I gotta ask you one thing," said the six-term assemblyman. He was a diminutive fisherman of old but insignificant wealth who had the bug of politics so badly that he was willing to cut deals and live with the tension of public life, all for the fun of going up to Albany and competing in a truly sleazy arena. You figure it out. "Are you really serious about all this tax-cut stuff you got in your ads?"

"Sure I am," said Edward with surprise that there was any doubt. His eyes flashed a little too quickly. His set of jaw and body stance suggested he made few jokes. And it was true. Edward seldom made people laugh intentionally.

"Just wondering, just wondering," Jimmy Fish said with his hands up in mild protest at the way Edward stiffened. "It sounds a little like pie in the sky to me, but if that's your issue, God bless."

With that they turned to face the reporters. Only now this other van came accelerating up the drive. It screeched to a halt so loudly I think it got them nervous in the guard towers, as the sound of forty bolts pushing bullets into barrels reached our ears.

Out stepped this little bushy-haired guy with a portacam on his back, utterly oblivious to what now looked like a distant firing squad peering down on him, us, the sunny day sending the serrated shadow of a few dozen riflemen pointing carbines toward our group.

He didn't seem to have come from a television station. There was no tacky logo on the door.

"Oh, here he is," said Jimmy Fish.

"Who is?" said Edward. "Here who is?" he said with squinting eyes fixed on his new political ally.

"My ad guy. He's terrific. Do you believe this? I have to make an ad for my stupid primary. And I'm being primaried by a little Ripon Society liberal."

Jimmy looked at us with genuine shock. Here he'd been a veteran of the Rockefeller wars with the Conservative Party, always siding with the more moderate candidate. And in this year of all years, when he'd finally made an uneasy peace with the Conservatives— he'd voted for capital punishment for cop killers when it had come up in the Assembly—he was suddenly being primaried by this rich, quality-of-life type whose issues consisted almost entirely of cleaning up the Hudson River and all but shutting down the prisons that were the county's livelihood. And this meant that if Jimmy Fish wasn't to be wiped out in the cross fire between Nate's moderates and Edward's right-wing crazies, he had to get off the stick and side with Edward. Jimmy was enough of a pol to do what was necessary to stave off the challenge, but you could see that it puzzled him, this switch in circumstances.

So he went through the endorsement, with the things that tied Edward and Jimmy together stressed over the things that divided them. At one point Edward balked at the recitation of their respective positions on everything from abortion to xenophobia and he got a little hot under the collar. I hovered near to keep him calm, even using my hands to motion as if I were pushing down a mattress on an imaginary bed in a slow, exaggerated manner.

When the news availability was over, the radio reporters slung their recorders over their shoulders and made for their cars. I thought it was a funny gesture, though no one else seemed to get it, then when we came to the door that would let us into the huge old prison, Edward waited until our traveling reporters caught up with us and, opening the door for them, he very politely said, "After you."

## —— CHAPTER THREE ——

I THOUGHT SAMANTHA SANCHEZ of the *New York Daily News* would pass out when the door clanged shut behind her. Her eyes rolled up and she grasped my arm for just a second. I kind of liked that. Because I didn't like being here any more than she did.

The warden, a jolly man who did not seem cut out for the job, was jabbering to Edward about the rehabilitative powers of hard work as eight of us, including the one-man advertising agency with his portacam on his back, followed them down the well-swabbed hallway.

We were here because I had insisted that Edward, before he started calling for the death penalty for juvenile jaywalkers, at least see the way Official Death would be delivered. Considering the funerals I'd been to in the last year, this was something I did not wish him to be cavalier about. Plus it made a great media event.

But we were here as well as part of our deal with Jimmy Fish, who had cut a separate deal with the governor. The governor had no wish for another problematic Democrat in the Assembly, and even less for an attractive liberal Republican, and he was quietly pulling every string to get Jimmy reelected. If that included letting Jimmy stand next to Edward in front of the electric chair and point behind him with his thumb as if they controlled the voltage, even when the governor had staked his liberal reputation on vetoing the use of the hot seat, so be it. The governor was a decisive man who knew how to make a two-cushion shot.

But Samantha Sanchez was queasy and I can't say I was all that much better. I have troubles enough with tunnels and bridges, but prisons are in a different league, and in this case, it seemed we were twenty thousand leagues under the sea. "Yeee," I said to her with my neck constricted and a rigor-mortis grin flashing on my face. "Aaaaah" came her equally distressed reply.

She was young and new on the beat, having been called up from City Hall to do a Senate primary her editors had not expected they would ever have the need to cover. She and I had a number of friends in common from my *Downtown News* days.

I liked Samantha being the reporter covering us for the *Daily News*, because she would be able to get only about four hundred words into the largest-circulation tabloid in the city, and such was her knowledge of Republican primary politics that about one-quarter of those words would consist of either Edward or me putting our spin on things. So long as she was traveling with us, we were allowed to be the Sherpas. The wit in our quotes, we implied, could carry her to the top. And she should trust our interpretation, because we knew more about politics than she did. We could rebut any of the charges Uncle Nate or Uncle Ethan made, though they were clearly on the defense these days.

Arthur Begelman from the *Post* was quite typically bitching about everything: about having to be here, about the food on the plane—he claimed he was on a diet, all the while he mauled the sandwich tray—and most especially about Edward. Those two just weren't suited to each other, though Edward went out of his way—some would call him patronizing—to make sure he was polite, to make sure Arthur got his message. Arthur was a dialectical materialist, a flat-out Commie if the truth be told, and I was told his copy tended to be completely reworked by the desk. Thank Heaven.

Arthur had just come off the road with Uncle Nate, who by now actually was campaigning, showing off the pork he'd delivered a particular upstate city, trying to invoke good feelings by releasing tally sheets covering various industries to show how many New York jobs had been created through his efforts. Nate tried to ignore Edward except where he could slam him, though never by name. The reports I'd gotten from our spies said that Arthur was as much of a pain to Jim Surrette and to Nate as he was to me and Edward, and there was a certain relief in that, a certain expression of democracy. We were made equally miserable by him.

Aubron Powell of the *Times* was with us and he turned out to be something of a treat. He was a tad pretentious, a tall, thin man who dressed in these double-breasted suits and Turnbull and Asser shirts with bright paisley ties, but he certainly kept Edward amused. He was the one reporter I knew who seemed to grasp how historic it would be if Edward defeated Uncle Nate by bashing him from the Right, all the while running a campaign based on economic growth through tax cuts. Aubron had covered the most recent presidential primaries and he returned from them with this glint of understanding in his eye, through he slurred his words after lunch sometimes. It was Aubron who had written in "The Week in Review" that the success of Edward's campaign, coupled with the recent victory of Prop 13 in California, signaled a significant development in American politics, with taxes becoming a major political issue.

Aubron was a little tough on his colleagues, sometimes laughing out loud at stupid questions. He didn't care whether he hurt the feelings of the upstate reporters who nervously questioned Edward with an eye on their city-slicker competition, or whether he was snickering at the chief political reporter for the *Post* or the *News*. His inability to put up with bullshit from other reporters, his total lack of collegial politesse, endeared him to Edward, who tended to go off on his most lucid flights with Aubron. They were both snobs who were students of populism. And this worked to our advantage, for it was Aubron's coverage of Edward's proposals that set off nibbles from the networks, op eds in the *Journal,* and liberated the race by bringing the issues, and not just the crazy personalities, to national prominence. It was after one of Aubron's better pieces that former California governor Ronald Reagan began to request our campaign material.

I was glad Aubron was on the road with us, because he was one reporter you could talk to about something other than the horse races or the Yankees, and most importantly, because he genuinely challenged the candidate.

Quiet Charlie Sullivan was here from the *Buffalo Courier-Express*, and he was going to do a big Sunday scene-setter for the final weeks of the campaign. He was a tweedy, somewhat gruff guy with short graying hair and a penchant for Wallabees who happened to write vividly and with absolute fairness. He would gently grill us on who was in the room when certain decisions were made, and the next week we would read an almost novelistic account of that particular meeting. I liked him. He could get a seat on our plane anytime.

I still felt as if we were in some cloying school building, and then there they were: prisoners. We passed through the next clicking lock in our descent, and we pushed into their midst, their depth, their world. The cons bounced against the periphery of our vision like predators in an underwater dream. Samantha was clinging to me and I longed for Laurie, whom I would see again that night, though it wasn't soon enough. I wanted outta there.

"Uh, Edward?" I said as we continued to walk into a world of milling maximum-security prisoners. This prison was the end of the line for those criminals who had gotten their mugs on the cover of the *New York Post*. Its farm league was the Tombs. "I think I've changed my mind about being here." But Edward walked on smilingly, confidently, and I was left to mutter. The guy with the portacam now turned on his light and he looked like a miner about to enter the depths.

We moved from this dark corridor around a corner where we could see through the bars to the prison yard, and it was as advertised: a couple of guys sitting around looking conspiratorial, a few shooting hoops, the dazed and the idle sunning their massive bodies. Over there were prisoners lifting weights, and if they could not leave the prison, they seemed determined to make their bodies *resemble* the prison; they could pump iron until they looked as though, if they huffed and puffed, then surely they could blow the house down. But then a curious thing happened, something I thought about for days afterwards.

A number of prisoners took notice of Edward, of our little entourage, of this fellow with the portacam, and most especially of Samantha. She'd thrown all journalistic bravery to the wind as she sought, in the inverse of these bodybuilders, to make herself as small as possible. But here were these guys pointing to us from the yard, the schools of criminals still swimming by but now slowing down to look, dull eyes sweeping from side to side.

"Hey, Edward Daley, man. Yo!" yelled one smiling guy as the entire yard froze to look at us. "Fuck. What are you doin' here? You're a celebrity!" And with that, a group of them began to laugh and sort of wander over to us.

"Oh, Jesus, what do we do now?" said Samantha, and the bushy-haired cameraman began to film as Jimmy Fish made certain he was standing next to Edward for the confrontation. The warden looked a tad worried, a trifle concerned, as if one of his children had just thrown mashed potatoes onto the carpet. We could see him nod to the men in the towers and to this little security brigade that so blended in with the prisoners it was tough to tell them apart.

Aubron Powell and Charlie Sullivan were taking notes, while Arthur Begelman stared on bemused, though I thought I could hear him curse me for not having allowed a *Post* photographer along for the ride.

And there they were, emissaries from Hades, and they were smiling and going, "Sheee-it, man, what brings you here?" with these big gap-toothed grins on their faces.

"Yeah," said one smiling guy who was six feet by six feet of solid land mass. He looked like a map of Siberia, or else like the rock of Gibraltar. "You getting thrown in jail, man?"

I have never, before or since, so understood the power of celebrity, nor of television's trick mirror effect. I never before so understood television's role not only in providing fame, but at the same time in declawing it. For here was Edward, who had been on at seven hundred fifty gross rating points for months, airing some really tough crime spots. He'd threatened to use the Navy to blockade our own coast if that's what it took to stop drug traffickers. He'd used thirty-second spots to talk about "law and order" so much we began to get slammed for it by *Newsday*. They claimed to catch an unsavory whiff of the right wing.

And now we were in the midst of hardened criminals who just wanted to come and gawk, as if we were the plumed cockatoos in this particular zoo.

All my life my family had been notorious, the public's opinion subject to the ebb and flow of our success. Yet Edward now was heavily on television with an *effort* to cause an affront to this particular group of people, and all they wanted to do was jive with him.

Of course I should have realized that a great deal of their day was spent parked in front of the television set—what other legal anesthetic did they have? But I never thought that a bunch of murderers and rapists would ask my older brother for his autograph, after he'd gone out of his way to insult them.

But here they were, chuckling and kidding, and Edward stood there, a little rigid, but game. He looked like the good-natured first lieutenant dealing with the soldiers fate had placed in his command. Edward was cool and it did not go unnoticed. Jimmy Fish, however, knew that being in a landing party greeted like Cortez before the Aztecs was not quite the footage he wished to pay for, so he waved away his cameraman.

That's when a guy we later found out was in for life—for having raped and murdered a nun—pulled himself up to his full six feet nine and said, in this nearly incomprehensible fashion, "How come you like the deaf penalty?"

Edward was under the scrutiny of perhaps six or seven hundred prisoners who were in the yard or hanging around the cellblocks. They were pressed around the corridors, in a semicircle behind him. There were faces pressed against bars. We were surrounded, Kemo Sabe. And Edward stood up to him and said, "I think that someone who cold-bloodedly takes the lives of innocent people forfeits his right to live." Oh, great, Edward.

He just stood underneath the big guy and said that in this deliberate fashion until the guy blinked and stepped back. "I thought you was going to say that," he said and then sort of grinned. A number of us exhaled and a number of the prisoners laughed. And with that we began to walk away, Samantha breathing normally again, Aubron Powell scribbling as he walked. We headed down a row of cells the warden wished to show off, the flicker of television sets jumping out and prisoners lying groggily on bunks even as we looked in.

We ascended a wide spiral staircase that overlooked the prison yard and all the dusty pockets of loafing and activity. We were on our way to see the electric chair.

It was a pretty shabby agent of death. It sat stark, for years unused, with rows of witnesses' seats in front of it looking as if they'd been uprooted from the chapel of some outlandish fundamentalist religion.

I was still a little shaken by the confrontation in the yard. There was something really bothering me now. There was something that didn't sit right, and it wasn't the electric chair per se. It wasn't the perverse genius of making the holding cell for the condemned man's last night the only cell in the prison that had windows looking out, so he could be face-to-face with God's green earth. So he could see what else his Maker had made as he prepared to meet Him. (How cruel? How unusual?)

What got me was not the vision of those men lying in bed while the TV sets blared and the hot afternoon arrived secondhand on the cellblock floor. They looked drugged by the time that lay upon them. It was just perverse that their time was so amorphous when their days were theoretically numbered.

It was the fact that the guards were listening to the radio, and here on death row, I swear to God, came a teenage Mick Jagger insisting that "time, time, time is on my side." Yes, it is.

But not on ours. There were only three weeks left in the campaign, and I wanted to peer over the shoulders of the reporters who would spend almost every waking hour with us to see what they were writing. I wanted to see what we got off for good behavior.

## —— CHAPTER FOUR ——

THE CARS WERE LINED up and set to take off as we breathlessly burst into freedom. I think Samantha Sanchez actually did kiss the ground. Edward and Jimmy Fish walked toward the cars as if they were the best of buds, as if they'd been allies for years, though their alliance was an uneasy one at best. The cameraman looked disappointed, though with some skillful editing, there was one shot—the prisoners marching toward us—that could be put to effective use. If only there was a way to wipe the grins off their faces.

There was a dusty phone booth just outside the prison door, I guess where escapees could call for a cab or pizza or something. Since Edward and Jimmy were talking, and Tim Verkhovensky sidled up to me to ask how it had gone, I did not queue up with the others for a chance to check in with the office. I wish I had.

Arthur Begelman squeezed into the booth, and if he'd lost his balance, that thing would have toppled. I should have known we were in trouble from the grunts of delight he uttered. "Ha!" he exclaimed. "Ooooooh!" he winced happily. He sounded as if he were being served a fourteen-course Szechwan dinner. I didn't pay attention, however, because my thoughts were on the prison, the pleasant day, the rally that awaited us in Syracuse.

I felt a little blindsided, my reverie quite snapped, as Arthur called, no, he fairly commanded that Edward end his discussion with Jimmy to come and face the press.

"Edward," he called, as though Edward were a schoolchild playing too near the highway. Edward looked up slowly, with the perfect amount of upper-class insolence. He instinctively exuded his right to ignore the command of someone who dressed and behaved like Arthur.

By now the other reporters knew that Arthur had some information, so they pressed forward as if they were the offensive line come out of the huddle, though only one of them knew the play. This would be an audible. I noticed Jimmy Fish was enough of a pro to make good his escape, and he drove away in the van with his cameraman.

"What's up, Arthur?" Edward asked with just the slightest edge of wariness. He'd come a long way as a candidate; six months ago he would have exhibited a certain hostility based on fear. Now he had this slight bit of playfulness about him, a show-me-what-you-got taunt that was cocky and at the same time attractive.

We were standing in the shadow of the prison we'd just left, and all eyes were on Arthur, and, boy, did he like that.

"Senator Stanton held a news conference in Manhattan this afternoon." Arthur actually took out his pipe and slowly lit it before going on. "He says [puff, puff] that you used the funds raised by Vietnam Vets for Victory for two years as your income, and never declared any of it on your income taxes. How do you plead?"

The reporters were switching on their microcassettes and holding them to Edward's face. All of them looked accusatory, Charlie Sullivan less than the others, for his was a nearly perpetually benign presence. The skeptical look on Aubron Powell's face was nonjudgmental, even magisterial, as befit the impartiality expected of the Paper of Record. There was a haughtiness there, though, that made even me wonder for just a second whether Edward might be guilty.

Edward blinked for just a few seconds while he quickly gathered his thoughts. "That is the statement of a desperate man. It's sad, well, it's especially disappointing that a man in public life as long as Senator Stanton has been would stoop to such a charge. He must be seeing something in his polling that suggests he's in a slide."

"Yeah, but is it true?" Samantha Sanchez wanted to know. She eagerly wanted to know. Our chumminess with her wasn't going to get us anywhere in the face of genuine news.

"It is utter bog rot," Edward said, pronouncing every syllable precisely. "Nothing could be further from the truth. In fact, I underwrote VVV. I personally paid every bill we didn't have the funds for. Now, I paid myself back, mind you, for some of the expenses. But I'll tell you what I'll do. I'll take the extraordinary step of going back all those years and I'll release my income taxes to you. And, while I do that, I'm going to challenge Nate Stanton to release his income-tax returns for the years 1964, 1965, and 1966. I think the voters have a right to know what kind of insider trading he was involved in."

I was just about to applaud him for the swiftness of that move, when Aubron Powell bored in. "The issue is whether or not the money you say you were paying yourself back was declared."

"Every penny of it, Aubron. Every plugged nickel, every stinking dime. And I'm going to the lengths of actually handing over to you the returns from the years I was chairman of the triple V. His charge, my opponent's charge, has no basis in fact. It's a diversionary tactic at the very best! In fact, the mere fact that he's making this charge, which has no validity, suggests to me he knows this race has turned around and that he is in deep, deep trouble."

There were a few more skirmishes along this theme, but Edward had answered their questions. He'd actually made pretty good copy, certainly relegating anything that happened in the prison to the fourteenth graph of every story. And I hoped he was right about the income taxes not revealing anything, though with Edward you sometimes got the feeling that from fourth grade on he had lived his life with an eye to a political future.

Edward had scored a few points here, not least because any attack by the better-known incumbent provided him a chance to counterpunch. And because he'd stuck to the journalistic convention of going to some lengths to disprove the charge against him, and then had gone on the offensive. The headlines the next day would probably be a wash, charge and countercharge. But the substance of the story, I felt certain, would favor us.

Yet there was to be an element of mystery in the next day's copy, for when Edward used the little pay phone to check in with the office, he spent something like fifteen huddled minutes talking to our cousin Owen. And when he stepped out of the phone booth, he was visibly shaken. I mean, all you had to do was look at him to see something was wrong. The next day, the papers would reveal that after being questioned on the finances of Vietnam Vets for Victory, Edward had canceled the flight from the prison to Syracuse, and had given for an explanation only that he had to return to the city for "personal reasons." That would not look good.

In the car delivering us to the plane I turned and stared at him in the backseat and waited for him to tell me what was wrong. "It's Daley Motorworks," he said as if in a deep depression. "The banks gave us a notice of foreclosure. It's imminent. Christ, just before the election. And you know what this means," he said, and he was wrong. I didn't. "There's no place left to turn but to that asshole Lazlo Fortescu. He's the only one now who'll bail us out."

I turned away from him as the car shot past the cornfields. The corn was as high as the Oldsmobile's aerial. I didn't want to look back at him; I didn't want to think. I wanted to get the image of a triumphant Lazlo out of my mind. I shuddered to think of Annie.

That's when Edward said, "Hey, Charles." I turned to look at him. "There's some good news too," he said with this really kind smile.

"What's that?" I asked with hopes very low indeed.

"Sam's home."

# ⸻ CHAPTER FIVE ⸻

SAM WAS BACK! MY brother was back! Back because the statute of
limitations had run out and his life as a fugitive could end. Back
because he missed us and he wanted to come home. That was worth
just a little break, just a tiny respite from the pressures of a primary
campaign. Sam was back, bringing his wife and children with him.

We each spent a day taking them on tours. It was my lucky task to
briefly split from work and climb to the top of the Statue of Liberty.
Sam's boy, Charlie, who was named after me, proved to be a rugged
little kid. When we finished with Miss Liberty, he insisted we take
him to the Bowery "to see Kojak roust the bums." That's what he
said. He was eight.

Claire, Sam's wife, was wearied by New York far more than she
was by her children, among whom I included Sam. Her children she
could deal with, but every moment in Manhattan justified her desire
that they go back to Oregon. Claire was ever so slightly cold, and
with her short black hair pushed back severely, clothes slovenly hip,
she fit right in in Soho. Her eyes were radiant and her cheekbones
were such that she could have walked into any modeling agency in
town and walked out with assignments. It was obvious what Sam saw
in her when he married her nine years before, Sam who followed
her around the way Charlie and little Lisa did.

Just being with them for a morning made me wonder about
Sam's imperfect magic. For all he'd been a fuck-up, he was the only
one in my immediate family who was simple enough to enjoy a conventional life relatively free of irony. Aside from his legal situation,
of course.

That night he had to leave us for a while to attend to some lawyerly
business having to do with the statute of limitations. So after he
departed, Claire and I went to the Public Theater to see Laurie on
the stage. She liked Laurie, but she didn't like the play. It was "de-
pressing." The kids were left with the Grecos, and when we returned, we spun the dial of the TV set in my little apartment in the
building, trying to find the new negative ads Uncle Nate had begun
to air.

Laurie came over later and she brought Camille. Sam came back, his visit uneventful, though he wouldn't talk about it other than to say that his problems were over, it was all worked out. So we sat up to celebrate, all of us but Laurie drinking wine I'd looted from the closet I had stumbled upon during my tour of the building.

I got this, I don't know, *glow* from this little gathering that made me wonder if this is what normal families were like. I had no basis for comparison, and maybe I'm romanticizing normalcy, but it sure felt good. The kids at last were sleeping upstairs in what once had been the Map Room for our far-flung empire. My brother was sitting with his untroubled look on his suntanned face, his healthy wife woozy and ever so slightly sanguine in our midst. I wanted to hold that feeling forever.

In a strange way, I found myself a little jealous of my sweet older brother. He had a wife and children, and in a family as large as ours, that's a virtuous reward you were expected to yearn for. Worse, he was so damned cheery. Of all of us, he was the one given to unreflective happiness. Of all of us, he was the least self-absorbed. And that seemed to pay. Which was contrary to my worldview.

Oh, sure, there was trouble when he had been a teenager at home. He wasn't very athletic. He never got good grades, as the rest of us did. He got sucked into some vicious spirals when the drugs he gobbled turned on him and there wasn't anyplace to hide. Maybe he wasn't tough, but who needed toughness when Claire was around. And he was a genetically distinguished mechanical fucking whiz.

Laurie and Camille and I sat up with Sam and Claire. Outside, Park Avenue was dead; and inside, the black-and-white television made shadows on the walls as we sat there giggling into the night. Sam was back.

## ⸻ **CHAPTER SIX** ⸻

OUR ETHICS AD WENT on the air and it caused an immediate stir. "Sleazy tactics," pronounced *Newsday,* and the *New York Times* denounced it so harshly that I was reminded of Uncle Ethan's warning about Nate's friends in high places. It was generally agreed that the ad was effective, but some of Edward's tonier acquaintances called to question whether it conformed to the Marquis of Queensberry's rules. "When somebody pisses on you," I heard Edward tell one complainer over the phone, "you don't call it rain." I suppose we hadn't needed to worry about Edward's resolve.

There were times when my own was in doubt, however, times when I wondered whether it was worth it, this war with the Stantons. I'd lost my dog, our family fortunes seemed permanently in decline, and never again would peace reign in Mingeboro, unless, of course, Blake drowned off the coast of Maine. But then there were times when I knew why we were doing this and it all seemed worth it.

Like that night we spent upstate when Edward debated the chair. Nothing electric, just an ordinary chair. It was a Friday, a day when Edward had been battered at an editorial board meeting for indulging in what some pompous little moralist termed a smear campaign against Nate Stanton. The guy treated Nate as if he were a saint and Edward as if he were a monster. I could see it had gotten to Edward a bit, not enough that it would make him pull the ad, but enough to make him pull his punches at a news availability we had at a high school later in the day. It was Oneonta or Oswego or some such place that resembled Iowa more than it resembled New York City. I know where it was. It was Pinders Corners. We were in the town because there was a debate scheduled at the county fair, and since Nate had long since declared he wouldn't be there, and because the county executive was a Daley supporter, it had been arranged for Edward to debate an empty chair.

Edward stood on a platform built over the pitcher's mound of one of two adjoining baseball fields. The sun was going down and a crowd of about seventy-five sat sullenly in the bleachers. In the other field a local Little League team was getting trounced, but these seventy-five townspeople soon appeared riveted as Edward held forth on a variety of issues that would certainly have come up had there actually been another debate with Nate.

The light was golden and the air was fragrant with the smell of the fields, and I sat there mooning at the vision of my brother airing his views before these citizens, the squeal of the young ballplayers in the small-town Norman Rockwell background. I audibly sighed. *This* was what we were doing this for. This made it all worthwhile. I felt pretty good about things until the very end, as we were leaving, when this old man came up to shake Edward's hand and told him that in his opinion there was no question about it. The chair had won the debate.

## ── CHAPTER SEVEN ──

WE WERE IN THE season of county fairs, and by coincidence, through a scheduling commitment that had to have been preordained, we found ourselves in Mingeboro on a Saturday night after Edward had spoken in nearby Rhinebeck. Sam had come along to see for the first time his older brother campaign, and so Claire brought the kids to the Dutchess County Fair. The kids seemed more interested in the elephants, in the reptile garden, in the octopus and the Ferris wheel than in their Uncle Edward's speech to indifferent farmers in their cleanest overalls. Afterwards, we all went home, and as I stood out on the deck that overlooked the lake, sizzling steaks for the family, my sister Betsy complained that we weren't being tough enough on Nate.

"This campaign, near as I can figure it, has been way too soft on the old buzzard. I thought we were going to go negative."

Everyone's a critic when you work in politics. "What do you think having an ad on the air calling Nate a crook is? A testimonial?"

"All I know is that Nate's particularly vulnerable on one thing, and that's his drinking. And from where I sit—granted, I haven't been following the campaign all that closely—you've been letting him off lightly."

"Wow. The Daleys attacking the Stantons for being drunks. That would be interesting. Anyway, the *New York Times* had an editorial about our campaign today entitled 'Knock It Off, Guys,' and you think we should be tougher. Is this what you're like on Wall Street?"

"Absolutely," she said without the slightest trace of humor intended.

"Hey, kids," said Sam as he stepped barefoot in khakis onto the deck. "Can I help, Charles? I always used to cook the steaks when we were kids."

"Somehow over the years you were replaced, Sam," I said, flipping steaks in this great flaming wave.

"You know Claire's vegetarian, don't you?"

"Yeah, Sam," Betsy said, "she and Annie and I are having our own salad."

"Okay," he said and then stepped off the deck and began to wander toward the cliff where you could see across the lake to the sun going down between Mount Targa and the next ridge of the Berkshires. It just dropped like a coin rolling into a slot. The cliff had been Sam's favorite place to sit and get stoned.

Edward stepped out of the living room and onto the deck without benefit of his shirt or artificial arm. He looked a little unbalanced, but an hour before, on this rare Saturday afternoon not spent out on the road, he'd just destroyed me on the tennis court. It was slightly awkward watching that one-handed serve, but he still got velocity on the thing. And spin? Amazing spin control. "What's up?" he said distractedly before walking around the corner of the house out to the driveway. You never would have suspected this skinny, one-armed guy had seventeen paid staff members and scores of volunteers trying to elect him to the most exclusive club in America. Or that he'd so far spent more than two million dollars of his own money, money he'd earned.

"Poor guy," I said to Betsy.

"How do you figure?" she asked.

"Ah, you know, having to be a candidate and all."

Seconds later Edward came walking back with this loud, for him, Hawaiian shirt on. The thing practically hummed "Pipeline." He had

had the shirt for years; a relic of those months he'd spent in the VA hospital near Pearl Harbor. He kept it in the Porsche he used for Mingeboro transportation.

With the touch of sunburn he'd picked up on the tennis court, he looked about as relaxed as I'd seen him in months. It had been a rough week, with more than its fair share of the usual campaign bothers. Nate's cheap accusation about Vietnam Vets for Victory had been a time-consuming distraction, and worse, Nate seemed to be making some inroads in the Nassau County Republican organization we had thought was ours, lock, stock, and phone banks.

We found things were not all they seemed when Edward's campaign helicopter had landed at Jones Beach the previous Saturday afternoon. The plan, which we had cleared with the party apparatus, called for him to campaign among the dunes and then lift off for Long Beach. But no more than thirty seconds after the chopper touched down in this swirling sandstorm, Nassau County cops were arresting him for trespassing, and somehow they had this photographer from *Newsday* along for the ride. Something was definitely up in GOP headquarters or that never would have happened. I mean, that's what they usually did to the Democrats! This wasn't just duplicity, this was a disaster. I had Tim Verkhovensky, an Island boy, working on it.

On top of that, there was this little problem with the rotation of our spots. We began to suspect something when within days of each other supporters called up complaining from Buffalo, Rochester, and Binghamton. They couldn't make sense of what we were trying to accomplish by having those first ID ads airing all over again. We couldn't either, considering the spots we'd told Harry Fox to put on were "Ethics," "Panama Canal," and both the thirty- and sixty-second versions of "Supply-Side Man." I mean, it made no sense to be on the air with the introductory spots now that polls showed Edward was identified by everyone in the state who was smarter than a corgi. It quickly turned out that some reefer-steeped kid in Harry Fox's office had packed off the wrong ads to the stations. So with much fanfare, we'd sent off a convoy of young volunteers in rented subcompacts, armed with the cassettes of half-inch tape, checks that would buy us a gross amount of gross rating points, and route maps so they could wend their way from the city all the way to Canada, dropping in on every radio and television station between here and the St. Lawrence Seaway. I felt as if we were blessing the Children's Crusade. It was imperative to be on TV.

Now Edward stepped through the door into the gazebo with a beer can in his hand. He leaned back against a deck chair with his feet up on the glass table. Moths began to bounce like toy projectiles against the screen.

Betsy was sitting with a magazine in her lap, her hair drying over the back of the chair. She looked as if she were waiting for her nails to be done. "So how do you like being a candidate, Edward? I mean, now that you've been doing it for a while. I've been wanting to ask you."

"It's okay," he said as if he were reassuring himself. He sipped the frosty lager.

"What do you like about it?" She curled up in her chair as if she were about to get catty. All her life she had teased the boys in the family, Edward most of all.

"Seriously? I like the motion. The activity. And I like arguing," he said with a laugh.

"And what don't you like about it?"

"The same thing." He laughed again. "I don't like *that* much motion. Traveling, even in a private plane—especially in a private plane with Charles and his reporter friends—is exhausting. And I find myself obsessively grooming, you know, spending all this time in bathrooms on the road. Because it's the only time I have to myself!"

"I'm really glad you said that," I said. I'd had to spend an embarrassing amount of time trying to coax him out of airport men's rooms in order to keep the schedule. "I thought it was vanity."

Edward raised his eyebrows and looked at me, and though now Sam came walking back up the path to the house and I could hear Charlie and Lisa playing with Annie and their mother in the kitchen, for some reason this wasn't enough to give me that glow I'd felt the other night in New York. I missed, well, my parents for two, and I'm not certain how weird this is, but I missed Fido almost as much. Fido would have made this perfect even without my parents. I wish Charlie and Lisa could have met him.

"Hey, Edward."

"Hey, Sam."

"Some sunset. You think the family knew what they were doing when they let us buy this place off them?"

Edward laughed. "If the price they charged Dad's Estate is any indication, they knew what they were doing. It may be the only deal in the last five years in which the family showed any business acumen."

Sam sat down between Edward and Betsy, his rightful place in the family order. "Things are pretty bad, huh?"

"Let's not talk about it now, Sam. I am finally, thoroughly, hopefully irrevocably relaxed," said Edward with his head back in an unnatural angle against the top of the pillow on the deck chair. Half his face was washed in the orange light of sunset.

"And in a minute you are also going to be stuffed. Annnn-niiiiieeee!" I called, and in a moment I could see her in the kitchen, her blond hair tied back in a braid, a T-shirt from the Stones' "Some Girls" tour hanging out of her blue jeans. She began to carry out the salad, for the two of us, as the youngest, had always done the work at barbecues.

"Here she is!" said Edward, and Annie came over and messed up his hair after putting the salad on the table. If you did not know they were brother and sister, you would think there was something going on between them. They couldn't keep any of their three arms off each other, ever.

"Tuck your shirt in, Ann," said Betsy.

"No, Betsy, I don't have to tuck my shirt in," she said with resolution, and when she went back into the kitchen to fetch the wine and the rest of our supper, I nodded to Betsy as if to say, I guess she told you.

"Can I help?" asked Sam in a cheery voice.

"No," I said. "You're the guest."

"Well, I'm not exactly a guest, am I?"

"You know what I mean."

Charlie and Lisa were at the screen door that opened from the living room. "Oh, boy!" said my namesake. "Steak!"

"C'mon out, tigers," I said, and there was Claire behind them, a T-shirt tucked into a pair of wondrously ancient jeans. She was marvelously well constructed. We'd all discovered that late this afternoon after returning from the fair when she sat at the pool in a one-piece bathing suit, quietly overshadowing Aunt Melissa, who huffily panicked when all the male attention for once went elsewhere. And the attention was different, too, because Claire was smart.

"Howdy, Claire," I said and she just smiled and quietly pushed her children in front of her. I picked up Lisa and hurled her into the air to her manifest delight. "Uncle Charlie," she squealed.

"Come sit over here," said Betsy to Claire. They had taken to each other as if it were the opening day of high school and they sensed kindredness of spirit.

The family politics here were that Annie and Sam didn't have much to say to each other, partially because they'd barely seen each other since Annie was about six, mostly because Annie was scandalized, or afraid she would be, by Sam. And Annie was clearly uncomfortable around a woman as pretty as Claire who failed to shave under her arms. "Guuross!" was how she put it, but I think there was a spot of jealousy at the way Claire carried herself, and that she was accepted by Betsy.

Betsy and Sam had always been close, having kept up a reasonably steady correspondence, when for me a letter from Sam was like the appearance of some mystical comet. In the time since he'd left I had seen Sam but twice.

The first time was when I went out with my father to rescue Sam from some commune in Mendocino that claimed he owed them money. We met him on the front porch of the commune's main lodge after they had expelled him for "capitalist tendencies." Poor Sam. He even got kicked out of communes, though we suspected this particular one had learned the use of prep-school extortion and were expecting my father to buy Sam's way back in. He didn't, and Sam was awfully sad.

I stayed with him a few days one summer vacation after freshman year in high school. As I recall, he and Claire hadn't been getting along at the time. She was supposed to be off in Portland living at a collective for women, which seemed pretty intimidating, then and now. Months later, when we found out Claire was back and was pregnant with little Charlie, I remember even my mother joining in our long-distance champagne toast, which we accomplished by riding up to the House of Lazarus and all of us shouting into the squawk box.

Now having spent a few days with him, I could safely declare he was a creature not of this family. To begin with, he hadn't the slightest interest in the pop culture we were so obsessed with. He couldn't care less about gossip, not even about us, and had hardly any interest whatsoever in politics.

You added all this up and the one thing for me that was utterly impossible to understand was that Sam's only interest in the family was in our emotional support, in pride in a homestead, a return to which he had long been denied. His interest in Uncle Wolfy centered on talk about engines and aerodynamic designs.

Being with Sam was like being with a relative, oh, not just different from being a brother, but a relative on a different evolutionary scale. And I could not tell whether it was he who had evolved to a higher order or whether we had headed back toward the ooze.

"Great steak, Charles," Sam murmured appreciatively when we began to eat. "And this salad, Annie, well I can't tell you the last time I had a salad this good."

"That's funny, Sam," said Claire. "I made the salad." We all cracked up, Sam's face getting a little red even now as darkness came to match the stillness settling through the pines by the lake.

"Dad!" said little Charlie, and he kept on laughing for a minute after the rest of us had stopped.

"This is the first time all of us have been together since . . ." And then Betsy had to think. "Well, this is the first time we've all been together!" she said.

"Yum yum yum yum yum," said Charlie.

"Quit playing with your food, Charles," said Claire, and I sat bolt upright, and chewed, getting down to business. Oh, she was talking to Charlie.

"So how's your love life, Bets?" asked Sam innocently.

"You don't want to know," she said. She took a quick swig of wine on that one.

He had never been one to have much tact, that much I remembered, so it wasn't surprising that Sam kept on. "No, seriously, you going out with anyone in particular?"

Annie, Edward, and myself silently turned to look at her. "Well, I'm going out with this guy from work. Wade," she said with a smile. "But it's not all that serious. I would have invited him up, but this weekend seemed special."

"I thought you were going to get married to that guy Gordon."

"Sam," I said gently.

But then Betsy went on with mock cheer, "Yeah, but that was before I found out the only way he could get off was by tying me up with nylon cord, Sam. Do you want to know more about it?"

"Nylon cord?"

"Sam!"

So then Sam, diplomat that he was, utterly without shame, turned to Edward and said, "So what's going on with Daley Motorworks? I thought I'd take the kids over there tomorrow and show them around."

"Well, you'd better do it quickly," Edward grumped as he leaned one-armed and beaverlike over an ear of corn. Darkness was now moving in so quickly I couldn't see my brothers' and sisters' faces clearly. The kids were eating quietly, fascinated by the adult talk. I wish we had a dog.

"Things are that bad?"

"We should talk about this later, and at length, Sam," said Edward, who, if you knew Edward, had just all but pleaded to be left alone. Usually Edward was the confrontational type.

"Why, Edward?" Betsy asked. "Are these things to be discussed only by boys?" Annie and Claire sat there silently, but you could see them staring at Edward.

"Look, this is not a happy subject, and this is the first time I've been home in a very long time. But, hey, if this is how you want to spend the evening, what the heck. I'll tell you about it.

"As you know," he began, "the decline of the Daley Motorworks actually began with the Lazarus. There was unbelievable demand for the car, but no way for supply to keep up with demand given our inability to set up a dealer network. Detroit must have been pretty heavy-handed about it, they must have laid down the law, because no General Motors dealership wanted us to compete with the Corvette, and Ford had it in for Grandfather on account of his going independent on them. Remember how the company had to sell the Lazzy that one year through the Abercrombie and Fitch catalog?" We didn't, but we were riveted. I hadn't heard all of this story or thought about any of it for a long time.

Edward leaned back from the table, his dinner now done, spoiled by the questioning that had resulted in this family history, though I thought he actually was digging it. Annie lit a cigarette and we all stared at her until we could sense that she was getting self-conscious.

"The irony," he continued, "is that just at the time Wolfy and Blitz were winning big races, just as the Lazzy was being written about as perhaps the greatest American sports coupe in decades, because we couldn't get them *out*, we began to be viewed as unreliable, and nothing kills the allure of a specialty car so much as an image of unreliability. People don't want a car, no matter how beautiful it is, if they think they aren't going to be able to get parts for it, or if it takes eight months to arrive. And on top of the sense of unreliability that was part of Detroit's active campaign against us, well, Grandfather, as you know, was an erratic financier. And if you recall, at that moment when the Lazzy was hot, Grandfather had disappeared and we didn't know what happened to our money."

Edward sipped his beer and we all stared at him. "That was the beginning of the end, really, of our family business, until eventually we couldn't continue to produce the Lazzy. It wasn't just the family's ongoing fight with the UAW. It was cash flow. It killed us."

"Daley Motorworks was still an independent company," I protested, as I had heard my old man protest a dozen times to reporters who had come to Mingeboro to do pieces on the rise, fall, and modest rise of the Daley Motorworks.

"Yeah," said Edward, "but we were subjected to the whims of the Big Three. Dad had to design things for Detroit, not for us. The dream of putting out our own cars was killed when we couldn't continue with the Lazzy. We were disciplined. We got the back of Detroit's hand for the sin of independence, for the sin of entrepreneurship, for the sin of having challenged big business. But that was better than the situation we have now, where with the complicity of the Stantons, we are about to go broke. I mean truly broke. If I hadn't challenged Nate . . ."

"Edward, that's horseshit."

"It's not, Charles. To be beaten by Detroit is still better than to be broke, which is where we are now, to make a long story short."

"Unless we borrow money," said Betsy.

"From Lazlo," said Annie in the most neutral fashion. You never would have thought, from the way she said that, that Edward, Betsy, and I continually wondered whether Annie had lain naked with that Canuck.

"Wait a minute," said Sam. "How's the fuel injector doing?"

"It's about to come off the assembly line, and we have orders for it. But we're busted," said Edward with some exasperation, "and we'll never fulfill those orders unless we get some cash to get us out of the hole."

But that didn't seem to faze Sam, who was sitting there with a great big grin. "So, the fuel-injector system works, huh?"

"Yeah, but it's a moot point if we don't have the money to get it out of Mingeboro. Why are you so curious about it?"

" 'Cause Dad and I designed that together."

"You're kidding."

"Oh, no, we'd been sending—we sent—each other designs for it right up until he died."

"Dad wrote you?" Betsy asked. In all the years we'd been away to school, I don't think any of us had received a letter from Dad. It was impossible to think of him in the act of writing. When I thought of Dad, I saw a guy with a smock on sitting in the House of Lazarus working through the intricacies of wind-flow dynamics and other aspects of the world he saw that I will never understand. He was lost in this world, and while it was fun communicating with him, it had always been on my initiative. He was an engaging, sad, ultimately impossible guy. To think that he and Sam had a correspondence going—but then Sam lived a little in that same world Dad had, a world where theoretical abstracts became mechanics, oil was blood, and nothing talked back.

"Yeah, we worked together for two years on it, and he even told me about a plan he had for the Lazarus."

"You're kidding, Sam, what was that?" asked Betsy. She was intrigued.

"He wanted to get Ford—he'd actually talked to some of the people he knew from when Grandfather still worked for Ford—to modify a Mustang the way they had the Shelby GT, only this time call it the Mustang Lazarus."

"What a great idea," I intoned. You know, actually it was. It was similar to the marketing plans Edward had had. "So Dad had some surprises right up until his, well, final surprise."

"Yeah, but how did he expect to keep the company afloat?" Edward wanted to know. "He knew the company was going to have rough sledding financially, and that was before the Stantons began using their might to fuck up our credit. He told me that once when we were talking about investment banking houses. It was one of the only pleasant conversations I had with him. I mean, you may have written him letters," Edward said, "but Dad and I hardly spoke."

No one contradicted him; it was Mom, not our father, who liked Edward. Sam now perked up, as if things were so obvious that we were simps. There was a look of surprise on his face, as if he couldn't believe he actually knew the answer to a riddle Betsy and Edward hadn't figured yet.

"He was going to get the money from the Stantons," he said, as if it were the most obvious thing in the world.

"What the hell are you talking about?" I asked, as Edward leaned forward in his chair.

"Yeah," said Edward. "What's this?"

Sam sat there blinking, as if he couldn't figure our puzzlement, as if there was something so obvious anyone could see it. He looked to Claire, but she wasn't much help; she looked just as curious as we did.

"Dad was going to ask the Stantons for our money back."

"What money back?" said Edward with some excitement mixed with exasperation.

"The money Grandfather Daley loaned Nate Stanton after Governor Stanton killed himself. Didn't Dad tell you about this?"

Edward sat at the edge of his seat with his hand outstretched toward Sam, and closing inward, trying to coax him to say more, the same way a ground crew tries to urge an airliner into its dock. "Hold on a second. How much money, Sam, and how do you know this?"

Sam looked as if he were about to cry, he was so frustrated that no one else knew what to him was a long-held fact of life. "The three million dollars Grandfather told me about."

"Told you about when?" I asked, and all of us now leaned as if he were a quarry we were not about to let get away.

"Just before he died. When I was in trouble. Mother and Dad told me I had to turn myself into the police, so I got in touch with Grandfather and asked if I could borrow enough money to get away."

"And what did he tell you? He spoke to you?" asked Betsy.

"Yeah," Sam said with further frustration. "He was speaking again. Well, a little. This was just before he died."

"*And what did he tell you?*" asked Edward.

"Well, that he couldn't get any, to begin with. That Dad had taken away his access to the cash when he came back from India. But that if I really needed some money, I could get it from Uncle Nate. He said Nate would give it to me if I told him Grandfather had said to."

Edward looked at me sharply. "I think we better get Wolfy here."

"I'll call him," said Annie. She slinked toward the Trimline.

And Sam just sat there with his eyes blinking, all but begging with his facial expression that Claire take him and the kids away, way away from all this family mystery.

## ── CHAPTER EIGHT ────

WOLFY STOOD WIDE-EYED on the deck. Sam had just told the story about Grandfather's trip to Kathmandu. "I would dearly love a drink," Uncle Wolf now said, though no one rose to get him one. The little ones were being put to bed by Claire, who was rather unimpressed by the importance of the meeting, by the clues her husband held, and it seemed especially by his digression about the black rose. "You mean he bought that fucking rose in a flower store?"

"Yeah, well, actually on the streets of New Delhi," allowed Sam.

"You mean that thing we worshiped as if it were a living shrine was as common as poison ivy? It was housebroken? He bought it like a carnation?" Wolfy growled.

"Well, you know, maybe you should think of it as a rare orchid. The thing didn't just grow from Burpee seeds in a pot." But Wolfy took no solace from Sam.

We were hoping to get on to the business at hand, but Wolfy wasn't finished with the black rose. It had been an object of veneration in his house when the old man was alive, and when he died, when Wolfy and Blitz went on a tear, well, they'd drunkenly gone organizing games in the Jungle Room. One of the young women a racing friend brought along for the wake had stomped on the weary old flower, which set off my Aunt Morgan to excoriating Wolfy as if he had just gone and pissed on their father's headstone. Wolf had been feeling guilty about it for years, for he'd actually thought the old man had crawled hip-deep in Hindu muck to steal the thing from some temple in Madhya Pradesh. And now he found they sold three to the rupee in some bazaar in the Old Quarter.

"Tell us again what Grandfather told you about the money," Edward commanded Sam with this unconscious trace of a Gestapo accent. If he'd had a lamp, he would have shined it in Sam's eyes. We were still on the deck, sitting in the gazebo that was attached to it, Wolfy having been collected from a quiet night with his girlfriend. Sam had told us the full story in a rush, but now was to go through it with Wolfy present, for perhaps he could fill in some blanks we might not know.

"Grandfather told me . . ."

"How often did you talk?" interjected Wolfy. Wolfy was too nervous to sit down. Either that or standing was the only way he could keep from drinking. He was dressed for safari, in boots and a khaki jacket, and with the moths bouncing off the screen, and with the occasional lone honk of that pathetic goose out there, it was as if a campfire was burning somewhere at his feet.

"We talked from time to time," Sam said a little defensively.

"Grandfather loved Sam," I told Wolfy, for it was true. Even when he was screwed up on drugs and was beginning to be known as a family problem, Grandfather and Sam would spend time poking around the Jungle Room. Sam was the only one of us entrusted to water the black rose.

"Grandfather told me that some time after Grandfather Stanton shot himself . . . Well, let me back up," said Sam. "You know that Grandfather Daley and Grandfather Stanton went into business together."

"Yeah, the Dixie Five Hundred," said Wolf impatiently.

"The three million dollars of Grandfather Stanton's money was the only real money the Stantons had. The rest was tied up in All Odds and trusts up the wazoo."

"Yeah, that part we know, Sam."

"C'mon, Wolfgang, let him tell it," said Betsy, with whom you did not want to mess. Wolfy glared for a second as Sam went on.

"Grandfather Daley went into shock when Grandfather Stanton died. He was his best friend. His oldest son had married one of Stanton's daughters. And Grandfather Daley went silent when he had to acknowledge that one of his typically long-shot investments had wiped out his buddy. He told me—'cause I pressed him a little, as I recall. It was strange to me that he would send me to Uncle Nate for money when I needed help. So he told me that a few years after Grandfather Stanton died, Uncle Nate came to him and accused him of using his family's money improperly, and implying that he'd killed Grandfather Stanton, if not directly, then indirectly. And I guess Uncle Nate was a U.S. senator and a pretty impressive man then . . ."

"Those were the days," said Edward.

"And he told Grandfather that we owed them. And rather than

throw him out, he was so stricken about the death of his friend that he loaned Uncle Nate three million dollars, even though that money was critical to Daley Motorworks."

"Loaned?" said Edward.

"He told Nate he was going to *loan* the money to him?" pressed Wolfy.

"Are you sure about that part?" asked Betsy, who was always at the ready to intimidate poor Sam. She could do it long-distance, over a WATS line from her office.

"I'm sure. Grandfather loaned Uncle Nate, or one of the trusts, three million dollars on the condition that after it had earned back the money that Grandfather Daley lost, he was to give the money back. I can't believe you guys didn't know all this."

"Wow. I wonder how much money Uncle Nate made with it?" I mused.

But Betsy was already doing the math. "Let's say that the Stanton trust was zeroed out by Grandfather Stanton's bonehead decision to listen to Grandfather Daley and go in on some cracker racetrack. And then, well when did this happen exactly, Sam? When did Nate contact Grandfather?"

"I think about 1963 or 1964."

"That's right when we needed the cash for the Lazzy," said Wolfy.

"And just before Grandfather headed off to India for his fucking rose," said Edward. "If only Dad had wrestled away the power of the purse earlier."

"So he got three million bucks in 1963 or 1964, and he invested in all those companies you're nailing him for, Edward, in that soft, gentle ad. That is a lot of money by now," Betsy said.

Wolfy looked at her, and we all looked at him.

"And you said you told this to Father, right, Sam?" I said. Annie was beside me practically trembling with excitement. Annie loved money. Oh, crap, we all did.

"Years ago. After Daley Motorworks got into trouble financially, Dad must have suspected something. He pretended he was only curious about how much Grandfather told me, pretended he knew all along, so I told him all that I knew."

"Dad had a poker face," said Annie.

"But then he admitted it was news to him and that this was our secret."

"But why didn't he say anything?" asked Betsy.

"Because he couldn't stand the idea of me and Blitz thinking he couldn't run the business without your grandfather's help," said Wolfy.

"Some help, when he gave away the money we needed at a critical time just so he could assuage his guilt," said Edward.

"And getting what's ours isn't an admission of ineptitude," I said.

"But Sam's already told you," said Wolfy. "Your old man was going to try to get our money back from those bastards. Events just overtook him," he said discreetly.

"God," I said. "They just never gave it back. How did they think they could get away with it?"

"For one thing, because they must have thought the old man was nuts, and, they thought they could pull it off in the same way they thought they could get away with Nate's trading in stocks he had inside information on," Edward said. "They're Stantons. They think they can get away with anything."

"They've done a pretty good job of it," said Betsy.

"And we're Stantons too, Edward," Annie said with a trace of defensiveness, as if hoping someone would provide an argument against this fact of life that she could use if people turned on her later on in life.

"They may be corrupt," said Wolfy, "but face it, we're inept. We never knew to ask for the money back. And anyway, Annie, you still have the soul of a poor person."

"What a nice thing to say," I said with admiration. And then, as a family, without lawyers and advisers, we sat down to come up with a plan to get our money back.

# —•— **CHAPTER NINE** ————

BLAKE WAS BACK TOO. Oh, that was clear. It wasn't just what happened to me; he was spotted.

On Sunday, just before revving up the beloved Bavaria for the trip back to New York, I decided to go for a long run in the hills that circle Mingeboro. In preparation, and knowing that the roads of Connecticut lack the amenities of Central Park, I first drove the seven-mile circle I would run in order to stash several ten-ounce bottles of club soda in the weeds at the side of the road. One bottle was even hidden in a cool stream underneath the bridge near the turnoff to Falls Village. People drove by in pickup trucks, old Impalas, and even an Aston Martin DB5, giving me strange looks, though the looks were no odder than what I usually got around here simply for jogging.

I did have the feeling I was being followed. A couple of times I anxiously looked in the rearview mirror down the long edging straightaways with the blue silhouette of the Berkshires for a backdrop. Nothing. It was only later as I was trying to make it from water bottle to water bottle, cursing myself for having gotten so far away on a day this hot and humid, sweat streaming down my face like Bish Bash Falls, only then I realized I should have been on the lookout for a particular purple Porsche.

For the bottles were each and every one filled with what appeared to be piss. There was only one person who was a methodical enough sociopath to have followed me and done this, and that's Blake.

What an awful lot of piss he was filled with. I was all set to call Uncle Ethan and tell him his worst nightmare was back from summer camp when Annie came out to the front steps with more buckets of ice water and the news that Ethan was on the phone.

"He's back."

"I know," I said, somewhat relieved to hear the tone of voice Ethan used. He sounded half scared to death, which was not a familiar sound from him. I decided to bust his chops. "I thought we had an agreement."

"We did, but there's nothing I can do about it. He's not staying at All Odds. I think he's staying up the mountain with some Targies."

I had to laugh a bit at that, though it wasn't funny in the least. Two hundred years ago, redcoats sure had found the combination of Targies and Stantons to be lethal.

We agreed to keep each other posted on Blake's movements, and if necessary, we agreed, Ethan and I, we would see cousin Blake behind bars. The man was a menace to my family and to Nate's political career.

Nate would have bigger problems this week, especially when I showed up to demand our money back. I had Owen working to find out about Nate's campaign schedule, because it was important that I meet him somewhere I could talk with him without his having the ability to check in with Ethan. Surprising Nate into doing the right thing was important, and that meant dealing with him without his sleazier brother, my despicable Uncle Ethan, who was my ally only when it came to dealing with Blake.

From Dover to Brewster I drove with the image of what Nate's face would look like when I asked him for the three million dollars he owed us. Even as I drove, eager Daley beavers were tearing through the House of Lazarus and the Motorworks factory to find the actual record of that loan, in case Nate played legalistic games. Owen was going to lead a search of the New York town house, figuring such documents as these were most likely in one of several acres' worth of filing cabinets that forlornly sat in empty offices, moldering, probably surprised at our family's complete lack of interest in them. For a family that was obsessed with our own myth and fantasy, we were curiously uncurious about the historical record.

Owen was even trying to track down old secretaries, ancient retainers, accountants long since put to pasture, on the theory that if no documents existed, their presence in a court of law might be enough to make Nate back down.

What we had going for us was that privately, I was told, Nate was obsessed that we had punctured his aura of piety. It was all the worse considering that as a Stanton he was supposed to be above such money-grubbing actions as insider trading. That was something they left to the likes of the Daleys. "They." I kept thinking of the Stantons as others.

I suppose I should have been most curious about what possessed my grandfather to loan money he could ill afford to give away, money that was necessary if his company was to expand to take advantage of the popularity of the Lazzy. Money that was the material reward for a lifetime of mechanical success. I was filled with nonspecific guilt, we all were, but something in my sense of admiration for my grandfather, I guess, made me think that he was immune from the disease.

It just didn't make sense to me that he would give away all that dough. I mean, I wouldn't do it, even if I really was guilty of something. I'd keep the money and just feel, well, guiltier. More rotten every day, delightfully guilty, but with some money to console myself.

Whatever it was that bent a lifetime accumulator of wealth and power into the simpering moralist who redistributed his *own* wealth was beyond me. After all, even Nate, when he became a power in the Senate, put enough loopholes in the tax code that all the wealth that was redistributed was someone else's. Grandfather's giving away our money went beyond my family's other self-destructive moves. In the end, I guess, it didn't much matter why he had given the money away, and especially to *them*. What mattered now was that we get it back.

## —— CHAPTER TEN ——

WHAT I'D LEFT FRIDAY at a hum was now at a screech; this campaign howled. Wind whipped the offices from the motion inside, as volunteers stuffed envelopes and the phones rang and rang. I got to the headquarters near seven-thirty, but already things were in tumult, like an aviary where Time is the fox. It was going to be a very difficult Monday.

Rick Morgan, the mysterious communications director, was barking out orders over the squawk box, while Owen was pulling out his hair. "That son of a bitch," he said to the air as he pushed his way by me to the volunteer's loft. The receptionists were struggling to keep up, the phones rang everywhere, the place was a pigsty, and clusters of people I had never seen before moved self-importantly in the hallway. I found two Italian teenagers sitting on my desk without the slightest embarrassment or surprise when I asked them, politely, to get out. The phone lines were all lit up so it was impossible to get a line to call Edward, who was campaigning by car on Long Island, and plan our Stanton loan strategy further.

Edward had his hands full. Uncle Nate had the afternoon before warned that if Edward was elected to the U.S. Senate, property taxes around the state would go up, schools would close, policemen would be the first fired in a fiscal crunch, hence widows and orphans would be stomped in the streets. Fathers, he implied, would have to choose between trying to help their daughters as they were raped by gun-toting teenagers or trying to save their homes from repossession after the state had sued for back taxes. It was a suitably apocalyptic charge for a candidate going down, and I was trying to find a way to see what our people had come up with to rebut it.

I'd suggested something dignified, like a simple recitation of all the times Nate Stanton had voted for a tax increase as well as every record of praise he had ever had for governors—a code word for Nelson Rockefeller—who had themselves raised taxes to pay for state extravagances.

"Hope you had a nice weekend," said Owen malevolently as he trudged back into my office and plunked onto the sofa, which was stacked with computer tapes, *New York Post*'s, week-old containers of pizza crusts, and assorted debris that had floated in on the campaign's internal winds.

"Sam was home," I said not defensively, since there was just no way anyone could make me feel guilty for seeing my brother.

"Oh, I'm not bein' critical," Owen lied. "We got ourselves a problem, however."

"That being?"

"Mechanical, Charles, mostly mechanical."

I waited for his litany.

"Remember that mail house in Chinatown Simon Ford said was so sophisticated it could take your zip code, divide it by pi or some such hooey, add your name's last letter, and then spit out the exact direct-mail piece tailored to your ethnic group, height, weight, and sexual preference?"

"Yeah?"

"Well, they'd have done great if they hadn't sent fourteen thousand letters addressed "Dear I-talian American" to people named Matzanaga, Okaido, and Mitsubishi."

"Jesus." I let out a whistle.

"You ever heard of the Japanese-American Anti-defamation League?"

"No."

"I hadn't either."

"Oh, boy. Anything else?"

"Nassau. D'you know that the federal government just appropriated four billion dollars to military contractors in Hempstead? Well, I didn't either, until we couldn't get any damn Republican in the county to return our calls. And you know, of course, who filibustered his damn lungs out to get the damn dough. Your Uncle Nate is a peach. Spends all his time worrying about these quality-of-life issues, then in the election year he's takin' care of more pork than a North Carolina barbecue."

"What else you got?" I asked.

"That media buy."

"I thought that was fixed," I said.

"Oh, we fixed it. But I'm telling you, if Edward loses by one point, it'll be because we were off the air when Nate was on there heavy."

I slumped for a minute. Though Labor Day was rapidly approaching, it was as hot as July outside, and the air-conditioning in the headquarters had long since snorted and heaved to a stop. Owen looked as if he'd been sleeping on the floor, and of course I had to remind myself that he had. He appeared much older than his eighteen years, and I had to wonder about what kind of genes Quentin Claydo had that could have produced such a natural politican as Owen.

"Is there anything going right?"

"Right?" Owen smiled. "Well, shit, I'd say if nothing happens in the next few days to blow things, we are still on track for victory. Yes, suh. And I've got a bunch of volunteers lined up to start searching the files at the town house this afternoon."

"Great," I said, and reached for the phone—one line was unlit—to try to reach Edward.

## ── CHAPTER ELEVEN ──────

AFTERWARD, WHEN I WAS describing the cabin of events to Edward, I left out the part about the bathtub. He didn't need to know that we were bathing, Laurie and I, and it was very early in the morning. We were in the Motorworks apartment I had gone from looking at as a place for an emergency bivouac to an encampment that was mine by birth. The ceiling-length door to the Park Avenue porch was open just enough to let the soot of New York air revive us on this Tuesday morning. It had rained, and already the streets were busy with the taxis' glide, and I was nuzzling Laurie, my feet by her waist at one end of the bath, her feet playing tic-tac-toe on my chest.

"So the family's holding up," she said.

"Admirably," I said. I was looking at her pale skin, which was almost translucent in the bath. It had this becoming underhue of blue visible in the clinical whiteness of the ancient bathroom. This was a bathroom in which you could hold court; it seemed as large as the West Side apartment I'd had to abandon so hurriedly just weeks before. It was two floors up from my actual digs, but who was going to see Laurie and me sneak to it at five-thirty in the morning? Mr. Greco? The shape of Laurie's calf was architectural perfection.

"And Sam's just going to stay up in Mingeboro for a while?"

"Yeah," I answered distractedly. I was tired. We had not had much sleep. "After all, he's been away for years."

"And the kids don't know anything at all about their daddy's difficulties, right? Did I guess right?"

"Actually, they do today, I believe. Sam was supposed to be telling them last night, emphasizing the fact that it was long ago and in crazy times that he fell in with a bad bunch of people. I think his intent was to play down that he's been a fugitive all these years."

Laurie and I had had dinner in the West Village. I'd told her all about the tale Sam told, and when we returned home, we had to pick our way through the Motorworks building, which looked like someone, Nazis, maybe the IRS, had gone rummaging through carelessly. There were papers all over the carpets, the marble staircase, drawers from filing cabinets at best left out, at worst dumped on the floors,

Mr. Greco in a red-wine-steeped foul mood. He threatened to have cleaners come and throw out all the files, which was a little ungracious. The chaos was obviously the work of the crew Owen had dispatched to search for evidence of that loan to the Stantons.

"So how long do you think Sam and Claire are going to stay" asked the clear soul at the end of the tub. Christ, I was glad I had met her in the rocket's red glare. Thank you, Blake, for something. I wanted to spend all my time with her. Oh, was I looking forward to the campaign being over. Not necessarily to our winning or losing, just being over and done with, with our fate resolved.

Laurie I wanted to see, to study, to watch the way she got dressed, slept, ate food. She is the only person I ever met who could sift through my family's latest crazed gesture with utter calm. There wasn't a thing I brought to her, an action by a Stanton or a Daley, that struck her as our—or their—having gone too far. I didn't think I really wanted to meet her family, if she could handle mine so effortlessly. What kind of people could she have come from that made her so unimpressed by mine?

We were talking playfully in the tub when the phone rang two flights below in my apartment. "Who could that be?" It was about 6 A.M., but few enough people had this number that I had to guess it was campaign related. I got out of the bath dripping and swearing. What a mess I made, even with the towel around me.

I nearly slipped on some old files at the top of the stairs, which would have been interesting, the drop to the ground floor being five flights. The phone was insistent as I nearly tripped ass over teakettle in the rush to get to it. "Coming, I'm coming," I said under my breath as I slipped and slid down the marble staircase under pictures of Lazzies. We had a Lazzy by Vargas, and one by Roy Lichtenstein with a Steve Canyon–type race-car driver wondering, Can I make the next curve? Good question—I nearly wiped out a time or two trying to get to the phone.

I plunged through the door to my apartment. "Hullo?" I demanded as I stood there in my towel, dripping on the tattered Persian.

"Charles, it's Rachel."

"Yeah, and this is Hank, Charles."

Of all the people in America who would get me out of a tub at this hour of the morning, I would least have expected these two. My *Downtown News* bosses.

"Well, hello," I managed.

"We've been thinking . . ."

"Yes, this hasn't been easy . . ."

"Because our roles as journalists . . ."

"And our friendship with you . . ."

"Come into conflict, you see."

I didn't, but I said I did. What were they talking about?

"We received word last night . . ."

"From Paddy Mack . . ."

"That someone from the Stanton camp was calling reporters telling them if they were interested in a fugitive radical whom the FBI has been looking for since 1966, they should drive up to Litchfield County today when the FBI arrests him . . ."

"Omigod. Today? They said today?"

"Oh, yes," said Hank.

"Holy . . ."

"This is your brother Sam, right?"

"Yeah, but the statute of limitations is up. He told me." I was still on my feet shivering from the ancient rumbling air conditioner near my rumpled bed.

"Look, we're not going near it. Even Paddy was offended that Stanton's press person was gauche enough to try to sell that one to us."

"But the *Post* . . ." said Rachel, letting the phrase hang.

"Wow," I said, as it began to be obvious what was going to happen. "Listen, you are both sweethearts, and I won't forget this kindness."

"Oh, don't mention it," said Rachel.

"Charles?"

"Yeah, Hank."

"When the campaign is over, come see us. We should talk. You still have a home here."

He said that as if the paper were an orphanage. Past baggage aside, I kind of liked the idea. In the meantime, I stood there dripping as alarms went off and I immediately called Sam at the house in Mingeboro.

The phone rang and rang and rang. I was about to hang up when I heard the phone get picked up and a tiny voice say, "Hullo?"

"Charlie, it's your Uncle Charles. Is your daddy there?"

"He's asleep."

"Would you get him for me, pal?"

"Okay."

A minute later Sam came to the phone. "What is it, Charles?" he said sleepily.

"Who told you the statute of limitations was up, Sam?"

He paused for a minute, trying to make some sense out of my early-morning query. "I asked Uncle Nate's office. They'd been keeping me apprised of my situation. Uncle Ethan called me about it himself."

"And told you you could come home?"

"Yeah. Why?"

Shit. They'd gotten us good on this one.

"Sam," I said, "you've got to get out of there."

"Why?" he asked, and then said, "Wait a minute, there's someone at the door."

"Oh, Sam," I said, and hung my head. I knew who it had to be.

## —— CHAPTER TWELVE ——

"RETURN OF THE TERRORIST" screamed the headline on the front page of the *Post*, as Mitch Sheedy, our normally unflappable pollster sat all but weeping in the green room. Owen just glared, but if you looked at Edward, at Simon Ford, Harry Fox, even Tim Verkhovensky, you might have thought it was election night and we'd just lost.

"I think maybe we just lost," said Simon Ford. "Goddamnit, Charles, how could this happen? You're supposed to tell us about this kind of shit, and even more than that, you're supposed to be smart enough to head something like this off at the pass."

I looked over at him, but I didn't say anything. If I threw him out the window, it would mess his natty suit.

"No one saw this coming," Edward said slowly, taking it like a man. Harry Fox just smirked. There was this aura about him that made me suspicious, as if he was pleased he'd just found his alibi if the race was lost. "It was a trap Ethan sprung, and Sam, not knowing any better, just fell for it."

Sam being fingered on the front page of the *Post* was bad enough. But now came word that the *New York Times* was going to do a front-page Metro Section piece on the history of Sam's escapade a decade back. The reporter I spoke to seemed a little disappointed that Sam had no revolutionary rhetoric to espouse, then or now.

I had to admit it was a royal screwup not to have seen this one coming, not to have seen how far Ethan would go to throw a monkey wrench into our smoothly running campaign machine. Goddamn them.

"We need this like a hole in the head," said Mitch Sheedy kindly. He appeared, in his off-the-rack fatman's suit, to be the weary embodiment of the kindly uncle. I know the type only from literature.

Except for Uncle Andrew, who while weak, nonetheless was kindly. He called from the courthouse stuttering in his description of the camera crews and pencil press that converged on poor Sam as he walked up the steps with the family's hastily summoned lawyer. He reported that Sam had walked firmly, however, had politely asked a reporter to get out of his way, and had entered the place with dignity. His demeanor apparently did not break when the judge ordered the decade-long fugitive held on one million dollars bail. That last one was a shocker. But so was our financial situation.

"To top this all off, the campaign's broke," said Simon Ford.

"Just as our numbers were really moving," said Mitch with a shake of his head.

"And Nassau County's no longer in the bag," said Tim Verkhovensky.

"Though Stanton's ads are just pitiful," said Rick Morgan over the squawk box.

"How are we possibly broke?" I asked. We'd been pumping out direct-mail fund-raising letters to conservative lists around the country, and things were reported to have been going well, the Post Office delivering bags of checks.

"Because while you were up in Connecticut with your brother the radical, the campaign here has been spending everything, including the volunteers' lunch money," said Simon just before I lunged.

Owen caught me with both his arms just as I got to Simon, who jumped back with his hands up in protest. "Okay, okay, I'll keep personal matters out of this. I didn't know any better, okay?"

It took a few minutes to calm me down, and Simon and I gravitated toward opposite corners of the room. "I know where we can get the money we need," I said.

"Lazlo Fortescu," said Harry Fox, the know-it-all. I thought right then and there how happy I would be when the campaign was over. It was beginning to wear me out, dealing with the same people day in and day out, the same nemeses in the press corps, or on the other side, but especially within the campaign.

"No, not Lazlo Fortescu," I said. By law he could give only a thousand bucks in the primary. "Nate Stanton."

They laughed for a minute, but Edward didn't. "Hey," he said as the rest looked on with puzzlement. "That money goes to Daley Motorworks," he said, and we were the only two in the room who understood what we were talking about. "That's the money that means the company doesn't have to deal with Fortescu," he said softly. He looked very determined.

"Don't worry, Edward, I'll get us the three million dollars we're owed, and I swear it will all go to the company. Uncle Andrew will be able to pay off the debt and make payroll next week, I promise."

While Simon Ford and Harry Fox began to beseech Edward to make him tell them what we were talking about, I walked toward the door. I was going to deal with my Uncle Nate. But first I had to find him.

## CHAPTER THIRTEEN

ON MY FIFTH CALL, I got lucky. They told me the senator was in. "Charles," he said neutrally, with none of the warmth I had been greeted with in the past, but none of the rancor I could have expected either. "I'm so very sorry about Sam."

And he meant it. Uncle Nate in particular loved Sam, and once, in a very incautious move, he had joined my fugitive brother on a bird-watching trip to British Columbia. He had always taken a shine to

Sam, but then everybody did, even the reporters who were assigned to cover his departure on bail from the jail in Litchfield County.

When I told Nate there was something I had to talk with him about that involved, well, Sam, and my mother too, he suggested I come have breakfast with him early Wednesday morning at his co-op on Gracie Square.

Given the fact that he was heading upstate to campaign in this final week of the primary, I thought it not unusual that he had me come for breakfast at six-thirty. By then "MY STORY" by Sam Daley was on page eleven of the *New York Post,* now that he had been bailed out by an unnamed benefactor. In his post-release news conference he had so thoroughly beguiled the cameras and reporters that what at first was thought to be a story of a young, rich punk who'd long staved off justice emerged as a cautionary tale of what happens when a nice kid does drugs he can't handle and falls in with the wrong crowd.

Told in the context of Daley family lore, it was perfect for the tabloids: the handsome young man whose innate sadness and romanticism draws him into trouble, but who pulls himself up by his bootstraps, ultimately to run his own foreign-auto/repair empire, which was duly photographed by a wire service and shown to be a bustling concern in the rainy Northwest. As to what it meant for the campaign, we just didn't have sufficient numbers.

It was clear and hot this late August morning as I rode toward Nate's co-op. I dreaded the afternoon's campaigning by helicopter throughout the Hudson Valley and back again to Queens. Edward was due at the Orange County Fair up near Middletown, at a luncheon in White Plains, a rally in Nyack, and finally, at a door-to-door media event to show there actually were Republicans at work in Astoria. This strain of having to deal with Sam's problem—or Sam *as* problem—just seemed unfair right now. It was another example of our personal grief being dragged into the public domain, and another example of our having to try to manage the tone of the news about things that were very personal. I was exhausted; we'd been at the headquarters until midnight as the phone banks ran and the last of the direct-mail copy was approved.

I say approved, because even as the computer was spitting out the names that would receive our little missives—the equivalent of plastic explosives under Nate Stanton's image—we didn't have enough money to get them in the mail. I couldn't believe the campaign was broke. We weren't even on the air. Meanwhile, the family was so broke we couldn't even bail Sam out by ourselves.

I had Carmine, my driver, park on York Avenue and I walked across the street with the *Post* tucked under my armpit. As a child I'd come here with my mother for Nate's famous Christmas parties, but this promised to be something else again.

The doorman was reading Sam's hastily dictated story in the *Post* in a manner I took to be a little carefree, given who resided upstairs. I was surprised, I'm compelled to say, at just how skillfully Sam had turned this thing around, even finishing by saying he knew that of the two of them, Edward was the hero, for Edward had served in Vietnam in a war Sam had been just too chicken to fight. None of this dithering about morality or politics, just an out-and-out expression of gutlessness. That took balls.

The doorman showed me to the wood-paneled elevator. "The Senator's expecting youse." And so he was, or at least so was Cabbot, my Uncle Nate's longtime valet. "The Senator's on the porch, Charlie," he said with ever so slight contempt. "You take care not to wake Mrs. Stanton, yuh hear?" And with that I was left to find my way outside.

I padded across the Orientals, past the cut flowers on the dining-room table. The portrait of George Washington that hung over the fireplace in the living room seemed a curious thing under the circumstance. I think I was expecting something more in the order of a portrait of Jay Gould.

I always loved the way Nate's home in New York was so evocative of Mingeboro. There were paintings of flushed coveys that could only have come from the grouse-stuffed woods of All Odds. From the rocking chairs to the colonial chests, this was a country home, not the home of a politician who had his limo downstairs ready to take him to his campaign plane. It did not seem the home of a man at a precarious axis of power here in the modern world.

The sun was coming up over Queens as I stepped through the doorway and caught Nate eating a strawberry. I say caught, because I seemed to have surprised him enough that he spat it back into the crystal bowl. "Uncle Nate, how are you?" And instinctively I walked up to him and kissed his florid cheek. It seemed I'd spent a lifetime kissing the cheeks of relatives.

"I'm very well, indeed," he said, coughing and motioning me to my chair. There was a bowl of strawberries waiting for me, and I had to chuckle at the big box of Frosted Flakes he'd had placed beside him on the table. "Fit for a general election," he said, spooning up another strawberry, a big fat one drenched in cream. There wasn't a sign of a Bloody Mary anywhere. Maybe he was telling the truth.

"You look well," I said nervously.

"I am well, and so, I see, is Sam, if we are to take the word of the morning newspaper. Did you ghost that piece?" he asked casually.

"Oh, no, sir. I'm not qualified."

"Hmmm," he snorted. Snorting became him. He had this aquiline nose, which before alcohol had fattened it somewhat, had been his most regal feature. Now it resembled nothing so much as the huge strawberry he lifted from the bowl. "Your brother is very lucky. Edward, that is."

"How so?"

"This business of Sam." He paused from his breakfast for a moment to look up at me as if I were a dummy. "This could so easily have harmed Edward, don't you think? I've been rooting for Sam's release, but there are those around me who were not."

"There are those around you who set him up," I said.

"We're all a little surprised at the way Sam was able to turn this thing around."

"There is that," I said. No one expected yesterday's puff piece in the *New York Times*. Preppies from Montauk to Katonah must have nodded their heads in recognition at that Metro Section panegyric.

Cabbot stepped out onto the porch and poured us each a cup of coffee. After moving the bowls to the side of the table, the valet went into the dark living room and returned a moment later with a plate of perfect scrambled eggs and then silently walked away.

"Let me ask you a question," said Nate. "is this what you thought politics was all about when you worked in my office that semester?"

That was tough. During the term I worked in Nate's Senate office, I'd lived in his home on Kalorama Road and traveled to work with him every morning. I'd learned about such senatorial courtesies as the elevators for senators only, the privileges of membership in the most exclusive club in the nation. Most of all I learned that Nate was one first-class horse trader, a superb negotiator except when he let his emotions get in the way. I learned that from seeing him in the cloakroom or on the Senate floor, when the bidding price for votes would go from cheap to priceless. I didn't have any grandiose notions about how democracy flourished, but I had thought it worked

—I had thought Nate worked—in a fashion somewhat less shabby than that which had recently been revealed.

There was an awful lot of love elbowing me back in my forward charge toward him. Edward and I thrived on politics as much from our genetic connection to this species across the table as from anything environmental. And as I was about to answer him, Nate looked up from his untouched eggs and said point-blank, "You think I am corrupt, don't you?"

"Uncle Nate, I . . ."

"Because if you don't, then why are you running ads that attempt to ruin me in the process of beating me?"

"Edward's just being pragmatic. God, if he put on the air some of the ads we've suggested—that have been suggested—" I said, quickly stopping myself. "Well, some of those around us have pushed for ads that were even tougher."

"I have colleagues who tell me they have not seen such an ugly primary in their lives."

Enough was enough. "Uncle Nate, it is your side that started this campaign on friendly footing when you told the *New York Post* that Edward had been fragged. Uncle Ethan told me from the start that this would be dirty. He promised it. And then he delivered when he tricked Sam into coming home. And remember your nephew Blake? He tried to kill me at a downtown club, and then he succeeded in killing my dog. Your nephew butchered my bluetick hound. Okay, so we put out information about you that doesn't make you look so hot, but the information was accurate. Wasn't it?"

"I never earned an illegal penny," he said in a low roar. "Any goddamn fool could tell that stock in Sikorsky Aircraft was a good investment in 1963. You should be pleased those investments were made. They made an awful lot of money for your mother, God bless her soul."

"Uncle Nate, I don't care what your rationale was. What you did, however, gave us a great political weapon, and Edward's used it."

"Nothing I did was illegal!"

"I don't care. It looks lousy."

"From today's vantage point."

"From any vantage point. Look, your brother is trying to make Daley Motorworks go bankrupt by using your name to screw us with the banks we need to raise money from."

"That's preposterous."

"That's true."

"Ethan doesn't have that kind of clout."

"Maybe not, but you do, and he's invoked your name. Plus we got a lousy credit rating to begin with."

"Well, that I'm afraid is your own fault. It's not my problem."

I had him. I'd been hoping to get him and I had him. "It's our fault?"

"Your father was a lousy businessman, and word on the street, Charles, is that Andrew's a pleasant incompetent. You'll be more appreciative someday when you're starting a family that the money you get from the trust flows the way it does. I haven't noticed you and Edward turning anything over to an orphanage."

His face was red, and if the table wasn't glass, by now he would have pounded it. It was his trademark. But this last reference to an orphanage was on the south side of the belt.

"So the money problems of the Daley Motorworks are entirely of our own making due to . . . what did you say? Incompetence?"

"Charles, I asked you to come to breakfast because you had something to discuss. To begin with, life is too short to spend it talking about the Daley Motorworks, but to be specific, I am due this morning in Rochester, where I am to denounce your older brother, which is not difficult, considering the drivel he espouses."

"Uncle Nate?"

"Charles." I could tell I had about two minutes more of his attention and that I was then going to lose the opportunity.

"You made a reference to our problems being due to my father's having been a lousy businessman. I have to say, you in particular aren't in a position to make such a judgment."

"If you're here to talk about your father . . ." he said, glancing down at his gold Patek watch.

"I'm here to ask for our money back, Senator. I'm here, you see," I said with a grin, "to ask for the three million dollars you owe us. The three million you mistakenly seem to have taken to have been a gift, as it were. My grandfather loaned you money you thought you should have gotten from your father, and you didn't bother with niceties like reporting it to the IRS. And we want it back." Now I was the one with the red face. But mine was from exertion. Why did Uncle Nate's face still glow red?

"Who said your grandfather lent me money?" he asked in this eerily calm voice.

"My grandfather. He told Sam. Sam told us."

"Can you prove it?"

He asked that like the headmaster of a British boarding school officiating a dispute. "Not yet. But we don't have to prove it, really. I guarantee you I could get it on tonight's news. Oh, and on the front page of the *Post* by noon, easy. Wouldn't that be nice? 'The money Senator Nate Stanton used to invest lucratively in war stocks, having had a jump on buying them because of his Senate committee assignments, was provided by a loan from the Daley family, a loan he never reported, and which now, according to his challenger, he won't pay back.' Like it?"

"It's creative, but too complicated, and hence of little use to you."

"Are you denying its potency or its truth, Uncle Nate?"

Nate slumped back in the cushion of his chair like a sixty-five-year-old man with a long day ahead of him. He exhaled sharply and just sat there. I listened to the sound of a helicopter, perhaps Nate's, as it made its way toward the 60th Street heliport, and from York Avenue came the honk and beep of rush hour. Bees were buzzing Uncle Nate's carnations, and I wondered where they came from. In front of me, my Uncle Nate was looking as old as Betsy had hinted when she thought we should attack him for possibly not being able to finish out his term.

"I bailed out Sam, you know."

"Yeah, I thought that was you. Thank you for that. Edward thought it might be Lazlo Fortescu in one of his periodic attempts at currying favor, but Annie told us he's out of town on business, so I doubt he even knows. Well, of course he knows. It made the *Times*. But thank you for that, Uncle Nate." I was a child again, thanking him for his Christmas present.

"I heard you were a little short on cash."

"That's very funny," I said.

"It is," said he, and we both laughed for a second. And then he let out a big breath. "Your grandfather was a very strange man. He had this hold over my father that we absolutely resented. He amused Dad. He represented, God, I don't know, the Great American West, the virility of the South. Something the governor had mythologized. Entrepreneurship. And when he told us, when Dad told us he'd put up cash for what was supposed to be a joint venture with Charlie Daley, we told him he was a fool. And he proved to be, though there was no way of talking him out of it. After all, he had been Governor of Connecticut and fancied himself a pretty shrewd judge of character. And I sometimes think that after he lost the money, he killed himself because he couldn't face telling us what had happened and having us, in turn, say, 'We told you so.' "

Nate was looking at me with the sincerity he saved for network cameras. "I always thought there was something fishy about that deal with Charlie Daley, that joint venture my Dad went in on. Something just didn't sit right. In the year or so after Dad killed himself, back when we were still maintaining he'd died in a hunting accident, I must have written your grandfather a half-dozen letters asking for the details on the venture. I'd just been elected to the Senate but, I wouldn't let it go. It took my hiring a private investigator to find out that while the rewards for the so-called joint venture were equal, the risks were not. My father put up one hundred percent of the capital in that goddamn deal, and your grandfather not a dime. That took me until 1963 to find out.

"Your mother had told me about your grandfather's dumb act, which she had seen through. It was obvious to her that if the old man had had a stroke and couldn't talk, then he damn well shouldn't have continued to lay claim to any power over the business. But he did, and it drove your father crazy.

"So, one summer day in 1963 I paid a visit to your grandfather unexpectedly. I found him sitting in the patio by himself with none of your aunts around. I found him utterely different than I had ever before seen him. He wasn't the titan he tried to be at your parents wedding." Nate smiled his wizened old snake charmer's smile, and I admit it was infectious. "Your grandfather wasn't the little Irish know-it-all he tried to be whenever he would come up to All Odds to get away from you all, which he did more often than you might think. He was shaken, and when I suggested he might help us make up the loss I assured him was ours alone, the ultimate loss, of course, being my father's life, well, he went into the next room to his desk and just wrote out a check. It was for three million dollars.

"I said, 'I'm not asking for you to give us our money back. My father lost that on his own. I'm just asking for what should have been your share to begin with.' At that time, we all thought your grandfather was fabulously rich, because, you see, when Charlie Daley moved into Mingeboro, he came with bucking broncos and British tutors and Spanish nannies and this incredible road show of cars and little Daleys, your father among them. It was quite intimidating, especially when your family moved in and took over the lake beneath our mountain. And, I suppose, when your father walked off with my little sister. But I thought your grandfather's being able to write out this check was rather an easy thing for him to do, though of course I realize from your subsequent financial woes it was not."

He breathed heavily and reached for his glass of fresh-squeezed orange juice. I was practically holding my breath.

"So your grandfather said, 'Consider this a loan.' And I said, 'For how long and at what interest?' He said, 'Until you've made back the money I lost for your father. Then just give it back.'

"So I went out to make back the money as quickly as possible. Things were booming, but as fast as I tried, your grandfather was clearly dying. First he just disappeared, with all that international brouhaha. Then when he returned, the couple of times I saw him, he barely recognized me. Or he would shut me up when I tried to speak with him. Your mother told me he'd gone bonkers, and I believed it. He died without my being able to pay back the money. And when he died, I was waiting for one of your uncles—Your father and I were barely on speaking terms, over politics, in fact your father once threatened to primary me. Did you know that?

"Edward is not the first of your family to challenge me, just the first to go through with it. Well, I was waiting for one of your uncles to zoom up the driveway in one of their flashy cars and demand the money back. And they just never did. Ethan and I used to puzzle over it, but truly, I always thought there would come the day when one of you would come to collect. And then we wondered if the old man took the secret with him to his grave."

He looked truly mystified that after all this time the person he would end up talking to was me. A mere nephew, and one who once upon a time had been close to him. "Since, about 1967, I've been waiting for someone in your family to ask for the money. Sam came, but that was for chicken feed. What's kept you, Charles? What's taken so long?"

"We didn't know," I said in protest. "The only person Grandfather told was Sam, and Sam didn't think anything of it, until now."

"I'm not going to venture into figuring that out."

"Well, Uncle Nate, I want to figure out why you never came to us on your own." But Nate just shrugged. He was in a fix and we both knew it. But I knew a way for Nate to get out of the fix he was in. I would have mercy if he kicked in the cash. I wanted to give him a chance to assuage any feeling of . . . Wait a minute. I wanted our damn money and that was all there was to it.

"Uncle Nate, we're asking now. We want—we demand—our money back right away."

"Settle down, Charles. I told you, I have always been prepared to settle accounts." He sat there for a minute looking at me as if he were relieved, but I don't for a minute think that could have been the case. I think I just happened to ask him at the one moment when he was utterly vulnerable to us. Is that fair? Who's to judge?

"I don't mean in two weeks, Uncle Nate. I mean, well, we need it today."

I expected him to laugh, but he was serious.

"I don't think there's any way I could get it today. I'm a little strapped for cash right now," he said with a sly grin. "You see, I'm in the middle of a campaign."

"Yeah, well the money you owe us is the only thing that stands between our family business and bankruptcy, Uncle Nate. We need it, and you owe it to us."

"Charles, you don't have to threaten me. I'm not your Uncle Ethan. But it's going to take forty-eight hours to sell off stocks and some bonds. I can have it by Friday morning, I would bet. After all, it's the Stanton Trust that owes you. In a sense you owe yourself."

"Great." Yippee! "But there's one other thing," I said.

"And that is?"

"We don't just want the three million dollars you owe us."

"Oh?" He looked wary. And he should.

"No, we want another two million dollars in interest." I looked at Nate to see if this would break the back of our deal.

He sat staring at me for a moment, the lids of his eyes flapping on a very slow rhythm. Then he just waved his hand as if with all he had trifling over a mere two million would be petty.

"I was going to say," he said, "I'd do it if Edward would get out of the race. But I know that Edward isn't going to get out of the race."

I allowed myself the luxury of feeling sorry for him, for he was blood, he was family, with all the attendant confusion in allegiance that can muster. It was morning in New York with a long campaign day ahead of both of us. Already Edward would be getting into the elevator in his apartment not far from here, ready to descend into a busy day.

We had prearranged that I would call him in his car on the way to the airport, but I had another call I wanted to make first. I wanted to call Laurie and tell her that I had gotten back the approximately two hundred thousand dollars that Ethan Stanton had stolen when she had been in trouble. And then I would tell Edward that we had, in addition to the money that would keep our family business alive, enough money to pay for the final weekend's worth of media and then some.

Cabbot showed me to the door, but it was Uncle Nate who walked up to me as I was standing there waiting for the elevator. Without saying a word, he took me in his arms and pressed me to his pin-striped chest. Forgiveness. It still was important that we now beat him. But my feelings were being torn into confetti.

"Stop running those goddamn ads," he said.

## ── CHAPTER FOURTEEN ──

WE GOT BAD NEWS from Mingeboro and it reached us on the plane. Against the drone of engines, we agreed, Edward and I, that once again Blake had gone too far.

We were flying back from Albany, where Edward had just debated a panel of eggheads on a show that this final weekend would be broadcast statewide on public television. And I have to say, we were in a pretty upbeat mood. I was chatting with Aubron Powell of the *Times* in the front of the plane, and I was certain he heard everything when one of our pilots pushed back and told us what had been radioed by Owen.

It seemed Blake had discovered that to amuse himself while on bail Sam was spending his afternoons tuning up the Lazzies. While Sam's boy played with a toy version of the Lazzy that I had unearthed for him, it was Sam's intention to work on our lovelies.

Blake must have staked out the House of Lazarus, or had a Targy do so for him, and watched as Sam lovingly tinkered under each Lazzy's bonnet.

Yesterday, late in the afternoon Sam had left four of our family sports cars outdoors, and after locking up the House of Laz itself, he'd gone with little Charlie for a swim in the pool. It wasn't until dusk that he'd hiked back up to put the cars away and discovered someone had taken a crowbar to the bumpers, a baseball bat to the windows, and something on the order of a sledgehammer to the roofs, the hoods, the door panels. Four of our Lazzies were smashed, disfigured, hopelessly marred. Four of our outstanding creations had been smashed by our maniac cousin, and I had one question: Was one of them mine?

"I'm going to take care of that son of a bitch once and for all," I whispered to Edward across the narrow aisle. It would not have been unreasonable for Edward to have said, "You and what army?" Instead he looked at me briefly, with this air of resignation that surprised me, suggesting a fatalism I had never seen there before. He looked away at the clouds we were flying through as we began our descent into Teterboro, but for a second there I saw a look that suggested nothing would surprise him now, and that a romantic fool such as I should be tolerated.

Instead of Edward, it was Aubron who leaned over the seat and said, "Who? Senator Stanton?"

"Aubron, will you bug off?" I said, and he seemed content to do so, eyes lowering beneath the business side of his half frames. He lived by a different etiquette than the others.

But now Arthur Begelman and Samantha Sanchez, who had been playing cards in a childish fashion in the back of the plane, wanted to know what we were talking about.

"Just a little family business," I said.

"Your family business is why we're on this plane," deadpanned Samantha.

"For just a couple more days," I said a little petulantly. "Until the general election," I said, catching myself. It would be pleasant when we no longer had to worry that every utterance one of us made might be a headline in the *Post*. Arthur was taking notes.

As we came in for the landing, I was a little expectant, and not just because of my anxiousness about my car. Owen had had a busy— and successful—morning already, or so we'd been told. We'd sent

him over to Ethan's office to pick up the check that Nate had promised, and I could almost hear the chorus of workmen in Mingeboro
bellowing hosannas. Apparently, Ethan hadn't even had the courage
to deliver the cashier's check himself; he'd had his amazon secretary
do so. Which was fine, as it turned out, with Owen, who now had a
date for tonight's show at Tier III, where my cousin Camille's band
was playing. I was going to go there too, with Laurie. But first we
had to go to Montefiore Hospital in the Bronx, where we had scheduled Edward to visit a wounded cop who was willing to say on camera
that if he lasted until Tuesday, he would vote for Edward Daley,
because Senator Stanton "coddled the scum what did this to me." At
least that's what my driver, Carmine, who claimed to be a cousin of
the wounded officer, had assured us this morning. I had Tim Verkhovensky checking it out.

It was a bumpy landing at Teterboro, and Samantha and Arthur
had gotten into an argument that was truly juvenile, so our nerves
were a little on edge. "Am not." "Am so." "Am not." "Am so." I kept
on thinking of Sam and the Lazzies and hoping that the children
were safe.

"All right, folks," I said to the reporters when we were finally out
on the tarmac, "we're going to Montefiore for an endorsement."

"From who?" demanded Arthur, sort of swaying in the airport's
greasy light.

"From whom," corrected Aubron.

"From that cop who was shot. Whatsisname. Zepoli."

"You're kidding," said Samantha. You could tell she was disgusted.

"I kid you not," I said, and looking over at Edward and the way he
was looking at me, I could tell he was disgusted as well. A month ago
I would have been too. But this was politics. This was news.

Our van for the reporters showed up on time, and as Edward and
I got into the Buick and waved to the reporters, of course we didn't
realize that we'd be making front-page news for the next forty-eight
hours. The only person who could possibly have known that was
Blake.

## —•— CHAPTER FIFTEEN ————

TONY ECHEVERIA, LIKE a paparazzi, was waiting at the entrance to Montefiore. He had his camera crew staked out to film the candidate as Edward gently stepped from the car door that Tim Verkhovensky had rushed from seemingly nowhere to open.

"How's it look?" I asked Tim.

"Pretty good. The cop's all lying there in his hospital gown with his service decorations pinned to the sheet and his cap on his head, and he claims he holds Nate Stanton personally responsible for the kids who shot him."

"What's the reasoning?"

"Nate sets a low moral standard."

I looked at Tim and shrugged. "That oughta do it," I said as the press van pulled up and our weary reporters followed us through the entrance to the hospital in the glare of the CBS crew's lights.

"Long day?" asked Tony in a friendly fashion. He had outdone himself this time, for this truly amazing linen suit he was wearing would have had to have been pressed about every two hours to keep looking like that. When Tony was doing pieces, he got all friendly and goofy, but when he went on the air, he looked as sober as a hanging judge. Right now he was in the friendly and goofy stage, and he had Edward giggling.

The hospital administrator came up to my giggling brother and said, "Welcome, fellow freedom fighter."

"Hey, that's a pretty snappy greeting. Did you hear that, Charles?" Edward asked enthusiastically. The administrator was just a little guy in a cheap suit with glasses held by a strap around his neck. That pompadour must have been something else on a marauding Bronx teenager in the 1950s. Now it just looked tacky.

"I'm also the assistant county chairman for the Conservative Party." That explained everything. "You spoke at our convention in Albany the last two years."

"Of course," said Edward to the administrator, as if he remembered the exact conversation. It looked as if the guy was about to tell him that they'd had.

"If there's anything we can do for you while you're here, just ask," he said as he made sure he stuck close to Edward the whole time the camera was on.

Patients looked up from gurneys, weeping relatives stopped just long enough to see what was going on, and nurses and doctors seemed a little nettled that their mortal struggle was the backdrop for a photo op.

"I would like to see some, you know, handicapped kids before I leave," the candidate said sincerely, rubbing his metal arm. Beautiful, Edward, I thought. I had to peer over Samantha Sanchez's shoulder to see if Tony's film crew was getting that.

We were still on the first floor, about to take the slow-moving elevator up to where the wounded cop lay waiting to make his endorsement, when there was this sudden collective intake of air that spelled trouble. "Everyone get down!" someone yelled, and, boy, we sure did. Arthur Begelman hit the floor with a thud that was a testimony to the strength of concrete. Edward, who was the most rational and puzzled of the crowd, seemed to hesitate, but the security guard who had come sweeping down the hall with his lungs blaring warning pushed him, and hard, to the floor.

"What the . . ."

Tony Echeveria was crouched down, motioning his cameraman to keep filming, and he did, lying on his back with the lens like a periscope above the crowd on the floor beside him. That's when the security cop seemed to get rattled and he pulled his gun. The bystanders scattered.

Edward was on his back and the cop stood above him, waving his pistol as if it were a magic wand. It must have worked, because whatever was out there was now nowhere to be found.

"What is the matter with you?" Edward asked with exasperation.

"There was," the cop began, "a guy with a gun [huff, puff] who shouted he was going to shoot that Daley bastard . . . well, you," he said. People around us gasped. Tony's cameraman kept filming.

The security cop was about five feet five, and for a perverse second I wondered if he had this job because he failed the police department's height requirements. But though he was a dumpy dummy cop, he looked a lot bigger with the service revolver in his hand.

"Would you mind putting that away?" said Edward as he stood up. He looked a little pissed, if the truth be told, and I couldn't figure how this would come across on camera.

By now Aubron Powell had jumped up and rushed over to the officer. Arthur Begelman was struggling to get off the ground, and in an odd way, I worried when little Samantha Sanchez offered him a hand. But, risking her ability to remain upright, she provided him the leverage he needed to stand.

The cop was still breathing hard and every second or so would smile like Flipper to make light of his exertion. "There was this guy with what seemed to be a gun . . ."

"You're sure of that?" said Aubron Powell, a notebook in his hand. His expression was utterly calm, though all around us chaos reigned.

The cop looked frightened, more frightened of a reporter than he had been of a guy with a gun. When Arthur Begelman got to him, his eyes went all shifty.

"Where is the gunman?" Arthur demanded.

"I don't know! I chased him into the stairwell down there," he said, pointing behind him. "Just as I got into it, well, he flipped me over onto the railing, and . . . and I've got this hernia, see, and see, he got away."

The cop was beginning to sweat.

"You all right?" I asked Edward.

"I'm fine." He wasn't. He was white as a sheet. Little did I know at the time that he was wondering whether it might be Earl "Swamphut" Mosely, who he had reason to believe was to be released from prison after serving all this time for shooting his first lieutenant, Edward. In retrospect, I'm grateful that Edward had the sense not to ask the security cop whether or not his assailant was black, at least not with the cameras rolling. Then again, with a close primary, maybe that would have helped.

The hospital administrator, who was standing there wringing his hands, no doubt regretting he had ever let us into the hospital, now suggested we all move down the hall to his office. This seemed to be a smart thing to do, because all around us was this caterwaul, with patients wandering out of treatment rooms to see what was going on, women and children staring at us rather sullenly, I thought, and at about a half-dozen real cops flooding through the lobby. "What's going on?" asked one of the cops.

"Someone tried to assassinate the candidate over there."

"Who's that?"

"Don't you know? That's Edward Daley."

"No shit? He's got my vote," said the beefy officer with the rather pink face. I took that as a good sign.

We walked into the administrator's suite of offices, and there was this bank of plump women working the phones. Every light on the console was lit up and the phones kept ringing.

"Who's with Mr. Daley here?" asked one of the women.

"I am," I allowed. Edward at that moment was sinking into a couch, and Samantha Sanchez, unlike Arthur and Aubron, who were trying to find the phones, went over to him and in a very kindly voice asked how he was doing. That was nice of her.

"I got phone calls for you from WABC-TV and radio, WNBC-TV, WPIX, WNEW, WINS radio, and a whole lot more," the switchboard operator informed me.

"Can you tell them . . ."

"I ain't tellin' them nothing. You can return your own calls."

I was about to say something, but I stopped myself before saying something I might regret. "What are you going to tell them?" asked Edward. I thought for a moment. There probably wasn't time to reach Simon Ford and others in the campaign before we'd have to make a decision about what to do.

"I'm going to tell them we'll be having a press conference in an hour at the headquarters."

"Yeah, and what am I supposed to say about this?" He didn't seem the least bit nervous about asking this in the presence of reporters.

"You're going to call for the death penalty for assassins." I felt guilty saying that, I mean after seeing the electric chair and all, but this was politics.

And this was a lucky break. On the eve of the election, here we were about to get a ton of press over something that had been done to Edward. It's not easy making a thirty-five-year-old right-wing multimillionaire into a victim, but somehow this had happened. This was great!

I looked over to Edward where he was sitting with Samantha Sanchez, who was now ruffling his hair affectionately, the two of them looking into each other's eyes. I was glad for her sake that the cameraman had been left outside. I don't think her editors would have approved.

The press conference in an hour would be perfect, I just knew. Edward's voice would quaver, he'd have just had his brush with death . . .

And then I thought, Who *was* the guy with the gun? And where was he now?

# —— CHAPTER SIXTEEN ——

YOU COULD BLAME IT on my level of campaign burnout, but after we were done with the dramatic press conference, after we had made not just the affiliates but the networks themselves, I met Laurie and headed to Tribeca for some loud rock 'n' roll. Camille was playing with Carlisle Jones, and the Avengers were in from San Francisco for their first and last time, and enough was enough. It was time to thrash around like a normal person.

By now the story of the attempt to kill Edward was being printed on the front page of morning papers from here to San Diego, and before I left the Motorworks building, I made sure to catch the eleven-o'clock local news. A quick turn of dials revealed a full hit of lead-in news, with the footage by Tony Echeveria's cameraman starting off in the dark, isolated, tragic tone of another American assassination. There was this inevitability about it once you saw Edward walking down the hallway. Thank heaven this time the ending wasn't tragic.

The lights were out in the Motorworks building except in my little apartment. Though the place was makeshift, it was home. It was my preserve among the Daleys. Within these walls was my family's corporate history. In the files, in trap drawers, and on dusty shelves lay immeasurable baubles of family lore, a lore we were conspicuously uninterested in unless there could be divined some clue to the resolution of our fortune. We'd never found the proof of Grandfather's loan to Nate Stanton, but in the oddest way, Nate was still a man of his word, still a man of personal honor, and once caught, he actually had coughed up what was owed. Of course, our threat to go public may also have had a bit to do with it.

There was something a little schizzy about the joy I felt living in the family's relic town house, and the rub lay in the fact that until Edward's race came along, I was doing well deliberately staying away from the family. As far enough away as was possible in order not to be rude, and even then sometimes I'd pushed it. Now here I was myself, several months after having given up my independence, using Edward's campaign as the mechanism for resetting our place in the world to the manner that I had sometimes—in a childish way —resented we had become accustomed. I wasn't just trying to manip- ulate our image to the outside world by carefully constructing the Potemkin village in which reporters were allowed to tread. I was sucking on the collapsed bosom of the family, and I was digging it.

After the news there was one more ritual, something I just had to do, and it involved "Live at Leeds" and loud volume on the stereo. Mr. Greco was heard to crack his door open to make sure it wasn't some madman leaving as I let the front door slam and headed for St. Marks Place, near where I would pick up Laurie at the Public.

I was waiting conspicuously, my arms folded across my black T- shirt, when she looked out from the doorway. Her face was set ner- vously before she recognized me in the dark, and then she bounded down the back steps. Yellow light cast her shadow wide down Second Avenue toward the Bowery.

"How'd it go?" I asked as I took her in my arms. Her face was freshly scrubbed from taking off her makeup, but even without makeup and even in the dark, her tugging me toward her could have been accomplished without hands.

We stood kissing under the shadow of the Public Theater as the slow, dangerous foot traffic swirled sporadically around us, and some cars had the urge to honk as they drove past.

"That was nice," I managed.

"Ummmm."

It felt good to walk, to be out of a suit, to be downtown with my girl on an evening that was too early to be Indian summer, but one that had rid itself of the oppression of August air.

"We're going to Tier III?" she asked.

"If you'd like."

"Is that where you want to go? Yeah? We'll go there, then," she said, and I felt so good about life, about her, about the end of the campaign and the chance to hear loud music, I didn't even tell her someone had tried to kill my brother just a dozen hours before.

## —— CHAPTER SEVENTEEN ——

WE WERE PRESSED AGAINST the wooden bar when the Avengers hit the stage. Within seconds there was a punk-rock roar that loudly filled the club. I was looking for Camille, and if she was there I would have found her, since it was a tiny little club, Tier III, with an upstairs parlor and a downstairs bar. For months the best bands in New York had been playing here as a slightly less seedy alternative to CBGB. There were fewer kids and more consistently great bands.

Now as the bodies beside us thrashed and pogoed away, Danny Furious bashed his boxes and the chick singer with the hard cheekbones commanded that we "Ask not what you can do for your country/but what your country can do for you!" I looked around me at the dancers' eyes. Bliss in the reversion of an ethos.

There was no way we could move, and no way not to move, the power chords crashing down in buzz-saw rhythms, any attempt at actually *dancing* overridden by a super command to jerk and flop spasmodically. No matter what else was going in the city, in my life, this band now held sway. I believed in something. I believed I had to move. It was all I could do to every few seconds touch Laurie to remind her I was there. "I believe in me, one two three four," crunched the Avengers at a furious pace. By that time the brief set was over, there was no place other than West Broadway where we could cool off and let the sweat dry.

Under the penumbra of the World Trade Center, punks were sitting on car hoods, smoking cigarettes and brandishing bottles of domestic beer in the darkness of late-night downtown. Everyone was doing his damndest to be cool. Passing cabs and other cars were few and far between. I sat myself down on the hood of a Jaguar someone had stupidly parked on the street, and I wrapped my arms around Laurie's waist as she leaned back in the night air to try to cool off. I saw Carlisle Jones walk up the street toward us from Canal, and there beside him . . . yeah, it was a leather-clad, newly blond short-haired Camille.

"Jesus Christ, Camille, did you do your hair yourself?" I asked when they got close and she proffered her cheek for a kiss in a manner she'd inherited, of this I was sure, from her mother, my Aunt Rose.

"Isn't it just awful?" Carlisle said with a benevolent smile.

"Yeah, it looks worse than mine did when she cut mine," I said, shuddering at the memory.

"This is," she said, "my own creation." There was a slightly contrived haughtiness that hid the smile playing at her lips. "Hey, babe," she said to Laurie, kissing her on the cheek.

"You look like a punk Marilyn Monroe," said Laurie approvingly, perhaps a little amazed at the transformation. Laurie's blond hair fell down her T-shirted shoulders with a luxury that was now conspicuously absent in what had once been Camille's nicest feature. Actually, her nicest feature you would not ordinarily look at unless you'd saved your copy of that issue of *Hustler.*

A door opened briefly. "If and when you come," sang a voice over the sound system, "I will see you there."

"You guys see the Avengers?" Carlisle asked.

"They were so-so," said Laurie.

"They were excellent," I said.

"We were a little slow gettin' here," Carlisle drawled, his eyes flashing at Camille. She pursed her lips defiantly.

"We saw the news tonight, oh, boy," said Camille, and she reached up to stroke my cheek. "How is he?"

"He's okay. He's holding up. We got him convinced it couldn't have been Earl "Swamphut" Mosely by checking with the Pentagon."

"How's who?" asked Laurie. "Sam?"

"Someone tried to kill Edward this morning," I said.

"Haaaaa," she gasped. "Where were you when this happened?"

"Am I a suspect?"

"Where were you?" she asked anxiously again.

"About two feet away."

"Charles!"

"It was Blake," said Camille. "It had to have been." The light caught her hair from behind, and what had once been a caramel-colored wreath was a glaring pert bowl. I saw she had put a beauty mark on her cheek, and the effect was alluring, but in a brittle, sluttish manner. You wouldn't want to roll in the hay with her anymore. Maybe do it in the stairwell, but not roll in the hay.

"The thought has crossed my mind," I allowed. Uncle Andrew had one of the men from the newly saved Daley Motorworks checking up on Blake, if possible following him to make sure he didn't attack the family's outposts, burn down our forts, fob off with our firstborn.

"But, man," said Carlisle Jones, "how are you really doing?" He was standing there in droopy darkness as the club called him inside for the set his band was to play, backing up my pretty cousin in all her black-leather blondness.

"I'm somewhere between militance and catatonia. I could probably go hole up, fetal positioned, in my very own cave."

"You ever thought of writing country western tunes?" he asked, I couldn't tell whether seriously or not, but at that moment Carlisle's drummer wandered out a little agitated about the delay when there was a set to play and they didn't even have the song order figured.

"See you after the set," I said to Camille, hugging her for perhaps a second longer than it is proper to hug your female cousin when she looks, as Camille did, like a punk-rock sex goddess.

When they were inside, I sat there on the Jag with my arms around Laurie's waist as she just stood there, her back to uptown, staring me in the eyes. "Why didn't you tell me about Edward?"

"Because you are my respite, my relief, my little buttercup."

"Can it. Why didn't you tell me?" She was serious.

"Because, I guess, I wanted one evening between now and Tuesday when I didn't have to incessantly babble about the campaign."

But she didn't much buy it. We went back in and before too long the place was cooking like a juke joint from the rockabilly-surf sound of Carlisle's guitar, the stand-up drummer's backbeat, and the bluesy harmonies of Camille and her legendary boyfriend. Some of their songs were soulful enough to take your breath away, and some of them pronounced it was time to body slam. Laurie smiled at me as I watched Owen obscenely pogoing with Sheena, Uncle Ethan's six-foot secretary, of all people, but there weren't many other smiles out of her that night. We rode back to the Daley Motorworks' building early in the morning in a cab that smelled of cigar smoke, the all-news radio repeating the message that there were no leads in the attempted assassination of Edward Daley, whom the *Daily News* was now projecting was running neck and neck for the Senate nomination three days away.

## ——— CHAPTER EIGHTEEN ———

SATURDAY MADE ME FALL in love with politics all over again. We sat in the headquarters and laughed and laughed while Edward, with a respite from the road, sat giving one on ones to reporters from all the Sunday papers. A few of them actually wanted a reprise of why the voters should unseat Senator Stanton in Tuesday's primary election. Most simply wanted details of how he had felt upon being told that someone was standing there in the hospital hallway intent on doing him in. Edward played it like a Stratocaster.

"Goddamn," said a hung-over and seemingly well-laid Owen when he read the *New York Post*. "How could he say such a thing?" We weren't laughing about Uncle Nate. We were laughing about our inevitable, or so it seemed today, general-election opponent, Hamlet O. Cattanasio.

Somehow the *Post* had laid its hands on Cattanasio's diary entries in regard to Nate and Edward. "I'll crush them into dust," read this particular excerpt from around the time of the debate last month. "I'll smite them, drive locusts through their well-larded kitchens. I will bring them down from the heights of their assimilated kingdom. I will lay them low." It went on like that for several more paragraphs, but you get the point.

It was particularly fun to read the explanation by Julia "The Whip" Luca, Cattanasio's spokesman. She claimed the passage came not from Cattanasio's diaries, but from a mail-order creative-writing class he was taking, and she denied it had anything to do with the Stantons or the Daleys. It was a nice try.

Everything seemed on track for Tuesday. The phone banks were at full pitch, the mail had finally dropped, and within forty-eight hours, six million missives, targeted to specific voters by an extraordinarily complicated formula, would be hitting people's mailboxes. We were once again heavily on the air, with a judicious mix of final jabs at Nate and high-minded, feel-good spots that reminded you of all the ads Edward had had on the air since his announcement of candidacy. It was meant to seem like a nostalgic culmination of a long-running sitcom.

Tomorrow we were to go back on the road, hitting our upstate base, coming back Monday for a quick helicopter ride out to a rally in Nassau County. We now believed that in spite of their switch to Uncle Nate, we could override the party organization with our non-stop media barrage. A great deal depended on it; perhaps the election.

Nate was finally slugging back with some spots that stressed his sure hand, his vast experience, with cutting remarks about the zealotry of rich kids. It was supposed to be a populist slam at Edward; my sense, and this was borne out by our polling, was that it merely rubbed in the fact that Nate was part of an Establishment people were ready to rebel against.

It was a fun Saturday. Uncle Wolfy came by with platters of food he and his girlfriend had made at Wolfy's Fifth Avenue place, a friendly gesture that evoked his newfound peace and the confidence that stemmed from having finished his book. It might not sell as well as his ex-wife's book—not many books did—but he clearly had greater celebrity this late summer than Rose did, and I was certain he would finish on top when the book was finally out.

For Rose's television show was beginning to languish, and whereas at first her guests had been the hippest of the hip, when I had turned it on a few weeks ago, she was enthusiastically introducing these two well-coiffed types from Vegas who made tigers jump through walls and disappear. It could only loosely be called peformance art. She looked a little desperate, and it was perhaps mean of us to take advantage of her fall by buying lots of ads on the adjacencies to her show. But we did it.

It was hard to see how anything could go wrong now that Edward was surging in the polls. He was actually two points ahead in the *Daily News* poll, and while, to be honest, Mitch still showed him to be a few points behind, the trend was all in our direction. We had a good shot at overtaking Nate on Monday, but things could just as easily swing Nate's way.

Television crews wanted to accompany our final fly around, and it was expected that wherever we landed, Edward would be greeted like a conquering hero. County chairmen who had been the least helpful were letting us know that they had secretly turned their people loose to jump on our bandwagon. I was a little upset that Laurie was upset with me, but that could be worked out. Everything could be worked out. The feeling of winning, of riding that surge of voter sentiment over the top, is an absolute high. Nothing could stop us now.

# —— CHAPTER NINETEEN ——

MY HANDS GROPED FOR the light that at last snapped on unmercifully. "Wha . . . Hullo?" I was in the Holiday Inn in Binghamton, and I'd gone to bed, a good boy, an hour earlier. This wasn't so obvious an act of abnegation as it sounds. We were to arise early to fly to Utica, and the women at the bar downstairs were so unspeakably lumpen, I couldn't bear to witness the members of the large contingent of press pick another one of them up.

"It's Owen." Owen? Oh, Owen.

"Yeah, Owen, what's up?"

"They got cable up there?"

"I'll let you know in the morning."

"I take that to mean you haven't seen what your chum Tony Echeveria did to us tonight on Channel Two."

"Tell me." Uh oh. I was wide-awake now, sitting up in bed, bearing down on the phone as if it were a lifeline.

"He went on the air with the footage, right, of you and Edward at that hospital. Only rather than play it as he did the first night, now he's sayin' the police are sayin' that this security cop there confessed the whole thing was a fraud, and that he was paid five K just to say he saw a guy with a gun. Apparently, the cop thought he'd get away with a falsified report."

"Wow." I looked around the room. Stark plastic conformity. Home away from home.

" 'Course Tony then made the necessary connection of saying that 'veteran political observers . . .' "

"He means himself," I interrupted.

" 'Course he does. He's sayin' that these 'observers' have observed the only person to gain from a falsified assassination attempt would be Edward."

"Oh, shit. Where is this cop? Who does he say bribed him?"

"I dunno the answer to either one of those, Charles. But we better find out quick. This things going to blow like a refinery fire."

I groaned.

"You sleep tight now, hear?"

"Ummmm," I said, and got up to tell the candidate before he had to read it in the morning paper.

## ── CHAPTER TWENTY ──

"HOAX" READ THE FRONT page of the *New York Post,* but in its subdued manner, the *Times* was by far the more damaging. I stood in the lobby of the Binghamton Holiday Inn blinking in the early-morning light and reading the story by the *Time*'s Metro Desk crime reporter, of all the people to put on a political story, about how the police had determined the assassination attempt at Montefiore was someone's put-up job. The one thing the police had confirmed was the security cop had not acted on his own; he had blubberingly produced forty-nine hundred of the five grand in cash he'd been paid by the hoax-ter, whoever that was.

"Morning," said Aubron Powell with his usual politeness. He was dressed in a charcoal-gray double-breasted suit the likes of which this lobby had never before witnessed. He looked rather grand.

"Morning. Aubron, can you tell me? How the hell could the *Times* run this piece and not bother for a react from our camp?"

"I don't suppose it really called for a reaction, Charles. It doesn't accuse you of anything; it only says your tiger had the most to benefit from a phony assassination attempt."

"Let me read it to you then. 'Authorities tonight were seeking to interview members of the Daley campaign's staff to seek information about their knowledge of the fraud.' What the hell is that supposed to mean?"

"Shhhhh," said Aubron with his finger to his lips. "You'll wake all the guests, Charles, and I don't much like being yelled at. You have a problem," he pronounced with great deliberation.

"Someone paid an obscure security cop to engage in a criminal act," Aubron continued, "the filing of a false report with the police. And with all journalistic objectivity, that news is fit to print. And from where I sit, having watched a campaign that was willing to spend millions and engage in some pretty harsh tactics to win—there are those who wonder whether this whole campaign might have more to do with settling family scores than in your brother simply becoming a solon—it is not inconceivable to me that you might have set the whole thing up."

I was going to explode. How could he think this? "How could we think we could get away with this, Aubron?"

"Precisely. And if I doubt you, wait until Arthur Begelman gets out of bed and calls his desk for instructions." And with that, he calmly left to go eat breakfast. He was about to discover that the Holiday Inn in Binghamton did not have pickled herring.

## ── CHAPTER TWENTY-ONE ──

BAD NEWS SHADOWED OUR plane like a cloud. From Utica to Plattsburgh my ears rang with the questions my poor brother had been asked at his early-morning press conference, and I began to suspect the journalists who were traveling with us were having sport at our expense.

"All right, Begelman," I said, whirling in the aisle on Arthur.

"What did I do?" he asked innocently, his pudgy hands in the air, his pipe clenched between teeth. And then he broke into giggles and so did a number of his colleagues.

"Why don't we have a little interview session?" I said. "That way you can ask the questions you want without having to in front of the local reporters you love to impress."

It was true. Arthur loved asking the nastiest question he could as the opening act of a press conference on some dismal little upstate runway, in a bald-faced effort to rile up the locals. There was no telling what manner of craziness he could inspire.

"Okay, I'll ask him now. But that's no guarantee my desk—I mean, another question—might not come to me later." And that set them off in hysterics again, all of them save Samantha Sanchez, who was strangely quiet on this trip. The rest of the pack hit us with their best shots.

Actually, the news wasn't all bad, especially the revelation that *New York* magazine had a cover story that was a marvel of inside knowledge and astute speculation. The reporter fingered Blake upfront as a maniac, going so far as to reveal his role in the death of my doggy. I was told that in addition to a lovely photo of Fido and me, which could only have been provided from family vaults, there was a watercolor of the smashed aquarium in Blake's wake at Club Blech. The sharks in the picture were directly contrasted with a picture of Uncle Ethan and Uncle Nate. I kind of liked that.

Owen read me the piece at a cost of about twenty dollars a minute over the airplane phone. It began to be clear where the reporter had received a large measure of her information. And what information it was!

The reporter described with an amazing amount of inside knowledge the business deal between my two grandfathers going sour. What a picture: the erect and tweedy governor wandering through the track site in the hills of South Carolina while the fast-talking southern sharpie points to imaginary concession stands, bleachers, and pits, money shimmering at the end of the imaginary straightaway. She was a good writer, and I say that because she captured with unbelieveable detail my meeting just last week with Uncle Nate, wherein the financial scores between our families had been settled.

Christ, I don't know how fast she could write, but there was information in the article that was current up to the time that assassin either did or did not stalk Edward. *New York* must have had editors working all weekend. All the lines were beginning to converge on tomorrow, and it was clear, absolutely clear, that *New York*'s source for most of this was someone in the immediate family. I suspected Betsy.

Judging from the results, I couldn't be mad, because it made the Stantons look so much worse than we did. The reason for that was Blake.

The piece portrayed Blake as the rogue attack dog of Stanton foreign policy, baring his fangs on anything and anyone who would challenge his ability to sit back and sponge drug money from his relatives. Until he got his hands on his share of the trust, of course. There was a fragmentary photograph of him from that time when he was kicked out of Yale, and he looked real mean.

From what I could tell from what Owen read to me, it was obvious that Blake was behind the assassination attempt; the trick was in proving it before the election tomorrow. Who was the source? I mean, the description of the hospital coconspirator fit Blake to a T!

There was considerable argument back in the headquarters in New York that it really didn't matter, that by the time the news had sunk in, the polls would be closed. I'd had it babbled to me by Owen, but I didn't much buy it. I didn't buy it because I knew that everywhere across the state, when people woke up in the morning, the article they would read about the Republican Senate primary would focus on whether or not the Daleys had engineered a hoax to push their man over the top. We couldn't afford to have that happen.

We'd been good at bluffing the Stantons lately. We had to do it one more time.

## —— CHAPTER TWENTY-TWO ——

THE KING AIR SPUTTERED and coughed over the treetops of Plattsburgh. For a moment we saw the squat outline of Dannemora Prison, and I thought with a little luck we could have Blake soon singing Christmas carols there. The trick was in making Uncle Ethan see that it was in his interest to throw his nephew to the dogs. I wanted to accomplish this not least because I still blamed myself a little for throwing my dog to his nephew.

The plane landed bumpily and there was more bad news outside. No marching bands up here in the mosquito barrens, just a minor-league team of reporters who had elbowed their way past our assembled campaign volunteers, their eyes not so much on Edward as on the press people who got off the plane with us. Our supporters had driven from the ends of Lake Champlain, responding to the eleven thousand or so phone calls that Tim Verkhovensky had overseen at just our North Country phone bank alone. We needed bodies for these final rallies, something I trusted would be my final media manipulation of the primary campaign.

We pushed the reporters who were traveling with us out onto the runway, and taking gulps of air, we prepared to tumble forth. "Anything special you want me to say here?" Edward asked me when he saw the reporters, Arthur Begelman in particular, were standing away from the metal staircase that dropped from the airplane's belly.

"You gotta come down hard on the people who would, uh, perpetrate such a hoax as the one you were a victim of."

He looked at me as if it would take some convincing to pull that one off. He began to rub his metal arm, which he always did at times of anxiety.

Just as he was about to get off the plane I told him, "I'm going to try something here. I'm calling Ethan as soon as the reporters are finished with you."

"To say what?" He was edgy, as he should be when the subject turned to Ethan. Our supporters were waving. He made no move to move.

"I've got to persuade him that it's in his interest to turn Blake in."

He laughed for a second. "I've always admired your sense of humor. How are you going to pull that off?"

"We'll think of something," I said, gingerly stepping onto the tarmac.

It was clear something was up from the way all the reporters who were traveling with us were now fixated on a tear sheet from the AP wire. They hardly looked up as we walked over toward them. Edward waved to the crowd, which was kept at a distance, standing in their egregious mix of colors and hats and old shit-kicking boots. They were standing dumbly next to the terminal, penned in by our advance men.

"Hey there," said Edward to the local reporters.

"Who's Charles Daley?" asked a no-nonsense television reporter who was carrying the boom mike himself.

"I am," I said, my voice all squeaky. Christ, all the press conferences I'd managed for Edward, and when the prospect arose that *I* would have to answer questions, I was scared half to death. Standing there on the runway, there was no way of putting the reporters on hold, no way I could ask if we could speak off the record. I would have felt a whole lot more comfortable if that reporter had been holding a telephone rather than a microphone.

"The New York City police this morning released information that says the person who bribed Officer Lancelotti—the security officer at the hospital—was named Charles Daley."

"Not me!" I looked around for a character witness. It was clear that wasn't going to be Edward; he looked as if just maybe he would visit me in prison. Aubron Powell and Samantha Sanchez came to my rescue, sort of.

"The police revealed that sorry little hoaxter says the person calling himself Charles Daley didn't fit your description. Apparently, he was a much bigger guy." Thank you, Aubron.

"And they aren't even putting out a warrant for your arrest. Yet," said Samantha. Thank you, I think. "They do want you to call them, though."

"How do you explain this, Mr. Daley?" asked a slick, blow-dried television reporter you could tell was just itching to get out of Plattsburgh. With luck, he'd make it to Albany or Hartford in a year.

"I can't explain it. It's inexplicable." I didn't want to throw them Blake, for that would simply turn this into a charge and countercharge exercise I suspected now would best be left to private diplomacy.

I remember the rest of the press barrage, though not very well, and then Edward stepped forward and said somewhat impassionedly —a rarity for him—"Can't you see? We're the victims of this hoax. Contrary to what 'political observers' have said, we have nothing to be gained from this. Let's put it behind us. Tomorrow is a day when the Republicans of New York have to make a decision about whether they want lower or higher taxes. They have to decide whether they want a stronger America or an America that capitulates to the Soviets. They have to decide whether they want a senator who will fight for them in Washington, or will continue to be the tool of the special interests. Let's put this silly thing behind us and talk about what's important in this campaign."

Edward had, I noticed, been pulling his punches ever since Nate handed over the five million bucks. Could it have been a very sophisticated bribe?

The locals scribbled down his answer, our traveling press stared off into the clouds, and while the cameras whirred, we walked toward the crowd. I could tell no one was convinced. The convincing could only be accomplished by the other side confessing. I left Edward with our local contacts and headed for the phones.

## ── CHAPTER TWENTY-THREE ──

THIS WAS NO TIME for consultants. In a way, what needed to be done had less to do with the campaign than with the family, if the two could be divorced. Blake hadn't thrown a table through our campaign headquarter's window. He'd knifed my dog, not some abstract campaign mascot. His rockets had buzzed cousin Camille on Independence Day, and the bottles of piss he'd left by the side of the road weren't intended for our campaign workers. No, we could settle this one ourselves.

Except, a thought did cross my mind there at the airport. While Edward, in the safe hands of local coordinators, spoke to the crowd outdoors, I persuaded the head of a charter company to loan me his office for a few minutes, and I sank into his chair to make a call.

I was trying to reach Angela. A friend now, a friend of Laurie's and mine, the last time I had seen her was at brunch at Raul's on Spring Street some weeks before. I thought I would try to enlist her in a little scam, because I needed the help of a reporter. And since she had written that piece on my family, her career had taken off. You should have seen the feature she wrote on Truman Capote.

A receptionist whose voice I didn't recognize, and who didn't know who I was, told me that Angela was away on assignment. When pressed, the new receptionist admitted Angela was on the road with Hamlet O. Cattanasio, whom the *News* had already endorsed for senator. So, scratching my brow, sitting underneath a photograph of the President of the United States, I asked if I could speak to Paddy Mack. I noticed Carter's huge teeth set in a grin that was at least half the size of his face, and I mused on that as I waited to see if I would get through. Paddy was sure to be in. Didn't he just sit there awaiting his instructions from the Politburo?

"Charles Daley, of all people. You'll give me a bad reputation."

"Hello, Patrick."

"Are you callin' me from jail?" he asked in his lilt.

"Not yet, but if I do go to jail, I'll start a hunger strike that would make you proud."

"That's my trickle-down lad. You called for a purpose. I can't imagine you're calling idly. And I doubt it's to gossip about the alibi *New York* wrote for you."

"I need help." I didn't know any other way of saying it.

"I've heard," he said. "They're saying the person who set up your little media stunt used your name. Sloppy, Charles, I must say."

I bit my tongue. I needed to ask Paddy for help, but there was no reason to expect it. Our old times weren't anything to call upon. He had nothing to gain from it. But I had no other reporters I could turn to for fear what I asked them might of itself become a story. Paddy couldn't get into print until after election day. So I plunged.

"Patrick, the person who set me up is this sicko cousin of mine, the son of Nate and Ethan's younger sister."

"Your cousin Blake Abbott, if I recall."

"Yeah, I forgot how well versed you are in my family," I lied, remembering that obnoxious piece he wrote about us. "But, you see, he's been engaged in a variety of stunts that have been getting increasingly threatening, right? And to be honest with you, I think he's been doing it on his own. I can't see Ethan being stupid enough to have put him up to it, even though Blake used to work for him."

Paddy was listening and it was time to make my pitch. "I'm sitting here in a little charter terminal in Plattsburgh, and we're traveling with a host of reporters who have nothing to write about other than the suspicion that Edward and I have been fingered as having set up that stupid hoax. Now, I'm positive that Ethan is either at Nate's office or at his campaign headquarters sweating this thing out. He has to know it was Blake, either because Ethan had a hand in it, which I doubt, or because he's smart enough to put two and two together. And Ethan is not a completely unreasonable guy . . ."

"He is the scum of the earth," Paddy said in his vague brogue.

I crossed my fingers. "Okay, but he's a practical son of a bitch, and if a reporter were to call him suggesting he knew the connection between him and Blake, and from there the connection between Blake and the assassination attempt, it could get him to see the wisdom of separating himself from the slimy punk who's responsible for the position we're in."

There was an audible sigh from the other end of the line. "Ah, Charles, I know exactly the position you're in, but I can't help you. It would be wrong, both as a journalist and as an . . . activist. I can't help your brother; he's as bad as Nate Stanton and worse. I'd like to help you, but I can't."

"I understand," I said, instantly regretting the waste of time. I forgave him for it, but as I hung up the phone I cursed my luck. I would have to reach Ethan myself.

## ── CHAPTER TWENTY-FOUR ──

NOW, THERE WAS A marching band, and it made the hair on the back of my neck stand on end. I squinted involuntarily as I looked through the tin blinds to the lawn outside the air terminal. Pudgy majorettes dropped their batons as their tubaed brethren farted a hideous arrangement of "New York, New York."

So I drew the blinds and went to work finding the number of the Stanton headquarters on West 45th Street near the old Peppermint Lounge.

Ethan was surprised I'd tracked him down. "What in the name of Fuckwad do you want?" he demanded, and I told him we were still hoping for his endorsement.

"So, you've still got your sense of humor, huh, Charles? Is this gallows humor or jailbird humor?"

"Why don't I get to the point."

"That would be a novelty. I'm just sitting here planning our victory celebration for tomorrow night. There'll be lots of big show-biz names. Starlets, Charles. Easy starlets. You should come, provided, of course, that Edward makes a gracious concession speech, and early."

"Listen, Ethan, don't spend what you don't have." That's not the family motto, I admit. Of course, we were considerably better off this month than we had been last month.

"All right, Charles, what do you want?"

"Blake."

"I haven't seen him since he got back from Maine. I've been spending very little time in Mingeboro, what with the campaign and all. Now that you've behaved like a highwayman, I'm not certain I can afford my house."

"I believe you, Uncle Ethan. But you see, when we get back to New York this afternoon, and Edward holds his final press conference in which he blames you personally for sending Blake to mastermind his little hospital stunt, your life could start getting awfully complicated."

"You've tried this sort of thing before, Charles, and it's not going to work. Good-bye."

"Uncle Ethan, this is a promise. Just like it was a promise when you said to me, 'Just don't say we didn't warn you,' exactly two days before my dog was butchered. You keep your promises; you're a great inspiration to me. So I promise you, in one hour, we're going to fly to Albany, and from there we go to New York. We're going to land at Butler Aviation at LaGuardia in time for the evening news. We've got this little rally going, see. I'm sure every network will be there when Edward stands up and says that he's learned it was you who put that dumb shit officer up to faking the assassination attempt."

"It'll never work." His calmness was transparent.

"Oh? You know, I was taught a lot about politics by you, Uncle Ethan. And one of the things you taught me was that you can have a twenty-four-hour press strategy. There are things you can say just before an election that you can't say in the middle of the campaign. You can make a charge, and it's up to the other guy to disprove it. Our back's against the wall. This election's tight. We're not going to let you get away with this."

"Listen, you little cocksucker," he now said to me, "you're the one in the fix. The guy who bribed that cop was named Charles Daley . . ."

"There isn't a reporter in the state who can't see through that. Even Arthur Begelman. And besides, the cops have already said it wasn't me. If they thought it was, I'd be arrested by now. Ethan, we can hang this one on you. You're going to spend years after the election trying to dig yourself out from underneath the rubble. You wanted war; we're going to leave you looking like East Berlin. You've seen the piece in *New York*. And that was written without our cooperation. Wait until you see what happens after the campaign when we begin to cooperate with any muckraker in town who wants to go after you. I'll trundle out witnesses who'll get your facial tic hopping. Maybe I'll do the writing myself."

"I have to go now, Charles."

"You hear that ticking sound? You know what that is?"

"I'm not buying today, Charles," he said, and with that he hung up on me. I listened until the recording of the operator came on the line. Outside came the sound of some big old galoot who thought he was a stem-winder. Oh, yeah, the county chairman. Hmm. He'd defected to us. I kept hearing his big words booming across the crowd. I slowly stood up and went to the door, and as soon as I whipped it open, the head of the charter company nearly collapsed at my feet. He had been crouching with his ear to the door.

"So, uh, politics fun?" he asked. He seemed eager to please.

## ── CHAPTER TWENTY-FIVE ──

IT WAS ON A charter plane to Teterboro that Edward's campaign had been born, and now upon this final leg we were downright giddy. On that first leg back from South Carolina, we were surrounded by our family. And here we were months later with the reporters showing nothing but relief that the primary was almost over. My emotions on this last leg were part nostalgia, part suffused desire to rush from the King Air the moment we set down upon the ground.

Perhaps it had been a mistake to have planned that rally in Albany, that island of Democrats in a sea of Republican farmland. We knew something was wrong when, in the middle of Edward's remarks to a group of perhaps one hundred supporters, Mayor Erastus Corning began spontaneously to extemporize on the other side of the Capitol steps—and three thousand Democrats, mysteriously released from work, sober, attentive, enthusiastic, forged their way forth to listen to him. "This looks ridiculous," said Edward in a stage whisper, and he was right about that one.

When we checked in by pay phone we were told by Owen that the progress we'd been making in the polls was arrested. "The only new arrest since the hoax," Edward said glumly, forgetting that Officer Lancelotti now languished on bail in his home in Jersey City.

But while no single night's sample told the tale, the tracking polls could indicate the trend, and the trend they picked up was the end of Edward's rise. We were dead even the day before the election. Perhaps we were dead, period.

But we couldn't show gloom to reporters. One whiff of that and we were done for. When we got on that plane for the final flight, Edward was stoic but relaxed. It was as if having discounted predictions of a Harvard victory, now he had to keep the Yale team spirits up. He was lighthearted, perhaps the word is resigned, for there was nothing we really could do now. But stolid as he appeared, he really was quite loose, and I remember thinking that if he could have behaved this way with reporters over the course of this long race, Nate Stanton would never have had a prayer. And prayers were something we now silently reverted to.

"So what happens if you lose?" Arthur Begelman, with a midafternoon scotch in his hand, asked Edward. He had rather noisily been getting tanked since morning.

"I won't have to deal with assholes like you, I suppose."

I guess in print that doesn't sound like the perfect rejoinder, but the effect on the plane was electric. Reporters actually burst into applause, until someone realized that either way, win or lose, Edward would still be on the ballot in November, because he was the Conservative Party's nominee. But I knew, we all knew, that should he lose the Republican nomination, he would be hard-pressed to muster the energy to run on just that one line in the general.

I was proud of my brother, I don't mind telling you. I was proud, first and foremost, that he'd been such a better candidate than I had expected. I was proud of the experience of having worked with him

—for him—for the months since I'd cashed in my independence and voluntarily immersed myself in the family. It was in large part due to Edward that, once immersed, I hadn't drowned. I was willing these days to push under the swamp water the head of anyone who slammed us.

"What are *you* going to do if you lose?" Samantha Sanchez then asked me.

"We're not going to lose."

It was awfully clear what Samantha and Edward were going to do, win, lose, or draw, and that was tear each other's clothes off, and maybe before they could even get to the privacy of Edward's home.

I tried to be motivated for the subsequent helicopter ride to Nassau County, but I couldn't. We swept down over the massive homes of Tuxedo Park, with all those English gardens and statues and columns in the parkland, and then we took the turn that brought us over the boring normalcy of row upon row of Bergen County developments. I'd lied when I told Ethan we were going to land at La-Guardia; it was Teterboro where we began this air war, and there where we would end it. There was no press conference planned.

We would no doubt have a nice turnout for our rally in Hemp-stead Township, since we had had Conservative Party members from all over the state bused in for the event. Nearby Suffolk County had provided us with almost every school bus from the Town of Islip, and I thought about the children there, trying to get home, wondering where the row of yellow buses had been spirited off to. Our hope was that even in Nassau County there were enough dissidents who, in the safety of the crowd, would risk their chances of ever being a drain commissioner to support a Republican primary candidate who did not have the blessing of the party. It helped that, in Tim Verkhovensky's lingo, we'd been carpet bombing them with television into some kind of submission. Maybe back into the Stone Age. There were times when you've just got to love Democracy.

Edward had that steely look on his face. He glowed like a girder when he was doing his duty. I imagine he had looked different when Mr. Earl "Swamphut" Mosely blew his arm to smithereens. But on this particular flight, that steel was tempered by a look of warmth that for too long had been missing in him, for too long had been the missing vital spark.

The plane lurched and bumped as it landed, and there was a smattering of applause. It was five-thirty, and we were right on time, a condition of our campaign. If we lost, I thought suddenly, I would spend as much time as I could with my time unstructured. I wanted time to be sloppy, to be frayed and rent by whimsy.

We waited until the reporters had gathered up their belongings for the last time in the primary. When they were all done, Edward made his way up to the cockpit and thanked each of the pilots for the job they'd done over the course of the campaign. "Good job," he said to the captain.

"You too, Lieutenant," the captain replied, and Edward grinned for a minute or two.

I didn't expect there would be anything but the most functional greeting party waiting for us on the runway, just enough people to get us to our helicopter and the reporters to the one we'd chartered for them. But there was Owen, with a wide smile on his face, and there was Mr. Greco. Stanley, our old driver, stood perspiring in his winter coat as the sun shone down upon us. Betsy actually had taken time off from work—and from leaking to *New York* magazine—to be out there on the tarmac, ready to hug our brother Edward. And there was Annie with tears streaming down her cheeks. And also this strange bearded fellow lurking behind them, and I knew from the metallic cackle he let forth that it could only be Rick Morgan, the campaign's reclusive communications director. There were about a dozen clustered members of our campaign standing in the clear September light. And the strangest thing, well, the thing I couldn't figure, was they were all huge with joy, beyond the call for normal end-of-campaign backslapping.

Owen stepped forth importantly. "I don't know what you said to him, Charles, but Ethan just went on Tony Echeveria's five-o'clock news. He fingered Blake."

The size of Edward's grin was presidential.

## ⸺ CHAPTER TWENTY-SIX ⸺

WHATEVER IS THE STATE of New York's ordinance about champagne in helicopters, we were breaking it as we flew over Manhattan. Its arteries were clogged, the traffic heavy, but Edward and I were giggling and clinking stems while we choppered over the East River and across Queens. From the Whitestone Bridge on our left to Coney Island way over there on our right, all I could see were voter households, and I wondered how many, if any, would be mobilizing in the morning to vote for my brother besides me. These suburbs were a lit-up pinball machine of Democratic votes. We were moments away from their mirror image Republican machine.

Maybe it was the champagne, but I was tempted to give the reporters in the helicoper behind us the slip, to do something irresponsible like turn the chopper around and head for, oh, I don't know where, but some place other than Hempstead. Some place other than the site of Edward's final campaign speech of the primary, which if things continued at this rate, he would deliver with a load on.

The highways were roiled with the tight red stream of brake-lit cars, and as always I was happy to be above it. We passed over homes in woody hideaways, over shopping malls and the endless rows of suburban grid, over the highways that had ruthlessly cut around the estates of robber barons and over the potato fields of plain folks. Edward was leaning back, his face contented in sunlight, his eyes a little bloodshot, his victory within reach. Then the pilot seemed to get busy on the radio, though we couldn't hear a word above our forward spinning whine.

The pilot leaned back toward me and motioned to a headset. I'm a quick learner, so I put it on. "There's a radio message for you, Mr. Daley," he said in the cavernlike roar at the heart of my earphones.

"Okay," I said into the little microphone at my lips.

"The person who's sending it, a Mr. Owens, is concerned that others will hear the message."

"Tell him if it's important enough just to go ahead."

Edward was oblivious. He would have been up in the clouds if there were any.

A moment later, the chopper pilot once again crooked his neck toward me. "All right, Mr. Owens is coming through."

And with that I heard "Charles?" in this incorporeal voice as if Owen were radioing down from Venus.

"What's going on?" I asked, not thinking there was anything that could break our champagne-laden reverie, the feeling of being lighter than air. I can't tell you how many times I had been dragged to a phone for "emergencies" that were the political equivalent of a hangnail.

"We got a real genuine problem." I thought he was going to say a phone bank was down, or some county chairman was bitching about not having "walking-around money." But this was bigger than that.

"Apparently, five minutes after Ethan went on CBS to finger Blake, Blake tore out of All Odds in his Porsche. He had a gun."

"My God. How do you know that?"

"Uncle Andrew had someone from the factory watching the house, and the guy actually came through."

"Yeah?"

"And accordin' to Andrew, Blake headed up toward the foundry and there is lots of Targy activity."

"So?" I couldn't tell what he was driving at, or why this should be of such concern to us when tomorrow Edward here could be the party's nominee.

"Sam and Claire and the kids went up there for a picnic this afternoon, and they haven't come back yet."

"Oh, Jesus," I said, ripping off the headset so hard I knocked the champagne bottle in Edward's hand into a fizzy puddle on the floor. "Pilot," I shouted, "there's a change in our destination. Turn this fucker around!"

"What is it?" Edward asked, but I was back on the headset talking to Owen.

"What do you need me to do?" asked Owen.

"Get Andrew to drag as many people as he can up there pronto. If he needs transportation, break out the Lazzies, but tell him to get up there fast."

"All right," said Owen. "Uh, over and away, er, out."

I quickly told Edward what was up, and when the pilot continued to skim above the highway out toward Hempstead, the two of us nearly throttled him.

"I gotta tell air traffic where we're going before I can turn it around!" he shouted rather desperately into his mike. "Where we going?"

"Mingeboro, Connecticut, and we need to be there *now!*"

"That's up near the Lime Rock Race Track?"

"You got it."

Suddenly the chopper turned in a smooth arch over the Long Island Expressway and began to fight against the winds. We were soon aiming for Shea Stadium and the shores of Flushing Bay. "What do I tell the other chopper?"

"Nothing!" Edward and I both shouted, though by the time we got to the Whitestone, they were tagging along behind us.

There was a minor victory at work here, in that Arthur Begelman, who had been convinced there wasn't going to be any news coming out of the trip to Hempstead, had headed back to the newsroom by car to file a story on Uncle Ethan's dramatic indictment of Blake. Aubron Powell and Samantha Sanches, as well as this guy from the AP, were the only ones in the chopper on our tail. Aubron was still there, as he put it, "in case he gets shot on my watch."

I was glad Arthur wasn't along for the ride, but it would have slowed down their chopper, that's for sure. We rode in silence for the longest time, watching as New York City finally gave way to Westchester, and once we got to the Hudson River right about at Tarrytown, we began to head due north.

There was something building in Edward, I could sense it, though he would wait until he could stand it no more before he'd talk about it. I didn't know what we'd find up on Mount Targa, but one thing I was sure of was that Sam knew the top of the mountain better than any Targy. It had been his domain back in the old days when he hung out with the Targy kids. So while Edward's fretting increased moment by moment, I had the mitagating knowledge that Blake, gun, Porsche, and all, was on unequal footing when it came to Sam and the woods.

We'd spent many a summer up there, Stanton and Daley alike, uneasily accepting the fact that in August that mountain was shared turf. My mother practically lived up there in the summer, sailing in what had once been limestone quarries. When we were kids and we'd summered with our Stanton cousins up top, I'd had my first inkling that Blake might be more than just a simple bully—he'd taken such pleasure in torturing frogs; he'd shown such joy in putting lye on the salt licks, projecting the megadeath of deer.

"This is all my fault," Edward finally said. The river was wide as we followed its twists and turns. It wasn't hard to figure out why the towns had names like Rhinecliff and Rhinebeck.

"That's bullshit."

"Sam and Claire and the kids wouldn't be in danger if it weren't for me."

"Hush," I said, tapping him gently on the arm.

But then he turned away and was silent as we flew east over the farms of Dutchess County, over the estates of Millbrook, and slowly, steadily, with the reporters in our wake, began to hone in on the mountain that produced the iron that had forged the Republic.

## —•— CHAPTER TWENTY-SEVEN ———

FIVE KNUCKLES ON EDWARD'S good hand showed white as we swept across the lake. Mount Targa loomed closer and closer and Edward quit his grip on the back of the pilot's seat, easing back into his own. "The view down on you Daleys from the mountain is very clear this time of year," Ethan had scrawled to me back in the spring. Now we were swiftly coming up on All Odds and our view down on it was as clear as a bombardier's.

Edward had guided us masterfully, like a commanding officer ferreting out the enemy. His nose was high in the air even as he stared directly down onto the lake. I wonder what the townsfolk thought as our helicopter convoy swept by at one thousand feet, though they'd probably guess wrong, it being Uncle Nate who regularly returned home in this modest fashion.

Shadows loped across the old farmhouse, and I looked for Blake's Porsche. Please, I prayed for just a moment, wishing that the hunting was good and that Blake was already home with a rabbit to stew for dinner. We saw neither hide nor hare.

Soon enough, as we sent whitecaps lapping on the shores of the small lake on the top of Mount Targa, we knew we were at the right place. There at the side of the old dirt road were the remaining seven Lazzies that Blake hadn't smashed. This is terrible, I mean we're talking about a life-or-death situation, not just of my brother, but of his wife and little children, but I couldn't help letting my eyes linger for a minute on the Lazzies as we landed, hoping to find my violet baby safe. Thank God, it was there. Now where the hell was Sam?

We landed on the spot where the old dirt road from Mingeboro and the pocked road to New York State met by the side of the lake. There were some cars other than the Lazzies abandoned here, several with their doors open, one with its motor running, jeeps and station wagons that members of the family and others had piled into as the news spread of Blake's departure with a gun. And over there in the clearing underneath the sycamores, over there by the path to the foundry, was Blake's purple Porsche. I prayed we weren't too late.

Edward and I unsnapped our seat belts and were out of the chopper before the pilot could get the blades turned off. I had to remind Edward to move forward, not around the tail, because it was viciously whirring like a buzz saw at a mill. It was clear that his senses were still a little clouded from the champagne we'd drunk in celebration —hah!—not an hour ago. We stood on the dirt road, not sure where to go, the cars all around us, the forest deep. Above us came the sound of the other chopper trying to find a nearby spot where it could land. I was grateful they were struggling, especially if as they landed they would set down upon my demented cousin. Where was everyone?

One mile down the path from the lake was the crumbling old foundry that had once produced cannonballs to be fired at the British. Now it was a hulk, a relic, a fun place to picnic. Now it was a repository for Miller Lite bottles, Zig Zag wrappers, and condom packets.

Given the placement of the cars, given that one of the Lazzies no doubt carried Sam and Claire and the kids earlier, it was likely that they had trudged down this path, probably picnicking with a large wicker basket. Blake would have guessed this. He must have seen them coming up here before he got the word that Uncle Ethan had ratted on him, before finding out that this was no longer his happy home.

We tore down that mountain path as if we were children again, as if it were Capture the Flag and we were shirts versus skins. Except we weren't playing. Edward's steel arm flashed in the light, its surface brighter than anything that had been produced in the foundry during the War of Independence. I was right on his tail, and I marveled at his balance as he skipped over rocks, over tree trunks, in his cordovan loafers and his baggy blue suit. When we were one hundred yards into the forest, we stopped for a second and listened. Our heartbeats. The gurgling of water. The distant repetition of the chopper blades winding down, the mechanical equivalent of a dog in its pant. If Fido were with us, we would have found them already.

Then began the harrowing march. From every quarter we could sense Blake's eyes, the scope of his rifle on our necks, our elbows. Where were the Targies? Was this all a trap to get Edward up here the evening before the election?

Edward had been through this before, this searching in an arena where bullets could fly, though to be honest about it, he didn't appear to be any more secure for the experience. He stepped purposefully, even now he stepped purposefully, but there was an ever so slightly perceptible cringe on his face each time he placed his foot down. A twig snapped and we jumped. A fly buzzed my face, it practically adopted me, and I realized I was sweating right through my suit. There in front of me was Edward, ripping off his jacket throwing it aside. "What are we doing without weaponry?" he asked.

Overhead the second chopper whirred, and I was glad the reporters were still suspended. There were some family rituals we could just as soon stand to have out of eyesight of reporters, and one of them was beating Blake to a pulp. If we got our hands on him before he got to us. There was very little Blake could do that would surprise me by this point, other than renounce his ways, become chemical free, and do volunteer work in a hospital. We would see him in a hospital, all right.

There were noises across the small stream that burbled by the path. Edward stepped warily, until we realized that the voices we now heard were a familiar blend of the Mingeboro lockjaw, the affected Daley stutter, the slight drawl that was one part southern legacy, two parts hipster snobbishness, and they sounded conversational, almost gossipy. What was going on?

We forded the stream from rock to log and hardly got wet. I felt less like Ethan Allen and his Green Mountain Boys than someone late for his reservation at the Russian Tea Room on a hot, sticky day. We rather breathlessly burst into the clearing, and the first person I saw was Melissa, sitting on a tree trunk filing her nails. That T-shirt she was wearing was mighty fetching.

Then there was Wolfy, who was looking not the least surprised to see us, filled as he was with clear-eyed bonhomie. There were a half-dozen cousins, some of them giggling, and even my Aunt Morgan, that wizened old bird, was girlishly amused by our grim-faced entrance. Uncle Andrew stepped forward with pained relief on his face, as if the final redoubt had been rescued by generals. Aunt Lizzie looked wasted, happy, but wasted. Again, I wondered, What the hell is going on?

"Where's Sam?" demanded Edward in a manner wholly desperate. Sitting on a rock next to the foundry was Claire, and she was holding little Charlie and Lisa to her as if they had tried to run away. Other than that, she seemed completely at ease.

The group looked back at us with utter calm, at Edward, who was dripping sweat and who was drenched through his white shirt, and at myself standing at the edge of the clearing panting like a dog that had just been run. I'd expected Targies and gunfire, not a wienie roast in the forest.

"Sam's up with the Targies, chasing after Blake," said Wolfy, as if what he'd just described was something as banal as walking the dog.

"The Targies turned on Blake when they found the person he was after was Sam," and Andrew utterly impressed. "Luckily they found Sam first."

"Yeah, they remembered Sam from years gone by. He used to fix their cars," said Melissa, as if until that moment the notion of social contact with a Targy was unspeakable.

"Where are they?" I asked. "And how long have they been gone?"

With an offhand manner that made me want to throttle him, Wolfy said, "They went thataway," and he gestured behind him up the mountain with his thumb. "About twenty minutes ago, I'd say. Between Sam and the Targies, I'll bet Blake will be here in about, oh, five, ten minutes."

"And so will the reporters," I said as Edward and I just looked at each other and took off at a gallop.

The path was crooked as it headed back up toward the top of the mountain, though in a more pronounced incline than what we had just come down. I tossed my sports coat to the side the way Edward had, only the way I wrestled with it made me feel like an uncoordinated Otis Redding throwing his jacket to the crowd. "Will you come on?" Edward puffed through gritted teeth, and I struggled to catch up. I wasn't used to jogging in oxfords.

"Damn them," I said as I slogged up the trail along with my brother.

"Yeah, they just sit on their asses and expect the Targies are going to save Sam's life."

"So long as they don't have to get their fingernails dirty . . ."

"Or their boots muddy . . ."

"A bunch of spoiled, lazy brats, the whole family, you know . . ."

"Oh, don't I know it. No one in the family kicked in a dime for my campaign. Not a dime."

"A bunch of cheapskates," I added.

"Ain't that the truth."

"They're louts."

And then, as we came around the bend in the woods, they appeared, a small group of slovenly Targies walking stiffly toward us and all but singing "Heigh ho" as they marched. Some had on Boston Red Sox baseball caps; all of them wore T-shirts or flannel work shirts too warm for the end of summer. And in the middle of them, lumbering toward us, was Blake, being prodded and none too gently by Sam, who was carrying the same rifle Blake had used to shoot at me some months before.

"Sam!" Edward cried, and we both ran toward him, throwing our arms around him, my brothers and myself now hugging while Blake looked up disgustedly and the Targies made sure he was covered with weapons of their own.

"We caught the sucker, Mr. Daley," said one gap-toothed gentleman I recognized from the time he had come by trying to sell us apples he'd picked from our own backyard when he thought we were out of town.

"Red-handed," said another one whose face looked familiar, and I remembered it had been in the *Mingeboro Gazette* after he'd been arrested for selling illegal venison to an undercover game warden not long ago. Flies were annoying us and sweat streamed down all of our faces, Blake's most of all, as Edward gleefully asked Sam if he was all right.

"I'm fine. I'm just glad Curtis here remembered how I fixed his car once."

"We didn't help only for you, Mr. Daley. This jerk here's a blight on a good community. At least we shoot deer without flashlights."

And Blake just stood there glaring. He glared the whole way down the hill, as we walked, my brothers, the Targies, and our prisoner, to go down and join what was, after all, our family. To join the family in a celebration of just what, as a family, the good Lord had given us.

## —— EPILOGUE ——

WHEN IT WAS TIME for the balloon drop, I had long since ceased to look at this as losing. Oh, sure, Edward was getting trounced by Hamlet O. Cattanasio and would not get to play in the United States Senate, but in a real way, I realized now, the game all along had been to beat Nate, and weeks before we had done that handily.

The ballroom here at the Waldorf was filled to capacity as election returns came in and everyone tried not to look ashen. I realized that winning the primary in September, while an ephemeral pleasure, had been a vast strategic mistake. We had needed Nate on the Republican line to draw votes from Cattanasio. In a three-way race, Edward would have won. Though I suppose in the long run, and I mean the longest run, it was worth it to lose now to Cattanasio for the joy of having whipped the Stantons in September.

I'm not really talking about Nate, I guess, when I talk about the thrill of victory. I felt rather sorry for him, and I have to admit, in the general election his willingness to campaign for Edward was an enormous plus. He simply refused to acknowledge he'd said anything bad about Edward during the primary and went on to trash Cattanasio. What I felt particularly good about was the disappearance of Blake behind the walls of the Payne Whitney Clinic, and I only wish we still lived in an era where shock treatment and lobotomies were customary. Uncle Ethan had a host of problems, from a spate of lawsuits filed seemingly moments after it was certain his brother would no longer be a United States senator to a rather pesky and well-publicized assault by the Internal Revenue Service. Hardly a day went by that some new revelation about his sleaze was not depicted in the Metro Section of the *Times,* and even Angela had a few scoops on him in the *Downtown News.*

Edward gave it a good shot, the general election, though it was hopeless from the outset. We spent the first ten days after Edward became the nominee dealing with the news stories that arose from the AP wire photo. It was the picture of the five Targies marching Blake at gunpoint down the slopes of Mount Targa, my relatives and me with the solidarity of linked arms sort of goose-stepping behind them. Edward looked as if he'd been dragged out of a swamp, his shirt all mud-splattered, his gruesome arm draped over Aunt Lizzie's shoulder. By the time *Time* had run the picture side by side with yet another family portrait—and I thought I could hear the faintest edge of editorial laughter in the soap operas they wrote about us— we were on the defensive, and it didn't take much encouragement for Hamlet to scribble devastating passages in his diary.

One diary entry he released to the press had him moaning, straight-faced, about his deprived background as the son of an immigrant. "A fight in my family, alas, consisted of Uncle Anthony spitting grappa into Papa's face. No one smashed our sports cars. But from this humble background, I now feel confident I will soon be a United States senator. America is a wonderful place."

Even when we took the campaign upstate to our base, I sensed people looked at Edward as a bit of a freak. I mean, after all the news coverage of our family as certified oddities. But as I looked down now, the balloons dropping onto the ballroom floor, I could see my sister Annie with her nice new boyfriend, a young law student who'd worked on our Ballot Integrity program. She'd given Lazlo Fortescu the old heave-ho shortly after the primary, and his intentions, or perhaps it's better to say his style, were made evident by how swiftly he stopped buzzing around our garden. For in the general election he hadn't raised a dime for Edward.

And down there on the floor I saw my sister Betsy dancing with Wade, a smile on her face in spite of Edward's loss. I could see Owen, who would start Yale in the spring in time for the baseball season, and tonight he was dancing with this cute girl who'd volunteered in the general election. Sam was there with Claire, sitting with the kids at a table along the wall. Little Charlie was attempting to drink a soda and eat party snacks all at the same time, and Lisa stared ecstatically at the balloons that kept dropping even though we were mere moments away from Edward's concession.

I saw Wolfy with his girlfriend Abby and a cluster of his fans around him, and he was standing there modestly, no doubt talking about his book, which was due out in the spring, this big, wide, healthy grin on his face. Within moments, Camille and Laurie would return from the ladies' room and would come up here with me as Edward conceded, the networks going live with it, my former journalist brethren in a penned-in corner sitting at tables with live phone lines to their desks.

I did not know whether I was soon to reenter that world. Didn't much know what I was going to do exactly, though I knew I was going to do it with Laurie beside me. One thing I would not be doing was working at the newly revitalized Daley Motorworks on that prototype of the Mustang Lazarus that Ford had sprung for and that Sam was to design. I would not be working with my family, but only because it was time to move on, time to go beyond this obsession with them that had weighed upon me for an unhealthy length of time. I didn't know what my next step would be, though I was glad this one was over. I would have been happier if Edward had won, but if he could take it with good grace, then so could I. I was grateful to have gotten to know and respect Edward, to have been a part of this with him, this campaign that in many ways had been for me a reconciliation with the family over a breach no one had been aware of.

The balloons having fallen, a hush came over the crowd. I felt a hand brush mine, and I turned and saw Laurie, her hair tied back, this sleeveless gown highlighting the fine points of her collarbones. Beside her was Camille, totally inappropriately coiffed for the occasion, and she was leaning over the balcony to wave at someone below. The crowd was expectant, and then Edward swiftly made his way to the stage with his head held high, as if he were about to declare victory instead of defeat. There was this burst of applause that turned into sustained and boisterous cheering. And as the roar got louder, I stood there applauding, a part of the crowd, but quite proudly a part of the family as well.

## ABOUT THE AUTHOR

As deputy press secretary in the 1984 Reagan–Bush campaign and then as press secretary for Jack Kemp during the congressman's presidential bid, John Buckley established himself as one of the most prominent and oft-quoted press attachés on Capitol Hill. He was formerly a reporter for *The Soho Weekly News, Rolling Stone, The Village Voice,* and the *Saturday Review.* He is currently a political consultant who divides his time between Washington, D.C., and Sharon, Connecticut.